Gabe

GLEN ALAN BURKE

An unusual butterfly lit upon a flower

Fear not flower I will only be here for an hour

Take your time fly but remember there are limits

For your time is measured not in hours but in minutes.

Art design by Tyson Burke

This book is dedicated to my daughter Tifany.

PART 1

CHAPTER 1

Clayton figured if he stared at it long enough, and held his mouth just right, he could make it work. He had meandered out of the ALFA Insurance agent's office meeting to check his smartphone for the text that he had been patiently, sometimes impatiently, waiting for.

Shannon loved to send messages to her husband. Usually about unimportant things: *Hi, on my way home from school;* or *Picking up some milk from the Piggly Wiggly, do you need something?* or *I love you, honey, really!* But today was different, important. Today he was waiting and timidly wondering how the doctor's visit went.

Clayton couldn't concentrate on the dull, insufferably boring insurance talk anyway. Along with the trepidation of the pending doctor visit, good thoughts were occupying his mind. *Jerusalem, Alabama, was a damn fine place to be in the fall.* The leaves were just beginning to give up their photosynthesizing process to the inevitability of the autumnal equinox, or as they say in Alabama, *the leaves were changing color.* The smell of Crimson Tide football was in the air, and they were winning. *"A damn fine decision to bring Nick Saban to Tuscaloosa,* "Clayton thought, and *yes...* Life was good.

If only the doctor had good news, then life would be even better. Clayton fumbled about his new smartphone, dilly-dallying with the apps wondering why they called them smartphones. The thought occurred to him: *"I know why. You have to be smart to use them... There it is... text... touch. "*

"We're Pregnant!!!!"

"YES!" The word popped out of his mouth reflexively. The other agents in the conference knew what he was anxiously waiting to find out. That's why he heard the not-so-subtle cacophony of chuckles and laughs reverberating from the room when he let out the irresistible "*Yes!*"

Clayton knew they knew, but the evidence he had in his hand was too sweet for a man who had been trying for over two years to have a child to keep to himself. He wanted congratulations, but mostly he just wanted verification. "*Yes indeed, it does say 'We're Pregnant.'*" What else could explain why a grown man would so proudly parade a text message to every person in the office?

As he made his way around the room, he remembered that he did the very same thing that time he caught a 550-pound Marlin. "*What the hell,*" he thought. Life was good, and he was glad to be a man, free on the earth, and now, A FATHER, DAMNIT!

Clayton and Shannon had been trying to get pregnant for five years actually, two years with medical help. Clayton had come to a universal conclusion about fertility. He knew the scenario: couples all over the world that were successful, had plenty of money, and desperately wanted a child had to use test tubes, Bunsen burners, electrodes, egg beaters, and such to get pregnant.

The more money you have, the less fertile you are. *A broke-ass couple living in abject poverty with five kids can accidentally bump into each other in the hallway and get pregnant.* The thought always amused him. "*As the bank account goes up, the sperm account goes down.* "

Clayton was a confident man, but only stood about 5'7", and would often find himself in useless reveries about this very subject. "If I could have a son," he often pondered, *would it be too much to ask that he be six feet tall?* Shannon was about 5'4". *What would that make my son's height?* The anguish that a man goes through who is below normal height is only known to short people.

That didn't matter now, though. He didn't even care if it was a boy — *just as long as it grew up healthy, 6'2" tall, weighed 225lbs., played running back for Nick Saban at the University of Alabama, and won the National Championship and the Heisman Trophy—that would simply be enough.* Just like the fertility of rich people, his own thoughts entertained him most of the time. He actually heard himself chuckling.

Dr. Kimberly Cummings was an old-time family practitioner. She didn't believe in loading her patients down with a bag full of pharmaceuticals. She did believe, however, in the good old-fashioned way to cure diseases: good food and outdoor exercise. One might say that she was a combination of a natural and traditional doctor. The curious thing about Dr. Kim was that she would remind one of a hippie. Clayton thought it was because of her very long hair and the round John Lennon-type glasses she wore.

Nonetheless, it was Dr. Kim that gave Shannon the herbs and vitamins that allowed her to finally conceive. *"It was the alfalfa tablets,"* Clayton figured. *"It had to be. She took 20 tablets of the damn things a day."* Whatever the case, Dr. Kim was the reason that he was about to become a father. That and God, he guessed.

Clayton didn't believe in miracles. He wasn't even sure he believed in God anymore. Shannon did, though, and she would periodically drag him to church. Clayton would reluctantly acquiesce because he figured sitting through an hour and a half of boring songs and a hyped-up preacher was easier than an argument and hard feelings that he knew would soon ensue if he snubbed church again.

Clayton was a practical man. He believed in science, which, he concluded, anyone who believed in the Bible had to suspend. But still, he felt ashamed of himself if he didn't go to church. He didn't know why he felt it. The obvious answer was, of course, that he lived in the heart of the Bible belt. It was simply shameful not attend church on Sundays. It was akin to not liking NASCAR, which, by the way, he didn't.

Second, his wife was a Born-Again Christian and a true believer. It was simply one of his duties as a good husband to support his wife and her activities. Third, Clayton had been raised in church, saved, and born-again himself when he was a child, aged eight or nine, best he could remember. There was a gnawing at his conscience when he didn't go to church, but why?

He concluded it was some Freudian, psychological, subconscious something or other reasons for the guilt he felt. On the other hand, he had been to college and had biology classes, and science classes, and psychology classes. All of them can point to reasons why human beings exist and act like human beings, and none of them have anything to do with God.

Still, he didn't want to be disrespectful to his wife, her family, and his, and most of his friends. Not believing in God was simply a matter you didn't bring into a conversation in the heart of Alabama. *Don't rock the boat, not now, not when things are good. Life is good. Keep your mouth shut, now and forever*, was his mantra.

Besides, he could be wrong. That possibility was always in the back of his mind. Like an ugly thought from a frightening experience in childhood, the gnawing thought that he could be wrong lingered under the surface of his educated brain. So he usually went to church. It was just easier that way.

It didn't much matter in either case. What was important to him right now was that his wife was pregnant, and he was going to be a father. *Oh, one other thing: "Did you hear that Alabama was winning? And I was going to be father! Should I stop and get my son his first Alabama football cap on my way in from work?"* The silly thought pleased him, but he was easily pleased these days.

CHAPTER 2

"Oh my God, I don't see how I have any guts left." Shannon was coming out of the bathroom, wiping her mouth with a towel and looking rather piqued.

"Is morning sickness supposed to make you this sick?" Clayton had already asked this question at least fifty times by now, but he didn't know what else to ask. He wanted to show sympathy to his wife, who had to carry all the burden of the pregnancy alone. Men get a pass.

"If I could, I'd take turns with you babe." Clayton wasn't very original, but he was sincere. Shannon could tell he was sincere by the way he looked so helpless every time she emerged from the bathroom after puking her guts out.

"I know you would, and I wish you could, but I guess this is part of the job description. I knew that morning sickness was one of the conditions when I signed up."

"I guess it is," sighed Clayton, "I just didn't realize how much a woman throws up."

"I didn't either." Shannon said, sounding irritated. "I knew that there was throwing up, but not this much. I hate to sound like a wussy, but I think I need to see Dr. Kim again. I'm not supposed to go to my OB-GYN for another week, but I'm a little worried."

"Probably a good idea." Clayton ventured, looking for something to agree to. "Dr. Kim can most likely give you the answers anyway."

"I hope so. I'm expecting to see a lung come out any minute." Shannon suddenly looked dreadful at Clayton, "I mean one of my lungs, not the baby's".

"Oh babe, I knew what you meant." Clayton chuckled mostly to himself as he moved to put his arm around his wife, who had just stirred up a loving feeling in his heart.

"It's just that I don't want anything to happen, Clayton." Shannon was trying to hold back tears that were ready to erupt, and the tenderness of her husband's arms around her was hurrying them along. "I love you, and I love the baby. I want to do this right."

Clayton was searching for words. "You're going to do fine, babe. I promise everything is going to be fine." Clayton thought he was hitting the right tones. "This son of ours is going to be healthy and strong."

"How do you know it's going to be a son? We won't know that for about another month or more." Shannon was sniffling as she nestled up under Clayton's arm.

"Well," Clayton paused and looked around the room, as if he was about to say something profound. Even though he wasn't sure that the wisdom he was about to spout was true, he was going to fake it anyway. "I read somewhere that if you have more severe morning sickness, then the mother is more likely to have a boy."

"Really?" Shannon was trying not to sound skeptical, although she could tell Clayton was probably making this up. She wanted to go along with her husband, who she knew only lied to her when he was trying to be supportive. "Well now, exactly what magazine did you read this in?"

"Well it was called, ah, oh I know. The article was called *How to Tell That Your Pregnant Wife, Who You Are Madly in Love With, Is Going to Have a Boy*. I believe the magazine was called *Expectant Fathers Quarterly*." Clayton grinned wryly as if it were the gospel.

"That's so sweet Clayton. We're going to be all right, aren't we?"

"I'm telling you, Shannon, right now, our son is going to be an important man when he grows up. A big man in this world."

Shannon appeared nervous as she filled out the sign-in sheet at Dr. Kim's office. They must have just opened the doors because she was the only one in the there. She was about to take one of the empty seats when, through her peripheral vision, she saw the strawberry blonde hair of Dr. Kim whiz by an open door that led patients to the back examining rooms.

"What are you doing here?" Dr. Kim's abrupt question caused Shannon to flinch as she was hunting for the correct chair to sit in. Anxiety hindered her ability to make even the simplest of decisions, like which one of the twenty empty waiting room chairs to sit in.

"Oh Kim," Shannon turned and worriedly answered, "I'm throwing up so much I'm worried. "I know that morning sickness is part of this, but man, I empty my stomach every morning, and it lasts until lunch sometimes. Is this normal?" Shannon was hoping to hear a *yes*.

"Well, what's happening here is your body is changing. You're producing a lot more estrogen. Sometimes a reaction to the increase in hormones can cause nausea. It happens." Dr. Kim was smiling sympathetically and sounded reassuring— just what Shannon wanted to hear.

"I have an appointment with my OB-GYN on November 15th. Maybe things will be better by then."

"I'm sure they will be, and if they're not, Dr. Matheson will give you something." Dr. Kim didn't like to give medicine to anyone, especially expectant mothers. "Listen, when you get to craving something, eat a piece of lemon. Keep a freshly cut lemon with you and sniff on it. It might stop you from throwing up."

"Sniff a lemon?" Shannon was amused but didn't want to sound too skeptical because Dr. Kim might be serious. "Yeah, sometimes it helps," the doctor affirmed.

"Sounds goofy enough to work. I'll try anything right now."

Shannon left Dr. Kim's feeling better. If not physically better, then spiritually.

CHAPTER 3

Shannon and Clayton walked through a seemingly endless corridor to Dr. Matheson, OB-GYN's office. They were quite familiar with the good doctor and the peculiarity of pregnant women having to navigate such a long corridor—fully loaded.

They had seen him before, years ago, but this was the first time they would see him while Shannon was wholly pregnant. They enjoyed him for his gusto, and just like Dr. Kim, he didn't give up easily either.

The atypical thing concerning the fertility problems with Clayton and Shannon was that there were, in fact, no diagnostic problems. For Clayton, all the tests were normal:

- 400,000 sperm per milliliter—normal
- Morphology—normal
- Motility—normal
- White blood cells—normal
- Fructose, volume, pH, liquefaction—normal

For Shannon, all the tests were, likewise, normal:

- Hypothalamic Dysfunction—negative
- Hyperprolactinemia negative
- Polycystic Ovarian Syndrome—negative
- Ovarian Reserve—normal
- Endometriosis—negative
- Adhesions, Pelvic Inflammatory Disease, Tubal Occlusion—No!

It was a head-scratcher. No one seemed to have an answer as to why this couple could not get pregnant. It wasn't until Dr. Kim and her bag full of magic herbs that Shannon finally conceived—Clayton was afraid to ask if she traded her milk cow for those tablets. Whatever the reason was, why or why not, didn't matter now. They were going to see their obstetrician as a family, and even the troublesome morning sickness could not kill the romanticism encapsulated in that single word: *family.*

"Well, I am so happy to see you under these circumstances instead of the alternative." Dr. Matheson said smiling warmly.

"Me too." Shannon replied, delighted but with a twinge of exasperation.

"Me three." Clayton added, sounding half exasperated, half delighted.

"I've heard you have been having some severe nausea in the mornings."

"I've been puking my guts out doctor." Shannon wanted to cut to the chase.

"Well you don't seem to be dehydrated. How is your weight?" Dr. Matheson was fumbling through her chart.

"I just weighed in at 122 pounds. I've lost about 10 pounds. Is that dangerous for the baby?" This was one of the questions that Shannon was most concerned about. Shannon and Clayton both appeared as if they were afraid to hear the answer, yet courageously braced for the worst.

"No, not necessarily. Weight loss in the first trimester could possibly affect the development and size of the fetus, but 10 pounds is not insurmountable, and I'm not too concerned about it right now." The doctor reassured. "We'll do a complete checkup. Estrogen levels, odor sensitivities, the whole gamut. And I'll do an ultrasound and get some idea of the size and time frame."

"Will you be able…"

"No, I won't be able to tell the sex," The doctor was chuckling at Clayton when he cut his question short. "We can't tell that until she gets a little further down the road, Clayton, old man."

Clayton shook his head with a submissive crossing of the arms.

"You know, one of the reasons that women throw up during pregnancy is that it's a reaction from the body in an effort to flush out toxins you ingest in your food. It's simply a defense mechanism. So, wash everything you eat thoroughly," said Dr. Matheson, sounding really professional.

"We've actually read *that* and have started steaming all our vegetables," chimed Shannon.

"Well, look, this is not out of the scale of normalcy. We'll do a thorough examination and have some solutions. So, stop worrying; everything is going to be fine." The doctor assured.

Clayton left his wife in the examination room with a reassuring kiss on the cheek, but dread had internal control of his visage as he left the room. Shannon recognized the look easily, which immediately sent her confidence level to zero, but they had been through worse things before.

One hour later, Dr. Matheson opened the patient waiting room door and made the motion with his head for Clayton to follow him back. Clayton was trying to analyze the look on the doctor's face, but there was none to analyze. The thought occurred to him that the doc must be a hell of a poker player. He was trying to make himself think of something— anything—except what he was about to hear from the expressionless doctor.

"Well I have made an examination of Shannon, so sit down beside her there and I'll tell you what I think."

Clayton was about to search for his wife's hand, but her hand found his first instead, and squeezed it tight, then suddenly let go, and that was followed by several short pats. Clayton looked at Shannon curiously, and even more curiously, he thought, was the fact that she was looking straight ahead and smiling.

To Clayton this meant one of two things: either he was going to hear very good news or very bad news. In either case, he was ready, *so bring it!* Shannon could hear a long exhale coming from her husband and a placid, stone look like prisoners hold just before they are read the death penalty. It amused her; she thought it was romantic, and she loved him for it.

"I can find absolutely nothing wrong with your wife. She's as healthy as any patient that I have at this stage of her pregnancy. She's lost some weight, but she's keeping hydrated, eating plenty, and taking her vitamins as directed." The doctor took time to smile. "In fact, those natural pre-natal vitamins must be working like hell."

"What do you mean?" Clayton asked, understanding why Shannon was so coy about the news he had just heard, and he loved her for that as well.

"Well, sonograms are pretty much useless in the first trimester. She is about 7 or 8 weeks along. The baby is little more than the size of the tip of your little finger, about 13 centimeters or so, except your baby is about the size of the tip of your middle finger." The doctor was making a demonstration using his thumb and middle finger.

"Well tell me doc, isn't that a sign that it's going to be a boy?" Clayton was smiling so big that he thought the sides of his face were hurting.

"I don't know what that means right now. It probably means we're a couple of weeks or more off on our gestational age, but as far as I'm concerned, everything looks normal, and I believe with the meds I've given her and the diet she is supposed to follow, the vomiting will stop, and everything is going to be alright." The couple of newly expectant parents left the office happy and feeling fortunate.

CHAPTER 4

"Honey, whatcha thinking?" asked Shannon.

"I'm thinking I sure do wish you would go to sleep right now," said Clayton, sounding like a wino, slurring his words out of sheer sleepiness.

"Tomorrow is a big day." Shannon was wide awake as usual.

"I know it is. Maybe the doctor can come up with something. One of us has got to have some relief." Clayton still sounded a little drunk, even though he was getting used to the irritating routine of his wife's insomnia.

The new symptom had started about two weeks ago. Shannon had noticed that it was tougher and tougher to fall asleep, and then it became tougher to stay asleep.

The peculiarity of it was the uncommonness of it. Most pregnant women find it easier to sleep and stay asleep longer. As with everything else with this pregnancy, Shannon was getting used to the opposite occurring.

In her twelfth week now, she had lost another pound. She should be gaining weight, not losing. The vomiting had stopped, but she found that her hunger and cravings had amplified. Her appetite was insatiable. She couldn't get enough to eat, and what she craved most was meat.

It didn't matter what kind of meat either, just as long as it was meat. She had turned into a full-fledged carnivore. If the steak wasn't cooking fast enough, she would open a pack of hotdog wieners and eat the entire pack. She remembered eating a pack of bologna, two pieces at a time. A can of Spam would last only about three minutes. And this was just while she was waiting for the roast to cook, or the steak to broil, or the chicken to fry, or the turkey to roast.

Clayton had dropped off a bucket of Kentucky Fried Chicken one afternoon. He knew there wouldn't be a drumstick, a wing, or even a lonely piece of greasy skin left when he returned. He didn't mind fetching the things his wife was craving, though; it rather pleased him. He pictured it as part of his job as an expectant dad. He had actually lain in bed, before Shannon had become pregnant, and imagined fetching his wife all kinds of crazy things that expectant mothers crave.

But he pictured things like pickles or ice cream—all 37 flavors, or however many there are now—or sardines. He had remembered this from an old *I Love Lucy* rerun. He envisioned Shannon wanting all three at the same time, the pickles and the ice cream with the sardines on top. He believed that was the way Lucy and Ricky did it in their show. It was funny, and he wanted it to be funny too.

It was sweet; it was romantic in a clinical way; and it was the way he wanted it. He wanted to share in his wife's pregnancy. He craved the idea of it almost as much as Shannon was craving pork chops. It was marriage; it was husbandry; it was fatherhood; and most importantly, it was life—a good life.

He loved the romanticism of his wife's cravings, but the insomnia was a different ball game. He wasn't so concerned with the fact that Shannon was eating so much and not gaining weight—at least she had stopped throwing up, and was holding her own weight-wise— but staying awake most of the night wasn't in any of the movies or TV shows he had watched as a kid, or even as an adult.

"You know what's weird about this, Clayton?" mused Shannon.

"What's that, babe?" Clayton lazily peered up from his newspaper. Shannon was mechanically mopping the floor in the kitchen like a robot maid with the switch set on high. Clayton had seen something that reminded him of this scene before—Rosie from the *Jetsons*, maybe.

"I feel wonderful. I've never had so much energy." Shannon's piston-like arms were in hyper speed, like the bobbin on a sewing machine. Clayton thought that the top layer of the ceramic floor might rub off with all the friction his suddenly "Energizer Bunny" wife was producing.

"Man, I've got to get me some of those vitamins you're taking." Clayton said in awe.

"Aren't they something?" Shannon fired back instantly. She not only was mopping faster but talking faster, like someone on crack. "I mean, I was told these prenatal vitamins were better than ordinary vitamins, but I never thought they were this good. I think that's why I can't sleep at night; I have too much energy to get sleepy. I just can hardly sit still. I try to sit down and watch TV, but I can only sit for a minute or two, and I can't hold a single thought in my head for over a second, and then I have to get up and do something." Shannon was chattering away with her head down, only half concentrating on mopping the floor.

"Is this a normal thing Shannon? Do all pregnant women have this much energy? I don't remember my sister being this way. Have you talked to other women who had kids? Do they have this much energy?" Clayton was shaking his head side to side as he was asking his wife these questions. They were only formed as questions so she could agree with him without sounding too overly concerned. He wanted her to come to the conclusion that something might be wrong with the vitamins.

"I remember hearing some women I know say that they had more energy than normal when they were pregnant. I don't remember who right now, but I've heard it said. Don't worry about this Dad, this is a good thing. If I feel this good, that means the baby must feel good. Whatever I feel, the baby must feel the same way, right?" Shannon still had her head down obliviously mopping and babbling away. Then she stood up and swayed her back to straighten up a minute and catch a breath. She flaunted a big smile at her still unconvinced husband.

Clayton was dubious but returned the smile back to his wife. She was beginning to get *that* radiant look as he noticed how her shiny hair flickered in the sun coming from the kitchen's skylight. Clayton had noticed for years the way an expectant mother seemed to glow.

They seemed to recapture cuteness, like the little girl they once were. Eyelashes appeared to turn up more. Eyes were brighter. Cheeks were fuller and rosier. He couldn't quite put his finger on it, but they're just prettier. He figured it must be the surge of the female hormone estrogen —or was it progesterone? — whichever one makes a girl look like a girl.

Whatever it was, Shannon was evolving those characteristics, and he loved her for it. Then he noticed something else as she leaned back to stretch her back.

"Shannon, are you showing already?"

Shannon noticed the bewildered look on Clayton's face and the piercing eyes that were fixed on her belly. She looked down to see exactly what he was talking about.

"Wow, I am pouching out there. I just now noticed it. I've got a little bit of a belly, honey." Shannon said, smiling all the while running her hand over the not-so-tiny bulge, being truly joyfully tickled by it.

"Are you supposed to be showing this early? I mean, you're only, what, 12 weeks? Isn't the baby only supposed to be the size of a pea or something?" Clayton looked up at Shannon inquisitively.

"Oh, Clayton, she's bigger than that. I mean, *he's* bigger than that." Shannon was playing with Clayton a bit. He smiled contently at the put-on Freudian slip, as Shannon knew how much he wanted the baby to be a boy.

"I don't think so, hon." Clayton said, getting back to the point. "I don't believe, at 12 weeks the baby is much bigger than a marble." He held his thumb and finger in an "O" shape to show how small.

"I think it's bigger than that." Shannon mimicked "O" shape. "There's all that embryonic fluid and stuff that's forming. You're just not used to seeing me with a little bit of a belly." She had made her way over, sat in Clayton's lap, and hugged his neck. "You're going to have to get used to it because it's going to get a lot bigger."

"I know it's going to get a lot bigger," Clayton said gently, taking into consideration the tenderness of his wife at that moment. "I just didn't think it would be this big right now."

"You gonna still love me when I'm out to here?" Shannon whispered softly her face curled in her husband's chest.

"I'm gonna love you more."

Shannon pushed herself up, smiling, put both arms around Clayton's neck and hugged him tight.

Clayton heard the same crunching sound his neck vertebra made when the chiropractor used to give him adjustments. Shannon continued to squeeze, and a sharp pain run through his neck like a nerve had been pinched.

"Honey, honey, your bony forearm is hurting my neck." Clayton grimaced and put both hands on his loving wife's wrist to extricate himself from the painful hug. He pulled, but nothing happened.

"Honey, let go. You've caught a nerve in my neck." Shannon quickly let go of her embrace when she realized Clayton was seriously in pain.

"I'm sorry, hon. I didn't realize I was hurting you," she said with a sweet chuckling voice, "Let me kiss it and make it all better." She gently gave Clayton a peck on the side of his neck, and then stood beside the chair to see if her expectant-mother magic had healed her husband. Clayton began to rub the side of his neck and move his head from side to side.

"Man, you've got a hell of a head lock. I think you got a hold of a nerve just right," Clayton said, half-laughing and rubbing the side of his neck. "I won't need an adjustment for a while, that's for sure. I think we need to get you to wrestle Hulk Hogan for the WWFFBB, or whatever the hell that title's called these days."

Shannon laughed out loud.

"You gonna be all right, Dad? Do you need to really go to the doctor?" Shannon asked.

"Nah, I'm all right. It doesn't hurt anymore," Clayton said, amused that his pregnant wife could hurt him. "Go on about whatever you were doing, mopping or whatever. I'm fine."

With that, Shannon bent down and gave her husband a quick kiss on the lips, then looked for where she'd put her mop. Clayton resumed reading his paper.

Things returned to normal —or the way they were about 15 minutes ago: Clayton reading his morning paper, and Shannon mopping the floor the way a crack head would.

Clayton distractedly returned to the paper as Shannon inched closer to the table and his chair. Not only was her rhythmic mopping distracting to his peripheral vision, but now she began to hum.

Clayton was trying to make out the tune. *"Hush, little baby, don't you cry..."* Yes, that was it. He thought this would be a perfect time to show off his virtuoso singing voice. *"Mama's going to buy you a mockingbird."* He looked up a Shannon to see if she concurred with his assessment of his talent.

"No, you dummy. It's 'Daddy loves you and so do I.'" Shannon was being disagreeable on purpose, just for the fun.

"Well, there's something in there about a mockingbird somewhere, right?" Clayton tried to be funny and disagreeable back. "Or was it 'Daddy's going to kill you a mocking bird'?"

Shannon shook her head and smiled as she continued to mop under the kitchen table. "That's the name of a book." She began to laugh as she approached Clayton's chair. "Raise your feet up a minute Dad." Clayton stuck his feet straight out.

"Hush Little Baby is the name of a book?" Clayton tried to look serious but couldn't help smiling. He put his feet back down.

"Yes, Einstein, you nailed it." Shannon smiled at Clayton as she unconsciously placed her hand on the back of his chair, gently sliding it two feet back from the table. Then, she began to mop fast-motion style where Clayton's chair had been.

Clayton tried to focus on the words that had, until now, eluded him when he suddenly realized that he had been slid away from the table, with the heels of his shoes lightly rubbing against the ceramic tile floor, but he kept his eyes on the paper, trying to focus.

Shannon speedily mopped the spot, put her hand on the back of Clayton's chair, and slid him tidily back to his original place, snug to the table. She looked around the room for any missed spots, all the while humming *Hush Little Baby*.

Clayton dropped his paper onto the table and gazed upon his wife with bewilderment. "Shannon, what just happened?"

"What do you mean?" she said while scurrying over to the sink to search for a potential unclean spot.

"Did you just slide my chair with me in it?" Clayton's bewilderment was still affixed to his face.

"Yeah, I guess I did." Shannon was studying whether she should put in a load of laundry or vacuum the carpet upstairs.

"What are you, Superman?" Clayton rose to his feet.

"Actually, I'd be Superwoman, dear." Shannon was still trying to make up her mind. Then, she realized what Clayton was talking about.

"Oh, the floor was wet where I just mopped, Dad. It was slick. Everything slides easily on a wet floor," Shannon said dismissively, with a flutter of the lower lip, and swiftly exited the kitchen for the laundry room.

"Oh yeah, I guess that makes sense." Clayton blew out a frustrated breath, only half-sure that it made sense. He did feel a little sense of relief, though. With the weird stuff that was going on with his wife right now, any explanation would make sense — or at least he hoped it did.

CHAPTER 5

Shannon's explanation for the chair made sense, but only clinically. Clayton couldn't quite let it go. It was still in the back of his mind and relentlessly inching closer to the front of his mind. *He was in the chair, all 170 pounds. She did use one arm. He slid backward and then slid forward. His head hurt. Stop thinking about this shit. What's the matter with you? Stop it, and stop it now. The damn floor was slick. OK...* "Damn! I just missed my turn."

Clayton had actually missed the turn into the ALFA office. Luckily, nobody saw him —he hoped. All he wanted to do now was get through the day and keep it together —, his shit, that is. *Nothing was worse than runaway shit*, he thought. Maybe it's the anxiety over the responsibilities of fatherhood. Maybe it's the anxiety over the tough pregnancy. He hoped it wasn't the anxiety over a stupid sliding chair. Nevertheless, *the stupid chair slid.*

"Clayton, you coming to lunch with us?" Roger asked, peeking his head in Clayton's office as inconspicuous as possible. He knew Clayton was unusually quiet and distracted today. Roger Summerall was Clayton's best friend, and like most best friends, he could tell there was a problem.

"Roger, I need to talk to you a minute. Could you shut the door and sit down?" Clayton asked of him.

"I knew it. Something *is* bothering you. I could tell the minute you walked in." Roger took a seat in the chair directly facing Clayton's desk. "What is it Clay?"

"When you and Melissa were expecting Austin, how did Melissa do physically?"

"What do you mean? She did fine."

"I mean, how did her body change?

"Well, she got a really big belly." They both chuckled.

"Yeah I know her belly got bigger, but did she seem to have more energy? I mean, more than usual."

"More energy? Well, I don't remember her having more energy per se. She was about like she always was. She didn't seem to have less energy, but I couldn't tell any difference really. Now, as she got further along, she seemed to have less energy, but I guess the bigger the load you're toting around, the more energy it takes. Why? Is something wrong with Shannon?"

"No, no, I don't think so. It's just that she can't sleep, and she seems to have a lot of energy. I mean, she can't sit still man. I'm talking crazy energy. Off the charts. Almost not normal."

Roger could tell that Clayton was bothered by this, probably more than he was letting on. He needed to say something to ease his best friend's apprehensions.

"Well, listen Clayton, I've heard some women say that they had more energy when they were pregnant. I believe it mostly happens on their first one. But, yeah, that happens, man. Don't worry about it."

Silence came from Clayton along with a disconcerting look, which prompted Roger to continue:

"What I'm saying is, Shannon is going through a lot right now. A lot of freaky things are going on in there. You know what I mean?"

Clayton nodded understandingly.

"I'm not a doctor, I don't even play one on TV, but I'll bet you that everything is normal and everything is all right."

With that, Roger got up and started for the doorway while whistling and singing "Don't Worry, Be Happy." He was doing his best Bobby McFarland, Jamaican impersonation, which sounded nothing like Bobby McFarland but made Clayton smile a little anyway.

Roger did ease Clayton's apprehensions, despite the ham-handed song at the end. It worked. He managed to occupy his mind with work the rest of the day, but then the anxiety monster started trying to tear out of its cage. *It was most likely merely the physiological changes that women go through,* he thought. *But, while I'm at the computer, it doesn't hurt to Google pregnancy.*

- *Breast may become unusually sensitive*
- *Sleep difficulties and fatigue*
- *Morning sickness and heartburn*
- *Frequent urination and constipation*
- *Weight Gain*

Nothing about having more energy or being stronger. But weight gain. Weight gain…, let's see, weight gain: '25 to 30 pounds on average'. Crap! She's losing weight and has more energy. Damn! Well shit, maybe it's all right anyway. She could be exceptional. You know, like those people that win lotteries. Damn, I'm not making any sense or making myself feel better. Get off this damn thing and get to work. I'm worry over nothing. It will be all right, Roger says so, the doctors say so, Shannon says so…I say so. So.

Clayton entered his driveway after a nerve-settling drive home. He usually did his best thinking and daydreaming while driving. Dangerous but effective. Sometimes, he'd overshoot the driveway, of course, but that's just a small price to pay when you're having a nerve settling daydreaming session.

Shannon was gone, the kitchen was empty. He had gone over all this shit in his mind on the way home. He figured he was just hunting something to complain about. *Why was he feeling this way?* He should be ecstatic that his wife was so healthy and felt so good and energetic. *It did beat the hell out of the alternatives, didn't it?*

He thought it would be nice if he started dinner —maybe spaghetti. Anybody can cook spaghetti. *Why, she'll start feeling fatigued and all the other symptoms as she gets further along, just like everybody else.* Clayton had put a pot of water on to boil. *God, it takes so long for water to boil. It's like watching paint dry.*

His eyes were drawn like a magnet to the steel chair. The same one he had occupied when Shannon slid him abruptly out of the way so she could mop the spot. He precipitously approached the chair and studied it for a moment. He casually pushed the empty chair away from the table. It easily slid a foot backwards on the slick ceramic floor.

Man, I didn't realize how slick ceramic was. He sat down and gave himself a push backwards with his feet. Again he slid a little, but only a few inches, and he pushed pretty hard too. Then he put pressure on the floor with both feet and pulled himself forward about a half foot at a time. Again, it wasn't as easy as he thought.

The chair would do fine until one of its legs ran across the grout line, then it needed more impetus with each grout line it encountered. *Wait! The floor was wet. YES! That's it. Anybody could slide somebody on a wet floor. What an idiot!* At that precise moment, Shannon entered the kitchen carrying a bag full of groceries.

"What are you looking so happy about? And did I hear you shout *YES* just now?" Shannon had an embarrassing look on her face —not for her, but for her weird-acting husband.

"Oh nothing, I'm just happy. What you got for supper? Cause I've already started spaghetti."

"I guess this is a hint you want spaghetti for supper."

"No not really. I just wanted to do something nice for you. You know, you being my wife and stuff like that. Carry my baby, you know, the little things."

Shannon smiled at the cuteness of her husband.

"Well, get this bag of groceries, and I'll finish your sweet gesture. You sweet husband, you."

Clayton wasn't going to argue. Making spaghetti required chopping damn onions. He hated doing that. He didn't understand how women could seem to do it without their eyes watering. He figured it must be a girl thing.

He reached out his hands to lift the jammed-full bag of groceries, but as he put one hand under and his other hand grasped the side of the bag, he could feel it slipping.

"Honey, don't let go. It's going to slip through."

"I'll just sit on the counter," Shannon said while simultaneously clutching hold firmly with her forearm to the slippery bag with Clayton's hand caught somewhere between her forearm and the bag.

She made two or three quick steps to the counter and then she began the motion of raising the grocery bag to the counter top when she noticed a definite resistance.

Two startled expressions met at the same time: Shannon looking down on the floor at her prostrate husband with half his upper body raised off the floor by two feet, and Clayton peered up helplessly with his hand wedged between a grocery bag and his wife's forearm… "Oh my God" echoed throughout the house…This would not be the last time.

CHAPTER 6

Awkward looks had become common place over the next three weeks for the weary couple. The one they were now sharing as they sat opposite each other in Dr. Matheson's office was as ubiquitous as the reassuring morning kisses that Clayton clinically administered every day before he resignedly went to work.

Perhaps "awkward" is insufficient to describe the look that Clayton possessed this time; "dread" might be more apropos. Shannon was a little more optimistic and only appeared awkward in her expressions to her husband because he so stubbornly refused to believe it could be anything other than a disaster.

They had talked ad nauseam about what happened in the kitchen three weeks ago. There was no consoling Clayton. His mind was made up that something was terribly wrong with the pregnancy. Shannon tried every logical explanation she could think of —and some she just made up —to explain away the freaky accident in the kitchen.

Shannon even went to the gym where she occasionally worked out—mostly after January 1ˢᵗ each year—to talk to Aki about leverage and illusions. Aki was the most knowledgeable person she'd ever known about exercise, diet, and body movement. He had a Bachelor's degree in something called Kinesiology. She believed it had something to do with how the body moves.

She would try anything it took to convince her husband that his wife, the mother of his soon-to-be child, wasn't some kind of freak. Shannon couldn't logically explain why she was so energetic or her apparent super human strength.

She did, indeed, feel stronger; she also, in fact, had endless energy. But it was also a fact, which she protested vehemently to her overly suspicious husband, that she was not *freaky* strong, or freaky energetic, or *freaky* anything. At least she didn't feel freaky, and Clayton was just going to have to trust her.

And so, when she explained what Aki had told her about the almost superhuman way a seemingly small person can position their body in ways that seem to defy gravity and appear to be super strong —is merely the use of leverage — Clayton seemed to become less doubtful.

Clayton figured it was because he wanted it *too* much. Bitter experience had taught him that when one wants something *too* much, a great equalizer in the universe —God, perhaps — has a way to settle the accounts. He figured that this was just merely account-settling: his punishment for misguided priorities.

He not only wanted a child but a boy. Not just a boy —a big boy. Not just a big boy —a great boy that would be a super athlete and make a mark in the world. *Too much, too much, he had asked for—too much.*

So this was his just desserts; his punishment for over shooting the mark. If only he had just settled for a normal, healthy child like everyone else. Boy or girl, whether he or she grew up exceptional or ordinary didn't matter at this point. He just wanted his child to grow up, period.

So, the two of them sat in the waiting room of Dr. Timothy Matheson, OB-GYN, exchanging uncomfortable glances. One anxiously awaited his fate from the doctor-executioner who was about to confirm that, indeed, something was terribly wrong with his wife and baby, and yes, it was because he had wanted too much. The other eagerly waited for the simple answer that everything was normal.

The nurse called the fidgety couple to the examining room, and they took their places: she on the table with the extremely long and wide piece of toilet paper; he in the small swivel chair beside her. Clayton noticed the chart on the wall of developing fetuses. He slapped his head like he could have had a V8.

"Today is the day we can find out if it's a boy or a girl." Clayton tried to put on his best dumbass expression. "I completely forgot that was today. That is today, isn't it?"

"I think so, I had forgotten that too. He is definitely going to do a sonogram."

"Yeah, I know he is going to do a sonogram." Clayton suddenly looked dejected again.

Three minutes later the door opened and a young lady stuck her head in the exam room and quietly, yet professionally, said, "Would you follow me please?" The young lady was not a nurse; she didn't look like a nurse, more like a doctor.

"Excuse me, are you a doctor?" Clayton asked curiously, already beginning to think that something was wrong right out of the gate.

"No, I'm a diagnostic medical technician," she answered properly. Clayton's mind was racing away from temporarily positive and toward permanently negative at breakneck speed. "I do the sonograms on all the patients." She turned and smiled at Clayton. He felt better, temporarily.

"The last time Dr. Matheson did the sonogram," Clayton informed.

"That was probably for something non-routine. This is just a routine procedure." Clayton still felt better, for the moment.

The lady technician put Shannon in position, squirted some lotion on her stomach and began to rub the transponder over her belly like she was floating concrete with a trowel. "How far are you along?" The technician asked Shannon with a slightly perplexed look.

"Why did you ask it like that?" Clayton interrupted.

"This is supposed to be my third month or about twelve weeks, isn't it Clayton?"

"Yes, about the twelfth week, we believe. Can you tell if it's going to be a boy?" Clayton let the words go automatically.

"Sometimes if the positioning is just right, but that's not what we're looking for today."

"Why did you look surprised when you asked us how far along she was?"

"Nothing, it's just she looks more like a 5 month from her abdomen size."

"I think so too." Clayton was nodding at Shannon.

The young lady was moving the wand all over Shannon's protruding belly, stopping at this position for a few seconds, then stopping at that position for a few seconds more, all the while never taking her eyes off the monitor screen and never losing the perplexed look on her face.

Clayton's heart began to thump harder and harder with each corresponding expression of puzzlement on the young lady's face.

"I'll be right back. I'm going to get Dr. Matheson." The young tech said as she turned and left the room with a quick step.

"I knew it." Clayton was pale.

Shannon shrugged like she didn't know, and it was no big deal.

Dr. Matheson entered the sonogram room, picked up the wand, and began moving the end to all positions while completely transfixed on the monitor. The same bewildered look was now on Dr. Matheson's and the young lady's faces too. They began to quietly whisper medical jargon to each other, pointing to the monitor. Clayton could only make out every other word. His heart was pounding so hard he thought he could hear it beating.

"Something is wrong guys," said Dr. Matheson, aspirated. "We have completely missed this somehow."

Clayton braced for the worst.

"She is much further along that I had calculated," the doctor said, still with a confounded countenance as he held the wand as still as possible while they got the measurements. "From crown to rump, this fetus is, ah…about 19, no, 20 centimeters long… about 8 inches or so. So she is actually about 21 weeks, or her fifth month… That can't be right." Dr. Matheson stared at the young technician, who was befuddled and staring back at him.

"What's going on here?" Clayton couldn't contain himself. He wanted to know if his worst nightmares were coming true or not. Secretly, he began praying to a God he didn't know.

"Well, either I'm crazy — which right now I'm not sure — but, ah, um, this fetus has all the development anatomically of about a 12- or 13-week fetus, but the size of a 20- to 25 -week fetus. Kerry, am I crazy?" Dr. Matheson sheepishly asked the young technician.

"If you are, then I'm crazy too," Kerry returned with a half-smile of amusement.

"What do you mean, what are you talking about?" Clayton's voice was lower in octave and slower in delivery, like a patient who was just told they had cancer—somewhere between disbelief, denial, and acceptance. Clayton's mind had seized upon the word *deformity*. It was the word he feared the most out of all the dreaded words that he halfway expected to hear from Dr. Matheson.

He could take the news that the baby was dead—non-viable, he believed was the clinical terminology—better than the horrific news that it was deformed. He knew that it wasn't the moral attitude to have, but it was the honest attitude, for him anyway.

He had heard time and again people describe having a baby with Down's Syndrome (*didn't they used to call that mongoloid?* he remembered) and other handicaps and deformities as a *blessing*. How can it be a blessing? *It's not a blessing, but a curse. And only complete idiots would think that a child would want to grow up as an object, not a person, but an object. Fill in your own word after object. Object of pity— object of ghoulish stares—object of anything but a human being.*

He knew it was wrong to hold these thoughts, but it was honest. *You can lie to everyone, except yourself.* He figured his own guilty consciences had brought him to this point. He was guilty. First, for wanting too much, and second, for the ugly thoughts that floated about in his mind every time he saw a Down's Syndrome child.

He braced himself for the verdict about to come from Dr. Matheson. But he already knew what the verdict was before he heard it; he guessed what he really was waiting for was the punishment. He secretly hoped for death. He didn't want to linger about in limbo. He got neither.

The doctor continued pressing the transducer that sent pulsating sound waves through Shannon's belly.

"I can clearly see that it is a boy. I can also clearly see the ventral and dorsal pancreatic buds. The limbs are long and thin. He is making a fist. See that Kerry?" The doctor looked over to get the technicians reaction, which was one of awe.

"You still haven't answered my question…Hey, a boy, did you say?" A half-smile slowly developed across Clayton's face and just as slowly disappeared. "What kind of boy? I mean, is he deformed?" Clayton was having trouble holding a particular thought in his head for more than millisecond because a thousand thoughts were vying for the same spot.

"No, Clayton, I see no abnormalities," Dr. Matheson continued, though confirming his bafflement by shaking his head, "The problem is the fetus is barely out of the gestational period and into the embryonic period. But he is — yes, there's no mistake — he is exactly 20 centimeters long." Dr. Matheson continued to shake his mystified head. "I know what you're about to ask me, and I have no good answers right now."

"You don't know why the baby could be more developed than he's supposed to be?" Clayton asked automatically anyway.

"Clayton, that's the problem. He's not more developed than he's supposed to be at 12 weeks. He's completely normal for 12 weeks. The problem is he's 20 centimeters long at 12 weeks." Dr. Matheson voice for the first time conveyed concerned instead of amazement.

"I mean, there is a range that fetuses can be in at these stages, and I've seen them vary as much as 50 percent before, but never, have I ever, seen anything like this."

Dr. Matheson continued to examine Clayton's son with awe and wonder, occasionally shaking his head and looking totally bamboozled at the young technician, who would in turn look totally baffled at Clayton, who would in turn look totally sickened at his wife, who had no idea who to look at.

"One other thing, Dr. Matheson," Clayton mumbled, considering not even bringing the subject up. But now, what does it matter? He figured he might as well, he'd already received the anticipated bad news. Might as well get it all out in the open.

"Shannon has unlimited energy and superhuman strength." Clayton had said the words so clinically and so matter-of-factly that Dr. Matheson acted as though he didn't even hear him but was transfixed on the giant baby boy instead.

Kerry, the young technician, did understand what Clayton had said and acknowledged it with an intrigued stare, as if she was almost expecting something else weird with this case. Shannon squeezed her husband's hand, and he squeezed back, but never took his eyes off his would-be son, whom he had already began to love — all 20 centimeters of him.

CHAPTER 7

Shannon's voluminous belly began to expand grotesquely as the days passed, but her personality began to contract into someone unrecognizable. She was less talkative, more introverted, irritable, and, frankly, a bitch. Clayton assumed the change was due to the discomfort of carrying a baby that was twice as large as it was scheduled to be.

She seemed perfectly satisfied with doing crossword puzzles, reading, and bitching at him. He knew that pregnancy brought with it changes in personality for some women, but he wasn't expecting this, especially from Shannon. The one stalwart rock that he could depend on was the even-keel temperament of his wife.

When things went terribly wrong, as things sometimes, or always do, it was he who would lose his head, and it was she who would find it, kiss it with the calmness and reassurance that a person of faith seems to possess, and make his head all better again.

That was the one aspect, the one side effect of Shannon's devotion to her faith that Clayton admired: her unshakeable belief that things were never as bad as they seemed. "I'm going to heaven and living in paradise when I die; how bad can things be?" she would say when bad news crept into her life, as bad news inevitably does to everybody walking the planet. The only difference was she shed bad news like a drop of water rolling off a duck's back.

The phrase would always rub Clayton the wrong way. He wanted Shannon to worry when he worried. He wanted her to be as upset and mad and as big an asshole as he was. But no, "I'm going to heaven and living in paradise when I die, how bad can things be?" was her answer to everything. It first annoyed him, and now, for some reason, it began to soothe him.

He figured that there must be some good that comes from religion and faith, or whatever you call it. He wasn't totally convinced that all that stuff in the Bible could be true, or that there was a man named Jesus, or some other old man with a beard that floats around somewhere in the sky granting wishes. In any case, the people who do believe this stuff seem to worry less than he does.

That's precisely why he began to acquiesce from time to time and go to church with Shannon; that and to keep the peace. He secretly began to desire what they had: inner peace and a less troubled mind. He tried to force out the ugly thought that they had less troubled minds because they had less intelligent minds. *Could they all be wrong, though?* This question was beginning to push away the ugly thoughts.

Just as Clayton had begun to go with Shannon to church more regularly, Shannon began to go to church less and less frequently. A cosmic transfer had ignited and began to expand in geometrical proportion along with the colossus belly… They were beginning to swap belief systems.

This wasn't like the Shannon he knew. She was changing physically, of course; that was to be expected, but he wasn't expecting her to be suddenly twice as strong as he was and twice as energetic to boot. He also wasn't expecting her personality, her soul, her very being, to change either.

Who is this person, who, well, seems to be smarter now? She could complete the crossword puzzle that appeared in the paper every morning in less than five minutes. She had never completed one before, as far as Clayton could recall. She would ask him if he knew a five-letter word for this, or seven-letter word for that, but she had never completed one much past half way, and inevitably boredom or frustration would end her futile attempts.

Clayton had found the crosswords lying on the kitchen table, completed only minutes after she opened the paper. "How the hell did you do that?" he asked, puzzled over the puzzle.

But what truly astonished him was the evening that "Jeopardy!" was on. Clayton usually watched the show just to see how dumb he actually was. Shannon was reading a book about vampires or some monster of some kind. Alex Trebek was posing the questions as usual:

Orange, Yellow… Wavelength About 510 Nanometers.

Shannon quickly answered without looking up, "What is Green?" Alex confirmed.

"In 1914, This Future Jurist Wrote The Book The Anti-Trust Act And The Supreme Court."

"Who is William Howard Taft?" Shannon said with no hesitation, still reading…Yes, she was right.

This Religious Movement Was Founded in Jamaica Around 1930.

"What is Rastafarianism?" she said quietly and matter-of-factly like she was asked, "What is two plus two?", then she became bored and got up to hunt something to do. She was right, of course, but left the room so abruptly she didn't hear Alex say, *"Correct."* Clayton sat wordless and dumbfounded by his wife's sudden acumen.

This is the person who asked me how to spell 'disrespectful' just a couple of weeks ago. And now she knows all the 'Jeopardy' answers? Clayton thought out loud as he whispered the thought audibly to himself. *If this were the only change happening to my wife, I could live with it.*

Clayton and Shannon were quietly sitting in the living room just after dinner. Clayton was surfing through the TV. He could do this so quickly that watching TV with him was like sticking your head in a strobe light. *Men seemed to channel-surf quicker than women*, at least, Clayton thought so based on the evidence he had.

Shannon was quietly reading the encyclopedia —*H*, it looked like. She had finished *A* through *G* the previous two days. She never seemed to want to speak to Clayton anymore; she only spoke when spoken to, and then in very short sentences. Clayton seemed to bore her now. He could only hope it was just another one of her crazy and mysterious symptoms of this crazy and mysterious pregnancy.

A mouse was tiptoeing along the baseboard of the living room, barely stirring — quiet as a mouse. The mouse had been in the house so long that Clayton had stopped trying to mouse-trap it long ago. "Speedy" was his name, Shannon had given it to him several months ago because of the way he moved so quickly it was hard to follow his lightning reflexes with your eye.

Speedy had, in fact, become a pet and an accepted member of the household. He was hardly noticeable anymore to the couple, and when he was, it was in a friendly manner. His antics had become a source of interactive entertainment. When it became apparent to Speedy that his adopted family meant him no malice, he slowly became brave enough to take a piece of cheese right out of Clayton's fingers.

Last Christmas Eve, they went as far as to buy him a small wedge of cheddar and took turns letting him nibble the delicate morsels out of their fingers before they retired for the night in their childless home. Clayton mused to Shannon as they went upstairs, "He's not the son I've always wanted, but he'll do for right now." They both laughed, but with an air of sadness.

Speedy was now inching his way around his favorite pathway from the living room to the kitchen. Even though he had no fear of his new parents, instinct encoded in his DNA dictated that caution should always be used when traveling.

Clayton didn't notice Speedy's movements but did notice, out of his peripheral vision, Shannon's right foot slowly moving from underneath her to the side edge of the small, claw-footed end table situated between the couch and the comfortable chair. Shannon was curled up with both legs under her butt, seemingly enthralled in what used to be the boring encyclopedia.

Her eyes never left the page she was reading when she launched the table with her foot so explosively that the magazines and doodads placed on top were momentarily suspended in midair, like Wile E. Coyote before he falls to the canyon floor.

Clayton would later recall that watching baseballs exiting a Jugs machine at batting practice was the only time he had ever witnessed something move as explosively as the end table that his wife nonchalantly foot-shoved across their living room.

It wasn't apparent to Clayton what her intention was until the load crashed and the red spray of blood and guts jetted into the air and up the wall.

"Finally got the little bastard," Shannon said with no emotion, slowly pivoting her eyes from the encyclopedia to Clayton's horror-struck face. "He won't have the guts to do that again. Would you clean that up, dear? Mice entrails would make me nauseous in my delicate condition." Her evil smile reminded Clayton of the movie *Rosemary's Baby* —the way all of Satan's dominions smiled at people with a half-coy, half-*I know something you don't know* look. It chilled him to the marrow.

All Clayton could believe at that moment was that his lovely wife —the mother of his child, his confidant, and best friend —was demon-possessed. What else could explain it? The inexplicable strength and energy, the lack of need for sleep, the personality change, the sudden distain for church, the super intelligence, and now performing acts of pure evil. *What else was left?* He was cursed, and he'd inadvertently brought his wife in on the evilness.

Clayton desperately wanted another explanation. He racked his aching brain for some other resolution. There could be some logical medical reason for this curse, he tried to reason. But not being a doctor —and not having the courage to confront Dr. Matheson with the new symptoms for fear of being carted off to Bellevue in a straitjacket — Clayton kept it to himself.

Believing your wife is demon-possessed is something you don't discuss at the water cooler at work. Clayton imagined how that might go:

Hey Clayton, how's Shannon coming along?

Oh, you know how things are. Her head is just now starting to spin around a little, and in a couple of weeks, we're expecting her to start floating off the bed — you know, the usual stuff.

"*Oh, shit, no!* "Clayton was shocked back to reality. He suddenly realized that he had to lie down beside her every night. What if her head *did* start spinning around and she *did* start projectile vomiting pea soup. A trembling fear engulfed him. He was scared of his wife, afraid to sleep beside her, afraid to close his eyes at night. *Could she kill me in my sleep?*

Clayton began to sleep on the couch, pretending he fell asleep while watching TV in case Shannon asked why he no longer slept in their bed. She never asked, and he wasn't pretending.

Three days later, Clayton noticed Shannon slowly and precipitously ambling down the steps. She looked pale, and she appeared tired. Her already large belly had grown bigger. Clayton thought she was struggling, and her rapid breathing confirmed it. He didn't know whether to help or let her be because he wasn't sure if she was his friend or his enemy. He made the instant decision that she was his wife.

"Oh, Clayton, I don't know why I'm so tired this morning." Shannon kind of sank into Clayton's arms when she had labored her way to the end of the stairs.

"What's the matter? I've never noticed you having any trouble before." Clayton was unsure and thought she might be tricking him. He hated to feel this way, but with Shannon's incredibly evil behavior lately, he couldn't the thought from creeping in.

"I'm so weak this morning. I must have slept ten hours last night, and I'm still tired." Shannon appeared scared to Clayton. The evil look she had possessed just a day or so ago was gone, and so was her strength and energy. She felt different in his arms softer. He was now holding his wife, Shannon, the whimsical, carefree, and loving woman he had married thirteen years ago.

The sudden change was mystical. She went to bed one person and woke up another. Clayton had been praying that she would. He didn't know what else to do. If his *disbelief* had caused it, then why wouldn't his *belief* fix it? He thought God wouldn't hear him. *Why would he?* Years and years of disbelief could not be rectified by mere days and days of believing.

Clayton could only remember a few of the sayings he had heard about God over the years. The one phrase he could recall right now was *"God works in mysterious ways."* Though he didn't feel worthy of a prayer being answered from a wretched sinner and non-believer, he was not going to question his apparent gift from God.

His tender and loving wife, Shannon, was now totally helpless in his arms. The fear of uncertainty was painted on the canvas of the beautiful face he had fallen in love with all so many years ago. She trembled and quivered like a scolded puppy. She was unsure, frightened, terrified, and she needed him. She clung around his right arm and wept. *"I want my wife back,"* he had asked. *God had answered him.*

Shannon began to gather her strength and color somewhat. Clayton wrapped her in a blanket and took her to Dr. Matheson's office. The doctor could find nothing wrong that a giant fetus inside the womb couldn't explain. Clayton was thankful even for *that* news, and from that moment forward, David Clayton Rinehart was a believer.

CHAPTER 8

Things began to "normalize" after the last doctor's visit. Normal for this couple would require an *Adam's Family* dictionary, as Clayton thought it. He and Shannon didn't talk about their overly large baby much. Not for lack of interest but for lack of words. What do you say to something like this? "Everything is going to be all right," or "We will get through this babe," or maybe "They'll figure out what's wrong and fix it." Neither one of them had much hope for the latter but would voice it occasionally anyway. Why not? No matter what each one said to the other, the phrase was always accompanied by a disquieting provocation: *I'll believe it, if you will.*

There were no more complications, health wise with the gestation. The only evidence that anything was different with this pregnancy than with any other was Shannon's ever expanding belly. The last visit on her 16th week revealed a perfectly developed baby, only instead of about 15 centimeter, which was normal, this fetus measured 31 centimeter, just a smidge past a foot.

As usual, Dr. Matheson had no answers; his colleagues had no answers; the University of Maryland Research Clinic only suggested the obvious: gestational diabetes or type 2 diabetes in the mother, except Shannon didn't have type 2 diabetes. Genetics of the parents? If anything, the baby should be smaller than normal according to birth weights on both sides of the families.

Dr. Matheson conducted test after test. Abnormal growth hormone excretions from the pituitary gland, maybe? No. Immunoreactive pituitary GH levels increase rapidly between 10 and 14 weeks of gestation, according to the University of Maryland, but the serum GH levels in the fetus were all in the normal range. Shannon was tired of all the tests and just wanted to be left alone.

Dr. Matheson concluded that the baby would just have to be delivered via C-section as soon as he was viable for living outside the womb. Somewhere around the 26th week. There was only one problem wrong with that plan…

Doctor's measure a pregnant woman's belly from the bottom of the uterus (pelvic area) to the top of her uterus. The mother's belly's measurement in centimeters should be close to your weeks in pregnancy. At 28 weeks pregnant for instance, the belly should measure 26-30 centimeters, or at 32 weeks pregnant it should measure 30-34 centimeters, and so on. Shannon's already measured 30.5 centimeters at 16 weeks.

He calculated at the present rate of fetal development, Shannon would measure somewhere around 50 centimeters at the 26th week. This would jam all of her vital organs upward to such an extent that she could actually die. Dr. Matheson was pondering what he should do, and how did this happen, and why… with no answers.

Clayton was pondering the same thing as the perplexed doctor, except he knew the answer why. It was him. He and he alone had brought this upon him and his wife. What else could it be? What else could explain why a giant of a child was growing inside his wife? Except that he put it there.

So it was with the greatest of ennui and the greatest of guilt that David Clayton Rinehart gave up his disbelief in God and submitted himself fully to Jesus Christ. It was a like a ton of brick had been lifted off his shoulders, he joyfully admitted to Shannon.

He was a defeated man before, and now he recaptured a sense of who he was once again. A sense of purpose, which had previously eluded him, had now a perch to light upon. Though he still had problems, he had a plan. Since it was he that brought this anomaly into his house, it would be he who would rectify it. How was he going to accomplish all of this? It was simple; by accepting it.

Though something was wrong with his child, he would take full responsibility for whatever happened. In fact, the *new* David Clayton

Rinehart had taken it a step further. He had made the decision to not only accept it but to think of this disagreeable prospect as a blessing.

Just like the people with the Down Syndrome children, whom he had just weeks earlier supposed to be great fools, he was going to bear-up and turn a potential problem into a potential gift. His wife Shannon, for a while at least, rejoiced and was exceedingly glad for him and for her.

"You about ready hon?" Clayton got ready first of course. He always seemed to get ready in half the time it took Shannon and that was before she was carrying a 19 pound baby boy in her stressed belly.

"Yes, don't rush me," panted Shannon, taking quick breaths in between words. Her vast abdomen seemed to get in the way of everything. Putting on clothes was exhausting. Talking was exhausting. And she was getting annoyed at Clayton for making her do both right now. Her super energy and mysterious strength had left her a few weeks ago, to Clayton's relief.

Dr. Matheson had Shannon coming in the office once a week now. She was having trouble breathing. She was having trouble sleeping. She was having trouble eating (even though maintaining the hulk child growing inside of her caused her to have an overpowering appetite to which only 5,000 calories a day could satisfy.) Eating and breathing at the same time was arduous.

Dr. Matheson was in a dilemma. He had come to the conclusion a few weeks ago that the only logical and safe thing was to abort the fetus. The inexplicable explosion of growth from the parasite (his words now) was surely going to kill Shannon. The David Clayton Rinehart from just three weeks earlier would have jumped at the recommendation; in fact, he had suggested it many times, even over the consternation of his emotionally, maternally stricken wife.

But, the new David Clayton Rinehart would no longer hear of it. The doctor could understand Shannon's position; he had to deal with it on a weekly basis from his patients. It was part of the job description. Young mothers, and sometimes not so young, never want to hear that they are probably going to lose the life that had fermented inside their wombs.

Thousands of years of maternally instincts would soften the heart of any would-be mother for the *baby*, not the *fetus* inside them. The distinction of the two words was important to note here from the doctor's perspective. He had started using the word fetus and stopped using the word baby weeks ago when the prognosis was inevitable. They taught him that in med school—they call it *bed side manner*. The old Clayton had begun using the same verbiage as the discouraged doctor.

The new Clayton, however, had *gotten religion* as the doctor would categorize it to his colleagues. The reprehensible prospect of letting his wife die was being rationalized on a daily basis by Clayton. His wife had always thought this way and heated arguments would erupt often times before. Clayton was being perfectly logical wanting to abort the fetus and save his wife; Shannon, on the other hand, was being perfectly irrational by her dogged desire to keep the *blessing* that she has struggled mightily to nurture.

But now it was two against one and the doctor was losing. So Dr. Matheson was in a dilemma, a race is more apropos. The fetus had only a 50-50 chance of survival outside the womb at 23 weeks. Shannon was only in her 21st week. As best he could figure, the fetus weighed somewhere around 22 pounds. Dr. Matheson had to be honest with himself. A morbid curiosity was lingering about in the subconscious mind of the good doctor.

He wanted to see it, alive if possible, dead if necessary, whichever the case, he wanted to see it. He wanted to examine it; he wanted measure it; and yes, he wanted to touch it.

He had to promise Clayton and Shannon that neither he, nor any of his staff, would leak the news of the fetus to the media. They would have it no other way. They didn't want to make matters worse by having a ghoulish, blood thirsty media to hide from every day.

This kind of news is merely fodder for an industry trying day after high pressured day to capture and hold an audience. What better news than that of a giant baby killing the expectant mother in backward-ass Alabama where it was most likely caused by inbreeding or sex with some kind of farm animal of some sorts. It would have captured the world's attention. This was trouble they prayed would pass them by.

Dr. Matheson promised to keep the news of the giant baby, who was killing its host parent little by little, day by day, confidential. Dr. Matheson had, though, told a couple of colleagues about the baby, in confidence of course. He had to. He had to tell someone or bust. How often does a medical marvel such as this happen? Not often; not in his lifetime.

He was keeping a meticulous medical journal on this case beside the regular medical file that is kept on all patients. He wanted to write about in the most prestigious medical journal of them all: *The New England Journal of Medicine.* He evermore had the ambition to write something praiseworthy, something big, enormous. This was it, figuratively and literally.

"My God Shannon!" The hardened and seasoned Dr. Matheson was struck by the size of Shannon's loaded belly, and he was the doctor, and he had just seen her last week. "I wish you would have let me had you admitted last week like I wanted to."

"You told me that it was only 50/50 whether he would survive in my 23rd week. I wanted to go at least two more weeks, if I could." Shannon was gasping for air and speaking in between breaths.

"I can't let this go any further," said Dr. Matheson with his fingers on Shannon's wrist. "Her pulse is 170, and she can't breathe. We're going to take it this afternoon. I'm sorry, but this is doctor's orders." The doctor didn't want to hear any more madness.

Shannon reluctantly nodded in agreement as Clayton helped her to get seated in the only chair in the examining room. "I think you're right." she said in her gasping manner.

"I know he's right," Clayton said firmly. "I'd rather have *you* alive than both of you dead. We've gone as far as we can go hon. This is it." Clayton gently kissed Shannon on the back of the hand. "We are going to get through this. I've ask God to help us. I'm sure he will fix this mistake and make things the way they should be."

CHAPTER 9

A cardinal, or redbird, in Alabama, was instinctively oblivious as it hopped from branch to branch in the Hackberry tree. Clayton had a trance-like glare out the window of the operating room at the unconcerned bird. Clayton's mind was having trouble discerning if this moment was real or if he was in the mysterious world of a dream.

"What is a window doing in an OR?" he thought. *"Don't they have curtains? Anybody could just walk by and look in".* Then he realized they were on the second floor. The sound of a dozen or so nurses and attendants scurrying around the room like a Chinese fire drill would momentarily distract him from his reverie.

None of this seemed quite right, or way it should be. In all the movies he had ever seen, what was happening now was the norm for a zany comedy. The thought that he had once watched a scene like this in a *Marx Brothers* movie dashed into his head. His eyes moved around the room to see if anybody looked like *Groucho*. *"Stay focused,"* he demanded of himself.

It was difficult, though. What he was witnessing was nothing like he had pictured. The quiet calmness of the hallway that Shannon was rolled down while Clayton dutifully held her hand was suddenly replaced by noise when they burst into the OR — a loud noise of talking, almost shouting, by medical personnel. Raucous, boisterous people filled the room. "Why are there so many people in here?" Clayton asked. He was ignored.

"Why are we in the OR instead of the regular delivery room?" Clayton asked again, this time addressing one of the masked men —a doctor, nurse, or anesthesiologist; he couldn't tell one from the other. Once again, he was ignored.

He was hurried into a small room, more like a closet, and instructed to put on the smock, mask, rubber gloves, and so forth just like he had rehearsed. This was the first time he had to do it by himself. It was harder to tie all those strings behind his back than he thought. It took several tries because his fingers refused to take his brain's orders.

He wasn't really concentrating on the garb, though, because he couldn't remove his eyes from his wife. The glass window in the closet allowed a clear view of Dr. Matheson and what looked like several other doctors — all men, with one woman. Shannon was lying on her back, almost completely naked, save for the tiny hospital gown that had squirmed its way up to her breasts.

Two attendants were contemplating how to hoist her from the gurney to the operating table. They managed it with great dexterity. For the first time, Clayton actually saw the cartoonish enormity of his wife's belly. *No special effects department in any of the Hollywood studios would have deformed a woman to this extent. "If Spielberg's DreamWorks studio attempted it, no one would believe it credible."* Clayton thought. He was having trouble focusing again.

The skin on her abdomen was stretched like an overinflated balloon. Clayton thought a bloated sausage left out in the summer sun was perhaps a better description. Her bellybutton was so distended that it actually would change the direction it was pointing with the slightest movement of the giant baby, who appeared was on the verge of bursting through with or without the doctor's help. It was almost like the baby was moving the stub of his mother's bellybutton like a periscope in a submarine.

Every movement of the baby could be seen from outside the almost transparent skin. The best way Clayton could describe his wife's ready-to-pop belly was as if you wrapped a sheet tightly around a toddler and threw him on a table, then observed the frightened child trying to extricate himself from the bondage.

Every movement of the arms and legs were transposed outward on canvas-like-skin. The baby had severe fits of movement before, but now it was so violent that Clayton could imagine the skin popping from within. A macabre thought entered Clayton's mind: *"Does he know that he can't stay in there any longer and is planning to tear himself loose, like a prison escape? Can he hear the doctor's plans outside his cell?"*

How could an infant, only twenty-three weeks old, move like that? It must not be human. "No, no, stop. Get a hold of yourself. Focus. He is normal, just big. They'll have an explanation for all this… Too much growth hormone. ..Yes. I'll bet when it's all over that's what it'll be.* Clayton was mumbling the words and began to stare out the window at the redbird again, who was now staring back at the loony scene with morbid interest. It was at this point Clayton realized this was not an ordinary delivery room. It was a stage.

Clayton was now dressed, with the help of a kindly nurse who seemed to be the only calm person in the room. She tied the last elusive string behind his back, made sure his cap and mask were secure, and then patted him gently on the back.

He started to exit the closet, but the nurse tenderly held his arm as if she wanted him to stand by her and out of the way of the mayhem. He took the unspoken hint and offered no resistance. What could he do? It all seemed like a dream anyway. He had no urge to move. Instinct told him it was time to stay out of the way and just let the morbidity happen.

His one-time fantasy of being the first to hold his child as soon as he exited the womb had evaporated. It was replaced by what another just as elusive fantasy — that his wife would simply survive this wacky scene from the science fiction movie in which he was an extra. Dr. Matheson was the director, Shannon was the second lead, and the main star was waiting to make his entrance.

Clayton's eyes slowly scanned the movie set to see if Stephen King was waiting to make his cameo. He remembered that Mr. King always makes some kind of cameo appearance in the movies made from his books. Surely, he was the author of this tale. *Focus, damn it.*

He began to wish he hadn't made fun of his wife for reading Stephen King novels. He thought they were so stupidly unbelievable and that only a dolt would waste their time with such drivel. The thought momentarily pushed its way through the haze of his brain—that this was Stephen King punishing him for speaking the macabre author's name in vain.

The incoherent thoughts suddenly regained their elusive clarity. The team of doctors, nurses, and technicians began to assume their positions, and the claimer soon dissipated. The calmness he had anticipated from the beginning lent a dose of relaxation to Clayton's frazzled nerves.

There were so many small tables and gadgets assembled around the bed Clayton couldn't see the main scene. The fact that the doctors and assistants were huddled so tightly didn't help either. He looked at the nurse, who still held his arm, for some kind of sign as to what he should do. She looked up at him and smiled with her eyes; then he realized she was there just to restrain *him*.

"Can we get closer?" Clayton asked the sympathetic nurse, like he was seeking permission from his Mom to go outside and play.

"If you like," she said softly.

Clayton was confused about what to do exactly. A part of him wanted to see what was going on, and another part wanted to keep his feet right where they were. Too scared to watch, too scared to not watch.

"Let's move just a little bit closer, okay?" Clayton was asking more than telling. The nurse nodded affirmatively. They slowly exited the glassed changing area and assumed a position about 15 feet from the delivery table. He could see Shannon's face mostly covered with a mask that the anesthesiologist had applied.

Clayton wondered what Shannon was thinking just before she went out. He hoped that she wasn't too scared. She was hurting so badly she was probably just wishing for any relief that would come. Still, he longed to see her face just before the mask was applied and the anesthesia worked its magic.

Dr. Matheson looked with a reassuring nod at the surgeon who was actually going to make the incision. The doctor had both his gloved hands raised in position to snatch out the overly developed infant—at least Clayton hoped it was an infant because at this point, he wasn't sure of anything—as soon as the cut was made.

An assistant swabbed the orange disinfectant, which rolled like tiny orange waves down both side of Shannon's surreal belly. The surgeons laid the scalpel lightly on the skin and seemed to barely apply the slightest pressure. The banjo-tight skin was seemingly splitting itself like an overly ripe watermelon.

The commotion at the table was blocked from Clayton's view. He had to slide a few feet over to the right to capture a somewhat clearer line of sight, just between tightly bunched shoulders of the doctor's and nurses' hands that were now madly working in unison.

His son's hand popped out like a hand would if it were trying to break from a sod-covered grave. One large hand, about the size of a two-year-old's hand, Clayton surmised, and then a bloody and membrane-covered head that looked like he was already mad as hell; moving side to side, up and down, this way and that, and screaming so loud that it reverberated a semi echo.

With both hands firmly under the infant's armpits, Dr. Matheson heaved the giant out of Shannon's belly, held him up to about shoulder height, and looked the squirming, fighting infant up and down.

Clayton, for the first time, saw his son. He was a massive, perfectly developed baby boy who was kicking and screaming like he was terrified by the introduction. It was an inauspicious prologue to the world. Clayton thought that he resembled a child's doll that he had seen little girls nurture in their make believe-worlds. Somehow, he knew how they felt. This seemed make-believe also.

Dr. Matheson sort of tucked him in a sitting position while someone else picked up the umbilical cord, which was the size of a man's wrist. *That looks like those big electrical wires that the power company hooked up to the breaker box in our house,* Clayton thought. *All twisted around each other.*

"The father is supposed to cut the umbilical cord," said Dr. Matheson forcefully while looking around to see where Clayton was.

"I'm here," Clayton bellowed after it took a second for the doctor's words to register in his wondering brain. "I want to do it."

"Hurry, Clayton, he's a hand full." The doctor was making the same grunting sounds he made when he was lifting his golf bag from the trunk of his car. He was having trouble holding the flailing child's arms still. "Let's move it, damn!" shouted the troubled doctor because Clayton was long on arriving.

"Hand him those scissors. Cut right here, Clayton, and then move back out of the way." The doctor sounded irritated while he held the umbilical cord up for Clayton to snip. Clayton was suddenly so jittery that he could hardly get his trembling fingers in the looped handles of the scissors.

"This is harder than I thought," Clayton surmised as the umbilical cord was more sinewy than he pictured. He finally cut through the last fiber and watched the blood flow from both ends, more than he was expecting at first. The blood coming out of Shannon's end of the umbilical spurted out the most. Someone put a clamp on both ends, and the blood immediately stopped.

"There it is," Dr. Matheson said. "He's out of her, and both are alive. Now move out of the way, Clayton, would you?"

Clayton turned his head slowly and deliberately toward his son. He had not actually looked at him when he was cutting the umbilical cord. Something in him was afraid to. Something innate. It's the same thing that *draws* our eyes toward the scene of an accident when it's someone else, and repels our eyes when it's someone we love.

"He looks just like a baby," Clayton blurted out the words as if no one was in the room, speaking primarily to himself. "Why, he…he's beautiful. He is actually beautiful." Clayton was now looking toward one of the nurses with a smile so large that the sides of his mask raised two inches. The nurse nodded agreeably.

Clayton was surprised that his child was beautiful and that he loved him. He had not actually considered that possibility after he had learned that his son would be born a freak.

Dr. Matheson then quickly hoisted the infant onto a smaller table, which had side panels about 10 inches high, just high enough that only half of the baby's body was exposed. The doctor and three others were trying to suck mucus out of the baby's nostrils, but he would have none of it.

"Hold his head still!"

"I can't!"

"Use both hands!"

Clayton couldn't tell who was saying what. He knew they were having trouble holding him still though. The baby was crying, more like angrily screaming, and Clayton could see his son's arms and legs floundering with nurses' hands grasping and missing.

"He's good. Wash him and weigh him," said an exasperated Dr. Matheson, both angry and amazed that three people were having such difficulty holding down a 23 week premature infant. "God, he should be on a respirator, clinging to life, but he's kicking our asses." The doctor smiled at the nurses bemusedly.

"Should we let the father do the washing this time?" asked an equally frustrated nurse who was securing a grip around her furious patient.

"Hell no, he's too much of a handful. In fact, why don't both of you wash and weigh and measure? Better still, why don't all three of us do it? I don't think the two of you can handle him. This is amazing."

The doctor then picked the baby up and raised him slightly above his head, turning him this way and that like he was looking for flaws in a piece of China. Clayton got to fully see the immensity of his son. Just like a regular baby, only four times bigger. The thought ran through Clayton's mind of a carnival. An old time carny is speaking through a megaphone:

"Hurry, hurry, hurry. Step right up folks, and get a look at the giant baby from parts unknown. He walks, he talks, he crawls on his belly like a reptile. Only 5 cents, one twentieth of a saw buck. Hurry, hurry, hurry."

Then, the master of ceremonies holds the giant baby up to a chorus of ooh's and ah's. Someone from the audience says, "Phooey, it's all done with mirrors. It's just a cheap trick. Nothing from this planet can be that big. I want my money back. Boo, boo, boo."

A momentarily dejected Clayton decided it was time to leave the delivery room. Two other doctors were stitching up his unconscious wife; three or four were washing and measuring his freakish son. *Nothing else to say or do,* he thought.

In a clinical way, Clayton knew his brain was probably just exhausted. He stepped just inside the glassed closet and began to disrobe of the sterile garb. He could hear in the background someone shout:

"23 pounds, 12 ounces." The carnival scene attempted to play again inside his head.

"32 and a half inches long" was barely audible as he flung the smock and mask at the hamper. *I need to eat something*, Clayton thought. *I wonder what they got in the cafeteria.* He was trying to occupy his mind with something else, anything else.

A powerful resolve then enveloped the new father: *Damn it, somehow we're going to be normal; a normal family. He is going to be a normal kid. They'll find out what's wrong with him and fix it. He'll stop growing so fast and become just a normal, big kid. There are big kids born every day. Stop feeling sorry for yourself and stop now. He's alive and healthy, and so is your wife.*

Clayton's step grew a little quicker and a little more upright with each reassuring thought. His strides soon matched his thoughts as he made his way to the cafeteria to tame a growling stomach.

CHAPTER 10

"Do you love him Clayton, as much as I do?" Shannon asked with a delighted smile while gazing through the observation window.

"Of course I do. I haven't had time to think about it much lately, but since I've seen him, he's precious to me, Shannon." Clayton took on the same nurturing character as his wife. The couple stood at the maternity ward window alone. It was the first time Shannon had seen her son without him being carried by a nurse.

Dr. Matheson had arranged for the baby to be in an isolated room. The startling image of a baby three times as large as all the rest would have been more like a freak show exhibit once word got out. *The two-headed fetus in the jar of formaldehyde*, Clayton pictured.

"OK, tell me which of the names you decided on. The nurses won't tell me, and I can't think to ask." Shannon was still peering with awe through the window at her son when she whimsically asked Clayton what decision he'd made. The short pregnancy and the suddenness of the delivery caught Mom and Dad without agreeing on a name.

Clayton hadn't seem too interested in deciding earlier, and Shannon couldn't make up her mind either. So just before she entered the delivery room, she grunted, gasping for breath for Clayton to decide.

"Well, it came down to Ethan, Caleb, Dustin, Levi, Elijah, or Gabriel. I narrowed it down to Levi, Elijah, and Gabriel."

"Why those three?"

"Because they're Biblical. And I can't help but think that God has his hand in this somehow. Don't you?" Shannon nodded believingly.

"So, I did some research while you were in recovery, and I decided on, drumroll please…Gabriel. Levi is his second name. We can call him Gabe."

Shannon was so pleased with Clayton appearing pleased that she didn't argue. She simply hugged his neck with all the strength she could muster, which wasn't much. Clayton had to assist his frail wife with the hug.

"I know Gabriel was an archangel who was a messenger, but what did you find out?"

"Well, Gabriel means 'God is my strength', and he foretold of the coming of John the Baptist and of Jesus. He basically delivered messages." Clayton looked prideful. "So I guess with great strength, he's going deliver a strong message to the world."

As on cue, newly christened Gabriel Levi Rinehart rolled over in his incubator, raised his head off the blanket, and then extended his massive arms and fully raised his entire upper body off the incubator floor, appearing to look around at his new environment.

"That's the same way a girl does a pus-hup, look honey."

"Oh my God." Shannon had her hand over her mouth and appeared dismayed. She looked to Clayton, who was grinning at this phenomenon with pride, like his son had just hit his first Little League home run.

"The doctors said that his lungs were fully developed, just like he was full term. They said they had never seen anything like him. Have you, honey?" Clayton seemed to be bursting with pride. The shock took the rest of Shannon's strength, and she fell into her husband arms. He helped her back to her room, and she wept all the way. Clayton assumed it was because she was as prideful as he was.

The couple, along with Gabriel, settled into their home and began life as a family. Though an unusual family, they may be. Clayton and Shannon both agreed they would just make the best of it and consider it a blessing. Shannon had tenaciously relied on her faith to help her through difficult times before. As a new Christian—or a new rededicated Christian—Clayton was just learning to rely on his faith. Both of their faiths would be put to the test…

CHAPTER 11

"Where is Gabe?" asked Shannon, angst. She had just arrived from the grocery store with groceries still in the car.

"He's in his room asleep. Why?"

"I just wanted to see him."

"You're going to have to stop worrying, Shannon. You can't go on like this, hon. We're going to be fine. We're just a little different, that's all."

"A LITTLE DIFFERENT!" Shannon left the room, red-eyed and visibly upset.

Clayton had grown accustomed to his wife's concerns and suspicions. Clayton himself had grown accustomed to it. "It" was their bouncing baby boy, Gabriel. Bouncing took on a whole new meaning with Gabriel Levi Rinehart.

Shannon stood over her son, who was fast asleep in his official Dale Earnhardt NASCAR bed. He was now 4 months old, 42 inches long, and weighed in at a slender 52 pounds. It was all she could muster not to break down into tears. What made it so difficult to bear was the fact that she loved him so much, warts and all.

And why wouldn't she? Gabriel was a most beautiful child. Shannon thought he had almost perfect features. She also thought that most mothers thought the very same thing about their newly arrived babies, even the ones that weren't so much, but in this case, hers really did.

Big blue eyes, not just blue, but bright sky blue, the color of the sky in early evening in May, just before dusk when the setting sun contrasts the sky. His doll-like eyelashes, the kind most little girls have naturally and women spend hours with eyelash curling tools to replicate what they once had free of charge, fit perfectly on Gabriel's figurine expression. His round face and full cheeks reminded her of the way they used to draw cartoon babies 50 years ago, Chuck Jones perhaps.

His tiny, pouted lips would part with a little-boy smile and subsequent goo at the slightest bit of amusement. Unabashed tenderness sent a maternal telegram to Shannon's heart that it was time to moisten the eyes and cry love tears that only mothers seem to have. Fathers are captured by all these charms, to be certain, but there is an assured degree of tenderness that overwhelms mothers. A connection that is unique in all of creation.

Shannon supposed to herself: *There is a bond between a mother and her child that a father and his child will never have. It's the bond that comes from a person being kept alive within your own body—kept alive from your own blood—kept safe from danger, from would-be boogeymen that love to snatch away such precious little trinkets in the wee hours of the night—all safe now, tucked away in God's loving pouch that comes as standard equipment on all mothers.*

It broke her heart to think that something was amiss with her baby. She didn't understand it, she couldn't understand it, but she was determined to never lose this feeling that serenity of motherhood had planted in her soul. She loved her son, and nothing was going to stop her from it. Whatever the reason that God had in mind for the unusual circumstances that were happening to her son, to her husband, and to her family was all meant to be, and that would just have to do for right now... What comes, comes.

Clayton, on the other hand, seemed strangely oblivious to the extraordinary episode that immersed his family. Shannon couldn't tell if he was in denial or simply trying to make the best of the hand they were dealt by the great dealer in the sky. But in her opinion, Clayton was beginning to take a bad situation and relish in it.

Every extraordinary feat that Gabriel would perform would invariably elicit a gasp from Shannon and an astonished, prideful laugh from Clayton, no matter how amazing or inhuman the feat may be.

Except the time when Gabriel climbed out of his antique crib with extra- high rails that were three feet tall.

"They must have kept babies in their crib till they were 10 years-old back then," Clayton joked when he showed it to Shannon. He'd stumbled on it at a garage sale, oddly positioned on the side of the road. They had told him that it was at least 75 years old and made out of solid 2X4 oak boards. Shannon was not amused at the crack that it could hold 10 year-olds.

Nevertheless, Gabriel managed to climb over the sides of the imposing crib and spill out onto the floor and crawled—more like dragged on his belly at first, then into a wobbly crawl—into the kitchen. Shannon actually irked at the sight of her son, whom she thought was fast asleep, safe, but now crawling around on her kitchen floor. She didn't even know he could crawl, especially since he was only four months old. Clayton, on the other hand, started laughing and clapping his hands to immediately let his son know his father was extremely proud of his herculean feat.

"How did he get out of the crib? Did you let him out Clayton? Did you know he could crawl and you wanted to surprise me?" asked Shannon incensed.

"No, I thought you sat him down in the floor to surprise *me*." Clayton had suddenly lost the prideful look and was now overtaken by concern.

"Did he climb over the sides?" Shannon's hands went to her mouth.

"I don't know. He had to, didn't he?" Clayton stared at his wife blankly.

"Oh my God, Clayton! What will we do to keep him in? What if he gets out in the middle of the night? What if…" Shannon started to tear up and Clayton ran over, took up Gabe, and then embraced Shannon with his free arm.

"Stop, stop," Clayton said, gently interrupting his weeping, frightened wife. "I'll put a top on the crib, or I'll do something, I don't know…" Clayton stopped talking and shook his head. First at empty space, and then at his son, all 52 pounds of him, who was now playfully goo-ing at him with his long legs dangling from his father's tiring hip.

Clayton was having a sudden case of reality check, though he was still optimistic that he would be able to make the best of this "unusual" situation; that his son was still a blessing sent from God; that somehow they were going to come out to the better, and he was going to simply have to *accept* the fact that his son was a lot more than "unusual."

Clayton sat Gabriel on the living room floor, then took a seat in his easy chair and watched his son slowly raise himself on all fours and begin to crawl about the room. Gabriel had the look of a baby boy on an adventure, excitedly yearning to make a new discovery of some unknown trinket or doodad that he could closely examine, usually by testing it in his mouth first, just like all babies do.

Except all babies don't crawl at four months old, and they don't weigh 52 pounds while doing it.

Clayton's mind began to wonder: *How could he be crawling at four months? How did he climb out of that crib? How could he pull his body weight, he's just a baby? How is that possible? He weighs 52 pounds! One of us had to absentmindedly sit him out of that crib and simply forgot it. But how is that possible? We forgot about it? Really? No. That's not it. Think for a minute…There is no other way…One of us, me or Shannon, had to sit him out of that crib. There is no other answer…*

Clayton became transfixed on Gabriel. He watched him closely, curiously observing his child navigate the living room. Gabriel would crawl, just like every other child of crawling age, but with a different approach to new objects. There was keenness, awareness, and intelligence in his eyes. Not an infant intelligence, and not an adult intelligence either, but something akin to what a 2-year-old would acquire. It was a sense of self awareness, of his own being, Clayton surmised.

Now, couple that with the absolute befuddled Dr. Matheson, and now the confounded Dr. Chong, his pediatrician, Clayton's thoughts began to muddle to senselessness. The uncertainty that had burdened his consciousness for all those months of the difficult pregnancy had suddenly infiltrated the positive thoughts he had struggled mightily to acquire. Dread had overtaken him, as a most unpleasant future for his freakish son now loomed in the darkness of his mind.

Indeed, what does the future forestall for an infant of only four months, who can now crawl and apparently have strength enough to free himself from his wooden prison? If he can do this now, what will become of him in a month, six months, a year from now?

Indeed, Mr. Rinehart, you have yourself in a pickle. Will the authorities find it necessary to take him away and study him in a laboratory in New Mexico somewhere? Just like they're studying and experimenting on those aliens that supposedly crashed. The neighbors are already becoming worrisome with their curiosity visits. Not so much to visit, but rather to gawk at the giant baby.

And then there are the phone calls, one after the other, from some newspaper or TV person. With the same tired script: 'Mr. Rinehart I understand that you have a very "unusual" baby in your house. I would like to interview you for our paper, or TV news show, or our magazine.'

You had the home phone number changed and unlisted, but how did they get your cell number? Oh yeah, that big billboard with my face spread all over it announcing what a good insurance man I am. I thought it was smart to put my cell number on it then. I didn't want customers to call the office. Since I paid for it, I wanted them to call me…Boy, they sure are, everybody but customers…How do you change a cell number? Clayton's mind was straining to stay focused and stop worrying incessantly.

Then, he had an epiphany. *Maybe this is a sign from God. I'm getting the urge to move from here. This Jerusalem, Alabama place they tell me is weird anyway. The only reason Shannon wanted to move here in the first place was because of the name and some weird-ass stories of miracles that happened here 30 years ago. I didn't believe any of it.*

To be certain, this place has had weird stuff happen—to us. I don't see the need to stick around here. I can take my insurance job to another state. The agency will even move any of us for free if we are willing to relocate to areas where we didn't have any offices.

Yes, a new start in a new location, away from all the gawking, rude, nosy, stupid-ass people. I believe this is what God wants us to do. Jerusalem, really? What kind of name is that for a town? Whether you believe all the rumors about miracles happening here or not, I do believe this is not the place for us to be right now.

Now, all I have to do is convince Shannon of it. Won't be easy. She's stubborn. And then find a place far, far away from this Godforsaken shithole. Some place secluded and not very populated where we can keep to ourselves. No busybody newspaper reporters. No rude TV cameras following us. Just plain country folks…Just like us.

Shannon's car pulled into the driveway abruptly. The skidding tires stopping angrily, interrupting Clayton's rapt soliloquy. He came to himself and made his way outside to assist her with the groceries. She carried in the groceries; he carried in Gabriel. It was a struggle for her to get him in and out of the car. Managing him from the car to the stroller back to the car was a gauntlet drill.

As Clayton unstrapped the hulking youngster and heaved him to a rest on his hip, the most stupid thought entered his mind: being raised on a farm, he remembered someone saying *that if they could manage to lift a baby calf every day as it grew, they would eventually be able to lift a full-grown bull.* The thought that he just compared his son to a farm animal made him embarrassingly chuckle.

Shannon was not amused at the moment. She looked positively pissed.

"What's the matter with you?"

"I was spied by that damn Hackman, or Hangman, or whatever his name is, that Jerusalem Times guy." Shannon was furious about the pesky newspaper reporter who was in constant pursuit of a photo of Gabe. He had asked politely several times for an interview and several times got turned down. He was a persistent fellow who had taken on more of the persona of paparazzi.

Clayton saw his chance. "I know what you mean. They're never going to leave us alone, you know that, right?" Clayton was waiting—hoping—for Shannon to agree.

"I know they're not," she sighed in disgust, as if it was just a matter of fact.

"Why don't we move from this place? You, me, and Gabe." said Clayton.

"Move! Just like that! How? I mean, what will we do? We have friends here. What will we do for money?" Shannon was so confused over the shocking question her mind began to ramble while she tried to wrap her head around the implausible words she just heard.

"The agency will move us for free; I'll be an agent just like here. They'll pay me 20 percent more salary and a relocation bonus. You won't have to teach. You can be a stay-at-home mom like you've always wanted to be." Clayton was more or less pleading at this juncture.

"I don't know, maybe you're right. I'm getting tired of having to hire men babysitters because most women can't lift him. At this point, I don't care." Shannon wasn't sure of anything. "Where would we go that would be any different from here?"

"One time they offered a big relocation bonus to some place called…Mountain Meadow, Montana. How's that for alliteration. Or, there's another place called…," Clayton quickly took a paper out of his back pocket, "Helpmein, South Dakota. Help-Me-In, get it? The population, I believe, was something like 5,000 or so. I believe the memo said that it had top-rated academics and sports facilities." Clayton was sounding like a used car salesman.

"South Dakota, hum, I do like the sound of Help-Me-In better than whatever Montana." Shannon was beginning to be sold. "That sounds like a place that our son needs to be alright. We need somebody to help us in," she said, trying to disguise a nervous laugh. "It sounds like an Indian name."

"You know as well as I do that we can never live a normal life here, not now." Clayton was sounding more confident. "Dr. Matheson or Dr. Chong can't stop Gabe from growing. I don't think anybody can. He's just going to be big, and that is all there is to it. Maybe if we get to a more secluded spot, we can keep him from the media better. They're just plain people up there, just like us…What do you say hon? Let's do this." Clayton had done his best.

"Fine with me." Shannon wasn't exactly jumping through her butt, but she had to admit that it made sense.

CHAPTER 12

"Hand me that lamp, please." Shannon wasn't about to trust a couple of minimum-wage moving employees with her family heirloom. The movers were both Native Americans, but that certainly wasn't the reason for her cautiousness. Shannon was very liberal when it came to people who were different, even more so now for rather obvious reasons. They both looked like they had just sobered up from a week long drunk, and it was a very nice lamp.

"Hey, I remember when we used to call you guys Indians," Clayton said jokingly, hoping the two burly movers had a good sense of humor. No reaction. Clayton felt a little embarrassed. Nonetheless, he was happy. Helpmein was much more beautiful than the brochure had portrayed. *How unusual*, Clayton surmised, *that a place actually looked better in real life than it did in photos.*

"What do you think so far?" Clayton asked, hoping Shannon was as impressed as he was with their new home. They both had a load of boxes, lamps, and other items for the house in their arms and could barely see each other's faces.

"The house is beautiful Clayton, much bigger and nicer than our old house." Shannon was hoping Clayton could hear her as she could only keep her eyes on the antique stone-cobbled walkway that led to the front door. She stopped just before the first step leading up to the screened-in front porch so she could take in the view of her new house with awe.

"I can't believe this house cost less than our old house. It's brand new for God's sake." Clayton's tongue had a rip-roaring case of the fulsome diarrhea. "I was so worried that the house was going to be a piece of crap. You know, punishment for buying a house without actually seeing it, but man, this is the coolest thing I have ever seen." Clayton thought back to a time when he was a kid and the surprises that Christmas morning brought. He was a little harder to surprise now though.

Clayton had been talking to the real estate agent for a month. He liked her, but being a veteran in the sales business, he knew how the sales game was played. He had to calculate about 25 percent off his expectations for lying. He caught what he had just thought and then amended accordingly: *I mean, sales enhancements.* His own thoughts entertained him at the moment.

"I think I'll give that real estate chick a great big sloppy kiss," Clayton chuckled.

"No you won't." Shannon tried to act jealous.

"Don't worry. If she looks anything like these guys toting in this furniture, I believe I'd just as soon kiss a mule's ass." Clayton's wry smile quickly dissipated when his eyes met the glare of the mover standing beside him instead of Shannon. "I'm not talking about you, of course." Clayton moved quickly up the steps and into the house with a face flushed red with embarrassment.

"How did you say that we got this place so cheap again?" Shannon was stunned by the spaciousness of the pristine abode. "I know I have to teach some at the elementary school, and you have to open up a new branch office, but I still don't understand how you did it. How it is so cheap?"

"Well my dear, it was all politics. Are you surprised?"

Shannon shrugged, "Not really, but how?"

"An Indian Representative from Congress made it happen. I mean, a Native American." Clayton caught it before he embarrassed himself again.

"You can call us Indians," said a booming voice coming from the living room. "We don't mind. Nobody cares… And no, our women don't look like us."

Shannon was looking at a shell-shocked Clayton for an explanation. Clayton put his index finger to his lips for a "shush" sound and whispered, "I'll tell you in a minute. These guys can hear anything."

"Yes we can," answered the same booming voice from the living room once again.

"Oh my God! We've been standing here yakking and forgot about Gabe." Shannon boomed herself with her hands clasping her cheeks. "Clayton, go get him out of the car. I hope he's still asleep." Clayton hurriedly started toward the front door before his frantic wife could get the last syllable out of her mouth.

In about three minutes, Clayton came up the steps and met his wife at the door with their son riding sleepily on Clayton's heavily taxed hip. His legs were limp and his feet came down to Clayton's knees. His round head lay snugly against Clayton's shoulder and almost seemed the same size as his straining father's.

The two rugged Indian movers came out of the living room ready to fetch another piece of heavy furniture out of the van. They stopped, stupefied in their tracks, with their mouths agape. Both men worked as guides for rich people that liked to hunt when they weren't working part-time for the moving company. Both men were wide-eyed when they saw Clayton lugging Gabe through the front doorway; like they had just happened upon a grizzly bear by surprise. Ironically, it was their turn to be embarrassed by their stricken stares.

"This is our son, Gabriel." Clayton could sense the men's awkwardness and decided to break the uncomfortable ice to which the men were standing dangerously afoul.

"Yes, ah, hum, how, how old is he?" One of them said stammering because he didn't know what else to say and remain polite.

"He's seven months," Clayton said while flipping his son slightly up to assure himself a better spot on his hip and to temporarily rest his aching arms.

"Seven, seven years?" The man who asked was sure he heard wrong or that Clayton had misspoken. *Surely that kid was older than seven, but why does he look like a baby in the face,* he thought.

"Seven months," Clayton said in passing as he lowered Gabe to the floor, and began to further examine his new house with an impressed air, while leaving his son standing beside the dumbfounded movers. His adult diaper was hanging loosely at the bottom, bloated with urine. Clayton regained himself from his fascination with his savvy new purchase, whirled around, and noticed Gabe's sagging diaper.

"Would you guys watch Gabe for just a minute while I run to the car and get his diaper bag?" They nodded, still not sure what they were looking at. Gabe was not sure what he was looking at either. He had just woken up and was a little groggy from his long nap. The irresistible hum of the car had its effect on old sleepyhead just like it does with all toddlers. He was trying to figure out how he came to be standing in front of two men he didn't know and to this strange house he had never seen.

He must have figured it out though, because he was off in a toddling flash, most likely in search of Mommy's voice that he could hear down the hall. He passed by the mover who inquired about his age with the top of his head even with the man's chest. Both men turned their heads in unison to observe the toddler literally taking giant baby steps. It was clear Gabe was just learning to walk with somewhat tenuous, unsure steps. His big blue eyes carefully studying where to place each foot. The baby fists precariously extended outward to each side for equilibrium, portrayed the essence of a toddler, viewed through a magnifying glass of course.

Mom came around the kitchen into the foyer in time to nearly bump into Gabe, who was overjoyed to find a familiar face. They swept each other up into a loving embrace, just like moms had done since time immemorial.

It is simply irresistible for a mom, or a dad, to behold little boys or girls toddling toward them with arms outstretched, waiting for the tender protection from whatever boogeyman that may be hot on their trails. Shannon was no different. She swept up baby Gabriel with a loving groan and placed his plump, round cheeks next to her own. Her eyes soon focused on the two movers who now possessed a familiar expression, which she recognized from many awkward past experiences.

"What's wrong with him lady?" mumbled the other mover that never talks, almost to himself, but Shannon heard the anticipated question. She had heard it before, about 1,879 times, she figured. *Maybe here it will only be 683 times*, she thought. The irony amused her.

"Nothing is wrong with him. He's just big," Shannon said with the same aloof, matter-of-fact manner that multiple repetitions instill.

With that, she lumbered with the little big man, as she sometimes thought of him—the name came to her by the remembrance of a movie she saw on TV once with Dustin Hoffman—to a rocking chair that had been justly placed by the now flummoxed and gawking movers.

She cradled her son in her arms and, with great difficulty, placed herself in her favorite chair and began to gently rock back and forth. Both of Gabe's legs dangled from off the chair arm.

The not-unexpected reaction of the two movers had set off her kindled, protective, motherly instincts, which had been bolstered on a daily basis by lookers-on who could not, or would not, understand.

The welling up of tenderness for her son, who she now cradled just like all mothers have done forever, began to overcome her. Her eyes moved to the two men, who, when they noticed that they themselves were being stared at by the giant's mother, regained awareness and started back to work. Then her eyes moved back to her child whom she held snugly.

A certain longing enveloped her soul. A wish. A wish for normalcy. Not for her, but for the sleepyhead whose bright blue eyes were growing heavier as she stroked his blond curls. She believed that she could see the same longing in his eyes too: a certain longing for *normality*.

Does he know? She thought. *Is he aware that something is wrong? I pray that he doesn't. He will find out soon enough, just not now. How could this happen to something this beautiful? What was God thinking?...* What indeed? Rationalization is impossible to impose on the irrational.

She slowly moved her fingers around the curve of the cute pug nose and across each precious, pooched baby lip. Then her thumb rounded the delicate little boy ears that send the heavy eyes of her little big man finally shut. Her heart's cup runneth over. She wept tenderly for her son.

CHAPTER 13

A great philosopher—Augustus McCrae—once said, "*No matter where you live, life is just life. If you want something too badly, it's bound to turn out to be disappointing. You have to learn to enjoy the everyday little things: like a sip of good whisky in the evening, a cool drink of buttermilk, or a soft bed,* or a three-year-old child that's five feet tall.

Yes, Mr. McCrae, we should all be thankful for what we got. That was David Clayton Rinehart's philosophy, anyway. Shannon could appreciate her husband's bravado, but her resolve for her giant son waned from time to time —especially when the toddler came zipping through the house with just his adult underwear on and no shirt and looked her damn-near eye to eye.

But then, after a couple of seconds of a mother-son staring contest—which Gabe would invariably concede by cracking a mischievous grin—he would whirl and flash off to another part of the house, looking for another adventure. The defined muscles in his back were the last sight she saw as he disappeared. "*He's just big,* "she would rationally conclude, almost convincing herself. Perhaps not logical, but rational.

Holding onto rational thoughts became progressively difficult, even for Clayton. Not only was his three-year-old son fast approaching a hundred pounds, but when it was Clayton's turn to be "it" in their latest game of tag, he found the toddler hard to catch. Gabe was frighteningly quick and agile.

He was beginning to develop outlines of muscles— not adult muscle separation but certainly not baby muscles either. He only weighed 97 pounds, but Clayton saw him dashing around the living room, avoiding imaginary tacklers carrying a 10-pound dumbbell as if it were a football.

It became increasingly difficult for Gabe to surprise Clayton anymore. But when he went from speaking baby gibberish, like all average three-year-olds do, to complete sentences in just a few weeks, Clayton was astounded once again. The time span between astonishments was becoming shorter as time passed by.

Yesterday Gabe learned to whistle; today he was trying to draw with a pencil; tomorrow he will learn to count to five. Physical and mental growth is what every parent expects—they count on it, pray for it, and demand it. Clayton and Shannon soon began to dread it. But just like the bright yellow South Dakota sun that beckoned the start of each morning, they could not stop it from rising. *Their son also rose.*

Clayton had garnered some confidence from his decision to move his family to this town. After the mostly American Indian population had satisfied their curiosity with a quick peep at the giant, they soon accepted the phenomenon as merely another quirk of the village. Clayton and Shannon felt safer here.

Helpmein was an outpost village about 100 miles or so northwest of Sioux Falls. Clayton was bolstered even more in his belief that settling in this innocuous spot of the United States had been wise when one of when one of the shopkeepers, a kindly gentleman named Itancan, told him that the word "Dakota" meant "*The Allies.*" The irony was not lost on either of the men.

Itancan (pronounced E-tan-can) humorously explained to Clayton, that it was his adopted Indian name for the tourist season. He chose it because he had a light complexion and would sunburn easily. Therefore, "I-can-tan," or "I-tan-can." The name was actually that of an ancient Sioux tribe.

Clayton liked Itancan from the start, and Itancan reciprocated in kind. One day, just out of curiosity, Clayton asked his new friend what his real name was. "William Smith," Itancan dryly answered.

"Your name is Bill Smith?" Clayton asked with a giggle.

"I know," answered Itancan, sighing. "That's why I changed it. Nobody wants to buy real authentic Indian beads and blankets and stuff from Bill Smith, so I changed it to a more believable and salable name."

"How long does it take you to make these beads and bracelets?" Clayton asked one day, bemusedly admiring some of the brightly colored trinkets judiciously placed on the shop's shelves.

"Oh, let me think." His friend rubbed his chin as though solving a linear equation. "It takes about 20 seconds."

"20 seconds?" Clayton looked dubiously at his new friend.

"Yeah, that's how long it takes me to get 'em out of the FedEx box. They're made in China." Itancan laughed uproariously. Clayton liked him from the start.

Itancan, too, liked Clayton from the start. He could sense Clayton was running from something the first time he wandered into his shop. *He has a lost look in his eye,* Itancan thought. *I wonder what he is running from. Everybody is running from something that comes here to live… A bad job, or a bad marriage, or a bad rap… What's after you, white boy?*

Itancan liked sad stories and wondered how long it would take for him to uncover his new neighbor's account. Today, tomorrow perhaps. Time and circumstance—that's all it takes, and in Heplmein, South Dakota, they had plenty of both.

The time part didn't take long to happen because the next day Clayton decided to bring Gabe to the shop with him. Upon first look at Gabe, Itancan knew what the circumstances were as well. He kept a cool composure about himself though, he thought, considering that a giant kid just walked right off the cover of some comic book and right into his shop.

Itancan's eyes were drawn upon the strange child like a loose piece of steel is drawn to a magnet. It couldn't be helped. It was the laws of nature at work—a magnet, a piece of steel—your eyes, a giant baby—they're both attracted to one another.

It took only a second of gazing for Itancan to switch his mesmerized eyes from the baby to the baby's father. In the eyes of the father, he could get the whole story, not the details, of course, but the circumstances. The anticipation that exuded from Clayton's sad eyes told all the circumstances he needed to know.

They were the eyes that had carried this look a hundred times before, maybe a thousand. Itancan had a quick decision to make at that moment. *Do I react like everyone else would when they see a toddler five feet tall, or do I give this father a break?*

"How can I help you, sir?" Itancan addressed Clayton with a receptive air. "And how can I help you sir?" This time addressing Gabe with a smile, just like the way he greeted any other little boy who had just meandered into a curiosity shop.

The kind gesture from Itancan was unsolicited, unexpected, and highly appreciated. Clayton found a friend that day, and so did Itancan. In fact, he found two of them, maybe two and a half. Itancan put the two-and-a-half part out of his head. He liked when original thoughts popped into his head, but not baby-and-a-half shtick. He also knew that he would get the details that went with the circumstances soon enough, but on the father's time. *No need to act curious, just accept that you made two friends today, and that's not always easy to do.*

And so it was that David Clayton Rinehart and Itancan Smith became friends that day. Clayton did confide all he knew about his son to Itancan; the tough pregnancy, the delivery, the doctors, the specialists, the disease they diagnosed him with, Acromegaly, or something like that, the move, the new insurance office —everything.

Itancan was fascinated. It reminded him of some of the old Indian tales he used to hear as a young boy. *Native American Oral Literature* was the politically correct term for the stories his grandfather used to tell all 30 or so of his grandchildren. They sat around the potbelly stove placed in every reservation shack in those days and listened with varying degrees of attention. Juh-*wert-a Mak-Kai* (The Doctor of the Earth), or something like that, was the word that pushed into his head.

"If I had known something like this was ever going to come up, I would have paid closer attention," he confessed to Clayton when he tried to tell some of the stories, he had heard so many years ago that they seemed like fog to him now. He didn't want it to seem that Gabe was so freakish that it somehow aligned with his grandfather's supernatural tales of giant badgers and woodpeckers and oxen, or whatever.

"It's just made-up bullshit, you know. I never bought into any of it as a kid. I believed in Santa Claus a hell of a lot more. Santa made more sense," admitted Itancan once after he had told all he could remember about one of the creation stories he was once told. Clayton never seemed to make any connection between the wild supernatural Indian folklore and his son. Itancan was relieved. He figured Clay (as he called him) had enough to worry about.

He sure wasn't going to bring up the one about the giants that used to inhabit this country—all of North America, in fact—not now. Not ever. Not necessary. It's all bullshit anyway, right? Better to keep a friendly relationship friendly and keep that one story to himself... Besides, the ravages of time had punctured his mind, and now his memory was leaking out what it once held tightly.

He didn't enjoy most of the conversations he had with the rest of his other friends. Clay was a different matter. It wasn't easy to make friends out here —they come and go so quickly. He wanted to keep Clay, and in a rather uncomfortable, clinical way, he wanted to be friends with Gabe too. It didn't take any special insight to know the boy was going to need all the friends he could get. Besides, Ike —as Clay called him, a nickname that Itancan rather liked (he'd been called worse)—liked Gabe, or perhaps he felt sorry for him. Sometimes, it was hard to tell the difference.

Though he was a child —a baby, actually —he was the best-behaved baby-child of his age Ike could remember. He was a far cry from the countless papooses that had frequented his store over the years. Invariably, a certain phrase —a rather unflattering one — that Ike had heard before came to mind to describe the little brat kids that inhabited his village: *"Like a bunch of wild Indians going to shit."* Running, screaming, breaking things, loud, bratty, spoiled kids.

But not Gabe. He would stand alertly, with a keen eye on all the goodies. Indian gift shop merchandise is an unbearable temptation to a little boy: drums, jewelry, colorful head bands, bow and arrows, mask, dance sticks and such —all hand made by 100 % authentic, native-born, genuine Chinese artisans.

It hardly mattered where they came from. To a little boy—or not so little, since Clay was usually the first to try on a Chief Headdress —the shop was simply irresistible. If Ike hadn't hated the bratty kids who treated his merchandise like on a basketball, he would have named his shop *Simply Irresistible,* after a song he'd once heard on the radio. He didn't particularly like the irony that thought cut with now.

Gabe, on the other hand, would wait for his father's signal before giving in to temptation. The signal, of course, was Clay making the first move. That was another thing Ike liked about Clay — he was just a big kid at heart, and his son was just a big kid, a well-behaved big kid. Ike could tell that Clay was a good father. It shone through, like sunlight through a white bed sheet does on a South Dakota clothesline. Gently, not to bright, just right.

Gabe didn't act like he was three-years-old. It was hard to notice at first Ike reckoned because you couldn't notice anything else in the room besides his size. He didn't act like a four -or five-year-old either, or even like a kid at all. He had a quiet amusement with objects and an intelligent curiosity about how things worked. That was the best way Ike could describe it: a quiet, intelligent curiosity. Not wild or boisterous, not loud, clamorous, rambunctious, or raucous —calmly intelligent.

"Look Daddy, this comes out and makes the pop." Gabe was demonstrating how the pop gun worked.

"That's right, son, Good boy." Clay was rubbing his son's head, reinforcing that it was good to figure things out.

"I couldn't have figured that out till I got in high school," Ike chimed in. "He is one bright little man." Ike cut the statement short. He didn't want Clay to think he was implying that his three-year- old was as big as a man. Clay never let on — just kept looking admiringly at his super-intelligent son. Ike could tell Clay loved his son —despite his size, or because of it, —either way, and in every way, he loved that overgrown son of his. And Ike loved Clay for his humanity. He knew he had a friend in Clay Rinehart, and he hoped Clay felt the same way.

Ike was right about one thing: Clayton loved that son of his. He was also right about another thing too; it was hard to discern if it was because of Gabe's enormous size that Clay was so at ease with him or if it was simply because was his son. One got the feeling that Clayton was going to love his son with all his heart no matter what, or how, he came into the world. Merely being born was enough for Clayton. Yet arriving under these circumstances had made the bond even more enduring.

For the first time, Clayton knew what the parents with special children felt. Accepting the *specialness* was the easy part, accepting the response from the others was the burdensome part. For Clayton, however, a child in a wheelchair or in leg braces might have left some doubt, uncertainty, or even suspicion about whether people they passed had truly noticed the child's disability. When they passed Gabe, there were apocryphal observations, no doubts, nothing equivocal. Your son is a freak, period.

It was in that vein that true love was born and nurtured in the heart of Clay Rinehart. He would watch his son for hours, observing the little things, the childish things, heart-melting things. Hands that engulfed the tiny figurines of soldiers on the battlefield, with the sound effects of pow-puh-bang emanating from little lips, would fortify that the 100-pound toddler was, after all, just a little boy.

His *mens,* as Gabe called them, were about to thwart another eminent monster attack, *this time they were going to get Mommy and Daddy for sure. B*ut at the last moment — just in the nick of time, — mighty Gabe and his band of plastic-coated brothers saved the day. The twinkling blue eyes that searched for acknowledgement that he had indeed just saved the day were met quickly by Clayton's moistening eyes.

An anguished feeling was quickly overtaking Dad as he watched his son play with his *mens,* and an uneasy, disquieted, foreboding feeling that he was watching his son play out his own future life. His beautiful curled-up eyelashes, that would blink quicker and quicker as the enemy would get closer and closer made the feeling that his days of little-boy happiness would be short and few.

Play on, son. I only wish the days would last. Please take me with you. I want to play too.

CHAPTER 14

Time appears and disappears quickly. It is the one inevitable constant in the universe. The world will turn, and days will disappear forever. And so the world turned and days disappeared for the Rinehart family as they did for all the families of Helpmein… The only difference was that the Rinehart family had a member was 5'11" tall, weighed 160 pounds, and by the way, had just turned five years old.

"He'll be fine here, Mrs. Rinehart, don't worry." Miss Pelham tried to sound reassuring. It didn't work. Shannon *was* worried. She had never left her son by himself, especially in a room full of other kids Gabe didn't know. She had no choice. It was the law. He had to go to school.

Money had been tight for the Rineharts. True, they did pay Clayton a bonus for relocating, and yes, he did get a 20% increase in salary, but there was a catch. He had to maintain a certain volume of debits, which was impossible. American Indians, or Native Americans —call them what you will —are not big on insurance. Clayton was now making less and spending more.

Everything pertaining to Gabe cost more. He could, in fact, wear the same clothes as his father for a while —a short while. Seemingly, he had to be bought new clothes on a monthly basis. The state-of-the-art medical center was just that. Politics had placed the facility in the middle of nowhere. Indeed, patients would travel hundreds of miles just to use of its technology and high —priced doctors. But there was a catch to this as well: it was expensive. Just the deductibles were eating up Clayton's dwindling wages.

The doctors wanted to run test after test —all expensive —and the results were the same as those from Matheson and Chong: negative. The doctors, to a man, all agreed: Gigantism, Acromegaly, or hypertrophy of the pituitary gland. Clayton and Shannon got so confused about which was which and what the difference was that they stopped listening.

As best they could decipher, both conditions were both caused by tremendous increases in growth hormone produced by the pituitary gland for various reasons. A tumor was the usual culprit —except in this case, of course, because there was *no* tumor. In fact, the growth hormone level in Gabe's blood *was* elevated but still in the high — normal range for a child his age.

Just like the hick doctors in Alabama, the fancy doctors at Dawkins Medical and Diagnostics Center were just as baffled. Distance and distinction did not make the diagnosis any more sophisticated: *I don't know why your son is a giant.* But *I-don't-know's* cost money. Clayton and Shannon both figured they could stay at home and get the same diagnosis for free.

So it was that they found themselves in a situation where Shannon would have to go to work as a teacher to make ends meet. And the biggest end to meet was Gabe's —no pun intended.

Shannon's apprehension was apropos. This would be the first time the well- protected Gabe would be exposed to other children, besides those who came to his house. The Rinehart's did make a few friends, and friends have children, and children like to play with each other — especially when one of them is a giant.

The conundrum was that the kids who did play with Gabe were twice his age. Not so much because of the obvious size difference—the kids who were twice his age were half his size—but because of the maturity level. Even at the age of five, Gabe was advanced beyond his years.

It was somewhat hard to gauge Gabe and his mental capacities while around other kids his own age, just like it's hard to gauge a Maserati at a tractor pull. Indeed, young Gabe was brilliantly smart — or at least his parents thought so. Brilliant and coy, and it was this (the coy part) that made Clayton and Shannon the most apprehensive. Not the fact that he was the size of a grown man and who would be placed in a room full ants compared to him, but that he would be placed in a room full spoiled brats compared to him.

Yes, the old axiom, *mature beyond his years*, did not apply here. *Coy beyond his years* was the better analogy. Clayton noticed, and Shannon also, a certain cleverness emanating from their son from very early on. More than intelligence, or mere cleverness, he was savvy —or cunning —in his approach to other children. He seemed to gain pleasure in toying with them.

It came to Clayton's attention first —the adroit way his son played with the other kids from the neighborhood, or toyed slyly with his outwitted opponents, who were even twice his age. At first, he became bored, and then it was merely a game to him. But not a game that a five-year-old would play — or even a ten-year-old, for that matter — but a game of wits an adult would consider as a challenge.

That was another eccentricity of Gabe's: his inexplicable competitive nature. Clayton thought himself competitive, but not so much out of nature —rather out of necessity, a byproduct of being shorter than most. "*Napoleon Complex*, "he had heard it called—a small man trying to prove himself equal to a larger man. That's understandable, and for a time, Clayton attributed his son's reluctance to concede even the slightest victory merely to an overly big kid attempting to be special in the eyes of his peers —other than just simply being bigger, of course.

But it went beyond that. Clayton realized that it went much further. One day, a friend of Gabe's came by to play. His name was Razz. Clayton thought it was obviously a nickname, but no —that was his given name. This was an anomaly of the village and all Indian people, Clayton figured. They had rather odd first names. Razz James, for instance, was typical. The villagers would have American last names and weird first names, as if they named their children what they believed to be nicknames on the birth certificate.

Nevertheless, Razz liked Gabe, and Gabe liked Razz —or so Clayton believed. Razz was nine years old and a typical third grader. He had seen Gabe at Ike's store one day and, surprisingly to all, instead of being taken aback like so many others, he spoke to Gabe. Then, they were off —like two peas in a pod, or perhaps like a pea and a carrot.

From then on, Razz would show up at the Rinehart's door ready to play with his new friend, and they pleasantly accepted him into their home.

But it was on this particular day, when Razz was over for a play session, that Clayton first noticed the way his son behaved around his new friend. As usual, a simple game of *hiding the Match Box car from the other* had turned into more than just a game.

Hide-and-seek was out of the question. How do you hide when you're the size of a grown man? Instead, it was game of hiding a tiny Matchbox car in a small bedroom, and the war of wits was on. Each child was to leave the room while the other hid the toy car. Clayton was watching from the den, merely out of curiosity. First, out came Gabe for about a minute, followed by the ready signal. Then Gabe would go in and find the car in about three minutes or so —no problem.

Then it was Razz's turn to wait outside in the hall while Gabe attempted to hide the car from sight. Clayton heard Gabe say, "I'm ready. Come find it Razz," and the door to the bedroom opened. Razz suspiciously entered and began his futile search —futile because Razz never once found the car. Clayton could catch glimpses of the frantic Razz going from this side of the room to the other, turning over this and looking under that, sliding open every drawer, carefully examining every nook and cranny. All in vain, for a tiny Matchbox car that had mysteriously left the room whenever it was Razz's turn to hunt for it.

"You have to be throwing it out the window somehow," a frustrated Razz would bellow.

"It's right in this room right now." Clayton heard his son return with a hoity laugh.

"Let me see your hands," demanded Razz. Gabe opened both hands —no toy car.

"Show me where it is, then. Cause it isn't in here, that's for sure!" Razz was angry.

"Sure, Razz". Clayton watched Gabe get up and put his hands on Razz's tiny shoulders. "Don't get so mad, Razz. They say you're not supposed to get so mad. It causes health problems, they say."

Gabe then turned, walked a few steps to a chest of drawers, opened the top drawer, and produced the car.

"I looked there, damn it," yelped Razz.

Upon hearing that, Clayton thought it was probably time to investigate what was making Gabe's new friend curse so.

"What's the matter, boys?"

"Gabe's cheating somehow, Mr. Rinehart."

"No, I'm not, Razz," said Gabe calmly. "Razz is mad because he can't see too good, that's all dad."

"I tell you Mr. Rinehart, nobody can hide something in plain sight like he can. Something is wrong. I'm not blind. I can see just fine. He's doing something—like magic or something. I don't know, but he's cheating somehow."

"Oh, it's just a game, boys. Y'all play nice." Clayton saw no point in refereeing a game of hide the car.

"I'll bet he can hide it where you can't find it either, Mr. Rinehart." Clayton sensed the challenge in Razz tone.

"I don't want to play. I'm too big to play. Y'all play. Gabe play fair now, okay?" Clayton thought he'd resolved the matter, but curiosity was piqued. Gabe tossed the miniature car into the air, catching it with perfect coordination. His coy smile seemed to mock his father, as though daring him to try.

"OK, I'll play. Hide it from me Gabe." Clayton felt odd about participating—not because he disliked playing with his son, but because the game suddenly felt serious.

"Really Dad?" Gabe walked up and hugged his father, a gesture of gratitude for indulging him.

"I'll go outside. and Y'all call me when it's hidden," Clayton said, stepping through the door.

"You go too Razz," Gabe said, nodding toward the exit.

"No, I want to see where you hide it."

"No, it's my secret."

"Come on, Razz, just play along. I'll show you how to find it. He can't outsmart dear ole Dad now, can he?" Clayton felt dumber by the minute. Reluctantly, Razz left

Clayton pressed his ear to the door, listening for the faintest sound— a drawer sliding, a door creaking— but there was nothing.

Then the door suddenly opened, catching him in the act of trying to gain an advantage over his five-year-old son in a stupid game of hide-and-seek. Gabe was smiling at the cuteness of it.

Clayton searched and searched, and searched, and then Razz joined in at Clayton's urging. And they both searched, and searched, and searched some more. They looked high, they looked low, in every nook and cranny, and whatever was left after nook and cranny has been searched. Clayton was actually beginning to get angry, first at himself, and then at Gabe for cheating.

Gabe lay on his bed, taking in the futility with great amusement. Clayton asked Gabe to show his hands —empty. He even gave his son a thorough pat-down, and again, nothing.

"Okay, son you've had your fun, where is the damn car?"

Gabe stopped grinning and took on a serious demeanor. He could tell his father was genuinely upset. He thought better of refusing, which he had considered.

He got up, walked slowly toward his father, never taking his staid eyes off Clayton's, put his large right hand behind Clayton's back, and removed the Matchbox car from the belt loop on Clayton's trousers, the tossed the toy to his father with a flip of the wrist.

"So you've been hiding it on Razz, just like you did me." Clayton sounded stunned. "That's why you hugged me," he continued mumbling.

"That's why you got so close to me every time it was your turn to hide." Razz had figured it out. "And why you touch me somewhere when I gave up. You took it back off me and acted like you were hiding it…"

"But it was in your hands." Clayton finished the discovered mystery.

"Boy, that sure is smart, isn't it Mr. Clayton? I wouldn't have thought of that in a million years." Razz was sniggering and sounding so relieved that the mystery was solved. He had been seriously worried.

"I wouldn't have thought of it either, Razz." Clayton wasn't chuckling or smiling, but was dead serious in thought, concerned.

How could he think of that? I wouldn't have thought of that. How could he? He's five. Five! Why is he looking at me like this?

Why indeed, Clayton. Gabe never took his eyes off his father. He had a contemplative glare at Clayton, as if he was trying to figure out why his father was so strangely serious over this childish prank. He was, after all, a child. Isn't this what children were supposed to do?

Gabe had long since acquired the self-awareness of his great size. It happened when he was about three. He noticed that *the other children were getting smaller,* at least that's how he phased it. They were *this* size, and now they were *that* size.

Shannon was showing Gabe a magazine one day that had pictures of adults and children conducting various activities. Gabe put his finger on one of the four or five-year-olds holding hands with their father and wondered to his mom:

"Why am I so big?"

Shannon was waiting for just such an occasion. In fact, she had rehearsed it.

"Because God wants you to be special, sweetheart."

"How am I special?"

"You were made bigger than most little boys and girls because God wants you to be a great protector and look out for others." Shannon figured if she could make Gabe's condition seem like some kind of blessing instead of a defect, it would cushion the blow for as softer landing. The world would be ugly to him soon enough —just don't let it be as a baby. *Do you hear me, Lord?*

But now, Clayton could sense that Gabe was coming to grips with the fact that he was smarter and more clever than the rest, and now, *was he actually smarter than his father?* Clayton was almost certain that this was what lay behind the cold, ominously contemplative stare. *Yes, Daddy — or rather should I call you Father? I see into your somewhat cloudy brain. I am bigger, stronger, smarter. I see that now, but what am I?... Clayton left the room...What next Lord!*

Shannon said goodbye one more time to her son, who was almost a half a foot taller than her. It's hard sometimes, she thought, to remember he is still, essentially, just a baby. Reaching up to hug your five-year-old will have that effect. She thought she should walk him in, but he insisted that he could do it by himself, embarrassed by the prospect of it actually.

Shannon drove to her parking spot at the high school. This was her first day on the job as well. She locked her car doors with her mind not on her son who was on his own for the first time, but rather her mind was on the thought that she didn't get the chance to love him long enough as a baby, she construed. She knew that was an absurd thought. Of course. she loved him, but oddly, not as a baby. The time got artificially shortened by his condition. She felt shortchanged because of it.

She could only hold him in her arms for a few months. She could only nurse him for a shorter time still. The gallon of milk per day it took to sustain him is easy for a Holstein cow to produce, for a 120-pound woman, not so much.

The gooey bundle whose sky-blue eyes would gaze deep into her own, for what seemed like hours, would much too soon be replaced with the uninterested glances of a wandering mind. The simple pleasure of giving baby bath, with splashes and assorted baby sounds brought about by the magic of warm, soothing water, reminding the baby of the warm, soothing embryonic bath in which he had spent several weeks inside his mommy —rent-free to boot — only lasted a couple of months. Now, a grown man seems to be in baby's bath.

Now it was all gone, all over, no more baby, no more toddler. All gone, replaced by a man-child who now occupies the body of what once was her little man... *Where is my baby?* She sopped, longingly.

CHAPTER 15

The disbelieving eyes of Gabe's kindergarten teacher, Mrs. Ellen Aberdeen, were affixed upon Gabe as he entered her newly decorated classroom. Mrs. Aberdeen had spent hours and hours making the colorful letters of the alphabet and meticulously placing them on the wall. She was proud of her work and herself.

She even managed to get her husband to help. In fact, Chuck Aberdeen was still there, adding the finishing touches when the bell rang for class to begin. He passed by Gabe entering as he was leaving. A backward glance over the shoulder caused him to broadside the door with a loud thud. Embarrassed, he left without turning back even once for an irresistible second glance at the giant. Gabe paid him no mind. He was becoming immune to startled eyes.

He was, in fact, such a striking figure to behold in broad daylight; it strained the limits of human incredulity not to walk right up to him and gawk. He was just five years old and, for the most part, had a five-year-olds proportioned body, but with broader shoulders and more muscle —a lot more muscle.

His shoulders were beginning to round at the ends. The long arms were showing signs of defined separation between the biceps and triceps. The muscles of his back delineated a clear outline between the trapezius and the latissimus muscles. His thighs had an outward sweep and defined quadriceps, which would be necessary characteristic if he had been doing a workout at the weight room as all the football players were required. But his body still retained most of the childlike characteristics of a five-year-old boy.

Gabe took his place in the high school desk that had been placed in anticipation of his attendance. Mrs. Ellen Aberdeen swallowed hard at the macabre sight of the tiny kindergarteners, all snug in their miniature desks, neatly aligned, and attentively awaiting their very first real-life school lesson. It was a bizarre contrast, almost as if one student was under magnifying glass, amplifying his resolution by three times. The young teacher was shaken but not necessarily stirred.

Kindergarten was not really a class for learning at Helpmein Elementary. It more of a day care for the middle-class working parents. It had great facilities, thanks to government grants and government quilt; dedicated teachers, thanks to the 30 percent higher salaries paid to all teachers who would come to the wilderness school. But years of low expectations and continual lax standards made the school below average as far as academics were concerned, even by reservation standards. In fact, it was the lowest in the state, and in fact, the lowest in the country.

However, Mrs. Ellen Aberdeen was going to change all of that. The letter she received from the Black Hills County School Board informed her that the board had a burning desire to improve all the academic standards of all the county's schools, and academic improvement was an integral part of their recruiting process. That and the $53 million appropriation's bill granted to the county also helped recruiting. Thanks in no small part —100 percent, in fact —to Congressman and tribal Chief, Guttmann Alliaceous (Star Hawk) Steadmire. The first Sioux Indian—mostly Indian anyway—ever elected to Congress.

Nothing like white liberal guilt over the Wounded Knee Massacre to bring home the bacon—and the pork. It was the Congressman's grandiose platitudes that sealed the deal, appropriating the money for the new schools and expiating the white man, at least temporarily anyway, of their sins. Funny how money seems to do that very thing…

In any case, Helpmein, South Dakota ended up with a top-notch school and one of the finest medical and diagnostic centers in the country. They had to put it somewhere, so might as well have been in this disenfranchised part of the country. Otherwise, the Congressman/ Chief might have conjured the Great Spirit to smite whitie on the cheek —or scalp'em —whichever the Great Spirit felt like that day.

It was on all the news. CNN had a field day covering the controversial bill. Nevertheless, it passed, and bod-a-boom, Mrs. Ellen Aberdeen was standing in front of her first class at Helpmein Grammar School calling roll. All of that, along with the fact that South Dakota has a town called Aberdeen—*a divine sign, don't you see*—sealed the deal on her decision to move to the wild frontier.

She didn't fully understand yet why this area of the state had the lowest achievement scores of any in the county. She thought that it was probably because of the parents habitually bad habits. She knew all too well that kids learn more when the parents encourage them. She had heard all the rumors whispered here and about that studying was not exactly an Indian strong suit. It had apparently infiltrated the white population as well because 20 percent of the enrolled children were white, or at least non-Indian. But she was going to change all the innocuous, and sometimes not-so-innocuous, whisperers.

First, she had to see just where these kids fell as compared to other children of the same age from Terre Haute, Indiana where she had taught previously. She thought she would surmise how proficient or lacking her students were in verbal ability by the simple task of asking them to tell something about themselves when she called the roll.

"Hoho Andrews."

"Here."

"What do you like to do for fun, Hoho?"

"I don't know…I like to fish because that's what my daddy likes to do."

"Good, Hoho." Not bad, she thought.

"Benjamin Caravali"

"Here, and I like to play with my computer."

"Really? That's wonderful, Ben. You have a computer. Is it Ben, or do you like to be called Benny?"

"My name is Benjamin, don't you remember?" Gabe laughed out loud. He was the only one that did.

Mrs. Aberdeen continued down the roll. She was somewhat impressed with most of the kids. "Typical kids," she thought. "No difference really from any other five-year-old kindergarteners." She continued the roll and came upon Gabe's name.

"Gabriel Rinehart"

No answer.

"Gabriel? Oh, there you are. You need to speak up, dear?"

"I thought you knew who I was. Don't tell me you couldn't see me." Some of the other kids laughed.

"I just wanted you to speak up and tell us a little bit about what you like to do, okay?"

"Well, let me think about it a minute." All the eyes and ears of the entire class were fixed on Gabe. Most of them just wanted to see if he could talk.

"I like to, ah, I guess the most fun thing to do is kill and eat little Indian babies. I like red meat," Gabe said stoically, with no emotion.

Gasps, and whispers, wild eyes cutting from one to another —the class was aghast.

Mrs. Aberdeen laughed out. Then sheepishly put her hand over her mouth, trying to conceal her laughter. She thought it was funny and beautifully delivered. She was the only one in the room that got the joke, unfortunately.

"These ignorant little papooses don't get this," Gabe said under his breath as he looked around for his expected laughs that never arrived.

Mrs. Aberdeen was still slyly giggling over the jest, but a sudden notion thumped her brain. *He did just make a RED meat joke in front of RED men, but these kids don't understand that. How does he understand that? He's supposed to be five years old.* She felt perplexed by Gabe's sense of humor.

Mrs. Aberdeen observed carefully her supersized student all through recess. His gigantic size made him an oddity, yes, but a dry, witty, comedic sense of humor didn't belong anywhere near a child who was supposed to be only five years old. Something was wrong with this scene, she thought: *an oddity on an oddity. What five-year-old has a dry sense of humor? Deadpan cracks would be clever coming from Leslie Neilsen, Christopher Walken, or Mark Twain, but a five-year-old? What am I saying?! What five-year-old is the same size as my husband? Where have I landed?*

CHAPTER 16

The students in Mrs. Aberdeen's class, Gabe's wee classmates, became happily acclimated to Helpmein Kindergarten, and the fact that a hero of old was in their midst didn't hurt. Gabe developed at a staggering clip. He seemingly, noticeably, grew every day. One day he was up to here; the next day, up to there. But not necessarily in just mere height —he began to expand outward in bulges of newly formed muscle.

He was simply impossible to take one's eye from. He was a bizarreness that would fit appropriately on the cover of one of Stan Lee's comics but was an aberration that our real-life experiences would not accept.

Everyone has seen 17- pounds giant catfish (or at least photos of them) when the average size for such fish is 7 pounds. There are giant squids, giant pandas, and giant centipedes, too. You've heard of the word giant in front of many animals —except one. There are no giant people, just very tall people or very big people. Save for carnivals or wrestling rings, giants are not associated with human beings —except one.

Clothes that were loose- fitting the first time Mrs. Aberdeen noticed him wearing the ensemble to class were tight-fitting the next. The thought actually entered her mind that if she put him naked in a chair and concentrated hard enough, she could actually see the skin expand. But as unbelievable as the child's physical growth was to comprehend, his brain was becoming just as muscular as his herculean body.

More than once, Mrs. Aberdeen had to snap herself out from a self-induced macabre reverie...*Fee-Fi-Fo-Fum...I smell the blood of Mrs.*

Aberdeen, and she is daydreaming about me again... She sure would go good on whole wheat right now... Yes, Aberdeen beef, my favorite. It's what for dinner... A sudden jolt of consciousness would catch her as she lost her place in class. She hazily wondered to herself whether she might wake up in a hospital ward somewhere, realizing that the insanity drugs had worn off. She even chuckled one or twice at the ridiculousness of it all. Ridiculous or not, it was happening, and she was witnessing it all before her disbelieving eyes.

The gigantic, muscular body of Gabriel was one thing; his gigantic, muscular brain was another. One was easy to see —no clouds in the way. Just open your eyes, and voilà, there it is. Like the Rocky Mountains, literally as big as life. All one need do is pull mightily on the yoke in the cockpit, and your plane might just gain enough altitude to skim over the top.

His mysterious mind was a little hazier than the Rockies, a little more cloud-covered to see through. Mrs. Aberdeen got the feeling that her plane, your plane, everybody's plane, was headed for a crash in the misty fog of Gabriel Levi Rinehart's brilliant mind. To her, this was a much scarier proposition to navigate.

Just as his father had observed before, Mrs. Aberdeen was also an eye witness to the humorous, clever, and sometimes cruel games Gabe made of his inept classmates. Everything and everybody was a game. His invisible strings manipulated his unsuspecting puppets like a giant Stromboli.

School work was a joke to him. "*Since he could read and write as well as I can, "*thought Mrs. Aberdeen, *I will get him tested and advanced as far away from me as they can get him —maybe to high school even. That's where he belongs.* Because it wasn't just merely his tiny classmates living in their tiny world with their tiny brains that Gabe satisfied his competitive nature upon. Now it had become his tiny teacher, living in her tiny world, because her tiny brain was a bit more challenging, you see.

"Mrs. Aberdeen, did you know that you have the same name as a town in South Dakota?" Gabe asked Ellen matter-of-factly.

"Why yes, I do. It's one of the reasons I decided to move here, Gabe."

"I thought so. You strike me as that type."

"What type is that?" It was taking a few seconds for it to register that a giant with a five-year-old's face had figured out what *type* she was. She unwittingly asked the rhetorical question like she would have to any adult. It was simple habit.

"The type that would like to see your own name on a map."

She didn't know exactly what to say. *Did he just insult me?* After a pregnant pause of an embarrassing length, she finally said the only thing she could think of.

"What do you mean by that, Gabe?" She really did want to know.

"I'm just saying that you're not all that pretty, and ugly people look for other things to give themselves stature, like their name on a map, for instance." Gabe wore no emotion on his face, just deadpan blankness.

Ellen was stunned into embarrassed silence. She had just been called ugly in front of the whole class by a kid. Anger flowed over her. She wanted to retaliate by saying, *"Look who's talking,"* but it instantly occurred to her not to say anything about his gigantism. Still, she was seething and wondering, secretly hoping something insulting would come to her. She didn't have to say a word, though.

"I was just kidding, Mrs. Aberdeen. Didn't you know I was kidding? You know that you really *are* pretty, right, Mrs. Aberdeen?" He said with the same dry demeanor.

What a damn thing to say to me. You damn thing from another world, she said to herself, sensing his insincerity. It was, in fact, a touchy subject with Ellen Aberdeen—her looks. She had spent many dollars and endured much mental anguish on her face. She was born with a cleft palate. But not just a cleft—it was so badly deformed that it repositioned her nose. It took several attempts to restore her face to normal, and the surgeons did a remarkably good job. No one could barely tell, *barely* tell. Very few people ever knew.

Nevertheless, there was the slightest speech impediments that was common in most cases of *cheiloschisis,* the medical term she learned to spell when she was four. Ellen was determined from a very young age to overcome even the slight lisp she had developed. Only the most discerning of ears could detect any malady in her speech. Yes, Mrs. Ellen Aberdeen was somewhat self-conscious about her face and her speech. She figured she was being paranoid again, a condition that children born with cleft palates develops naturally.

"Oh, come on Mrs. Aberdeen, it's not like you're a harelip or anything. For gosh sakes. What I'm saying is—YOU HAVE NOTHING TO WORRY ABOUT, RIGHT?" Gabe giggled childishly when he said it.

Ellen had a paralyzed stare and said to herself: *You little bastard, I mean you big bastard. You know, don't you? How could you know? You ARE from another planet.*

It was at this point, when she became the brunt of his capricious games of wit, that she became authentically scared of him. Up until then, he was just a gentle giant, an extremely over-grown child. But lately, he had become something else to her: something scary, some*thing,* perhaps truly from another world— maybe the underworld.

It was only a passing thing to note, an interest—the way Gabe interacted with the other kids in the class at first. The way he would see how many of his classmates it took to pile on his back and bring him to his knees…The answer: all of them. How many kids could he carry a distance of twenty feet? How far could he fling this one as opposed to that one? Everything was a game. His only competition was himself, and *he* always won.

The mind games were cruelly perpetrated upon his inferiors for his own amusement. Apparently, much enjoyment and important data can be gleaned from *hearing that flying saucers were landing near the school. He would convince every student in class to pile into the closet, claiming he would use his great size to protect them— only to be sitting blamelessly at his desk when Mrs. Aberdeen returned, clueless about the whereabouts of the missing children. Of course, he neglected to tell the children about the snake he placed in the closet before class. It's funny to watch kindergarten children melt down into pandemonium, isn't it?*

Mrs. Aberdeen was not amused when her students came trampling over each other as they hysterically escaped the closet upon discovering the rattler (a rubber one) coiled underneath a piece of cloth.

What did amuse her was Gabe's reaction to his prank. He took notes, carefully detailing who came out first, who came out the swiftest, and who showed the most dexterity and athleticism. She looked over his shoulder and noticed the categories. He had several notes on everyone in his class, including her.

Why she wondered.

And so, it went for the giant of Helpmein, South Dakota…unstoppable growth…incredible intelligence…undeniably cunning…unquestionably scary…

CHAPTER 17

He ducked his head with a practiced swoop as he exited his mom's car. Nine-year-old Gabe was used to ducking to get his 7'2" frame out of cars. The Ford Explorer's suspension creaked upward, as if with a sigh of relief. It had been hauling around 345 pounds of all man—or all boy, actually. The 33" wide clavicles would make him appear rather man-ish. The nine-year-old voice made him kind of child-ish. The 210 IQ made him definitely genius-ish. His maniacal cunning made him something else-ish. It was the something else-ish that had Clayton and Shannon Rinehart rather skittish.

"Here he comes, Dzoavits," whispered Juno Tenpenny, loud enough for Wiz Manso to hear, yet soft enough to stay out of earshot of Mr. Danbury, the 6th grade teacher at Helpmein Middle School. Mr. Danbury's patience was precarious at best. He had signed on as a well-paid teacher of sixth-grade kids, not as a study subject of some psychological warfare nightmare to which he had become an unwitting participant. Unfortunately for the weary teacher, the horrid games were afoot again today.

"Don't nobody let on nothing," Wiz warned his fretful classmates.

They had all become victims of Dzoavits (Lakota for *Tall Man*, or at least that's what Ike was overheard calling Gabe). Though they were twelve and he was nine—advancement testing rules would only let him advance three grades—they were still no match in their *war of wits* with Gabe, and they knew it. But it didn't keep them from trying, if only in vain.

A trap had been laid for Gabe, just like it had been a few days before. Retaliation, you see. A *revenge-of-the-nerds* type of thing, Gabe surmised, except he didn't call them nerds exactly. The word he used was *Nimrods*. Though they didn't know what it meant, and he never explained, they just accepted the fact that it was probably something that meant *stupid*. All they knew for certain was what *he* thought about *them*: not much, if at all.

Gabe's processor-like brain, however, seemed to be preoccupied with other matters rather than his insignificant classmates. When he cut his sky-blue eyes toward them, he was in deep thought, looking at them, but not seeing them. They were occupying the spot his eyes were resting on, yet he was seeing something else in their places. The something else was the scary part. What did he see? No one knew. It was just as well they didn't.

"Hey, Dzoavits, we have you a new desk and it's just for you," smirked Juno when Gabe saw the six-foot-tall desk. The same one that made *Billy Crystal appear* even smaller than he actually was for a movie scene—*perspective.*

"You know that Dzoavits just means *tall man*, right?" returned Gabe with the same snarky tone in which it was given. "It doesn't mean anything bad like you think it means. Of course, I wouldn't expect you to take in much, not with your limitations and all."

"We may be limited, as you call it, but we're not some GD freak from Mars or something." Juno had a terrible habit of cursing when he got mad or scared. Right now, he was both.

"If you had paid attention in class, you would know that Mars couldn't support even the lowest life forms—not even your dumbass."

"But with a processing unit of such limited capacity,
Your ignorant ass simply lacks the audacity."

Gabe had begun to mock his rivals in rhyme sometimes, but only when he seemed bored or angry. It managed to irritate his classmates even more, which was the point.

"We got as much capacity to process as you have. You just talk funny 'cause you think it makes you look smart, you big weirdo." Wiz was getting angry again also.

What Juno was referring to was the gigantic desk that was used as a prop in the movie *My Giant,* starring Billy Crystal. Mescal Standback, who was an administrator in the office, was surfing the internet and saw that the desk prop and some other movie paraphernalia were being auctioned online to raise money to preserve, ironically, movie props and other paraphernalia from yesteryear. The giant desk was a prefect replica of a school house desk, so she pointed it out to Principal Summerhawk, and they wrote the studio a letter and promptly appropriated the desk as a donation.

It was not meant to be a joke but as a practical matter of size and comfort for their one *special* student. Gabe simply could no longer fit in the regular-sized desk. More than once, he had stood up with the standard-issue high school desk still attached to his mammoth frame.

It was on the occasion of the desk's first appearance in class that brought about the anxious anticipation and the beginning of today's games. Juno and Wiz had actually witnessed the delivery of the prop to the school the afternoon before. They had both agreed that sabotage was the only logical answer to their "Gabe" problem. Embarrassment was the name of the game, and the game was not trending in their favor. It was Gabe 108; Juno, Wiz, and the rest of the class 0. Those weren't the correct figures, but as far as the two boys were concerned, it might as well have been.

Trying to beat Gabe the Giant, or Dzoavits, or whatever his classmates were calling him this month, in embarrassing, highly planned, and well-thought-out traps was as difficult as defeating him at basketball— "damn near impossible," Wiz would utter, as one after the other of their serendipitous pranks would be turned against them instead. These two recipients seemed to be humiliated on a daily basis.

Wiz was his real name, given to him by his father. "It was because my father had a premonition that his son was going to be clever," he proudly let slip in front of the class one day

"That's not what he told me," Gabe quickly snapped upon hearing the prideful revelation. Everyone's attention was then turned toward the booming voice of Gabriel Rinehart, class wise guy and a particular tormentor of one Wiz Manso.

"No, what did you hear my father say?" Wiz felt the pregnant pause was going on too long.

"No, he said he got the idea of your name because every time he thought of you being born, he had to take a piss."

Restrained giggles at first gave way to uproarious laughter. Wiz wanted to attack, but the folly of such nonsense was reinforced by his close friend, who wisely grabbed hold of Wiz's arm. "Don't be an idiot, just be patient, Wiz. We're gonna get him this time," cautiously whispered Juno.

"Why don't you try out your new chair, Gabe?" asked Juno pleasantly, no sarcasm.

Gabe eyed him suspiciously.

Mr. Danbury had just entered the room and noticed the desk, which was impossible to miss, of course. It was so enormous that it could only be accounted for as a practical joke, but he knew the desk was donated to the school, and it was no joke.

"Go ahead, Gabe and try it out," said the teacher. He was actually anxious himself to see how the boy would size up to such a ridiculous piece of over-the-top slapstick comedy. *Anybody else would like a two-year-old sitting in a grown up chair, but maybe not Gabe,* he was thinking.

"Go on, Gabe. It looks just like a king's throne, doesn't it?" giggled Juno, unable to hold back the soon-to-be amusement which would come his way when Gabe sat in the desk, and he and Wiz's carefully laid trap would be sprung.

"Yeah, you think you're our king anyway. Why don't you sit down and take a look at all your subjects." Wiz was a little more serious than his best friend, but Juno wasn't the one who had just been stung by the clever giant whose stinger was not only large but extremely pointed.

The day before, after class, June and Wiz got a handsaw out of the janitor's closet and meticulously cut the two back legs of Gabe's new super-sized desk just deep enough so that his 345 pounds would cause the legs to snap and dump Gabe's big, smart-ass on the floor. This time, the laughs would be cast toward Dzoavits for a change.

"OK, since you put it that way. I do like the way that sounds, Juno: *The king of the class.* Yes, I believe you just might be on to something, you insignificant ant."

Gabe went to the desk, pirouetted and sat down hard with a thud, stretched his long legs out, casually placed one size nineteen's on top of the other, then just as casually interlocked his fingers behind his head.

Nothing happened. No crash. Nothing.

"You are right about one thing," said Gabe leaning forward and glaring seriously at his dumfounded foes, who were staring blankly at the desk legs, wondering why it didn't crumble and spill out Gabe as planned. "You are definitely *my* subjects, and don't you ever forget it."

Their eyes soon focused on the pieces of 2 x 4 scabbed over the two cuts. They looked at each other perplexed and then at the victorious Gabe.

"Oh yeah, I came in after you guys had left and patched the chair legs as good as new. I even used the same saw you used. It really is surprising what you can find in a janitor's closet: hammer, nails, a saw, and glue, all kinds of glue. White glue, clear glue — everything you need really." Gabe was sounding more like he was a thirty-year-old diabolical mad scientist than ever. Mr. Danbury was not amused by the theatrics in his class but was becoming accustomed to it.

"Yes, the King and his court. I guess that makes you the court jesters. I believe they call you the *fools*." Gabe began to laugh, and he was soon joined by some of his other classmates. The other kids didn't want to laugh, but it was one of those embarrassing situations that no other response would do.

"All three of you go to the principal's office. I believe you know the way." Mr. Danbury uttered those words as casually as if he had said them a hundred times before, which wasn't far off.

Gabe jumped up and quickly exited the room. He was to be followed by Juno and Wiz, but they were having trouble getting up from their desk. Something was holding them in place. Finally, one, then the other, tore loose from the powerful grip their respective desks had on their pants.

Tearing sounds, almost simultaneous, was heard echoing through the room and down the hall. Both boys looked at the remains of their dungaree's bottoms glued firmly to the desk seats. They quickly used both hands to cover their exposed underwear. It was hard to tell which happened quicker: them fleeing the room, or their faces turning blood red. Most of the class agreed it was a tie, when they could stop laughing, of course… Foiled again.

The disagreeable thoughts of yet another victory for Gabriel Rinehart would come later for the class, but for now, it was just plain funny. And even when it's at your own expense, funny is funny.

Juno and Wiz were in a dead sprint. The thought of their underwear flapping behind them didn't matter at this point. All that was on their embarrassed, pissed-off minds was that this time, they were going to do something about it. Gabe had to pay for this. Giant or not, be damned, they were going to kick his big ass.

There is a mechanism, —a self-regulating mechanism —that comes as standard equipment on every man or boy alike. This regulator is located somewhere near the frontal cortex, as best anyone can figure. It sends a signal to the courage box, or common-sense box, or, more aptly, the self-preservation box, as most men of wisdom might suggest. It is located near the front of the brain because it doesn't take long to activate when applicable. This mechanism is what keeps a man alive. It has worked well for thousands of years.

Here is a good example of how the mechanism works: Juno and Wiz raced wildly toward Gabe with fighting on their minds. After all, they had just shown their asses to the class, literally and figuratively. What else could they do? This time was too much. There is a line that cannot be crossed, and Gabe had just crossed it. Not only did he ruin two pairs of expensive pants, which they were going to have to give an account for when they got home, *but it happened in front of the girls.*

Being humiliated is one thing, but to bear the burden in front of the girls? Not this time. They were going to tackle his big ass and pulverize the giant bastard. They had restrained themselves from doing this before. Something had always managed to stop them, but today would be different. They might very well get the worst of it, but men have to make a stand sometimes. That's what their fathers taught them anyway. That was what their brave warrior heritage demanded.

Gabe heard the advancing boys and turned quickly, suddenly, and menacingly. Seven feet two inches, with 33" wide shoulders — just the bones in the shoulder, not the 4" of rock-hard muscle attached to each socket. A barrel chest that tapered down to a waist that was so small that it resembled the emaciated Holocaust concentration camp detainees. His pants were so baggy around the waist that he was constantly in violation of the "Baggy Pants Law," the only dress code restriction in the school.

Veins were becoming more prominent, more distended every day, and even began to show clearly defined outlines through his ever-tightening shirts. Both boys slid to an abrupt halt just feet away from the hulking Gabriel. The mechanisms of self-preservation kicked in.

A man, a boy, a child, knows that when someone is this much bigger, this much stronger, and especially this much meaner than you, it's time to have a discussion about this dispute. No need to fight right now. Surely some understanding can be reached between reasonable people.

"You're gonna pay for this Gabe." Wiz was almost in tears at this point.

"Yeah, I know." Gabe returned philosophically.

"I mean it." Wiz wanted to hit him, except for the mechanisms.

"You guys cut the legs on my chair,
And when it was discovered, so easily you scare,
 Surely now, boys, you must confess,
 That your anger comes from your easiness to best."

This pushed Juno and Wiz even further. Those stupid rhymes. It was like pouring salt on an open wound; it stung. Gabe only used them when he got overly excited or angry. It was as if he couldn't help himself. They just popped out accidentally. *He* was even surprised when they came spewing from his mouth, as if he didn't understand the reasons for it either. But they did come through a clenched jaw, and just like the unstoppable South Dakota bitterly-cold, biting wintery winds, they were inevitable.

After his poetic soliloquy, the boys noticed —for a split second, anyway —a confused visage in Gabe. A look they had never noticed before today. As if he was embarrassed by the sarcastic poetry. But it was short-lived, however, and the cocky swagger of a superior being quickly returned to the face of Gabe, where it belonged.

"Again?" Principal Summerhawk had grown weary of his frequent quests. "Sit down." He was reading a letter or some piece of mail. "How do you like that desk, Gabe? You know that desk was in a famous movie, don't you?" The Principal was proud of his bargain.

"I didn't know that. Which movie?" burst forth a curious Juno.

"My Giant with Billy Crystal."

"Who? Never heard of it?" Juno gave the old shrug of the shoulders.

"I have," retorted Gabe. "It's about a tall basketball player, and it's hardly famous."

"It may not be all that famous," returned the defensive principal, "but at least we got it for you."

"You're right," Gabe thought for a minute. "It was a thoughtful gesture."

Wiz and Juno were speechless. They had been waiting for another sarcastic remark or at least to be *ratted* out about the attempted sabotage. Neither happened. Instead, Gabe was nice about it... This was scarier still.

CHAPTER 18

"Gabe, could you hand me that can from the top shelf there?" Clayton was pointing to the Turtle Wax can on the top shelf in their garage. Gabe was good at reaching things. When you're 7'8" and have 92" wingspan, it's what you might call *a decided advantage.*

A decided advantage, which was the turn of phrase that Clayton used to describe the fact that his son was two feet taller and a couple hundred pounds heavier than any of his teammates. *Teammates,* because Gabe was finally allowed to play varsity basketball this year. Clayton didn't want his son to feel any more superior than he knew he already did, but he didn't know how to prevent it.

It was hard not to feel superior, Clayton surmised, especially when you can score at will and, if the notion struck you, stop anyone else from scoring— again, at your will. He, in fact, could do whatever he fancied doing on the basketball court. It was his court, and his opponents, and often his own teammates, were mere court jesters.

It had taken an act of Congress, literally, to let Gabe be tested for advancement again, primarily, and in this case specifically, so he could play varsity basketball. Eleven-year-old Gabe had already been advanced three classes, the maximum under state law, but there was nothing in the statutes that forbade being tested again, and there lay the pathway to Gabe playing basketball with kids six years older than him.

Age hardly mattered, however. He toyed with whoever was on the court with him in any way. Age, grade, size, and even profession were irrelevant. Yes, profession, because the unnerving fact was that no NBA player would have had a chance and Gabe knew it. More importantly, Clayton knew it too. Not only knew it, but feared it.

Gabe could dispose of defenders on the basketball court as easily as he could have achieved whatever outcome he wanted on the *Certified South Dakota Advanced Placement Examination*. Gabe asked his father what he should score on the exam so as not to bring about more attention than could be absorbed. "I don't know, son. See what the minimum is to advance three grades and shoot as best you can for that mark," his father cautiously advised. Gabe heeded the advice, knowing the consequences of showing off.

Self-awareness had become the new obstacle to overcome for Clayton's son. But, as usual, Gabe was a fast learner. Suspicion was to be avoided at all cost. This was the lesson that Clayton was trying to teach his amorphously nebulous son, as he knew that high scores on tests led to suspicions. Suspicions led to investigations. And investigations led to Helpmein, South Dakota. And that, well, led to Gabriel Rinehart. More news, more reporters, more TV cameras, more trouble.

In a detached sense, Gabe understood why his father didn't want him to do as well as he could have on tests and in sports. He knew and understood that he was drastically different from other kids and other people. He could grasp the reasons why it was not always a good thing to stand head and shoulders above the norm (pun intended). But he had one particular flaw: he couldn't control himself from performing, from proving, from winning. "He has an innate competitive nature he was born with, an innate competitive nature he will die with," Clayton sorrowfully admitted to Shannon. She concurred with Clayton's unfortunate prognosis.

But Clayton knew that he couldn't give up on his son. Even though he was in a very real sense scared of Gabe, of what he was capable of, and of what he was capable of becoming, he still loved his son. He was *his* son. Thoreau said that *most men lead lives of quiet desperation and go to the grave with their song still in them*. Clayton was living a life of quiet desperation and had to contain his song buried deep inside him. The mere thought of singing his song sent the icy fingers of despair down Clayton's spine. He had a super being for a son and couldn't tell anybody about it. *Sweet irony*, he thought.

At least that's what he thought sometimes. Sometimes his thoughts went to other places. Darker places. Places reserved for that part of the mind left for the subconscious to sort out because the conscious simply couldn't accept the unbelievable.

For unbelievable was what his beloved son truly was. Clayton witnessed a transformation, more like a metamorphosis, from what once was a very large, playful child into something that the English-speaking world has no language for. How does one describe the indescribable? Mere adjectives are inadequate, just like his hapless classmates and opponents on the court.

For those who paid their money and witnessed his exploits of physical prowess, he was the stuff that dreams are made of. For others, however, he was a walking, talking, breathing nightmare. Humiliation seemed to be the goal, not the points. Anyone can score on anyone; that is a truism. But no one scored on Gabriel Rinehart without his permission, and permission was never given without dues first being paid.

The dues were your manhood. He took that like candy from the proverbial baby. He could elevate his almost 8 foot body from the floor with the slightest of effort, float in the air like he was suspended on one of Hollywood's invisible cables, catch the ball in midair only seconds after the shooter was sure that just this once he actually got a shot off against the mighty Gabe.

Upon lightly touching down, like a colossal ballerina, from Russia perhaps, a stare would follow: a blank stare, cold, emotionless, and straight into your disbelieving eyes. *I own you,* it said. *I own everything about you. While you are with me on this court, I own you. And I'm not selling you back at any price. The only way a repurchase can be bartered is when you leave this court, and then not all of you can go home. A part must stay behind with me, because I own it now.*

Which part must stay? *That part,* that part of your soul that acknowledges: *You are the best I have ever seen, the best there is today, and the best that ever will be. I, Gabe, am your superior in every way, and there is nothing you can do about it.* In essence, your manhood. He relished in *your* manhood, because it became his. He owned it, lock, stock, and barrel.

Clayton could see that. Gabe could see that too. But he couldn't do anything to stop it. He was being pulled from within and pushed outward toward something ugly. Father and son both knew.

Whatever Gabe's understanding of not holding back, of not drawing attention to himself through his physical and mental exploits, might have been, it mattered not; it was all rendered moot anyway. Attention was coming his way no matter what he did on the court. He was developing into a physical phenomenon that the locals simply could not comprehend.

The oohs and ahhs from the crowds—that's what nourished Gabe, and he was well-fed from the Helpmein crowds. Feeding frenzies were commonplace. They all, to a man and woman, agreed that he was a physical phenomenon, and the best athlete that had ever come from these parts—or from any parts. Unlike most high schools, this mostly Indian crowd was hard to impress.

There were usually only about 50 to 75 people showing up on a weeknight to watch high school basketball. Now there were 400 to 500, cheering, leering, and sometimes sneering in disbelief.

Something just wasn't right. Something was wrong with this picture. Most came out of sheer curiosity, to satisfy their morbid inklings. But 11-year-old, NBA-quality kids didn't just happen by every day—not here, not anywhere, not even from this planet. Their mouth's gaped open, and from open mouths came words, and words have a way of finding ears. They would soon be coming.

To Clayton, it was a bittersweet. He knew that something besides being very large was wrong with his son, and he also knew, as his fame grew, that anonymity would not last. People would seek him out. He might have to move again. He knew better than to acquiesce to the obsequious coach who literally begged him to let Gabe play. It seemed logical since Gabe had been beating the coach's best players since he was seven.

Still, he knew better. Nothing good could come from his son's fame but the vicarious allure of fame itself. Clayton's fame, Clayton's importance, was like a deadly nectar that seemed too irresistible not to sample. *Only a sip,* Clayton figured, *wouldn't hurt anything after all. One tiny sip, just to see what it tasted like.* Of course, all addicts start with this folly. Before long, a sip becomes a gulp, and a gulp becomes a guzzle.

Clayton knew he was guzzling his son's attributes and importance. He also knew he had to stop it or lose him. The problem was stopping Gabe. Not an easy thing. His son was very persuasive. Just his sheer presence, his mammoth physicality, was brutal to dissuade.

Clayton also had another little problem: the physical at the medical center. He had put the persistent doctors off for as long as he could. He was going to have to carry Gabe in for the exam because it was required to play varsity sports. He had no idea what was going to happen. He dreaded it bitterly.

CHAPTER 19

"Here are our basic findings, Mr. Rinehart," said Dr. Donald Simmons as he leaned forward and crouched over his desk apprehensively. Taking on a sheepish air, he seemed almost embarrassed to disclose the results of the physical his staff had performed on their prize patient. Clayton was anxious but wasn't really expecting to find anything new since their last visit over a year ago.

Shannon didn't want to go; the substitute wasn't available that day, and besides, she has heard it all a hundred times before. She had resolved herself to the fact that medical science had no answers for her son, who picked her up like a doll each morning to kiss goodbye.

The doctor began:

- Age: 11 years, six months, and 13 days.
- Height: 242.67 cm, or 7' 11"—Normal height: 52"
- Weight: 123.16 kg, or 371 lbs.—Normal weight: 79 lbs.
- Body fat: 0.73%, as measured by (ADP) Air Displacement Plethysmography—Normal top athletes: 6 to 12%
- Heart rate: 23 (HRrest)—Normal: 73(HRrest).
- Basal level GH (Growth Hormone): 10-20 ng/mL (normal)
- Involuntary Reaction Time: 250 to 300 milliseconds—This was the same as a Mongoose.
- Muscle Mass Percentage: 67%—Normal: 39%

"Ok, what are you saying?"

"I'm saying your son isn't human. Not in the sense that is measurable for normal human beings."

"Ok, what are you saying?"

"I'm saying, your son is not normal in any sense of the term."

"Ok, what does that mean?"

"Something is abnormal about your son."

"Do you know how many times I've had this same conversation? Huh? How much is this physical going to cost me? Whatever it is, I'm not paying a penny of it." Clayton wasn't really angry, just conveying information.

"There will be no charge for the examination or the test. We wanted to do it for our own curiosity, Mr. Rinehart."

"Go on and finish it. You left off an adjective in your sentence, doctor."

"I don't follow."

"Our own *morbid* curiosity, Dr. Simmons. *Morbid curiosity.* God, Gabe is right; we mortals *are* stupid, tiny people." Clayton caught what had just unconsciously slipped out of his mouth and looked sympathetically at the perplexed doctor. Clayton couldn't believe he said it either. Disgusted with the results, the waste of his time, and himself, Clayton stood up and made for the door…

"There is one other thing, Mr. Rinehart," said the doctor uneasily, like he didn't want to pile on any more bad news.

Clayton turned, angrily anticipating some more crap he already knew.

"We tested his IQ."

"I know what it is, uh, 210, or something like that. He has been tested before, Dr. Simmons," said a dejected Clayton, who continued out the door.

"Not exactly, Mr. Rinehart, no sir. That's not what we found." The doctor had to shout the last words as Clayton was out of sight. In a few seconds, Clayton came dismayingly back into Dr. Simmons's office and sat down in the same chair he had just left.

"What did you find?" Clayton looked like a man uncertain or scared of what he was about to hear. He'd been frightened and paranoid about his son's acumen ever since Gabe could crawl.

"We found we can't test him the normal way we test other ordinary people. He plays games with us. Answering impossible problems, playing dumb on easy ones, and so forth."

"Yeah, he does me that way too. I really don't know how smart my son is, Dr. Simmons. You understand then, don't you?"

"That's the way we felt also. So we did something a little different. We did a EEG on his brain."

"An EEG?"

"Yes, an Electroencephalography."

"I know what the damn thing is!" Clayton barked at the doctor, annoyed. Clayton desired him to tame both of their morbid curiosities though, the doctor's and his.

"It measures voltage fluctuations resulting from ionic current flows within the neurons of the brain."

The added information only amped up Clayton's impatience.

"Yeah, yeah, get to it."

"Well, alpha, beta, theta, and delta brainwave patterns vary widely in normal people depending on several factors, like age and activity, and so forth." The doctor peered over the paper at Clayton. "Let me give you an example: Awake and relaxed adults typically have an alpha pattern between 8 and 13 cycles per second."

The doctor stopped looking at Clayton and returned his eyes to his paper and became much more subdued and softer in speech. He held a long pause before he sighed his next words.

"We measured your son at 98 cycles per second."

"What does that mean?" Clayton sighed just as softly.

"With all his physical data and his brain activity, there is only one logical explanation, Mr. Rinehart…Your son is not a human being. He is from another world, not this one." The doctor never looked up.

Clayton didn't look at all surprised from the shocking, bizarre news. He simply got up and walked slowly to the window of the office, as though interested in what was going on outside in the real world.

"What is he then, if he's not from this world?"

"We don't know what he is. We just know he's not human."

"You could be mistaken." Clayton murmured, mindlessly flipping the window latch with his finger.

"His DNA, RNA, and Polypeptides have only half of the characteristics of a human. The other half is unidentified."

"What are you going to do?" Clayton was still murmuring.

"Nothing."

"Why not?" Clayton brightened and turned toward the doctor, surprised.

"People would think us mad. Besides, we don't have any real scientific proof."

"What about the tests? You were so sure, I mean…"

"All of it can be subjected to conjecture on our part. None of us are experts in any of disciplines of genetics and DNA. They will say we contaminated the samples and misused the EEG machine, which would be the logical explanation. I would say the same if somebody came out with something so preposterous."

"So what are you going to do?"

"Nothing." The doctor shrugged. "The way you took this news, you know, don't you? You know we're right, don't you, Mr. Rinehart?"

"I don't know anything, Dr. Simmons." Clayton was looking at the doctor but seeing nothing, only a hazy world in the distance. "I don't know how he got inside my wife. I know I'm not an alien." Clayton was so deep in thought he began to mumble again.

"One problem with that, Mr. Rinehart."

"What is it that's wrong with *that*, doctor? Do I look like an alien to you? Does my wife?" Clayton went from mumbling to shouting at the doctor. "We're normal, both of us. What the hell ever normal is." Clayton mumbled the last part again.

"The problem is, he has a strong resemblance to you in the face. Don't you agree?"

"Really? I always thought he favored Shannon more than me," he replied in a hazy, mumbling manner.

"Well, he does actually favor both of you. All your dominant genetic facial features come through in Gabe — from both of you."

"You know, I contemplated for a long time that Shannon had had an affair with some really big dude. I did, seriously." Clayton began to laugh, still in a foggy haze, still looking through the doctor like he was invisible, just barely loud enough for the startled Dr. Simmons to hear.

"Isn't that crazy? I mean, I was checking out every man in Jerusalem, Alabama, that I passed on the street," he chuckled, "looking for someone who was about 6'6" or so and weighed about 250 pounds. Every guy who was over 6 feet tall became a suspect," another labored, grunting chuckle followed.

"I quit after he was a few months old when I realized Gabe wasn't really human. You want to hear something funny, doctor? I mean really funny?" The doctor stared at Clayton sorrowfully.

"I had myself convinced —for a while anyway —that this was a blessing from God." Clayton began a disturbing laugh.

"I thought I was being doubly blessed —hell triply. Is that a word, Dr. Simmons? Anyway, you know what I mean." The doctor nodded. "I wanted a big, athletic son to make up for what I never was." The hysterical laugh came from Clayton again, "I guess I got it, I surely did."

"Then you've known he was an alien for some time then?"

"What?" mumbled Clayton, returning back to reality. "No. How could he be an alien and have *us* for parents? You said so yourself that he looked like both of us."

"Exactly, Mr. Rinehart. How indeed?" Though he tried to hide it, a suspicious tone exited the doctor's mouth along with his whimsical question.

"I've been asking you this a lot today, but what are you saying?"

"I'm saying we'd like to test you and your wife," said Dr. Simmons directly but quickly changed tone. "Just as a baseline, Mr. Rinehart. We don't think you're aliens or anything, but we need to compare your profile to his, —at least the part that we believe is indeed human. You understand? We're not accusatory, or at least don't mean to be." The doctor seemed far too apologetic to suit Clayton.

Clayton turned back to the window and looked toward the great Black Hill Mountains that stretched for what seemed a thousand miles against the bright, clear South Dakota sky. He caught sight of a soaring eagle floating on the thermals at least a mile away, high in the far-off sky. He thought: *Lend me your wings, Mr. Eagle, and let me float away too. Please. I would only need to borrow them once. What I wouldn't give to be you right now, bird.* He wept, while the doctor watched helplessly.

CHAPTER 20

"I look forward to the challenge, sir," Harrison said with such confidence that Principal George Olaska Summerhawk broke out in such joyous laughter. The sound echoed through the telephone receiver and stung Harrison Ford's ear. After all, Harrison was the first African American teacher hired by the school since its inception. The lack of diversity—particularly among African Americans —was a persistent issue that the board had brought to Principal Summerhawk's attention for years.

It wasn't his fault, the embattled principal rationalized to the board and himself. How could he be if Black people had no desire to trek to this out-of-the-way, nowhere place? And by the way, to be the only Black people in the village? Mr. Harrison Ford fit the bill perfectly. What a résumé! Principal Summerhawk couldn't have been happier with his new hire.

Harrison Ford and his wife, Melissa were hopeful that their Garmin model 1450LMT GPS was taking them on the right path to Helpmein High School. It hadn't done so well in pinpointing Black Hills State University. Spearfish, South Dakota, should be easy to find, right? "Damn GPS don't work up here," Harrison must have mumbled a hundred times —or at least, that's how many times his wife thought he had mumbled it.

He knew that this certainly wasn't the job he wanted, not the job he had driven 2,557 miles for, but it was a job. Right now, a job—any job—had suddenly taken top priority. He was going to interview for the new head football coach position at the university. He wished they had told him they had decided to hire another coach before he arrived for the interview. But it was his fault for not leaving them his cell number, and it hadn't occurred to him they would make a decision so quickly.

What really pissed him off was that they had hired another African American for the job. He should be happy for his fellow traveler, lucky enough to land a university coaching job. But deep down, he figured he would've been the better coach. He didn't like the ugly thoughts running through his mind right now. *Childish. And that was one thing he couldn't afford to be—not as a Black coach, not in this economy. Take the high school coaching job and be happy, fool.*

"I wonder what kind of talent they're going to have up here," Harrison mused aloud, not really expecting his wife to answer.

"What kind of talent level?" Melissa sounded aggravated at the question. "This is going to be their first year having a football team. They've got to travel for hours on a bus because the schools are so far apart just to play the game. And there are only six schools on your schedule, and you got to play each team twice. Most of them are Native Americans who've probably never seen a black man before. Talent is the least of your worries, baby."

"Right, and I still have all that stuff no matter what. But it would be a lot better if they had some talent. That's all I'm thinking…I can't believe what they're paying us to teach. Plus my coach's premium payment. I guess I better get used to it. You know, if you combine what you and I will get paid, it's almost as much as I would've gotten if I'd landed university job." Harrison was trying to boost his uncertainty.

"I know you're disappointed about missing the college job, Harrison, but it sure was nice of the dean to hook us up with that Helpmein High School. We could be peddling our black butts back home without jobs. And, not to mention, we're broke."

"I *am* thankful for the job. It's not that. I've been working my ass off at McNess. Two years as a graduate assistant. Two years as offensive coordinator. These were college players. Now I've got to go coach a bunch of Indian kids who've never seen a football before. I'm used to seeing big, fast athletes. Not to mention, black athletes."

"So, you've got little Indian boys to coach now. It could be worse." Melissa wasn't trying to be philosophical, but she *was* trying to be helpful.

"One little, two little, three little Indians. Is that how that went?" Harrison looked over at his wife, confused.

"Oh, I remember something like that from when I was a kid," Melissa said, just as confused as her husband. "It was four little, five little, six little Indian boys. I feel ashamed of myself. I think I left out some more numbers." Now she was sounding philosophical, Harrison thought. They both laughed.

"Little Indian boys. That's what I've got to coach. Little Indians. I'll bet there's not a kid in the whole damn school who weighs two hundred pounds."

"Now, Harrison Ford. I'll bet *they're* not used to being around a movie star either." She poked fun at her husband she got the chance about his famous name.

"I told you he wasn't famous when they named me. They'd never heard of him. I'm just not used to being around little athletes. I hope they've got just one big kid in that whole school somewhere. I'm used to being wowed… I got a feeling I'm never going to be wowed by any of these kids…"

CHAPTER 21

"I see you found us." Principal Summerhawk extended his meaty hand, which Coach Ford was content to accept.

"We're getting used to locating places up here. It takes a while to figure out *when* you're going in the wrong direction." Harrison laughed like a man who had experience at being lost.

"Yeah, you can sure do some driving up here."

"Summerhawk—I guess that's an Indian, ah, I mean, a Native American name," stammered Harrison, embarrassed by the slip.

"Nah, it's Irish." The principal couldn't hold his attempt at seriousness and began to chuckle. "And by the way, we're not too politically correct up here. You can say '*Indians.*' We know what you mean. What do we call you?"

Harrison suddenly found himself in a spot. What did his new boss mean by that?

"You call us 'Black' or 'African American,' I guess," Harrison said, trailing off insecurely.

"That's good to know, but I meant, do you go by Harry, or Harris, or do you go by Harrison?"

"Oh, whatever you like, Mr. Summerhawk." Harrison was embarrassed and wanted to change the subject. "I understand this is going to be your first season of football here."

"No, we have a football team here. It's going to be our first year as an *11- man* football team."

"11-man?"

"Yeah, we've been playing 7-man football for years, and now we petitioned the South Dakota Athletic Association and became an 11-man team. There are only 8 teams in the whole district."

"Oh, I didn't understand. That's better. Then they know something about football already." Harrison was agreeable about the surprising news.

"A lot of traveling for the games, but you'll get used to it," answered the principal, also agreeably.

"I noticed your facilities when we were pulling in. My God! They are more impressive than the college we just left. How?"

"Do you mean you want me to explain about the facilities, or are you greeting me again?" returned the principal with as straight of a face as he could. It took a second to figure out that the principal had a good sense of humor, and Harrison began to laugh. Almost simultaneously, Principal Summerhawk joined him.

"Where's your whip?" the principal asked, returning to the same serious face. Harrison was again caught off guard by the peculiar question.

"I don't believe in corporal punishment." Harrison was stammering and unsure again. "That was the rule at the schools back home. Do *you*?"

The principal burst out in a loud, rotund laugh and patted Harrison on the back. "No, I mean your whip from when you were Indiana Jones!"

Harrison got the instant feeling that he was going to like Helpmein High School. It was not at all like he had pictured. The principal was a jovial and good- natured fellow with a pleasant, dry sense of humor, and he seemed genuinely happy to have him on board. He hoped that his wife, Melissa, was having the same experience he was. It was her first day, too.

CHAPTER 22

"This is your room, Mrs. Ford. The English room," said Mrs. Paulette Craft, the vice principal, encouragingly, as they meandered the halls of Helpmein Junior School. Mrs. Craft had a spring in her step as she regarded her new hire. Melissa would be the Jr. High English teacher for grades 7-9. The Vice Principal had thought that matched her step: *Maybe her skin will be not only be darker but a little thicker than the others.*

Now, they had two African American teachers for the price of one, metaphorically speaking, of course. Economically, it would cost the school over $100,000 for the pair. The two principals mutually agreed that it was a bargain.

That's the thing about government money: *strings.* They had to have, at the very least, 12 % African American Staff. With each rejection from Black recruits, the wages offered went a little higher— a lucky break for the Ford family, or so Harrison and Melissa thought. A petition from the school finally got the requirement down to at least one Black teacher. Now they had two, which was 50% more than the minimum. This was a good day indeed.

"You can start in the morning, Mrs. Ford, since it's already 10:00am. We'll let the sub finish out the day, but you can sit in if you'd like."

"You don't think it will make her nervous, do you?" Melissa was trying to be considerate of the substitute English teacher, sensitive to what it's like to be monitored by a peer.

"She's a student teacher and has filled in pretty well for us. She won't mind at all."

"What happened to the original English teacher?" Melissa was only making small talk, not really caring, just thinking of something to say while still scoping out her new job site.

"Well, she quit. She was the third one this year," Mrs. Craft said inattentively.

"Really," Melissa returned offhandedly, as she was only mildly curious. "Why such a turnover for teachers at this school?"

"Oh… you know…it's hard for some young teachers to adjust to new things, new surroundings, a different kind of student. You know how it is," said the Vice Principal, flustered, like she had a slip of the tongue and was searching for the remedy.

Satisfied, Melissa said, "I think I will sit in for a while, if you don't mind. I might as well start to get acclimated."

"Of course. Just one other thing I should tell you before you go in." Mrs. Craft seemed discomposed. "We have a, well, unusual student in our school. He's kind of large and rather troublesome," she finished ambiguously.

"Oh, I don't care about things like that." Melissa wanted to put her apprehensive boss at ease. "You wouldn't believe how big some of the kids grow from where we come from. We both have taught in the inner-city schools. You talk about some big children. You've never seen kids as big and strong as these kids are, and a lot of them were troublesome. You know, from troubled homes."

Melissa wanted to put in a final touch of reassurance, "Don't you worry about me being startled over some big boy, Principal Craft, I've seen them all, honey."

"Ok, that's good to know. Good luck, Mrs. Ford, and welcome aboard," Mrs. Craft said quickly and ominously. She wheeled and walked away quickly, her echoing footsteps disappearing down the shiny, waxed floors.

Melissa thought it odd that Mrs. Craft would finish with such an apprehensive manner. It didn't matter to her. Teaching is teaching, and she had taken in quite a lot. She had taught in some tough situations before, and she didn't take any crap from any of them. When you are the wife of a football coach, you'll get that opportunity. *Little Indian boys, really, Mrs. Craft?*

I wish I had told her I had taught, or at least tried to teach, gang members before. Troublesome? Did you say? Indeed. These little boys and girls are like lambs compared to the street-hardened criminals I've sat in class with before, Mrs. Craft. No parents; usually only a grandparent, if that; no guidance; no discipline; no love; no hope. The only thing that protected me was two months of karate and my wits. If ever there was such a thing as a piece of cake, Mrs. Craft, this is it. The thought of the principal warning her about some hick *country* students made her smile.

Smile a little smile for me, Rosemary, what's the use in crying. For some reason, this oldies song darted into her head just as she was about to open the classroom door and introduce herself to her class. She had heard it and a good selection of other oldies on the everlasting drive to this far away land. There had to have been a thousand radio stations fading in and out, one song statically and irritatingly being replaced with another.

Smile a little smile for-me, Rosemary, what's the use in crying, was now playing in her head, and she couldn't shed it. She kind of liked it. She was not a fan of rap music, per se. The fact that she liked oldies and not rap, like the romance warning about a problematic student, made her smile. She was no stereotype.

She thought she would take the hint from the unshakable song, and a big, warm, hearty smile was just what she needed when she entered the room, and that's what she wore when she lightly tapped on the door. She'd seen the lovely Mrs. Obama enter a stage the same way, many times on TV. No better role model, she figured. Confidence is what a smile conveys. *Confidence is what the First Lady has; it shows through and can't be dissuaded, and damn it, neither can she. Little Indian boys my ass, give me that door knob.*

She opened the door briskly, "May I introduce myself?" she asked pleasantly. "I'm the new English teacher."

"Of course," answered Consuela, the student substitute with equal pleasantry.

Melissa crossed to the middle of the room with the confident swagger of Mrs. Michelle Obama herself, pivoted powerfully on one foot, held her chest forward, stood attentively erect, took a deep breath, saw the 8'4"—414 lbs.—42" wide—optical illusion known as Gabriel Rinehart and gulped, "OH SHIT!"

Gabe winked at her with a maniacal grin… Melissa fainted limply to the floor.

Meanwhile…

"Well, what do you think of our place here Coach?" Charlie asked whimsically, knowing what the answer would be before he asked. Charlie Bass was the interim coach until a new head coach would be hired.

"I've never seen anything like this for a high school. It doesn't seem to fit, you know what I mean?"

"I know what you mean."

"How?"

"Government conscientiousness," answered Charlie.

"That conscientiousness seems to stop at my people's neighborhood."

"We were in line first. It don't help that lines were getting longer neither."

"Amen, brother. So, tell me, what kind of athletes we got here?"

"Not like you been used to, I'm guessing."

"I just want to know what kind of hand I got dealt." Harrison was surprised by Charlie's frankness.

"Pretty damn bare." Charlie said with a very direct disposition. "They don't get into sports around here. Not like you'd think."

"You don't have one athlete in the school?" Harrison asked, lightheartedly. He didn't want to appear picky on his first day.

"Well, that's kind of a tricky situation there." Charlie had his hands in his pockets, appearing like he really didn't know how to say what he knew he had to say. "You're gonna find out about this sooner or later, but yeah, we got an athlete in this here school."

"Yeah, well, tell me about him. How old is he?"

"I'd say he's about 12 or 13 by now. That's probably wrong."

"How come you don't know how old he is?" Harrison couldn't quite figure out what was going on with the coach's evasive demeanor.

"It's really hard to tell how old he is." This made Coach Ford even more intrigued.

"Is he a Native American boy?"

"Indian. It's ok, you can say it. And no. He's white, I reckon." Coach Bass had a brief puzzled look about himself. "His mama and daddy are white anyway."

Harrison thought he would just keep quiet and let it leak out of the coach, because asking him questions was not getting him anywhere anyway.

"He'll be up here directly. You're gonna have to get hold and brace yourself. You ain't never seen nothing like him."

Coach Ford's brains began blasting thoughts, "*Oh brother, another white boy that I ain't never seen nothing like. White boys that I ain't never seen nothing like are everywhere. Every time some white boy that can run pretty fast or jump fairly well, I'm told I'm not supposed to have to ever seen anything like them. But I have seen something like them every day.* A smile cut across Harrison's face as he thought, *they're called the average black boy… If only white people knew what black people actually thought, they'd be in for a surprise?* This thought also made him smile at Coach Bass.

Still, the straight-talking Charlie Bass didn't strike Harrison as a person who would carry on over such things, so this white boy he was hearing about did sound interesting.

"So he's in what, the sixth grade?"

"No, he's in the 11th. He got advanced cause he's so damned smart."

This triggered a thought soliloquy from Harrison: *Well that's it, Charlie. I don't need to hear another word. Smart white kids are not athletes Coach. I'm surprised you don't seem to know that. Hey, and it's not just white kids either, blacks kids too. If you're smart, I mean really smart, there is no way you're a really good athlete.*

East is east and west is west, and smart kids are smart, and good athletes are good athletes and never the twain shall meet. Don't you know that's how God keeps the world orderly? It's why the world is run by smart kids and not by good athletes. Don't tell me anymore. I've heard enough, Coach Bass. In fact, I'm bored with this place already. God, if you only could read my mind right now. The fact that you can't, Coach Bass — well, I guess that's what makes the world orderly also. Again, his own thoughts made Harrison smile broadly, giggle even.

"Ok, coach. He must be a really smart kid to get advanced to… what did you say? The 11th grade. That's one of the biggest skips I've ever heard of." Coach Harrison continued philosophically, "It's usually the other way around in the world that I navigate in, Coach. Kids need to go back a grade or two to catch up. I'd like to meet this really smart kid."

"You won't notice he's smart at first. It'll take a few days, then you'll notice it." Charlie was putting emphasis on this particular point.

"Why? Is he bashful?" Harrison was trying hard to act like he cared, but he was distractedly looking this way and that. He didn't really give a damn about the smart white kid that this Yahoo thought was a good athlete. He just wanted to meet the kids he was going to have gin himself up to coach.

"Nah, he's just different from anything you've seen."

No, I'm not going to even think those thoughts again. It's too much work.

"He must be something, Coach." Harrison was anxiously looking at his watch, counting in his head how much longer till PE.

Charlie put his hand on Harrison's shoulder with a concerned look, "Just brace yourself, Coach." Charlie walked away, leaving Harrison amusedly chuckling about his carryings-on and then thinking to himself:

I don't care how pitiful this bunch is; I will not let it get me down. Kids are kids, and I don't care if we never win a game —they deserve the best I can do. I am a damn good football coach, and I'm a damn good man. Everyone deserves a fair shot, and that includes these people.

How different can they be? They're kids. No more sarcastic thoughts, Harrison. Start with this smart kid that I've never seen anything like. I don't care how pitiful he is; you will be nice to him. No ugly thoughts. He may be their best, but you will not laugh at him, not even to yourself. You will get through this until something better comes along. Don't laugh. Don't laugh. You're better than that. Being inferior is not this boy's fault. You remember that.

Coach Harrison paced back and forth, impatiently watching the sweep of the seconds hand and realizing how *long* a second took.

CHAPTER 23

The door of the gymnasium swung open, and the air escaping from the cylinder made a whistling, *swishing* sound. Kids popped through the opening one or two at a time. Coach Ford stood to the side and somewhat behind the door, closely observing his new players while staying unobserved for the time being.

A tall, skinny boy with long bushy hair —almost an afro, Coach surmised —two short, skinny kids, a kid just as short but heavier —all of them white. Then two boys who were obviously Indians, no doubt about it —both overweight, out of shape, and without an athletic bone in their bodies. Another Indian, the same, but taller maybe. More kids came through the door, all different shades of whiteness.

Whiteness —a good word, Harrison thought. *That's what I've got here, many shades of whiteness. Different colors, different shapes, different heights and different weights —all different, yet all with one common characteristic: whiteness. I kind of foresaw this.* He had braced himself, forced a smile on his face, and determined to greet the boys pleasantly and explain how much he was looking forward to coaching them this year.

As he took the first step toward his new students, the door exploded open. He jetted backward, barely missing his face. The handle slammed with such force against the wall that it shattered, with three- or four- pieces ricocheting across the shiny basketball court.

A blurry, enormous image flashed before Harrison. It took a full second for the startled coach to realize it was a human. Gabe had a basketball in his hand, took three long strides, exploded from the floor off his right size 23 foot in front of the goal, twisted in midair, and flung the basketball sidearm and downward at about a 45-degree angle into the basket with such force the net ripped off and cushioned the basketball when it landed about ten feet from where it was originally launched from the sky above. A twinkle of light gray smoke rose in a curvy thin line from the entwined ball, and Harrison could smell the odor of burning nylon.

Gabe lightly touched down after his 15- foot or so trip into space, fisted his hands on his hips; shoulder muscles bulging 42 inches; veins distended; muscles layered with sinewy definition; trapezius muscles that almost touched his ears. The monster was staring at Coach Ford and seemed surprised to see his horrified new witness, whom he just noticed.

Harrison shook his head vigorously and rubbed both hands over his eyes, apparently attempting to remove some invisible glaze that had just covered them. He stared at Gabe for a second longer, abruptly turned, exited the building, and walked around the parking lot in quick, worrisome steps, occasionally stopping to bend over and catch his fleeting breaths.

In his 32 years, this was the first time he had actually hyperventilated. He had heard all his life about hallucinations; he just didn't figure he would ever have one, not at this stage of his life.

He always assumed the shortness of breath would cause the hallucination, not the other way around. He remained motionless, bent with both palms on his knees, mind racing, trying desperately to have some kind of rational thought as to why his mind would allow his eyes to see such a thing.

Oh God, I'm sorry Lord. Please forgive me. Never again. No more ugly thoughts. Don't let it end this way Lord!

Harrison, for the first time in a long time, was scared for his life. What had he done? Was this a heart attack? Or a stroke? It ran in his family. He put his index and middle fingers on his carotid, fidgeting with different pressure points. As best he could tell, his pulse was rapid but not racing. He didn't feel faint.

What the hell just happened to me?

Harrison looked around, trying to gain his bearings. *Do I know who I am? Yes. What am I here for?... I'm the new coach at this Indian school. I saw something in the gym… Some kind of monster, yeah. It scared, me and I came out here. Yes. Okay, go back in and see that it was just a kid and your mind just played a game on you. When you get back in there, you will see that it's just a kid. A big white boy. Just a kid. Calm down.*

Harrison looked over his shoulder, right and left, to make sure nobody saw him just have a meltdown before heading back in the direction of the gym. He actually started chuckling to himself as he opened the door.

What an idiot. Just tell them you had to answer your cell phone that was vibrating. Maybe they won't wonder why you left so quick… Get it together, let's go.

Harrison opened the door. AND THERE HE WAS. BIG AS LIFE. *BIGGER* THAN LIFE!

Harrison gawked at Gabe and then at Coach Bass, who was staring at him.

"Well, Coach! What the hell are you gonna do about what just happened?" Harrison was screaming, more like pleading, at Charlie for some help coping with what his crazy-ass mind was telling him to deal with.

Coach Bass stammered around, not knowing exactly what the Coach meant. He walked up to Gabe and said harshly, "Damn it, Gabe. You're gonna pay for that door knob. And you can string up another net too. I told you the next net comes out of your pocket." Coach Bass looked at Harrison to see if he approved of how he handled the situation, but approval was short in coming.

Harrison walked slowly up to Gabe. He was breathing heavily. His steps got shorter and shorter as the giant appeared to get closer and closer. Gabe was staring back at the terrified coach, but amusedly. Harrison put his trembling hand forward and upward and gently touched Gabe on the shoulder like he was a baby. Gabe grinned at Harrison. His dimpled cheeks contracted and brilliant white teeth shone through thin white-boy lips at the crooked-necked coach.

Harrison looked at Charlie, Charlie looked at Gabe, and Gabe looked over his shoulder and winked maniacally at his solemn-looking classmates, who, in turn, were looking at their new, terrified, African American head football coach… All went as expected.

CHAPTER 24

Harrison pulled the Cadillac Escalade timidly into the apartment complex. He sat in the car, still not speaking to Melissa. It wouldn't have mattered much because Melissa wasn't in a talkative mood. Harrison wanted to register, pick up the key, and put this day behind them. They were supposed to go house shopping tomorrow, but for now, this apartment would have to do.

This was the first drive of any significance that Harrison could remember when his wife wasn't impulsively jabbering in his ear. There was something about being a passenger that loosened her lips with zealous abandon. There would be no need to pretend to listen this afternoon. Her lips were sealed, and her mind seemed lost in timid reverie, resignedly speaking in one-word answers, if at all.

"What's wrong with you?" Harrison asked morosely, trying to make up his mind if he wanted to speak of the traumatic event that had so abruptly rocked his world today.

"Nothing, Harrison, ah, I don't want to tell you right now…I fainted today, and they gave me some kind of sedative, and it made me kind of groggy."

This was not the Melissa Ford he knew. *Fainting? A sedative? Timidly speaking?*

"What happened?" Harrison asked, somewhat relieved that he would have time to gather himself before he had to manufacture the words to describe the jolly green giant he saw today.

"I stepped into the classroom and promptly fainted. I hit the ground like a sack of potatoes. I've been in the nurse's office for the rest of the day." She began to laugh, "I thought I saw some kind of giant, alien kid sitting in the front row and passed out. I don't know what happened after that. I woke up on a couch in the nurse's office.

"The paramedics gave me something to drink, and I slept most of the day away. Isn't that funny? I must not have been getting enough sleep with all the traveling we been doing." She was rubbing around the side of her neck like there was a kink in it, and she sleepily yawned with a wide mouth.

Harrison was staring wide-eyed at her.

"What's the matter with *you*?"

"I saw that same giant today that you just saw," he gulped. "He's real."

"What?! Real? You mean that thing I saw sitting in that big-ass desk was real?" Melissa had a tendency to forget her proper upbringing and go stereotypical when she got really excited or scared. "No way, Harrison. Not what I saw. That wasn't real. You're bullshitting your wife baby."

"Listen to me damn it. I came that close to fainting myself. I thought I was having a heart attack or a stroke or hallucinating or something, but I wasn't seeing things; it was real. Hell, I touched him." Harrison began a nervous laugh, "He looked at me like I was some kind of idiot. I touched him to see if I was going to wake up in a nuthouse somewhere." The nervous laugh returned for what Melissa considered too long.

"You know what's weird about all this stuff?" Harrison waited for Melissa to nod. "Nobody but me thought anything of it. This kid, this thing, was walking and talking around all the people. The coach, my new assistant coach, got onto him for ripping down another net," said Harrison, hysterically laughing like a crazy person. "That idiot Coach Bass tried to tell me something about him being some kind of growth hormone freak of nature. He was right about the freak part. He sure was," Harrison continued the crazy laugh.

"Ok Harrison, let's pull it together," said Melissa, straightening her dress as she got out of the car. "He's a giant kid with a pituitary problem. We're here; we got jobs. We can get used to him, no problem." Melissa was trying to convince herself.

Harrison jumped out of the car, slammed the door, and scowled at his wife.

"There's just one other thing. You weren't conscious long enough to notice, but I sure as hell noticed."

Melissa peered at Harrison. Harrison looked like the words had escaped him, or he didn't want to say the words he was about to, like he wasn't quite sure he had all his faculties.

"He's not right."

"Who's not right? The giant kid? Of course, he's not right, you fool. He's a giant."

"No, that's not it, Melissa. What do you remember seeing?"

With trepidation in her voice, she said, "Well, he was a giant-size kid." She looked down, searching for words. "Wide, muscles bulging, veiny, ah…like someone had drawn him for a comic book or something…I remember that he smiled or winked at me or something, and then I fainted. I don't remember anything else. I thought I dreamed it all."

"I saw the same thing you did. Except I saw him jump up in the air, his waist above the rim on the basketball court, and throw the ball *down* in the goal like he was skipping rocks across a pond. It ripped the net clean off the rim. Nobody can do that. It's not possible, but he did it, and nobody said anything and acted like it was an everyday thing to 'me." Harrison became stolid but continued:

"Shit, I wanted to start running, but nobody said a goddamn word to me, like they see this stuff every day. It was no big deal. Hell, they didn't even look at him; they looked at me instead, like they wanted to see if I would faint. I damn near did," he chuckled.

"What are you going to do, Harrison? Do you want to go back home and hunt jobs around there?" Melissa said resignedly. "Just say the word, baby, and we're out of here."

"Let me think about this a little while, please." After a very liberal pause, Harrison continued with a trembling voice, "I saw something else about him. I don't know how to explain it. I want you to see if you notice it too."

"So I guess this means we're staying."

"Yeah, I have to now. I can't run from this…I'll wonder about it for the rest of my life if I do."

"But what is this that I'm supposed to notice? If what I saw was real, there's about a thousand things to notice. I don't know what *one* thing to look for."

"I can't tell you. You'll have to notice it for yourself…" Harrison began to laugh, "Shit, we're probably gonna wake up in our beds back home any minute." They both laughed.

"That is, if we're both having the same dream, and we're both in it," chuckled Melissa. They both stopped laughing.

"Let's go in and check out this apartment. I'm ready to go to bed. I'm tired. We got a long day tomorrow, baby," Harrison concluded.

CHAPTER 25

Harrison was nervously tapping his wristwatch with the eraser end of a lead pencil. His first P.E. class started in five minutes. This period would have the monster in it, along with just regular kids —he hoped. The coffee he had gotten from the teachers' lounge was still hot. He sipped it noisily.

The three history classes he had to teach were behind him now. For the next month, until spring football practice started, all he would have to do was babysit two P. E. classes in the afternoon each day. He turned the infrared heater up a notch. It was March, but still bone-chillingly cold. Harrison figured out why teacher's pay was so generous here. *This damn South Dakota is a cold-ass place.*

Harrison heard the thud of footsteps thundering toward his office door. His coffee vibrated with little splashes, and ripples widened across the cup with each approaching step. Gabe opened the door, ducked his head, turned sideways, entered the office, and stood erect, peering down at the tiny coach.

"I thought I heard you coming," said Harrison, looking almost straight up with his mouth open. Then, sensing his mouth agape, closed it.

"Yes. From the way you acted yesterday, I wanted you to know I was coming. I didn't want you to faint like your wife did. Yes, she did fine today." Gabe's mouth slowly widened into a mystic smile. "I figured you'd like to know."

"You don't have to alert me you're coming; you're fine with me." Harrison was trying not to appear startled.

"Oh yeah, that's right. You people are hard to sneak up on. I forgot," Gabe said thoughtfully.

You people? Did he just say something racial to me? Harrison was having trouble latching onto the thousand thoughts ricocheting in his head because of the real-life giant standing five feet away, peering down at him. Gabe's head was no more than a few inches from the 9-foot-high ceiling.

"You people?" Harrison almost talked himself out of saying it, but it slipped out anyway.

"Yes, football coaches have excellent hearing. It was hard to sneak up on the last one…What with all the whispers behind his back about his coaching prowess and whatnot… What did you think I meant?" Gabe was still musingly smiling.

"Nothing, just talking." Harrison was caught a little off guard by the question.

"I guess with your heritage and the way your people get jobs and such, with affirmative action and all, I guess you hear a lot of paranoid whispers behind you that aren't there." Gabe was no longer smiling and obtained a serious demeanor.

What kind of conversation is this? Is he trying to get at me, or am I being paranoid?

"Football coaches are a little paranoid; it comes with the job, I guess." It was the only thing Harrison could think to add to this weird conversation.

"Yes, especially with a Black coach. I suppose that would be especially true. I'm thinking that with people, people in general, who think that you're inferior anyway. You know, with your race being held as property for 400 years and all, how could they not think that?" Gabe laughed smugly, and then the muscles in his face relaxed. Emotionless eyes target-centered on the coach's, and he continued stolidly in monotone cantor, like he was reading the news from teleprompters behind each one of Harrison's eyes:

"We both know you're here because this school would hire the first black that wasn't wearing prison stripes. You wouldn't drive all the way from where you were spawned if you could get hired anywhere else."

"Look, I'm here because I was offered a college coaching job and missed it. This one was handy. That's all. Sometimes people have to make the best out of the hand they're dealt." Harrison's anger caused his voice to raise a couple of octaves. "What damn business is it of yours anyway?"

"Forgive me, Coach, but the role of philosopher becomes you not… This is not the time to become coy with me, Coach Ford. We could perhaps help each other. We are both in the same paradoxical boat, if you will. I am the target of presupposition, and so are you. It is supposed that I am an alien from another world because I am superior physically and mentally.

"You and your people are under the simple supposition that you are superior physically." Gabe paused, stoically anticipating the anger brewing on Harrison's face as the coach attentively waited for the words to form on Gabe's huge lips. "Not so much mentally." Gabe began a pensive chuckle. "Let's face it. If it weren't for the fact that you can run faster and jump higher than white people, they wouldn't have any use for you at all."

What the hell are you? Did you come into my office just to show me how racist you are? What the hell do you want? Harrison thought but remained silent.

"You have to be thankful that these white people have guilty consciences, though, don't you? I suppose that a parent who has just whipped their mentally slow child for spilling a glass of milk would bear the same burden. Guilty, I mean, and the inevitable amelioration of the offense act, and the expiation of the unforgivable sin by overcompensation, such as a new play-pretty, a visit to the zoo perhaps…or new teacher hires under strict quota rules. I believe in our civics books, it's called *affirmative action*," Gabe laughed maniacally.

"What the hell do you want?" Harrison wanted to slap the hell out of this thing, save for the *mechanism* that was probably saving his live right now.

"They won't let me play sports around here." Gabe had returned from his trance-like stoicness to normalcy. "Surely you know how frustrating it can be to know you can excel at something and yet not get the chance to show it. You're probably a smart man, but you aren't awarded the opportunity to show it often."

What does he mean? Is he trying to gain sympathy now?

"What do you want from me?" Harrison was tired of the racial insults and mind games.

"I want to play football. It's that simple."

"What's stopping you?"

"The parents won't let their wee children play if I'm on the field with them." Gabe abruptly became angry. "And there is the *small* matter of the uniforms. I have offered to pay for the tailored uniform myself." He calmed, "If you could ease the parents' weak minds, I can guarantee that you will never lose." Gabe slammed his fist down on the edge of Harrison's steel desk like a 30-pound sledgehammer.

The Styrofoam cup of coffee flew straight up about two feet. Coach caught it with great dexterity, spilling only a few drops. Gabe looked admiringly at his graceful coach.

"I'll see what I can do son." The ringing of the slam still resonated it his ear. At this point, Harrison just wanted his angry adversary out of his office. *If he had hit me with that same fist, it would have caved in my skull like a coconut,* he thought.

Gabe stopped half way out the door, twitched his head back under the door frame, and glared at Harrison, saying blazingly;

"There is a time for all men, that's the rule,
A time for a hunt, a time for a catch; listen, you fool
I won't tarry about you impish wee people
What with you so useful a tool
Like my ancestors, I can sense, I can tell,
In the end you all will become as fodder, for... Gabri'el"

Gabe slammed the door, pulled the handle, and Harrison watched and heard the steel door crumble inward like an aluminum can. The door was now perforated in waves of metal around the handle, much like an accordion.

I'll never get this damn door opened. I'll have to crawl out the window, Harrison surmised. He took another sip of his rescued coffee and peered down at the corner of his smashed desk. The leg on the side which had just been angrily bludgeoned was bent at a 45º angle. He slid the desk to a new position in the room, thinking it must weight 300 lbs. Like the heavy steel door, the monster just crumbled it like it was paper.

This ain't gonna work. I can't let that thing, whatever it is, loose on other people's kids. He'll kill every one of them. He looked at the crumbled door and what used to be his desk. *What the hell just happened?* He laughed at his own incredulity.

CHAPTER 26

"Well, tell me something, baby, how was your day?" asked Melissa, who was in the process of closing the car door. Harrison had both hands tightly gripping the steering wheel, broodingly staring into empty space. It took a second for him to realize that he had been spoken to.

"Oh, kind of boring... I think that's how you would describe my day."

"Well, tell me the boring stuff anyway, and I'll tell you about mine."

"Well, you know, the typical things you would think would happen around here. A 9-foot-tall hulk from Mars crumbled my desk and office door like a tin can, and then I couldn't fit through the window. It took two hours for them to get cutting torches and cut me out of my own damn office. You know, the usual stuff." Harrison was still staring dreamily into space with little emotion.

"Well, I got into it in class also with you-know-who. Listen to this." Harrison stopped his daydream and turned to attentively listen to his wife's encounter with their mutual nemesis.

"Everything was going well," she began resignedly. "I was teaching away, then I posed a question to the class. *Who do you think is the most influential woman in the United States?* I was curious as to where they were politically. You know, I was getting a feel for how liberal-minded they were." Harrison nodded understandingly.

"The first response I heard was Michelle Obama. 'Good,' I thought. I waited for some more answers. Someone else said her name again; some more nodded in agreement. I thought, 'this is going pretty well.' Then, that Cyclops says, right out of the blue:

'Michelle Obama, really?
Why not Aunt Jemima, silly
One is as asinine as the other,
Are we surprised she'd pick a brother.'

"What a way to talk? I didn't know what to say, so I said, 'You disagree with the choice of Mrs. Obama, Gabe?'

'A duck, a goat, a cow, or a guinea
One black, I've heard say, is as good as any,
Is it surprising you would stick to your bed?
When to choose another, lighter color instead,
Would most profoundly, be over your head.'

"So I say, 'I'm not used to students speaking to me this way.' He says back to me,
'Why, I's be sorry, Mrs. Fo, I didn't realize you's don't be understandin' all dem English words and such. Why from now on, I be speakin' in dem Ebonics were's you be understandin' and thangs. Is tis here what you be used to, Mrs. Fo.'
"What do you say to that!? So, I try not to get mad at this thing because of the way he looks at you! It sends chills down my spine. He apologized and said he was just kidding. I didn't think so, and he knew it all the time. I can tell it wouldn't take much to set him off. I don't mind telling you, baby. I'm scared to death of him. He can insult me all he wants to. I ain't provoking that dude."
"I don't blame you," said Harrison supportively, "the same thing happened to me today. He was making hateful racial insults to me, like he was trying to get me upset and mad. But I'm with you. If he'd wanted me to, I'd have tied a rag scarf over my head and made him some pancakes."
Melissa was tickled at her husband's comments. She smiled warmly at his dry sense of humor, and they drove to their apartment silently, holding hands.

"So are you going to tell me about this Gabe thing, or are we going to walk around in circles all afternoon?" Harrison asked Charlie Bass. Charlie had asked the coach to walk around the practice field with him after he'd caught him hypnotically watching the giant acrobat put on his usual demonstration in the gym. The general performance usually included, but was not limited to:

- Dunks launched from between the foul line and midcourt.
- A dunk launched from the foul line carrying an unwitting 7th grader under his left arm.
- A dunk, with both hands, straight down between his knees into the basket, propelling himself away from the backboard with his hands, his entire body above the rim.
- And, of course, the classic routine, *where Gabe pretends to throw the basketball in someone's face, only to squeeze it so hard it bursts into a deflated piece of leather and cords, gently slapping the flinching victim.* Everybody gets a kick out of that —except Clayton, who sends a $40 check to school about once a week.

"I thought I'd get you out of there for a while. It's kinda hard to take it all in if you ain't used to it, ain't it?" Charlie grinned quaintly.

"Hard to take in? It's impossible to take in! What the hell is that?! And don't tell me about that growth hormone shit! I'm not in the mood to hear it! I've been around a damn little bit, and there ain't nothing like that on this freaking planet!" Harrison's voice was grew louder with each sentence.

"No, I know there ain't," Charlie replied timidly, like he was ashamed of it.

"You know what my biggest fear is? Man, you're going to like this one." Harrison's voice took on a manic edge "My biggest fear is that I'm going to gain some kind of consciousness in an asylum somewhere. That's what I'm most scared of!"

"You're not crazy or imagining this stuff, Coach. It's real," sighed Charlie.

"Well?" Harrison demanded, waiting for an explanation that wasn't coming.

"There's nothing to tell you. He came here from some shithole in Alabama about 10 or 11 years ago. His parents are regular, nice folks, and he grew up as a creature from another world. End of story," said Charlie matter-of-factly and looked down at his watch.

"The fact that he is superhuman is one thing, but why the hell is he so damn mean? He's made fun of me and my wife. He's called us every kind of nappy-headed nigger you can think of, without actually using the words." Harrison mused at that thought. "And what's with those rhymes? Why does he do that? He's so damn smart too. Brilliant."

"Yeah he is," agreed Charlie. Let me tell you about the time they sent that feller from the state down here to test him. That was a hoot." Charlie chuckled before continuing:

"The station wagon with *South Dakota Department of Education* printed on the side of the door pulled slowly in the parking spot reserved for the teachers and visitors. Wouldn't you know it? It was a Japanese guy named Kabayashi. I never knew if that was his first name or his last name. He wasn't around long enough for me to find out.

"They had administered that IQ test that they give every student at least twice during their time in school; you know the one I'm talking about. Wel, Gabe got every question right, of course, and scored a perfect 210. I believe that's as high as it goes. He did it twice: once in grammar school, and again when they advanced him up to high school.

"That didn't sit well with them, so they were going to administer what they called a *field test*. That's what they do when they suspect foul play. So they sent Mr. Kabayashi to do the test.

"About the time he was getting out of his car, a bunch of kids came strolling by, wouldn't you know it? One of them was Gabe—the very person he came to test. All Gabe our "wonder boy" saw was that Kabayashi was a foreigner and a little feller at that, and that set him off. He made straight for the state guy, and, well, you know how it is the first time you see Gabe.

"Kabayashi jumped back in the car and tried to get away, but Gabe picked up the back wheels of the station wagon two feet off the ground with one hand. The wheels were spinning a hundred miles an hour, but the car wasn't going nowhere. Gabe must have figured out who he was and what he was there and wanted to play with him. You know how he is.

"Gabe finally convinced him that he wasn't Godzilla and that he wasn't going to eat him—not literally, anyway. They finally made it to the office and went in one of the rooms. The little feller opened up his laptop and started the test. One of the office girls was close enough to hear what was said and told everybody what happened to the poor little guy."

"Okay, Gabriel, we just had some confusion over your test results. We would like to clear some things up. Do you mind if I ask you some questions?"

"You think I cheated on your test, don't you? How do you think that's possible?" Gabe began to deliberate cunningly. "The irony in this situation is delicious."

"I don't follow," said the little fellow, stumped.

"An organization that studies intelligence is, in fact, lacking in the very substance it tests."

"We are not suggesting, Gabriel, that anyone cheated, but that some anomaly happened in the administration of the exam. You see, no one can get all the answers right. It's just not possible so we, ah…"

"So you think I cheated," interrupted a sardonic Gabe.

"Let me just ask you a few questions. I'm sure we can get a true assessment of your intelligence in just a few minutes." Kabayashi was anxious to get this over with, and he didn't want to escalate this tense situation, which had become a *scene from his worst nightmare come to life.*

"Very well. Ask." Gabe eased his back against the wall as he sat on the floor (no chairs big enough, you see) and relaxed, exhaling with the customarily disquieting smile. The little man began to read his carefully selected questions:

"At the end of a banquet, 10 people shake hands with each other,"

"45 times," Gabe blurted.

"How many handshakes will there be in total? Yes, ah, please wait until I ask the entire question. Thank you." He continued a little flustered. "The day before the day before yesterday is three days after Saturday."

"Friday," said Gabe casually, cleaning beneath his finger nails.

"What day is it today?" The little man looked sharply at Gabe, then sighed.

"Which number should come next in the series 1, 3, 6, 10, 15,""21," Gabe whispered while idly contemplating.

"Your choices are 8, 11..." Kabayashi scowled at Gabe. "Okay, Gabriel, what got our attention— perhaps cast some doubt on the veracity of your scores— was that you took the math portion of the exam in only 3 minutes and 15 seconds, which means you had to be using a calculator, which is prohibited."

"You are aware that Japan has the highest IQ of all countries and has since testing began," said Gabe attentively.

"Yes , I am. Let's get back to the math portion, shall we? Now I'm going to ask you to do some calculating only in your head, and please answer as quickly as possible. You will have only 5 seconds to answer. Ready?"

"I wonder why your country has such a poor record when it comes to wars?" Gabe ventured, interrupting the tester.

"What is 123 plus 427?"

"550," Gabe answered within a fraction of a second.

"We have a pretty good record when it comes to wars. Check our history," said the tester, defensively.

Gabe laughed cleverly, "Yes, but the only one that counts is the last one. In that one, you didn't do so well. I wonder why that is, Kabayashi?"

"What is 123 times 427? And what does our war record have to do with anything?"

"52,521. It's just that I find it a rather perverse ambiguity, don't you?"

"What is this ambiguity you speak of?" Kabayashi said, even more defensively. "And what is the cube of 6, plus the square of 12, divided by the square root of 324?"

"20. And the ambiguous part is that for all your supposed intelligence, the most effective part of your military campaign was the kamikaze bombers." Gabe had a maniacal laugh that evolved into a serious tone. "When you get right down the irreducible minimums, your entire race is no more developed than the suicide bombers of the ignorant Muslim countries."

The tester was speechless and angry. Gabe began to study him deliberately. His eyes moved over his entire small body, observing but not commenting, and then he smiled and leaned his ponderous bulk against the wall again, and the coy grin returning.

"Next question, please."

The tester hesitated, closed his laptop, and picked up a calculator.

"Out of questions already? Good. Let me ask you one. Do you think you will ever marry an American girl again, Kabayashi, after this one cheated on you?" Gabe was looking toward the floor and speaking in a low, monotone voice.

Kabayashi was stunned into silence. He glared at the idle giant incredulously. His trembling lips finally formed the inevitable question: "How did you know I was married to an American girl? How did you get access to my file?"

"You wore your file to work this morning." Gabe continued to speak in the low monotone, never looking up. "Did you know that the average Japanese penis length is 4.75 inches Kabayashi? I measured mine hanging limply at 22 inches. The average female vagina is only 10 centimeters deep. We are both in the same boat, I'm afraid. I will never have sex with a girl, and most likely, neither will you."

"What about my marriage? How do you know?" Kabayashi asked morosely.

Gabe sighed, "Your fourth finger on your left hand has a faded ring around it. Up until about two months ago, you were wearing a wedding band. Your belt has distinctive ruffled wear in the notch above the hole that it is now in. You are a small man and have recently lost weight, presumably from not eating. Hard to eat with a broken heart, they say.

"Japanese men never buy their own clothes because that is a duty for the wife. Your trousers are from a Japanese manufacturer. A Japanese wife would only purchase American made clothes, immersing completely in the Western life style. Only an American wife would romanticize Japanese tradition."

"Your glasses have a glaze of semen on the rim. I read an article where men often fantasize about their cheating wives being with other men and masturbate more than usual, and sometimes the muddled mind is not as hygienic. It was merely a guess, but I can see from your reaction I hit very close to the target.

"And to answer your next question, you are thinking, being much too honorable to ask. Yes…she left you because of your smallness." Gabe looked up and grinned impishly, adding, "I mean, your height of course."

Kabayashi trembling fingers gingerly put his laptop and papers inside his satchel. He gravely returned to his car and drove away like an old man does, lost as to where to go next.

"He doesn't mind ripping out anybody's heart, figuratively or literally," added Charlie.

"There is another thing about him. Have you noticed it?" asked Harrison while momentarily stopping their walk to gain more of Charlie's attention.

"You're going to have to be a little more specific Coach. I mean, there's a lot going on with him."

"I mean about the way he moves."

"Yeah, he moves quick for a giant, don't he?"

"No, more than that. Do you not see it?" Harrison was getting flustered over everyone else's lake of observation. "I was hoping that Melissa would notice what I'm talking about and mention it, but she hasn't yet," said Harrison despairingly.

"I think I know what you're talking about," said Charlie as the invisible light clicked on in his head. "He moves like he were a little bitty guy."

"YES!" Harrison looked like he had just hit the jackpot. "Damn, finally, I thought I was the only one that saw it. I'm telling you he's not a human being. Not a chance. I don't know what he is, but he's not one of us."

"I know somebody you need to talk to."

"Who's that?"

"Everybody calls him Ike. He's been here so long I've forgotten what his real name is. He owns that shop that sells Indian stuff down there on Main Street."

"Yes, I've seen that store, but why would I want to talk to him?"

"He believes the same thing you do, and he's got some darn fool ideas about it. You'd like him."

"I think you just insulted me, but I'm going to get his opinion anyway. Hell, I've got to talk to somebody about this or go insane one."

CHAPTER 27

"Hello there, young fellow. I'm Ike. What can I get for you?" said Ike warmly as he held out his hand to the new football coach, whom, up until now, he had only heard of. Harrison took Ike's hand in the same manner it was presented —warmly.

"I'm Coach Ford. You can call me Harrison or Coach or whatever you want to call me. I'm actually here to talk to you about a student of mine. Is now a good time?"

"Well, sure it is. Pull up a chair around this stove and warm yourself." Ike had one of those old-fashioned, wood-burning potbellied stoves. Many of the homes on the reservation heated their homes in this manner.

"If you're as astute as I've heard you are, then you probably know *who* I want to talk to you about."

"Yeah, I know who you want to talk about," Ike returned contemplatively.

"I don't know where to begin," said Harrison chuckling.

"I know where to begin, Coach," said Ike dryly.

"And where's that Ike?"

"At the beginning."

"Beginning of what? Look, Ike, I don't mean to be abrupt, but I don't need any more riddles here. I get enough of that from you-know-who."

Ike chuckled heartily while patting Harrison on the back and slid his chair a little closer to his new friend.

"You have obviously noticed that something is terribly wrong with Gabe… I mean…other than the obvious things. You know, other than the fact that he is gigantic, brilliantly smart, and diabolically mean, etcetera, etcetera. You can see that something else is wrong with this picture, I hope." Ike was getting more animated with each word.

"Yes, I have!" Harrison seemed relived. "I was getting so frustrated that someone else hadn't noticed it. Ah," Harrison was so excited he momentarily forgot Charlie's name. "Charlie, my assistant coach, called it *moving like a little bitty guy.*"

Ike was bobbing his head and about to burst, "Yes! That's it. He moves like he's our size. It looks so weird to me."

"Me too. Hell, it was so maddening for me that nobody would say anything about it. I began to wonder if I was seeing things that weren't there. Hell, as far as that goes," Harrison said quietly out of the corner of his mouth, "I keep expecting to wake up in my bed, and it's the middle of the night back in Ohio. I've felt this way ever since I arrived at this place and first laid eyes on this dude. I can't explain it, but it's like I don't belong here. But I don't know how I know.

"I don't mean, like, I don't want to be here," continued the befuddled coach, "I mean, like I don't *belong here;* like I'm not supposed to be seeing *this.* Not like in a dream exactly, more like this is not *supposed to* happen. I'm not making any sense, am I?" Harrison looked at Ike repentantly.

Ike said, laughing, "You're making a hell of a lot more sense than you even know, my friend, because I feel the exact same way and have ever since I saw him." Ike continued, with each word easing Harrison. "That's because he's not supposed to be here. Not for centuries. His time has come and passed."

"His *time?*...He's an alien from another world, isn't he? I knew it!"

"Yes, he's an alien."

"What planet?"

"Earth."

"I thought you said he's an alien from another *world.*" Harrison was getting a little agitated from yet more riddles.

"He is definitely an alien, but from this planet."

"How can he be an alien from this planet? That doesn't make any sense."

"Well, let me clarify…not so much from this world, more like from a time."

Harrison was afraid to ask the next question he was about to ask, but since he already thought he was crazy anyway, what the hell?

"He's a time-traveling alien, right?"

"In a manner of speaking, I guess you could say he is a time traveler. Except he didn't use an H.G. Wells machine to travel in."

"How did he get here then? I feel so weird having this conversation." Harrison was looking about the souvenir shop disquietingly.

"He came in Mrs. Shannon Rinehart's belly." Ike was trying not to make too much eye contact with Harrison at this point for one simple reason: he had trouble believing the words that were now coming out of his own mouth.

"I've seen her in the car from a distance and have often wondered about his parents—what they looked like, how big they are, how smart they are, and of course, what damn planet they're from." Harrison began to laugh.

"Every time I think about this stuff, which is about every ten damn seconds, I'm reminded of the movie Coneheads. Did you see it? These aliens crash-landed on Earth and couldn't get back home, so they have to adapt to society.

They have a kid, and she has to go to school and blend in, except she has the big, tall cone on her head. And the funny part is that people hardly notice it. It's obvious to everybody watching the movie that she is an alien, except for the people in the town, who think nothing of it. Just like here.

The part I don't understand is why these people haven't reported this thing to the news media. I don't remember ever seeing anything about it. I would've told somebody. And that big-ass clinic over there, what do they say about that?"

"Funny you should mention them," said Ike, waiting for a second between Harrison's breaths to jump in. He hated to interrupt because he knew that Harrison had a lot to get off his chest. "They do have a lot to say about it. I'll tell you about that later.

But first, I have to give you some background on how I think this happened." Ike got up and poured two cups of hazelnut coffee. "Here,

I haven't met anybody yet that didn't like my coffee." Harrison took the cup graciously and pulled his high backed chair a little closer to the stove. Ike took a sip of the hot, aromatic coffee and began.

"You notice how Gabe can not only do incredible feats, but he is out of kilter among us mortal people. He moves at the same speed we do, not lumbering about."

"Yes," said Harrison. "I've hung around athletes all my life. I have a degree in Kinesiology, and there is one incontrovertible fact of physics: the bigger you are, the slower you move. Except for him."

"Yes, you know what it's like? It's like he was superimposed, like Hollywood does with their, ah, what do you call that a… blue screen, or is it a green screen? It doesn't matter in any case. You know what I mean. They always do giants this way. They sort of superimpose a regular person and make him bigger with a computer or something, and though he's ten times bigger, he still moves the same as the rest of them. Is that how you would describe it?"

"Yes, that's it." Harrison and Ike were both whispering to each other, though no one else was in the store at the time. With each fantastic revelation, their enthusiasm rose, while their voices lowered.

"It's like watching a movie except you can reach out and touch the screen. Best damn 3D movie I've ever seen," whispered Harrison.

Ike smiled widely at the accuracy of the description.

"How did this happen? What do you know about the parents? Are they aliens too, only smaller? What gives here, man?" Harrison was rattling off questions before Ike could start to answer the first one.

"First, his dad is one of my best friends. There's nothing wrong with him. Nice guy; straight as an arrow; runs the insurance office down the street; you'll like him, or you would've liked him. He doesn't come around much anymore. The last time I saw him he was worried to death. I mean, can you imagine living with Gabe in your house?

I tried to get him to talk about it, but his brain is pretty much fried at this point. He said he was going to have to kill his own son, or at least that's what I thought he mumbled. His poor wife too. She quit teaching school about three years ago. She spends a lot of time away. I haven't talked to her for a while. I'm going to tell them, though."

"Tell them what? Tell me what you know? Damn, man, I have to know what you know. For my own sanity, tell me everything you're thinking. " Harrison was about to the point of giddiness.

"Alright, I'll tell you the whole story. Wait a minute." Ike stood up and put his hand on his head, like he just remembered something. "I need to kill two birds with one stone here. I'll call Clayton and Shannon to come down here. I'll tell all of you at the same time. I don't want to have to tell this twice. All of y'all are going to think I'm crazier than a Bessie bug anyway."

Ike went to the telephone, made his call, put on a fresh pot of coffee, and began nervously fidgeting with the fire while he waited for the weary parents of Gabriel Rinehart. Ike and Harrison made small talk until they heard the twinkling of the bell that sat atop the door that alerted Ike to a new customer.

Clayton and Shannon slowly walked with downcast faces to the stove. Ike was shocked when he saw the couple. Neither looked happy to be there or anywhere, for that matter. Ike thought they looked hopeless. Perhaps this wasn't the time to tell them what he was about to tell them, but he figured that no time was a good time for *this* news. Besides, he also figured that he might never see them alive again either.

CHAPTER 28

Ike was alarmed, actually shocked, at the weight his friend Clayton Rinehart had lost. What used to be a strongly built 170-pound man now resembled a clothes hanger with a shirt and baggy pants hanging loosely from its wiry frame. Ike figured he couldn't have weighed more than 130 pounds — if that. His once amiable demeanor was enveloped by a hopeless, emotionless, rapidly aging face.

His wife, who once bore an optimistic and delighted smile, now carried the somber expression to her husband. She had aged 20 years in only ten. Deep lines around her eyes had furrowed to the edges of her once perky lips, like erosion deepens a branch into a river. Ike didn't know how he knew, but he suspected she hadn't laughed, or perhaps hadn't even smiled, in a year.

As he introduced the tormented couple to the coach, he wondered what the news he had to tell them would do to their obviously fragile hold on reality. He knew the couple had —or at one time had —a strong conviction in their Christian faith.

He knew before he spoke that probably one of two things would happen: they would reaffirm their belief in God's plan and His sometimes bitterly tough blueprint for some people, or they would hopelessly surrender to Satan, having had enough of this purgatorial existence. Sharing a life with a prehistoric species of maniacal giant that was never supposed to be living in this age of more civilized times would have this effect on the strongest of faiths.

"I wanted you to hear this together," said Ike, addressing all three of his guests. "Everybody pull up a chair and get as comfortable as you can. The news I have to tell is going to be tough, especially for you guys." Ike was looking at Clayton and Shannon as everybody scooted their chairs closer to the radiating stove.

"I know you've told me that you have been doing research on Gabe and that you had some news that you had to tell us, but why is the football coach here? What has he got to do with all this?" Clayton's voice was weaker than Ike remembered from the last time they talked.

"Coach Ford has observed the inhuman, mechanical way Gabe moves, and I knew that his curiosity might lead him to the wrong conclusion and bring outside forces upon us before we could come up with a plan of our own."

Harrison looked at Ike like he was crazy but held his tongue because he really couldn't formulate a question that made any sense.

"I told the Coach I would start at the beginning, and that's probably the best place to begin anything." Ike said, stirring his coffee with a plastic fork, searching for words. "Oh, by the way Coach, before you hear any of this, how is your relationship with God?"

"My relationship with God?" Now it was time for Harrison to search for words. "I'm a Christian, brought up in church, sang in the choir like most of the kids in my neighborhood. Why?"

"Well, your relationship is about to get a lot tighter, my friend."

"Don't say anything," Harrison said morosely. "I knew that God or Satan had something to do with this. I didn't want to think about that, but I knew —or, at least I thought I knew."

Ike nodded his head. "More than you know. I know both of you are Christians, Clayton and Shannon, and I know you've told me before how your faith in God has been tested to the brink, and you have no answers."

They both nodded gravely.

"It's about to be tested further still," Ike said as he picked up a notebook that was lying by his chair and started fumbling through its pages, trying to reason how or where to start his tale. Then he looked at all three of his increasingly impatient guests, started to speak, snapped his fingers, got up, walked to the door, turned the *OPEN* sign around to *CLOSED*, locked the door tight, and flipped the lights off. He slowly came back to his chair; the ruby glow from the red-hot stove cast an eerie air upon his face. He timidly began to speak again.

"I have done nothing but think about Gabe ever since I met him, ah, it's been 11 or 12 years now. Don't seem like it. Oh, I've done other things —the things people do —but when my mind is not forced to think about the things it has to, it automatically returns to ponder on Gabriel. I know it has yours, too.

"I hope I'm not going to offend you good people," Ike nodded toward Clayton and Shannon, "when I tell you he's not supposed to be on this earth. I know you've talked to me many hours on this very subject, Clayton. I didn't have any answers for you then, but maybe I do now. Maybe.

"I've heard all kinds of tales when I was boy from my grandfather. I never really paid much mind to them. Too damn fantastic, even for a naïve kid to believe. I've heard the creation stories and the flood stories, and hunting stories, warring stories —you name it and my people have a story for it that goes back thousands of years. Never written down, just repeated from generation to generation.

"I'm sure they've changed some over the centuries. Hell, you can start a rumor in town today, and by the time it gets back around to you tomorrow, it isn't even in the same category. I know because I've started a few myself.

"Many of the 1,000 stories I heard as a boy were about giants. Of course, when you're thinking about Gabe, you are naturally going to think about all the folklore stories about giants you can remember. I probably heard about 30 or 40 different stories about giants that once roamed the plains of this country, but there was one of those crazy stories that wasn't so crazy —it actually made sense.

"The problem was that it was located in the back recesses of my mind, just out of reach. That's the bad thing about becoming a feeble old man. You never can picture yourself becoming that old person you used to make fun of when you were a boy. If I'd known what it was going to be like, I would've held my tongue a little closer.

"I just couldn't grasp it— just out of reach, and when I did finally catch hold, it was only for a second, and then I'd lose my grip again. It was like trying to focus on those little bright, twinkly stars we call *devil's dots* that dance across your eyes when you raise up too quick in the heat of the summer. When you try to focus on one to see if it is indeed a tiny devil, they fade into nothingness… There is no dignity in getting old.

"All I could remember was that my grandfather said that they found some of the giants' bones when he was a boy, and they put it in the papers. That sort of stood out and clicked the little devil's dots to dancing in my mind. Since I can't seem to catch the devil's dots, and I don't have one of Mr. Peabody's Way-Back machines to talk to my grandfather again, I decided to go to the library. I spent months—years now—putting all this together.

"One article would lead me to another, and to another still. I must have driven a thousand miles, spent half my paltry savings, and talked to clergy in every denomination, to medicine men, to rabbis, and to Shaman. It became more than a quest for me; it was more than an obsession; it became this old man's… destiny.

"I know that I must sound like a crazy old fool to you. You think I don't know that? But hear me out now. What I'm about to tell you is the truth. It's the only truth there is. There is no other. It is more fantastic than any of the wild and crazy Lakota tales my grandfather used to tell. I had been waiting only for one more piece to arrive, and it finally did. I've not opened it yet. We will look at it together in a minute. I'm afraid to look at it by myself.

"You must never repeat this to anyone, but I'm going to tell you what I know so far. If I don't tell you now, I'm afraid I will die and I'll carry this song to my grave, never having been sung. You must know the truth, for as one of my favorite people once said, 'Know the truth, and the truth shall set you free.'

"Clayton, Shannon, and now Coach, do you want to know this?" Ike stuck out his hand toward the couple. Shannon took his hand, and then a second later, so did Clayton. They sat directly in front of Ike with the glowing stove warming their backs. They looked like starving puppies waiting to be fed by their master. Coach scooted his chair in closer with the same look in his eyes. Ike picked up the thick, voluminous notebook and cleared a lump from his quivering voice.

CHAPTER 29

"With the utmost respect to you fine people," Ike said apologetically, "I think we can all agree that the boy who's living in your house is not of this world." Clayton and Shannon nodded in despair, in unison. "But the question becomes: what world did he come from, and how did he get here?"

Clayton looked hopelessly at his wife and then turned to Ike saying, "One of the doctors at the clinic said he had alien DNA in him, but he didn't say where from."

"Well, he's partly right, Clayton," continued Ike gingerly. "The answer is not so much from where but from when."

Clayton, Shannon and Harrison cast resigned looks at each other. Ike opened his note book, took a pair of glasses out of his shirt pocket, placed them across the bridge of his nose, and began.

"I didn't know it, and I'll bet you didn't either, that giants really did walk the earth at one time. History is gorged with the evidence. Look here:

- In the Canton of Lucerne, an oak tree was toppled by a gust of wind, and to the amazement of the locals, a 19'6" skeleton was discovered. It was surmised at the time that the giant was buried with the sapling tree on top of the grave as a marker.
- In 1456, a 23-foot giant was found next to a river in Valence, France. It had clutched in its hands a sword that measured 14 feet long and weight over 300 lbs. The men that discovered the find were put on trial for heresy.

- A perfectly complete human-like skeleton specimen was found in 1613 near the castle of Chaumont in France. From skull to heel, it measured 25'6". A large hole was found in the skull, and the feet and hands of the creature were bound in shackles.
- In 1856, a miner fell through a hole in a mine in Italy and found an 11' 6" skeleton. The skull was found several feet from the rest of the body.
- In the late 1950s, during road construction near the Euphrates Valley in southeast Turkey, many tombs containing the remnants of giants were found. One of the femur leg bones was measured at 47.25 inches long. According to Joe Taylor, director of the Mt. Blanco Fossil Museum in Crosbyton, Texas, who was commissioned to make an anatomically correct model, the giant measured just under 16 feet in height. All of the bodies had been decapitated.

"Now, that was some of the evidence of giants in Europe, but as European settlers started spreading across the good ol' U.S. of A., newspaper reports of giants' bones started springing up almost as fast as their log huts.

- The most credible stories of giant skeletons were centered in the Appalachians, the Cumberland Plateau and Ohio Basin areas. They were typically found in graves lined with field stones. These graves were later recognized by professional archaeologists as the *Stone Box Grave Culture*. The average size was about 10 feet long. Curiously, the cause of death: broken necks.
- The tombs of seven giants were found in Clearwater, Minnesota. Each one measuring over ten feet. Again, just as oddly, they all had skull fractures.
- In 1833, soldiers digging at a pit for a powder magazine in Lompoc Rancho, California, discovered a male skeleton that was 12 feet tall. The skeleton was surrounded by carved

shells, stone axes, and blocks of porphyry covered with unintelligible symbols. The skeleton had an iron rod 12 feet long, weighing over 250 pounds, wedged between its ribs. These bones substantiated legends by the local Piute Indians regarding giants, which they called Si-Te-Cahs. By the way, the axes weighed 350 pounds each.

- In 1918, while working on a guano mining operation in Lovelock Cave in Nevada, workers unearthed a giant skull. My grandfather was one of those workers. Here's a photo. They called in some archeologist, and more bones and Neolithic artifacts were found. A complete man and woman's skeletons were retrieved, in addition to several detached supersized human bones. The male was said to be well over 20 feet tall but was probably more like 25 feet. Supposedly, most of the artifacts were lost in a fire, but the skulls are on display at the Humboldt County Museum in Winnemucca, Nevada if you want to see it. Those bones didn't get lost in a fire. I've seen them.
- Finally, in Browerville, Indiana, a 19'8" skeleton was excavated from a mountain as reported in the Indianapolis News on November 10, 1875.

"My God, have you ever heard about any of this stuff?" an incredulous Harrison asked the stupefied Rinehart's. They shook their heads.

"Why haven't we heard about this before?" Harrison was looking despairingly at Ike.

"I didn't know it either," droned Ike, "till I looked for it, but it's out there. My grandfather was right about giant bones being found in this country. To be honest with you, I always thought my grandfather was full of shit. That was before I found all of these articles. If I'd known all this, I would've paid more attention to him… Now here's where it gets interesting.

"I found that every Native American narrative tale of every tribe or culture, that I could find, has one legend that is common among them all. Only one. And that is the legend of the mighty, light pigmented, yellow-haired or red-haired giants living in the Great Lakes Region or southern Canada, who occasionally traveled southward into their territories, and at some point, had at least one war with the tribe. One war was all it took, by the way.

"You might imagine that the war didn't go well for the tribe. How could it? In fact, the slaughters were so vicious that the survivors had no language to describe the carnage. If these accounts —which are different from the other legends, as their origins are much more recent —are true, then the power and might of these giants are truly beyond a simple people's language to describe. These are the descriptions of the giants that are most common:

- Between 20 and 25 feet tall
- Red or blonde hair
- Weighing somewhere between 6,000 to 7,500 pounds
- Muscles without skin, bulging, rippling, with veins exposed all over the entire body
- The muscles on the sides of the neck (trapezius) extended to the ear
- Clever, intelligent, unbeatable in warfare with a penchant to torture their captives or use them for games… I don't know what that means
- Capable of such feats of strength and agility that so beguiled the enemy, they would often surrender without resistance and, while whimpering like children, beg for mercy. Unfortunately, mercy was short in coming from these beings.

There's one other little bit of information I found —kind of disturbing, though —and again, it was true in all accounts from every tribe that I could find any writings. The only way the giants could be killed is when they killed each other. In fact, the only way that any were ever found dead is by their own people's hand."

Clayton and Shannon were visibly distressed by what they were hearing. Their anguished faces showed that they had expected the worst —and were getting it.

"I know where you're going, Ike, but how did we manage to have one of them? How?" pleaded Clayton.

"I'm coming to that now. Ya'll just sit tight. This part is going to be tough to say," Ike said somberly.

"Around the turn of the 20th century, the distinguished Tuscarora anthropologist J.N.B. Hewitt began to study these legends and found the giant white people that once wreaked havoc —and practically decimated his own people —to be credible. He set out on a pilgrimage to get to the bottom of the 'why' and the 'how'. It became his quest… before it became mine.

"It took him over 20 years and cost him his life savings. He crossed over mountains and seas, transversed the Atlantic three times, and spent time in a Prussian prison, but he finally got his answers and put the story down on paper in 1924 in this notebook. I found it by accident in the cellar of his great-great-granddaughter when I was plundering through his artifacts. She and one other person —besides me, of course, are the only people to have read it. She let me have it after I told her about Gabe.

"There is one other of his notebooks that I've been nervous as hell waiting on, and it got here this morning. It was in a bank vault tucked snugly away in a safety deposit box in Sassarai, in the region of Sardinia, Italy. Don't ask me how I managed to get it sent, but I don't have nearly as much money as I used to.

"What I'm about to tell you is going to put you to the test as Christians. I know it did me." Ike was fumbling through the pages in an attempt to find the correct ones from which to start. His fingers were shaky, and he had trouble finding the mark.

Harrison stared contemplatively at Clayton and Shannon. He was wondering what they were thinking about right now. All he knew was that he wished he had his wife with him at this moment.

He knew well enough that he was about to hear something that was going to shake his world to its foundation. He didn't want to hear it alone. He wanted his wife, or his mother, or somebody he knew, with him right now. He couldn't restrain himself. "Let me go get Melissa, please," he said desperately. "I want her to hear this. I don't mind telling you people, I'm scared."

Ike flashed a smile at Harrison, and said gently, "Go get her. You're going to tell her all about this anyhow. Just don't tell anybody else."

"Are you kidding me," snapped Harrison. "Who the hell would believe it? Shit, man, I know it's true, and I still don't believe it."

CHAPTER 30

Harrison fled to his apartment and, with a shaken voice, explained to Melissa everything that Ike had told him. She was stupefied and humbled by her husband, and yet curious. A morbid curiosity is a strange animal to house. Despite its weight, it is a very picky eater and not easily fooled when it comes to the morsels it will digest. Its cravings can only be satisfied with truths, and it will regurgitate the unsavory and unbelievable bites as quickly as they're tasted. Only the palatable serving of the truth will satisfy a ravaging conscience.

When they arrived back to Ike's, the eerily dark shop and the foreboding red glow of the potbelly stove only heightened Melissa's sense of apprehension. But just like Clayton, Shannon, and her husband, she had a craving to hear the rest of the story.

Two anguished people —a man and a woman, parents of a giant who is roaming the earth, who are seeking redemption or damnation, in either case — craved to hear and know. They took their places in the red, warm glow of the stove.

Two other anguished people —a man and a woman, Black people living in a strange world of white people and a giant roaming the earth, also seeking redemption or damnation — likewise took their places within the radiant glow of the stove.

And a quivering old man, a native to this land, who had a giant in his midst roaming freely, merely seeking the truth and having found it, began to speak in the luminescent red glow of the stove with timid, timorous lips.

"Mr. Hewitt did it all you know. I just happened to stumble across his life's work. He discovered the truth. It drove him to the brink of madness, but he discovered it. The funny thing about discoveries is that the world has to be ready for them. I guess Mr. Hewitt figured that the world wasn't quite ready for the truth because he went to his grave and never told a soul —not even his own family. Here's the Reader's Digest version of what he found:

There are 66 books in the Bible, but those aren't the only books that ever written. There were more. Did you know that there was no specific accounting for what went in the Bible until Emperor Constantine commissioned it in the 4th Century AD? The books that make up the authorized King James Bible were chosen by men, not divine forces. Many forbidden books were excluded from the cannon because, well, some didn't seem to fit, or they were written by unknown authors. Some were considered absolutely too bizarre. At one time, as many as 600 books.

Ol' Constantine began purging all the books deemed unacceptable to the new doctrine of the church. Through a series of decisions by the early church leadership, all but 80 of those books, known as the King James Translation of 1611, were purged. Another round of further reductions by the Protestant Reformation brought the number to 66 in the *Authorized* King James Bible. Listen to this:

"When men began to increase in number on the earth and daughters were born to them, the sons of God saw that the daughters of men were beautiful, and they married any of them they chose." Genesis 6:1-2

"The Nephilim were on the earth in those days - and also afterward - when the sons of God went to the daughters of men and had children by them. They were the heroes of old, men of renown." Genesis 6:4

"We saw the Nephilim there (the descendants of Anak come from the Nephilim). We seemed like grasshoppers in our own eyes, and we looked the same to them." Numbers 13:33

This is in the Bible we know, right? This is what is written in one of the lost books —books mentioned in the Bible but supposedly never found —called The Book of Enoch:

In olden times of the ancient world, long after God had created the Angels in Heaven to offer praise to Him, and which He was most pleased, there did occur a rebellion, which God did allow, and of which God was most displeased.

All of God's creatures, whether angelic or human, were undeniably created with the time, space, and omnipotence of a sovereign Lord. This time and space are essential to our existence and to that of all His creatures, Satan and the fallen angels included.

So it was, and so it is, that the Son's of God are free to move about in this time and space, in which all of the created creatures exist and at the same time.

Alas, there can be seen in His mighty sovereignty the authority to allow man, to allow all His creatures, to *choose* whether or not they wish to follow Him of our own will. Some choose wisely, some choose poorly, in either case, there are consequences for creatures to endure. And so it was.

This is from a prophet named Nathan:

And so it was at this time that the devil gathered his dominions around him and he did say, 'it is time for my plan to unfold, and thus my sons you may choose your shields of three of any of the animals that creep on the earth.

And Satan spoke saying:

'You therefor may mate with the daughters of men and produce freely a mighty creature and cries of fear will echo from sea to sea and on the mountain tops also.

'And so being well shielded you must therefore also be marked with a sign of our world. As you roam freely our world beneath heaven will be seen by man but he will not know your sign of the world below.

"The exact number of books purged is known only to the church, and it is not shared knowledge. What is known is of one particular book discovered by Mr. John Arthur Gibson Hewitt. It's not really a book, but more like a diary or an accounting of a rather unpleasant time to be alive in Bible's times.

These were the *Forbidden Books* that were never considered part of the Bible and were ordered to be destroyed, but they weren't of course —just merely hidden away, patiently waiting for such a driven man as Mr. Hewitt to resurrect them. It seems as though they were kept alive for some unknown future purpose. I believe they were divinely preserved just for our discovery. How else can you explain the one-in- a-million chance I found it?

Written in some dead language that only a handful of linguists could comprehend, Mr. Hewitt had to travel to Italy to have it translated into modern English. But once it was discovered that he had it, he had to hide it away and flee for his life. What better place to hide something than in a bank vault?

The book arrived via FedEx early this morning. Before I read it to you, you need to know some background.

You know the story of Abraham. Through the seed of a woman was to come a Savior, and he had to come through Abraham. We're talking about Jesus, of course, but here's what you don't know: Satan had a plan to put his own seed in the land of Canaan. He got together with some of his angels —yes, Satan has angels —and decided to let them visit earth and mate with the women.

The aim here was to occupy Canaan in advance of Abraham. Satan knew there would be battles, so he gave his side an advantage. Thus, he allowed these Fallen Angels to each use the DNA of certain animals — three to be exact. They could choose any three animals they wanted, but only three per angel.

What it created was, well, this book I'm holding here is supposed to tell that story. I don't know what's written in here, but it will have our answers. Man wasn't supposed to see it until it was time. I think the arrival of Gabe has made it time for us to found out, don't you? Do you really want to know what's in here?" Ike looked up and into the eyes of each of his quivering guests. "It may change you."

"We're already changed, Ike," answered Clayton ashamedly. "We have to know, or we'll die."

"Well, hell, man," wailed Harrison, "our minds are so blown, it may be the only thing that can keep us sane."

"Do one of you want to read this, or do you want me to?"

"You do it, Ike; it's your find," said Clayton gravely, and then he embraced his knees and lowered his head. His heart was pounding.

Ike opened the book and began to read…

PART 2

CHAPTER 1

The noise is deafening. When they laugh, the ground trembles beneath our feet. My ears throb in pain.

"Where is my grog?" bellowed Behemoth, and then, catching me in the corner of his eye, he sends a backhand at my head. I duck. The mighty fist strikes Meehan in the mouth. His head explodes in a red mist of brain matter and skull fragments.

Behemoth springs to his feet. The jarring ground vibrates the five-gallon flask of grog I'm carrying to my master. I clamp my body over the top of the flask and rescue its contents without spilling a drop. Behemoth gives a momentary acknowledgement of my dexterity and then grimaces in pain.

He picks Meehan's tiny teeth out of the fleshy part of his hand and drops them into an empty flask. The last tooth he flicks in anger with his forefinger at a six-inch-diameter sapling. The tooth enters one side, explodes through the other, leaving a much larger hole of splintered wood debris.

The Nephilim are among us. The giants are our masters. We are their slaves. We must live with them and serve them —or die. This is our life. If you have not seen a Nephilim, you people would not believe what my eyes have witnessed. I hope whoever hears this can interpret my words. I hope I am adequate to tell the story, for hell has descended upon us. You must know what live is like on Earth in these times.

There are fewer of us today than there were yesterday. And there will be fewer tomorrow than there are today. But it will all be over soon. Almost all of us will die. We just don't know when.

Behemoth is the Master of this region of the Nephilim. They are all giants. He is the biggest and the strongest —for now. He may not be by the end of The Games. It doesn't matter to us who wins. Only three families will be alive to know —or care.

My name is Compel. We are being prepared for the Games. It is the Games that will be end of most us. Behemoth is almost drunk now. That's why he swung at me —and missed. Good for me, bad for poor Meehan. That's not true either. Meehan won't have to suffer the torture of guessing when he will die an agonizing death like the rest of us.

"Meehan is dead, "I say coldly. My wife, Lindsay, returns a nod just as coldly. "It was quick. He never saw it coming. I'm glad," I say as I lie down on my pallet. "He was a good man."

"At least his journey is over," says Lindsay with a sigh. "He is with the Father now." Lindsay is cutting up small pieces of ox meat for the stew that has just begun to boil. The ox had gotten tangled in the limbs of the large tree above our hut. It landed there by mistake. It was supposed to land on the hut of our neighbor, but Urobach was having trouble with his aim. Good —it is our gain. Whatever animal lands closest to your hut belongs to you and your family. Already slaughtered.

"Is he with the Father?" I was beginning to get angry again.

"Please don't think such things, again Compel." my wife says, attempting to keep me from losing my faith again. "It is all we have left, my husband. Please don't take that from me now. I am beginning to weaken too." Lindsay fights off a sobbing sound.

"I am lost, my wife. Lost in my own muddled thoughts."

The next day, the sun is bright, and the air clear. The Nephilim tribe is sleeping late this morning after being so drunk last night. It takes about two weeks to make a batch of grog. When it is ready, the seven Nephilim occupiers have a feast of three skewed oxen and twelve sheep while they consume the hundred gallons of grog.

We have to serve them or die before the Games begin. Either way, we die. That's not entirely true. Not all of us will die. There will be three families of survivors from the Games —or so they tell us. Three families. That is all that will be left from our village.

I try to remember what it was like before the Nephilim arrived that day. It is like trying to remember a dream. It is hard to tell which is reality and which is the dream. Did I dream our village before the Nephilim? My mother, my father? Or is this all a dream? How do I make myself awaken? My mind is confused.

The approaching thumping sound means that we are about to receive a visit from one of the Nephilim. Maybe he is coming to play with our minds, or play with our bodies, or maybe he is coming simply to kill us. One never knows what fate awaits. Dark shadows make the sunlight disappear from the cracks around and underneath our door.

"Come hither, my good friend Compel. I am in need of you." Behemoth's voice booms. It is impossible for them to speak softly. They have acute hearing as well, and they say they can call to each other from up to ten miles away.

I am afraid now. I have already answered one of their riddles. I didn't know if I was right or not, but I'm still alive, so I must have been right. It is all part of the Games. Only three families will survive.

"I have come to apologize to you, my friend." I open the door gingerly. It matters not why he came. I was going to open the door regardless, or risk dying on the spot. Their tempers are as acute as their hearing. I look up at the twenty-three foot man mountain. Behemoth kneels down to one knee. I stare gravely at his biceps with a 6-inch-diameter, distended vein that coursed through his bulging 45-inch biceps, level with my head when he is in this position.

"I am afraid I was intoxicated last night from the grog. You have been a faithful servant to me, and so was Meehan. I'm sorry he had to die before his time. He would have made good sport. It was a pity. I would have enjoyed killing him honorably."

Behemoth's voice actually sounds apologetic. Of course, it's impossible to tell if he is serious or if he's laying a trap. He may have been sincere about missing the chance to kill him in a more horrible way. They call this the games —the honorable way.

"What do you want of me Behemoth?" I ask cautiously and with forced friendliness. Friendly is the way to stay alive. Words must be chosen wisely. The wrong wording can mean the end. And sometimes the wrong look can be just as fatal.

Once, Jone, one of the best men in our village, made the mistake of frowning and mumbling at Urobach when he ordered him to come. He temporarily forgot that the Nephilim can read a man's lips from a half mile away. He never saw the spear that was traveling at 400 miles per hour, flashing through his temple, through the wall of his hut, through his wife's body, exiting the other wall of the hut, and burying itself so deep in a tree that it is impossible for us to remove it.

It is still there, wedged three feet deep in the hard oak tree as a daily reminder of the terminal cost of a misguided, sullen expression. We hate to serve them. But we hate to be skewered at the end of a three-inch spear more. If we were smart, we would made a downcast expression and die quickly. Better than what awaits us, we have heard. My talk is brave because I am a coward, just like the others. There is always a chance I might win and be spared. Me and two other families. That's why I never change the expression on my face. I might win. We all think this same thought.

CHAPTER 2

I want you to run an errand for me, Compel." The bright blue eyes of Behemoth appear as glass. His hair is shiny, golden blond and contrasts starkly with his dark, tanned skin. He is 6,500 pounds of bulging muscle. His arms are the size of my chest. I once saw him thump a man with the middle finger of his right hand and fracture his skull, killing him on the spot. I never take my eyes off his. To look away when in conversation with a Nephilim can be very bad for your health.

When the Nephilim engage you in serious conversation, the intensity of their stare stings your eyes. One can only maintain constant contact for a few seconds. Then you must focus on another part of their face —the furrowed brows, for instance. But never look away. They find that offensive. Your fate is at stake. Sometimes painlessly, sometimes not.

Their brains radiate intelligence that flows through their eyes. It is all part of the Games. The Games —that is what they call the insane struggle that will decorate our countryside with graves. Fortunately, it will eliminate all but seven of the Nephilim in this region of the world as well. That is a good thing. The more these creatures from hell discard each other the better.

"What is this errand I must do for you, Behemoth?"

"I want you to go to the next village and assess our competition." Behemoth's penetrating glare begins to hurt my brain, so I focus on his brow again.

"Do you mean spy on the other Nephilim?"

"Of course I do. Don't upset me with your ignorance now, Compel, for I desire you to be a winner."

"You mean you desire for us both to be a winner." I say with fake pride.

"I mean, if I lose, you lose. Do you understand that?" Behemoth frowns and intensifies his concentrated, painful glare. A sharp throbbing travels from the back of my head to the front. I put my hands to my eyes and bend in agony. Behemoth laughs. "I think you understand me well enough."

"Wouldn't you, master, be a better judge of the abilities of the others than I?" I am attempting to rub away the pain from the front of my head. "A wolf's ass is easier to spot than the flea on the wolf's ass, Compel." Behemoth turns his gaze away for a moment to spare me from further pain. He sighs deeply as he contemplates something off in the distance. "I want you to be my eyes and ears. Mine are too large, Compel."

He has what appears to be concern on his muscular face.

For he knows his life is at stake as well, but his life is of little concern to him. He craves what they all crave —what they all desire. The Prize.

The Prize is the reason they have come to earth. At least that is what the elders have told us all these many years. It is part of the legacy or prophecy, as the elders call it. I have never read this prophecy myself. We were all enchanted by the stories of the Nephilim as children, but we all doubted their existence. The stories seemed too fantastic to be real. We know differently now.

CHAPTER 3

The long track to the next village of Milo is tiresome. If I'm caught spying on the Nephilim of this village, it will matter not if I'm tired or fresh—I will be dead. I can only hope it will be quickly.

They could keep me as a volunteer. But, most likely, a massive hand will clutch my throat, and an immense, crushing thumb will snap my head off of my shoulders. This is the preferred technique of an angry Nephilim. More than once, I have been struck by a friend's spinning head h—cold, dead eyes, literally, staring back at me.

I lay myself atop a small rise of the rolling terrain. I can distinguish the village below clearly. Milo appears the same as it did when I visited before h—the same as our village had, save for the seven Nephilim that are roaming about, eliminating the weak.

Only the strong will survive until the Games begin. That is true for every village that has been besieged by the Nephilim. Seven of the giants —always seven—will gather at a village and announce to the dwellers that they have been chosen to participate in the Games.

They approach from seven different directions. The announcement is initiated by hurling a full grown-ox into an unsuspecting hut. The animal explodes against the exterior, crashes through the wall, and covers those who are not killed by the flying debris with ox blood and guts.

It is an effective way to communicate. I had heard of great announcements preceded by the blowing of a trumpet when I was but a boy. This is the way the Nephilim blow a trumpet. It works well. There is no doubt about what is happening—your village has just been

chosen. There is no escape now. Very bad things are going to happen—
bad things

It never seems real to your eyes at first. Everyone has heard the stories of the Nephilim from childhood. But no one has ever actually seen one. They grow into myths and legends, something parents use to scare children who misbehave: *Mind me now and do your chores, lest the Nephilim get you.* It works at first, but the more mature children stop believing such nonsense.

It always takes a while for reality to whack your brain when the invasion first happens. Your mind eventually accepts that it is happening, but it never seems real. I suspect the people of every village have the same expression upon their faces—the same as the people of my village. An air of unreal disbelief and confusion.

We all seem to be waiting for the one who is having this nightmare to awaken and release us. *Enough of your dreaming, my friend. You have caught me up in it, and I would be most appreciative if you would awaken now.* They are sound sleepers. Our screams for help travel through the air and disappear without so much as a yawn.

"The dreamer who is dreaming me must be drunk on grog," I once joked to Behemoth. Jokes would sometimes amuse the Nephilim, as long as they weren't the brunt of it. A mistake you only make once.

He beheld me for a second. I feel a trifling pain deep behind my eyes, but only briefly. Then his eyes traveled to the open plain, deep in revelry.

"I have wondered the same thing before, Compel. It does seem as though I am misplaced— a gnawing at the inside of my brain." His voice was as peaceful as I can ever recall it being. He continued to almost whisper to himself.

"I know why I am here, but I don't know how I know. I originated from one of your women—my mother. She died you know, giving me life. They all do. A part of me has a yearning to feel pity for you, for what we are doing to you minuscule people. Yet a greater hunger dispels the weakness, and then I recognize I must win, and I begin to feel nothing for any of you once again."

He peeked at me and his vast lips spreads. The muscles of his face contracted, revealing striations and veins crisscrossing the musculature.

The bright white teeth unveiled a handsome smile. It is insane what I am about to say, but at times—very few times, but a few nonetheless—I can almost have feelings for the Nephilim. One gets the impression they are here against their will. And then one of your neighbor's head is slapped off his shoulders so quickly that his headless body is still standing, and the feeling goes away.

"I will try my best, Master Behemoth." Though it is probably useless, I can't help but attempt to garner favor from a creature with no heart.

"Go forward, good and faithful servant," says Behemoth sadly.

"What, Master?" He couldn't have said what I thought he said.

"I heard that said somewhere, though I don't know where," he said even sadder.

"Is something wrong, Master?" I asked, hoping for sympathy, if it was indeed possible that it abounded in them.

"Yes, servant Compel, something is very wrong. We are going to lose."

"We may win, master. You don't know until the games are over." I say desperately. If they lose, we lose, and vice versa. Only the winning Nephilim team gets to choose the three families that get to live. This is no time for our Nephilim to feel defeated.

"You don't understand, Compel. Even if we win, we will lose." Behemoth's head was bowed, and his voice was soft.

"What, Master? I don't understand."

"Go, Compel!" Behemoth bellowed so loudly my ears pounded in pain. He was angry with me now. I vamoosed in a sprint.

I am about a half a mile away from the village. The villagers are tiny from this distance. The Nephilim that now own it *are not.* They are colossal— bigger than the ones that are the owners of our village, at least the ones I see. That is another trait of these creatures. They never stop growing until they are killed. They can live hundreds of years— thousands perhaps. No one knows because they kill each other before they reach old age. That's good.

These have lived longer than ours. I call them ours because, in a sense, they are ours. Each tribe of seven Nephilim captures a village and takes possession. There is no fight, no resistance, and no chance to fight them off. They are impossible to battle. I once heard someone describe us as appearing as grasshoppers before the Nephilim. The description is just about right, except a grasshopper would have a better chance. At least they have wings.

Imagine a creature standing before you that is 20 to 25 feet tall, weighs from 5,500 to 7,500 pounds and has no fat—only muscle. Shoulders six to seven feet wide. Covered from head to toe in bulging sinewy muscle and veins. The muscle on the side of his neck extends to the level as his ears. Can hurl a spear that weighs 100 pounds over two miles. Can run down the swift cats on the African plains for training purposes…There are no battles for a village—only surrender and pleadings for life…Anyone who says differently is a liar or a fool… There are only dead fools.

CHAPTER 4

I have keen eyes, but I am having trouble making out what is taking place at our neighboring village of Milo. There doesn't seem to be enough people scurrying about. I count only four Nephilim. *Where are the others?* I wonder.

From behind a clump of trees, I can hear a commotion. Then suddenly, I see a Nephilim dart out from behind a tree and speed to a spot that is marked with a large X sign scratched in the dirt. A man's scream breaks the silence, and the sight of him spinning in a spiral through the air appears from the top of the trees. He is spinning at about 1 revolution per second as he slices through the air.

The Nephilim who is at the X mark takes several steps backpedals and catches the screaming man in his enormous, yet cradling hands. He sets the petrified little man on the ground and fashions another X mark about 40 feet further back from the first.

The titan who had just hurled the man about 300 feet through the air steps out from behind the trees. Even for a Nephilim, he is a monster. He must be 26 feet tall and weigh over 7,000 pounds. Even mighty Behemoth will be no match for this creature. He is the largest and most powerful of them all. And collectively, they are bigger than Behemoth and his team. I know why Behemoth looked concerned about the Games. And now his concern is our concern.

These are the way of the Nephilim. They roam around the earth in groups of seven. I have only seen male Nephilim. I have only heard of male Nephilim. All we know is what we hear and what the Nephilim tell us. I don't know where the females are. I don't know if there are female Nephilim. I have been tempted to ask Behemoth, but I lack the nerve.

One does not engage them freely. I have asked questions before, but I am usually made to feel ignorant. They are much more intelligent than our people. Much more. They don't deem us worthy of conversation. To tell the truth, I don't exactly know what to talk to them about. It is a strange time when a man must be friendly with his executioner. Yet, I find myself strangely drawn to these mesmerizing creatures. I know I will probably die from one of their hands during the Games, or maybe before, from a sullen look, or a misplaced word perhaps.

It sounds morbid, but I'd like to know more about them. I know what I have been told about the beginning. I have often pondered the story. It actually makes sense now.

CHAPTER 5

I did not desire to convey what I had just witnessed from the village of Milo. Behemoth never takes bad news well. How do I say to the master, who can literally hold your fate in his hands, that he is outmanned? That he is going to lose? Carefully…

"What did you see, Compel? Don't tarry about. And don't be fearful. I won't kill you for what you are about to say, unless the news is bad, of course." Behemoth was not regarding me, but had his gaze solidly upon Ronwe, the Nephilim who speaks in unusual ways. He transferred his gaze upon me again and smiled. "I jest, Compel. Speak now before I fail to recall that I enjoy you."

"I saw, hum, uh, big men." I suddenly lost the ability to speak.

"His tongue is tied. Perhaps he his brain has died. Don't worry me, ant. For spare you I can't," said Ronwe in his strange language that he alone uses.

"No, Ronwe!" rumbled Behemoth. Don't frighten him. We need to know what he has seen."

"Speak easy, Compel. Don't let your tongue dwell. For I mean you no harm. Jesting is simply, my most enduring charm. " Ronwe faked an apologetic gesture. He is the cruelest of this team of Nephilim. His subtle riddles are difficult to figure correctly.

Though his riddles are subtle, his punishments are not. If you can't solve a riddle, he will sometimes spare your life if you will tear off one of your own fingernails. Charming indeed.

Once, while my friend Tupac was carrying a heavy platter of roasted goat to Ronwe, he asked him whimsically:

"Tell me, dear Tupac, and riddle me please.

What loves to eat, a weed, a shrub, a canvas piece,
  or even an iron sleeve?"

"A goat, "answered Tupac cleverly.

"I am afraid you are wrong. The answer lies underneath."

Ronwe presented Tupac a platter with a cloth on top. Tupac nervously removed the cloth, unveiling an iron sleeve. Ronwe snatched the sleeve between his two fingers and slammed into Tupac's mouth. Blood splattered. Tupac staggered backwards and wrenched in pain. He opened his blood-spurting mouth to reveal only gums. Then Ronwe said with a snigger:

"The creature is Tupac, without any teeth." All the Nephilim roared. Our ears hurt. Tupac had to eat cheese for his meals, but was alive anyhow.

"I saw them toss a man through the air for three hundred feet, master." I swallowed hard, and then said. "The one that tossed him was larger than you, master Behemoth."

Behemoth only made eye contact with me for an instant. Then he beheld his fellow Nephilim remorsefully. I had never perceived Behemoth in this manner. The others were waiting to see what their chief would do next. Behemoth was pacing back and forth with his hands behind his back, contemplating and pondering.

"They have allowed one of their own to live too long. They must be cowards," uttered Uroback. Behemoth stopped and peered resolutely at the utterer.

"It would be a certainty that you would not make such a mistake with me." Behemoth was now glaring at Uroback.

"A certainty indeed, master," mused Ronwe. "To do less would be a disaster."

"We would think less of us if you perceived us to be so weak," added Asmodeus. Behemoth is scowling at Asmodeus. He is the grandest Nephilim, next to Behemoth, and his constant nemesis. Behemoth never takes a lax breath around his antagonist.

But they all know that now is not the time to destroy Behemoth. The losers of the Games may well die. It is in all their mutual interest to coalesce behind Behemoth and win the Games. Yet, there is always the unceasing threat of betrayal. This is the persistent danger of creatures so vile. They hate each other as much as they hate my people. They hate, period. I have often wondered how this much hate could get inside these creatures.

CHAPTER 6

I understand why Behemoth struck at me and accidently killed Meehan when I approached him with the grog. He missed me because he was drunk. He struck out because he thought one of the others might attack him when he was most vulnerable. They all live in a paranoid world of suspicion. The only thing that can kill a Nephilim is another Nephilim. They are invulnerable otherwise.

They cannot be approached while sleeping. If they are awakened by a nearby sound, something in the vicinity is going to die suddenly. Once, an ox was pulling grass next to a tree where Andras lay napping. The ox coughed, as oxen do sometimes to dislodge a blade of grass. Andras backhanded his sword in such a flash, and with such precision, that the ox's head slid to the ground, and three seconds later, the headless ox toppled over, spurting blood.

Andras never opened his eyes. He merely changed sleeping positions subtlety. I was standing 100 feet away from the tree when it happened. "Compel," Andras blasted at me with his back turned away. "Yes, Master Andres," I answered as I quickly made haste toward him. "Drag this ox off and prepare it for food. Quickly, before its blood reaches me."

They have the ability to scan, in an instant, a scene with their hawk eyes, and recall everyone's positions exactly. In less than one second, any of them can count every person in the village, all of the oxen, the sheep, the chickens, the guinea fowl, the donkeys, and anything else that is in eyesight. They know straightaway if anyone or anything is missing. An accounting must be given quickly for anyone or of the stock absent.

To hide from them is futile. They can smell everyone's distinctive odor for a half mile. They can hear a leaf skittle from 100 yards away. They have panoramic vision, or so Behemoth called it. They can almost see behind them. Their reflexes are so fast, they can snatch a horsefly out of midair in a blur. It is easier to hear the movement then see it.

I sometimes ask questions; they sometimes answer. If they are bored, they will give quick answers, or angry answers, or no answers. You can never ask the same question twice of them. They never forget a conversation. You had better not either.

They don't enjoy answering questions, but there is the sense that it is part of the game rules to answer. They are ten times our superior in every way, and they are bored with us. It angers them for us to be in their very presence. To talk to us. To answer us. It is all beneath them. Yet, they are compelled to answer, to tolerate, to bear us in their presence. It is as if they are being punished. There is no joy in them. Only anger. Much anger.

I pace the ground back and forth. I most work up my courage to ask another question. But the question I am going to ask is delicate. I am afraid that I might ask the wrong question and die for it. They have a compulsion to answer, and an even stronger impulse to kill if they don't like the question.

"Master Behemoth," I ask him as he is relaxing on one knee and gazing out across the horizon in deep thought.

"Yes, Compel. You wish to ask me another question, don't you?" he says without looking at me, never breaking his gaze at the horizon beyond.

"If this is not a good time, I can ask another time, master." I always like to premise my questions in this cautious manner. A Nephilim only becomes angry with you once.

"What is this Prize which you and the others battle to win, Master?"

"I have been waiting for you to ask this question, Compel. If I didn't like you, I would not bother to answer you," he whispered, still gazing outward in thought.

"Have you not notice that there are no women of our kind with us?"

"I have assumed, Master, that there are gathered at another village waiting for the Games to be over.

"There are no women of my kind, Compel," he says, louder, with growing agitation.

"No women, master?" I am thinking to myself how they come to be, but I do not wish to press my luck, then I remember he said something being spawned from our women.

Upon hearing our conversation, the other Nephilim comes to where Behemoth and I are talking and gather around us in the same one-knee posture as their leader. They seem intrigued by our topic. I am amazed that they have all come at the same time, as if they are hearing this for the first time themselves. But this is not the case. They all know, but seem to desire to hear it again. I am amazed by this.

I am uncomfortable being surrounded by all seven Nephilim giants. I feel like the grasshopper, and I acknowledge the accuracy of the person who first used this analogy. They are not considering me, but are patiently awaiting Behemoth's next words. I am standing in a poor position for a disagreeable word to be uttered at this time. I inch myself closer to the security of Behemoth's massive knee.

I delicately put my nervous hand forward and stroke the top of my Behemoth's knee, which is at the level with my chest, and lean in closer to it, almost embracing it. I feel the heat of the pulsating blood thumping through the immense veins on his calf. I browse my eyes around and hope that Behemoth is not wearing a frown. He cuts a short engrossing smile at me and recognizes I am merely protecting myself with the shield of his authority. He is charmed by my quaintness. He once again beholds an imaginary target far away in the distance. He speaks quietly:

"We Nephilim are born from your women, Compel. Our fathers are not of this world. We are not sure who our fathers are, but they are not present when we are delivered. We are all born males. There are no female Nephilim."

"Except one, Behemoth. There is one," interjects Astaroth, the friendliest of the seven Nephilim occupiers. Or at least he has killed the fewest of us. He seems to smile much more and is less hateful. He is still a Nephilim and has no trepidations about killing the little people. There are no Nephilim who have any qualms about killing little people, except Behemoth, who seems to look disappointed when he kills someone, especially accidentally. This is a common occurrence.

"Astaroth is right," acknowledges Behemoth with a scowl at Astaroth for interrupting. "There is one Nephilim woman, and it is she who we will kill each other for.

"Indeed, indeed, for it is she that we'd,

"Would kill a sixpence to sow our seed. "added Ronwe in the only manner he can speak.

"Yes, yes indeed," retorted Behemoth answering Ronwe. A sixpence will probably die."

"You mean that six of you will die and only one will live to mate with the female mistress Nephilim?" I ask, while regarding the now stoic Behemoth. "Why does six have to die master?"

"Because six is a magic number," he droned hopelessly. "It is our magic number."

"But isn't that the number of…" I change my words quickly. "But there will be three teams of Nephilim," I countered. "I thought the team that wins the Games wins the Prize. Wouldn't all seven of you share," I added chummily.

All seven of the Nephilim glared straight at me. Then Astaroth uttered, "Do we strike you as the sharing kind, little man." And all seven of the giants began to maniacally laugh. One examining the other, who is scrutinizing the other. Louder, and louder they roared, until I have to cover my ears with my hands and I flee from their presence.

CHAPTER 7

In a treaty made long ago, the Nephilim agreed to hold, at a neutral site, a mighty competition called The Games. They used to kill each other indiscriminately. Not anymore. Alliances of seven would congregate together to hunt and for mutual protection against other Nephilim. I have never been told why seven. I don't believe they know.

Each Nephilim member of our team, and all Nephilim, possess odd proclivities. They say they are named after their fathers from whom they derive these peculiar personality quirks.

Astaroth—the prince that obtains friendship of great lords. He is the friendliest and a most distrustful. None of the other seven will turn their backs on him. Behemoth is the most leery of the idea that Astaroth would make an alliance with the enemy. He studies him suspiciously.

Ronwe—the prince of lingual knowledge. He can speak only in a limerick. It frustrates even himself.

Uroback—he is of the lower order. They have the least respect for him, and so do we. By far, he is the deadliest. Brutally powerful. He is the most likely to kill out of irritation. He is mortally jealous of the others.

Andras—the prince of discord and quarrels. He is the agitator of the bunch. He spreads rumors that one of the team may be laying a trap for the others. Like all his brethren, he does it cleverly. Always in the shadows, he would rather wait till the others have done each other in and emerge the winner.

Mammon—the princes of tempters. He lures our people to their dome with clever traps. The promise of rewards is usually meet with the anguish of a horrific death. He delights in sending gifts that are booby-trapped. He once lifted up a cow with one hand and held it about five feet above the ground so the children would have an easier time milking the animal. He neglected to tell them that earlier he had forced several adders to inject the cow with their deadly venom. Nice.

Asmodeus—the prince of vengeance. He holds grudges, forever. He is the most distrusted of all the Nephilim. All of the others at one time have had an incident with Asmodeus. They know they will pay; they just don't know when.

Behemoth—the prince of indulgencies. He is the oldest and the mightiest. I believe he is also the wisest. He is different from the rest. He is an oddity even for the Nephilim. He seems to be frustrated by something he can't quite grasp. An itch that even a massive finger can't scratch, because it lies just out of even his long reach.

They are all impatiently waiting for the Games, and the Prize—the giant female Nephilim. She is said to be the most beautiful creature to walk the earth. The winner will get to marry and mate with her. This is what drives them.

This is what I have learned from them. Every generation of Nephilim for hundreds of years have participated in the Games. The Nephilim kill each other until there are only 21 survivors. Then they gather from all over the world to meet at their point of origin, near the land of Canaan.

The winner will get to marry the queen Nephilim. They will mate and produce a child, one child, a female child. She will then grow, mature, and eventually become the next queen. The Games will determine who will be the King, and thus have the privilege to mate with the Queen. After mating and birth, the care of the baby girl is left to the little people of a conquered village. And so it goes, or so they have told me. It all comes down to the Games.

The Games, these are the highly structured battles that all the Nephilim are compelled to participate in. They all have an irresistible, inward yearning to be the King and to mate. They have no control over this hunger, this craving to be King. It is a longing that attracts the Nephilim every 100 years or so to this location.

The villages are obliterated by a takeover. As an incentive to do well in the games, the Nephilim agree to let three families from a captured village live. I hope to be one of them. This is also why these creatures appear as myths or folklore. There are very few survivors to pass along the information. Those who do tell the story are thought to be fools.

They use the little people as instruments and Game devices, paraphernalia, if you will. To be hurled for distance. To be carried as batons in races, and so forth. I do not know the details as to what the Games consist of yet, I will find out soon enough. I only saw the other village of Nephilim practicing the Toss and Catch. We have yet to practice.

They are all frustrated. I believe that is why they kill, some for the fun of it. It relieves their frustration. For all their immense power, and their monumental abilities, they are a group of suspicious, distrustful, paranoid, and miserable lot of God's forsaken creatures. They all seem to know it, but are frustrated as to how they know it. A taste of honey is worse than none at all.

This is why the great Behemoth scans the horizon deep in thought. He seems to endlessly pondering upon something. The others also spend much of their time in distracted thought. There is no fellowship among them. No friendship. No love. No feelings. They rarely speak to one another. On the rare occasion they do, it is a strange conversation to witness.

"Behemoth," Ronwe said softly one day while Behemoth was deep in contemplation. "I have often wondered while you're deep in thought, are you satisfied with what the elders taught?"

"Ronwe, why are we here?" He answered remorsefully. "Do you feel what I feel? Do you not sometimes desire what these little people possess?" Ronwe then asked, somewhat dismayed,

"And what is it that these ants possess,
  That we could not acquire?
  Could it be Behemoth, nevertheless
  That you've merely lost your desire?"

"Love, you fool, "Behemoth returned, disgusted. "We truly are damned." The master returned to his reveries, disappointedly shaking his 500-pound head.

Feeling the bite in Behemoth's words, Ronwe answered back:

"And what is love, but a word,
Its meaning is muddled and absurd.
But let pain be spread, enough to be heard
Then love takes flight, just like a bird."

"Maybe you're right, Ronwe. But you have watched these people willingly die for one another." Behemoth raised his voice to the approaching team of Nephilim who could hear their conversation and became drawn to the topic. "Tell me, oh great and powerful Nephilim. Men of renown, heroes of old, what say you?"

"I say you have gained a certain degree of humanity, Behemoth," said Urobach resignedly. "Are you going to weep for this people next?"

Behemoth returned his eyes off to the sky, and his voice softened, "I would if I could. You know we can't weep for anything or anyone."

"This is our finest blessing of all, you foolish imp of a leader," scowled Urobach.

Behemoth then posed a question. "Tell me men, if you win the Queen, are you going to love her, or lust after her?"

"What is the difference, you fool," shouted Andras, growing angry with this topic.

"Precisely." Behemoth's voice lessened to a murmur. "I don't know the difference either. But I know there is one… We are doomed. I feel it coming. Don't you?"

CHAPTER 8

The mighty Behemoth is standing on the crown of a small hill about a half mile from our village. He says calmly, "It is time we train, for the Games draw nigh." The power of his voice is remarkable.

The other Nephilim are standing at different points throughout our village and begin to motion for us to follow.

There are about three hundred men still alive in our village. The women and children will not participate in the Games, though they will have to watch. We are now huddled tightly together like a school of sardines waiting to be caught in their nets. Behemoth scans the crowd and then addresses us:

"There are 303 men standing here now." I can hear his voice echo off the mountain range beyond. "There will be no more of you killed. You know why you are here. You know what is at stake for yourselves. Nevertheless, I am afraid we have not been totally truthful with you."

A clamor stirs through the crowd. Heads turn to one another. Trepidation is evinced on every face. What is curious is that the other Nephilim are likewise surprised by their leader's unanticipated words. Behemoth begin to speak once more. The disturbed crowd quieted.

"You have been told that three families will live after the Games. That is true, *if* our team wins. If our team loses, however, the wining Nephilim will kill you all." The crowd is deathly quiet and somber. I was not surprised at what I have heard. And judging from their response, neither was anyone else.

These creatures are brutal, monstrous, and have strengths and abilities beyond the mind of mortal man to comprehend. Their minds are so superior that our meager presence angers them. I wasn't expecting that any survivors would be allowed. But now I believe differently. The master, Behemoth, may very well keep his word.

"However," he continued, "I have decided to make a change from what you were told. If we win the Games, *all* of you will live. You have my word." The crowed again seeks each other's eyes searching for solace, but their tongues are silent. They do not know exactly how to respond. They have every right not to believe what Behemoth is saying.

He very well could be lying. All of these creatures have a penchant for the trait. Just like their speed, strength, and cunning, lying seems to befall their very being. But something is different in Behemoth. I get the feeling he is telling the truth, because his fellow Nephilim are regarding each other with dismay and smirks.

"Practice is over," he said craftily, and walked away.

CHAPTER 9

The Games have begun. We are gathered together and are marching to the wide, open meadow. I am guessing it is centrally located between the three captured villages. There will be more than 1000 men there. I know precisely how many Nephilim —exactly twenty-one.

I am afraid we are not prepared for the games. We have not practiced any. I understand what Behemoth was doing. It worked because we are anxious to do well and we all live. But the others have practiced.

"Master Behemoth, "I say as gingerly as possible. "Why have the others practiced, whereas we have not?"

"We don't need to practice, Compel. Our skills are already honed," He answered casually.

"Why did the others practice, then my lord?"

"They were not practicing Compel, but merely displaying their skills for the spy they undoubtedly knew would be observing," he continued in his sublime manner. He doesn't appear to be concerned anymore.

"One more question master?"

"Yes"

"Why haven't you told us what the events are in these Games, so that we can prepare ourselves?"

Behemoth peered at me ashamedly and chuckled, "You don't need to know, Compel. Understand me, it is better you don't know." I am worried again. One thing has bothered me. It has bothered me ever since the Nephilim took over our village. *Why haven't we known of the Nephilim before this? Only the rumors. Especially since three families survive.*

I don't think there are any survivors. They just tell us this to get some modicum of willing participation. None of us will live. It only makes sense.

I had a vision once, just after the Nephilim seized us. A misty, dreamlike image of our villagers being decapitated. A Nephilim is walking about with his sword and whacking the heads off of the remaining survivors. It was a grisly sight. But what was most horrifying of all was that it was the women and children being slaughtered. I couldn't quite tell which one of the Nephilim was wielding the sword. I always assumed it was Behemoth. But maybe not. In any case, I don't believe they can allow anyone to tell the tale of the Nephilim Games. Better left as lore and rumors.

As we are marching to the games, Behemoth suddenly turns his immense head toward me. The muscles in his neck expose deep crevices of sinew and veins. He makes eye contact with me, but there is no pain. There is something I have never witnessed in a Nephilim before. I believe he had sympathy.

"Go get your wife and children and bring them here, Compel, "he whispers. I am scared again. I have always assumed that I would die, but my wife and children would be spared. Now I am not so sure. *What does he want with my wife and my two sons? Why did he look at me with what I thought was sympathy?*

"What do you want with them, master?" I meekly ask.

"Go now, Compel. It will be good for you," he said, still looking me painlessly in the eye.

I spring forward and run toward my family, who trail behind the men. My thoughts are raging in my head. I can only think of one horrifying thought. He does feel sympathy, and therefore he is going to kill us quickly as a favor. No one wants to die, quickly or otherwise. I can't think straight

Then another thought flows into my mind. *He wants to set us free.* I must believe this to be the reason. I have no choice but to believe it. My wife is not so easily convinced. She is suspicious of Behemoth's motives. She is terrified of watching her own children slaughter before her eyes. So am I.

"What are our choices, Lindsay?" I say coldly. "If we try to escape, we will be killed. If we do nothing, we will be killed." Lindsay cries and holds her sons to her bosom and kisses them. She is convinced we will all die. I don't blame her. She is probably right. I say as calmly as I can, "I think he may let us go."

"Can he do that?" She says hopefully.

"I think he likes me," I say, forcing a smile at my frightened sons. Lindsay nods, acknowledging my plan to keep my sons encouraged.

"Let's go, my sons. The mighty Behemoth is going to free us.'

"Did you hear your father? We are going to be free. Bear up now and follow your father." Lindsay is trying to appear relieved before her sons. It is our only choice. Maybe it is just as well. We could be facing a much worse fate later.

"We are making the slow track back to Behemoth and the others when something suddenly occurs to me. I have not yet prayed for deliverance. Before we were overrun by the Nephilim, I used to pray daily. But since I have been caught up in this nightmare, I have figured there was no use. I have obviously lost favor with God. How else could you explain our predicament?

Then I began to pray silently: *What have we done wrong, Lord? Have I not always done what is right? Why have you forsaken me and my family and my village? Are you not stronger than the Nephilim?*

Then something else occurs to me. I am asking the wrong questions of God. *Lord, I just ask that whatever is Your will Lord for me and my family, let it be. I pray that you will remember that we bore it well and that you accept us in heaven as faithful servants.*

We return to Behemoth. The other Nephilim and the men are wondering why they have stopped. We are a couple of miles from the Games site. Behemoth motions for the others to gather around.

"Come forward, Compel. Bring your sons and your wife. I have need of you." There is an air of satisfaction in his voice, and yet, we apprehensively come forward. I think maybe he is going to single me out for my uncomplaining service to him and make an announcement that he is about to grant our freedom.

"I will now show you what lies ahead of you if you think about betraying us to our enemy." Behemoth bellows so everyone can hear.

Then he picks up a net that is attached to the end of a huge pole about 20 feet long. He grasps me by the waist with one hand. I struggle, but he could easily squeeze me in half if he wanted. He drops me in the net. He looks me morosely in the eye and whispers under his breath, "This is what I truly think of you, Compel." He starts to whirl in sharp circles and flings me with a terrific grunt.

The wind whistles over my ears as I head toward the clouds. In that brief moment of time, as I am about 100 feet above the earth and passing over some trees beneath me, I hold the thought of my children. *Is he going to send them on the same death ride in the sky? They will be terrified. So much for prayer.*

It is truly amazing how time slows down when one knows that death is imminent. The thoughts that flash across the windows of my mind are not what I had imagined. Other than the brief sorrow for my terrified children, I could see my mother and father and a happier time. The day my wife agreed to be my wife. The first steps of my sons. And then suddenly they are gone, and I am now a bird without wings.

CHAPTER 10

I put forth my arms and spread them. I am a soaring eagle. The air is sliced by my hands, and I can twist my wrists to change the pitch of the whistling wind. My hair waves straight back, and my cheeks flutter against my jaws. I will soon be with my wife and sons. I will ask God to explain, for I have been told that all the answers to all the questions I have ever had will be revealed.

Then, I see a small pond as I start to descend back to the earth. It is in my path. It is rapidly growing larger. I might land in it. I hit the pond with a terrific splash. The water is cold, which helps to alleviate the stinging pain.

My skin is bruised from the hard impact. But I am alive! My breaths are short and quick. What luck for me! I am so stunned to be alive that it takes a few seconds for my thoughts to return. Unfortunately, my thoughts return to my sons and my wife. I can't expect luck to be bestowed upon us all.

No sooner do these thoughts enter my mind than I see an object in the sky headed toward the pond. A screaming woman's voice confirms it is my wife. The screaming sound approaches as fast as her tumbling body. A monstrous splash, and a great mist of water dampens my head.

I swim toward her, and just like me, it takes a few seconds for her to reach the surface. I take hold of her hand, and as she catches her breath, the same expression of disbelief that she is still alive is etched with a smile.

"My sons," she says with short breaths. Her smile and mine are soon displaced with anguish. We both get the same idea at the same time and turn our eyes toward the sky. Yes! I see two objects, with no more than twenty feet of separation between the first and the last, fast approaching in the same manner.

"Move, Lindsay!" I shout. "We don't want them to hit us." We swim as fast as we can to get out of the path of our two sons. One great slash, and a second later, another splash just as great as the first. "Let's get to them. They may not be able to catch their breaths," I continue to shout excitedly.

We are all alive and well. We are bruised, and the sting on our skin is like a swarm of bees has attacked. But my family is alive! We swim to the bank, and I can't get enough hugs and kisses from my terrified yet grateful family —grateful to God.

"The Lord has spared us." I am still embracing my wife and sons. "Behemoth thought he had done us in, but he is no match for the power of the Lord God."

"What would make him suddenly want to try to kill us like that, Compel? I thought you said that he liked you?" asked Lindsay, puzzled.

"I don't know and I don't care why he unexpectedly turned on me, but let's not tarry. They may figure out we hit water. Hurry, sons, up on the bank, quickly with you and be lively. We must make haste." I elatedly cry to my family.

"Listen to your father, sons. We have little time to get as far away from here as possible, "says Lindsay breathlessly. We are all trembling with exhilaration. "It is a miracle that we all landed in this pond," she continues with chattering teeth. Then she says:

"The last thing that Behemoth mumbled to me was, 'You're lighter; I hope I don't overshoot where Compel has landed.' Did he mean for me to land on top of your squished body? Was he trying to stack us one on top of the other like a pile of wood? What a vile and cruel creature he is."

Something in her words suddenly struck me. "Wait a minute. The last thing he said to me was, 'This is what I think of you.' "What did he say to you, my sons?" I ask them inquisitively.

"He said, 'I hope you follow your father'," answered my oldest.

I am astonished by what I have just realized. "Behemoth did this on purpose." I clutch my wife by the shoulders and passionately peer into her eyes. "He knew the pond was here. He targeted it, and with great precision and skill, he hit his target. Don't you see? He saved our lives."

My heart is overjoyed. I hated Behemoth with a passion just a few seconds ago. But now the opposite feeling has overtaken my soul. I will now die for him if need be. And need may be, for I fear the worst is going to happen to my master.

"Do you really believe he did this to save our lives, Compel?" My wife asked skeptically. "Why would such a monster like that care what happens to us? All he cares about is killing. You are wrong about this, my husband."

"Do you really believe, Lindsay that he stopped the caravan at this one particular spot along the route and suddenly decided to hurl us accidentally at this pond? Think of the words he said to us. He saved us at his own risk. I tell you, there is good in him. I don't know from where it came, but there is good in him." I say passionately.

"Whether there is good in him or not, we must make the best of our miracle and leave this land and search for a new village to live. We can't go to the remains of our old home. There is no one there, and there is the danger they may return." Lindsay is growing apprehensive by the look in her eyes.

"You go back to the village. They won't return. Take my sons and be safe, Lindsay. I must help my master."

"Help him! How can you help him? You are just a speck, Compel," she cried.

"A speck can be most irritating when it gets in your eye." I answer wryly. "Besides, I must try to help or people if I can. If Behemoth wins, I believe he will set them all free.

"You know very well, Compel that our people are doomed. Why do you believe that this monster will spare our people when he has killed so many of us at the slightest whim? And you also know very well that they are all liars. Don't be a fool, Compel. Let's go to another village." Lindsay was pulling me by the hand and pleading.

"He saved our lives and our sons. I cannot express with words why —I just I know I must help him and our people," I said sternly, and then I thunder, "By God in heaven, I will not turn my back on our people. Take my sons and go to safety. Go to our village. There is food and shelter there." And then I added triumphantly. "I will return with all of our people."

My wife and sons left, and I made my way to the Games. I had no idea what to do, nor how to do it. All I knew was that I must at the very least try.

CHAPTER 11

I have found the caravan of my people and our Nephilim captors. They are at the site of the Games. I am observing from the crest of a fairly tall hill. A group of men from the three villages are gathered in a circle. It appears that 300 to 400 are in each group. The Nephilim are holding poles with flags of bright colors attached to the ends. They appear restless as they hold hostage the trembling men of the conquered villages.

Behemoth is standing in front of his group. Two more Nephilim are doing the same for their groups. There are 21 Nephilim competitors in total. There must be close to 1,000 oppressed and hapless men total.

The three Nephilim leaders come together in a circle in the middle of the grounds. There is little difference in the stature of the Nephilim leaders. Oddly, the giant Nephilim I saw a hurl man with one hand is not even the leader of his group. Nonetheless, the leaders are magnificent creatures. What I am witnessing from my hilltop vantage point is truly something to behold.

Only from a distance can one put these creatures in proper perspective —the way they move, the way they dwarf average men. Their bulging muscles defy words to describe. I have to shut my eyes and reopen them quickly. I almost expect to awake from my dream whenever I do this. The fairy tales from yore are playing out before my very eyes. I feel ashamed of what I'm thinking, but I feel wickedly privileged to be witnessing this.

I can't quite hear what the three leaders are saying. I hear the sound of their voices, but I can't make out any words. They mostly seem to be locking gazes. Even when they are not talking, they never look away.

The tension of the chilling stares is suddenly interrupted by the booming sound of trumpets. They are so thunderous that their sound carries for miles. Then a procession appears, breasting a small hill. A legion of Nephilim marches forward, two by two. In the middle of the line, four of the giants are carrying a sedan chair. Someone important must be inside, for I have only seen slaves carrying a king in this manner before.

In a few more strides, I see the Prize the Nephilim will soon fight to the death for. It is the coveted Queen. Her majesty has arrived. I can't quite see her fully from this angle, and then they turn, and she is in full view of me. After a good look, I am once again ashamed of my perverse thoughts. *For the first and only time in my life, I wish I were a Nephilim.*

As exaggerated as the Nephilim men are in their prowess, the queen is adorned with indescribable beauty. Within seconds, I cannot remove my startled eyes and my blood begins to heat to the thumping rhythm of my lovesick heart.

When the giants set the chair to down, and she descends the steps, gasps ripple through the crowd. Her face is as if it were made from porcelain. Golden blond hair reflects bits of sunlight as it waves in the light breeze. Striking dark blue eyes. Stunningly smooth tanned skin. Blood-red, plump lips curl cutely and purse delicately as she slowly moistens them with her luscious tongue.

She seems every bit the most beautiful queen in the world —high and regal, with an air of mystery. Her pale blond eyebrows arch gracefully over feline eyes. A small, almost snub nose adds a girlish cuteness.

Her voluptuous figure makes her absolutely ravishing. Her breasts swell and bounce, seemingly trying to escape her tightly fitted gown. Her waist narrows exquisitely before curving out into enthralling, rounded hips and sensual legs, displayed boldly by the gown's split.

I was so aroused that I have to get off my belly and onto my knees to avoid the pain. The risk of being seen be damned; I am in love. My blood is boiling. Then, I suddenly realized that I was married and under an enchanting spell. In a bewitched, deviant moment, the thought runs through my mind that she would be worth dying for, just to get within a few feet of her. The ravishing queen has forged an evil lust in my brain that I'm ashamed to admit will never leave.

I wasn't the only one. All of the Nephilim men appear equally entranced. It is much easier to detect on these creatures, for their proportions leave nothing hidden.

I fully understand why they have the games —why they would die to win the queen. And to be perfectly honest, I wish I were a Nephilim. I would gladly die for the chance to win her. But I am not a Nephilim. I am merely a man. It is hard to remember that at this moment.

I understand a lot more about these creatures now. I can't restrain my mind from picturing myself as a Nephilim Champion, winning the Queen. I used to have similar fantasies as a boy —of being a great warrior, defeating a treacherous enemy, and saving the village. But I was a boy then. Now, it would be a better for me to keep my eyes off the Queen. *Dear God, help me keep my eyes from straying to her.*

I don't know why the other Nephilim are here. I understand escorting the queen, but why are they so heavily armed? Each one is carrying a sword. The twinkle of sunlight reflects from their razor sharpness. There must be hundreds. Where did they come from? Why so many? Did they come just to watch the Games? I don't understand what's happening here. Whatever the reason, the Games are about to begin. I will be a witness.

CHAPTER 12

I sense something of a commotion in one of the groups. A Nephilim is carrying a man like a loaf of bread to the middle of the field where the three leaders are gathered. He is bound with rope, and a cloth is tied around his mouth to silence him. By the way he is struggling; he does not look like a volunteer. What are they about to do with him? I fear the worst for the poor fellow.

The one carrying the hysterical little man stops when he reaches the circle and tosses the bound man in the air above it. In a flash, the three leaders unsheathe their swords, and all three slice at the doomed man at the same time. He is cut into three pieces.

I am aghast, along with the captives. The head flips through the air and rolls to a stop. Then the abdomen lands in a squish, guts oozing from the lower portion. Then the legs touch the earth a few feet away—a sickening sight.

The head is closest to Behemoth. The deliverer shouts, "Heads win," Then the deliverer of the sacrifice touches Behemoth on the shoulder. The leader closest to the stomach and guts is touched on the shoulder. The remaining leader nods his head, acknowledging he is last. What a vile way to determine in what order the Nephilim get to kill my people.

The first event is set up: The *Race*. This is an event to determine who is the fastest. Sounds simple. It isn't. A course is laid out about a mile long, with a pole adorned at the top with a flag flapping in the breeze.

The contestants race to the flag, which they must go around, and race back. There is a catch. The racers will be carrying a man, who is morbidly referred to as a volunteer. And they must pass the man to another member of the team, who races back to the starting line. It is called a relay race.

The two fastest sprinters from each group take their places. Behemoth is not one of the sprinters, but he is the scale to demine which one of the men in our village is the lightest. He places his hand on the ground with his palm up and his forefinger pointed outward. Each man stands on his finger, and he lifts him up and down. Then the next man, and so forth. Behemoth chooses the lightest and tosses him to Urobach , who lightly tosses him up and down to judge the weight.

Urobach is the darkest —skinned of the Nephilim. "Since you're dark Urobach, and we all know that dark Nephilim are the fastest, you'll be the anchor leg," says Behemoth. Urobach sprints to the flag.

"Andras, you will lead," barks Behemoth. "Since you are the most despised by everyone and are used to running away from us, you can take the start." Andras does not seem upset by the snide remarks. They all talk to each other in a satirical manner this way. If it weren't so gruesome, it would be funny.

I can't make out which one of our unlucky people Behemoth has decided to be the lightest man so he can act as the baton, as they call him. Whoever he is, he's tucked underneath Andres' arm like so much bread. His head is cradled in Andras' palm, and his feet are dangle from underneath his elbow. I have seen them carry people around the village this way before while the other Nephilim attempt to tackle the carrier. It must be comfortable for them to carry men this way.

Three Nephilim sprinters are at the starting line. The judge, the one who brought the unfortunate soul that was dissected to determine order, will be the starter. He is holding another man around the waist with his right hand. The man is squirming and trying to get loose. After I saw what happened to the first victim, I don't blame him.

The sprinters all have a baton —a skinny man —tucked under their massive arms. They spread their feet apart; put the hand not holding their man on the ground, and peer at the starter, waiting for whatever he is going to do with the whimpering man. Muscles pile in swelling ridges on the sprinters' thighs. Rippling, pulsating, sinewy muscle and veins seem to be all the creatures consist of when they flexed in this manner.

The starter flings the hysterical man in the air. He is tumbling some thirty feet up and falls flailing toward the earth. He splashes on the ground and the sprinters are off. Chunks of earth underneath their feet spit backward some one hundred feet in a flume of dirt and grass.

The legs of the sprinters are moving so rapidly they are merely a blur. The earth is peeled away with each stride. Faster and faster the arms are swinging in unison with the legs. Further and further the ground is spat behind them. My eyes have never witnessed anything like this.

The sight of these magnificent creatures in a dead sprint is enough to take a man's breath away. The must be traveling at near 100 miles per hour, for in just a matter of a few seconds, they have reached the flag pole, neck and neck.

They begin to sweep out to make the turn. As they turned their bodies sideways, the trench of earth they are digging gets deeper, and the dirt they are unearthing is much greater. The earth is being flung a good two hundred feet behind and to one side. They are snorting the way a horse snorts when in a dead gallop. The sight is truly indescribable.

The two relay sprinters begin to run toward the finish line with one hand held behind, palm up, fist open, anticipating their tiring partner to place the screaming man they are carrying gently in their awaiting palm. If they drop him, they lose.

Andras is a foot or so behind at this point. The other two are even with each other. The exchange is a tricky proposition. The hands of a Nephilim can reach around a man's waist, but Andras still has to be careful where he places our man. A fumble would be easy at this point, especially at 100 miles per hour. It could be deadly for the man, who I can now tell is Elon. I agree he is a good choice since he weighs less than 100 pounds. Why? A worm in his stomach, we have always figured, for he can eat more than any man in the village.

A worm is the least of his worries right now, for he is about to be passed from a Nephilim traveling at 100 miles per hour to another. Either one of them can squeeze a full-grown oxen in one hand and pull the spine out with the other while the ox watches.

Once, I saw Urobach become upset at the others because he wasn't consulted about a decision made by the group. He was sitting by a tree about a foot thick and 40 feet tall. When he heard what they had done without him, as he was angrily raising to his feet, he latched his mighty hand around the tree, pulled it up by the roots, picked up a camel, tossed it in the air, and batted it at the others with the tree as the club. They had to scatter out of the way as the larger half of the animal landed close by.

Now Urobach has to gently cradle the bony Elon in the same hands. Andras extends Elon forward and places him in Urobach's hand with a smooth transition. One of the other two racers is having trouble. He placed his man inside his partner's hand alright, but held on too long before letting go. The partner pulled his man into his chest, only to discover that he had only the top portion of his baton, guts were streaming in the breeze. A common mistake associated with this game of coordination; I was told. He is eliminated and stops running, chucking the remains of his baton in disgust.

This leaves only Urobach and the other sprinter. Behemoth is right, the darker Nephilim seem swifter than the lighter —colored. For Urobach is pulling away at the end. He finishes ahead of the other by 20 feet. I am so delighted for my group and poor Elon.

It takes several hundred feet for the giants to slow down from their top speed. I can see Elon clapping his hands as he peers out of Urobach's chest. Urobach is excited too. He is, in fact, overly excited and jubilant —a common characteristic of the darker Nephilim.

He raises Elon in his hand over his head and prances and struts with Elon flopping about. Then he alternates his knees up and down but stays in place, not moving, and then he slams Elon into the ground. Guts splatter for twenty feet. I was told that he calls this *spiking a man.* Bad for Elon, I suppose he won't have to worry about the worm anymore, and my people have one victory in the Games.

CHAPTER 13

I wait to see what will be the next gruesome game that will kill my people. My team of Nephilim has one victory. Since this is my first Games to witness, I have no idea what to expect. The leaders are talking to the judge Nephilim. I hear them say *Toss for Distance*. I know what this is.

Two Nephilim from the brigade bring forth the same pole and nets that Behemoth sent me and my family on a wingless flight into the pond and our freedom. Except I don't see any body of water for the landing of the volunteers. I don't expect they would use it if there was. I can only hope they will use a rock or an oxen, but I know better. This will be bad.

I learn as I listen that distance is not the only skill to be judged, but accuracy is also. I know for a fact that Behemoth is good at this event. He is the one to represent his group. He makes his way to the field. Since he won the *heads* in the human slice, he gets to go last so he will know the marks to beat.

There are three events within the *Toss for Distance* event. First, there is *Height*. This is simple. The one who can pitch a man the highest in the air is the winner. Judging the height is tough. In this event, there is also a *Catch* —literally. The one who does the toss is called the Jouster. He can take no stride or windup. He starts the net on the ground, then explodes upward and sends the man as high as possible. Then he must catch the man in the same net.

Sounds simple enough. The Judge then explains that the man must be able to walk away. Upon hearing this, volunteers begin to raise their hands. The fact that the *catch* is alive has spurred their courage.

Choose an event where you can live now, while the choosing is good, is their thinking. The next event might bring certain death. There are no volunteers for those. You get volunteered.

One of the Nephilim escorts sweeps a giant hand, and whoever can't get out of the way is the volunteer.

A Nephilim escort explodes in a dead sprint to the mountain, which is about three miles away. He climbs to the top for perspective on the height. He has a red flag that he will hold for the winner.

The volunteers scurry to get in line. They figure this looks like it might even be fun. When death is around you in every direction, the mind has ways of coping. A man can almost become a child again and think childish thoughts the same way I did when I was a wingless bird.

The first Nephilim flings his man. It is a good toss. I am guessing 400 feet or so. The man tumbles back to earth. The contestant makes no effort to catch him, and he splatters on the hard ground. The volunteers are wiping blood and intestines from their eyes and face and looking at the Judge in horror and disbelief.

He explains that the contestants get two tosses. If they don't feel the first would be their best, then they don't have to make the catch. Only the one that is caught is counted as an attempt. The volunteers try to scurry back but are restrained. He flings another man and catches him expertly.

It is time for the next Nephilim to take his turn, but he has trouble with the squirming volunteer, so he thumps him on the head with a snap of his finger. The volunteer is much calmer now. He is also not breathing, so he is dumped out, and another volunteer is placed in the net. This new volunteer has seen what attempting to escape the net can bring, so he remains still.

Contestant number two takes two quick breaths and explodes the net upward. The tumbling volunteer is silent —I no screams. He's almost out of sight, and then begins to fall back to earth. It is terrifying to watch, wondering if the contestant is going to catch or let drop his tossed partner. He catches him but seems unsatisfied.

Now it is mighty Behemoth's turn. He looks over the small herd and, remembering each one's weight with his finger scale, he systematically culls out the heaviest and calmly chooses the lightest of the remaining volunteers. The volunteer happily hops in the net, thinking that Behemoth will win this event easily. Behemoth sets his feet, takes a couple of deep breaths, closes his eyes, and tenses his hands on the 6-inch solid iron pole. Veins and muscles extend in grotesque ripples and a grunt that can be heard for ten miles precedes his explosion of prodigious power.

The volunteer is shot upwards but not nearly as high as the other two had before. The pole has bent in Behemoth's hands almost into a U shape. He is examining his pole as the volunteer is screaming toward the fast approaching ground. I turn my eyes, as I do not want to see a splattered villager again. Just before the man hits the ground, Behemoth extends his hand and catches him softly around the waist and sets him on the ground. The volunteer is limp as he has fainted.

Behemoth fetches another pole and places the unconscious man in the net. This time he moves one of his hands further up the pole and repeats the same technique. The volunteer is sent so high he appears as a speck, about the same size as the highest eagle soaring on the thermals. He tumbles back down, and Behemoth catches him easily. He rolls the man out of the net, still limp; unaware that he has just won the contest and his life.

The escort Nephilim returns from the mountain and announces that Behemoth was by far the winner.

"Who was second?" the judge asks.

"Why Nesbeth was second, judge." The escort answered, confused by the question.

The judge then says with a sigh, "I declare Nesbeth the winner." A commotion is spreads through the crowd of my fellow villagers. Behemoth glares at the judges with anger.

The judge continues: "You know very well that the man you use must be fully aware that he is being honored. This man is dead or at least unconscious. Therefore, Nesbeth is the winner of the *Toss for Height.*

Behemoth grasps the 6-inch pole with both hands, begins to bend and twist the metal, easily bending and twisting this way and that. Then he hands a perfectly shaped hangman's noose made of iron to Nesbeth and storms off to the next event.

CHAPTER 14

I am waiting for the second part of this event. It is the toss for accuracy. My village has one victory. We are tied with another village that also has one victory. Behemoth angrily lost the first part on a foul. This event appears to be more about concentration than strength. They all have similar abilities, though. The slightest slip is all that separates winning from losing.

It is a strange thing to watch the Nephilim when they are around each other. They seem to be studying one another in deep concentration, searching for the slightest weakness. They kneel on one knee, propping an elbow upon it, creating a bulging bicep that draws my eye in awing envy. They observe closely every nuance of their opponent's movement. I get the feeling they are not necessarily pondering just their abilities.

I have noticed this from the very first time I saw a Nephilim. What are they seeing when they look at each other? A Nephilim never takes his eyes away from another Nephilim for more than a few seconds. I have always gotten the feeling that they are in awe of their very being, that they themselves can't believe what they are seeing. When things were calm in the village, in the cool of the evenings, as they relaxed on one knee and pondered their thoughts, this was when it was the most noticeable.

I thought then, and I think now, that these creatures sense something is wrong. But I don't think they know what it is. Behemoth is the only one who has every expressed it. Not outright, but hidden in his words. I think he is more sensitive, perhaps even smarter than the others. It seems to anger him that he doesn't know the answers.

But it seems to anger him even more that the others don't sense their impending doom the way he does.

I believe this is why they study each other. They are trying to detect something. And if only they concentrate their eyes on one another long enough, it will suddenly be revealed. But it never is. They watch nonetheless, if only in vain. They all seem to be living in quiet desperation. I suppose that all men live this way, but the Nephilim even more so. Behemoth most of all. They all look desperate right now.

I see now how the second event will be done. Some of the escorts string together a net between two trees that are about ten feet apart. The contestants are to hit this target. It is a small window, especially from the distance they are standing. It must be a quarter mile or so. There are no volunteers for this one either. Only frightened men trying to avoid the random hands of the Nephilim guards. When you are caught, you are caught. No use to struggling. You have just become a volunteer.

I know now how chickens feel in their pen when it is time to catch one for supper. The men of my village scatter in the same manner as the chickens, desperately trying to live for another minute, just like the chickens. And just like the chickens, once you are in the clutches of your master, there is no point in struggling. Death is near; nothing you can do about it. I think I will free the chickens from their pen when I get home. They suddenly don't seem as tasty.

I have now noticed that the tossing nets are different. The pole is much shorter. The first Nephilim is handed three men from his village. Contestants can only use men from their own conquered village. This is a strict rule. If they use up all their men, they can't *borrow* others.

He places the men under his arm and clamps them under his arm pit. Six legs are dangling, occasionally kicking — for air, I suppose. He takes one man around the waist, clamping his elbow firmly on the other two, lest he drop one. He places the flailing man in the net, pulls the net back with a pinched grip of his thumb and forefinger — just like the hunting device called a slingshot I saw once — takes aim, and lets him fly.

The man is shot forward with such velocity that a mist of urine lingers in the air. He tumbles end over end, missing the net but partially catching the tree trunk on the right with his arm. When he stops rolling 200 feet pass the net, I can see that his arm is missing. He is dead. That's one attempt. He has two more men, two more tries at the tiny net.

They go in rotation. The next Nephilim's turn. He uses the same technique as the first, but he doesn't hit anything either. His man is dead too. If the target is not hit, there is no chance his "stone" —that is, the man —will survive.

They must be traveling over 200 miles per hour when they leave the net and handle. They usually come apart when they hit whatever is not the net. I don't know exactly what happens when they hit the net. No one has hit it yet.

Master Behemoth's turn. He stretches the net back, back. I can hear a twang as the net cords sing out with a higher pitch as it is being stretched tighter and tighter. He releases. He misses. One of the men in my village is dead. It is just as well that I can't make out their faces from here. I don't want to know which one of my friends has just died. I feel guilty that I'm free, and they are not.

Then the next round continues in the same manner: each Nephilim taking a turn, each missing, each killing another innocent, helpless villager, each landing with a splat.

I can see what the problem is. After a couple of tumbles, the man being propelled straightens with his chest to the wind. When this happens, he begins to move, dart, and jitter against the wind as he slices through the air. It is impossible to go straight. Their aim is not off; it is the confounding air that is forcing the helpless men off the center of the net. The contestants are trying to adjust, but it is pointless. They tell the men, just before they release them, to keep tumbling. But it seems impossible to maintain this against the power of the wind.

The first two Nephilim produce the same results on their final attempts: two more misses. two more dead men. Two frustrated Nephilim cruse at the volunteers, angry that they cannot maintain a tumble. I want to shout at them, *"Do you actually think these men are dying on purpose, just to anger you?"* But my tongue is brave when my mouth is shut, and becomes cowardly when it starts to open. It is much easier to be heroic against the Nephilim from a distance —and silently.

Behemoth has been studying and calculating. He talks to his last man-arrow. I can't make out the words, but they seem like instructions. The man seems to understand and claps his hands optimistically. At least he will die thinking that he has a chance.

I can see the strategy. The man is going to point his body stiffly, like an arrow, with his hands clasped together above his head. Behemoth pulls the man's feet and net at the same time and lets him fly with a swish. It works beautifully. The man slices through the air as straight as an arrow, literally, heading horizontally for the safety of the net.

Just before he hits, I begin to fear for his head and neck. What would such an impact do at that speed? I was concerned for nothing because he passes right through the tough netting without so much as causing a ripple. He hardly slows at all when he strikes a tree in the distance. One moment, he is a hopeful villager sensing safety; the next, he is a splattered mess.

Behemoth seems pleased with the victory as the judge holds up his hand. Then, as he is returns to his group, he glances at the bloody spot where his arrow splattered against the tree and bows his head in what I perceive as reverence.

CHAPTER 15

Now it is time for the Toss for Distance, the main event of the three exercises for which they are collectively named. This event is easy to judge: whoever can toss his man the furthest wins. There are no rules for the windup —any technique is permitted. Just take a volunteer and fling him in the air. This is pure strength, an attribute that my master has in abundance. There is one problem: so do the others.

I can't tell which direction they will pitch the man. Behemoth threw me and my family a good half mile with only a flick. These men might go a mile or so. I do not want to watch what is about to happen to these men when they land. The breath was knocked out of me landing in water at half the distance. Fortunately, they will soar so far away that I can't see the gruesomeness —at least, I hope.

For Behemoth, going last is a blessing. He will know the mark to pass. His opponents look capable. They are almost as big and powerful as he is. Almost, but not quite. Behemoth is truly a spectacular creature to behold —startling, even among creatures that are all startling. I feel Master Behemoth will win easily. My village has the lead in the Games, with another victory almost a certainty.

The first Nephilim is ready to launch his hysterical volunteer. It suddenly occurs to me that I know precisely how this volunteer feels — I was once in his very shoes. I did not have time to think or struggle. It's just as well I didn't. I was blessed in that way. It's ghastly when you think upon it. These men have time to think and struggle with their pending deaths.

Once again, I want to shout down from the safety of my perch —but this time at my own people. At the man who is struggling, squirming, and trying to free himself. *"What are you fighting for?"* I want to scream at him. *Do you think you can free yourself from these giants? Why don't you shut up and enjoy the few moments of life you have left? You are about to become wingless bird, you fool. Enjoy soaring in the clouds —it is the last thing you will ever remember. You are lucky in a way. In just a few minutes you can ask God why he has released the Nephilim upon his people. You will become wiser than me.*

Nephilim number one begins whirling round and round like a child's top. On the last revolution, he gives a mighty push upwards with the pole handle, but the man comes out of the net sideways, like the rotor blade of a helicopter spins in the air. The man's body is not as tough as the blade, and piece by piece is comes apart. First the head, and then one leg, and then the other. His torso plummets down a few hundred feet later.

There was no noise in the entire camp. Horrified looks pervade the faces of the men of each village. Some of the Nephilim smile, while other shake their heads and then smile. It is hard to impress a Nephilim, but this came close. I have now changed my mind about shouting out at the squirming man.

Behemoth's expression of friendship to me has become more precious. A man cannot dream such sights as I'm seeing —not in his worst nightmares. I was expecting the Games to be bad for the captured villagers but I could never have imagined anything as bad as this. I will never sleep well again.

The next challenger's turn. He uses a different technique. He whirls his pole and net end over end, like an ax, except in complete revolutions —over and over, faster and faster. The net begins to sag back, and back. The pressure from the speed of the revolutions sinks the man deeper and deeper into the straining net.

I remember this pressure against my back from my flight from Behemoth. The net straps begin to bury into your back. And when you are propelled out of the net, the pressure against your face is unbearable. And that was just a mere toss of half the distances that these men will travel, if they are lucky.

The Nephilim explodes his volunteer out of the net in a blur. Most of what a Nephilim does is in a blur. The man is off in his wingless flight. And yes, he looks like a bird. It is natural to hold your arms out like a bird — it was to me. There is no thought of it. It just happens. It is as if feathers might suddenly appear on your naked arms. I wonder what birds think when they walk on the ground.

The wingless bird is flying a long, long way. He appears as a mere speck in the far distance, about the size of a fly. It must be a mile or maybe more. Measuring is simple. Wherever the man lands, a Nephilim stands. This is the mark to beat.

I am glad I can't see the landing of the wingless man. Just a poof of dust. I hope that's dust.

Behemoth is ignoring the cries coming from his volunteers. I can hear them plainly. I recognize the voice of this future bird. It is my wife's brother. His name is Con. Con is a good man, with three sons. He is also a big man, larger than the average. It makes sense that a heavier man would travel further against the resistance of the air. Behemoth knows the exact weight of all three hundred men in our village. His finger scale is precise; his calculating brain never forgets.

I can hear Behemoth saying something to Con, who is sobbing for mercy. "There is a stream beyond the distance to make. Stop your whimpering, and I will try to make the water." I believe this is what he said. I am afraid to stand tall as to gain sight of the stream Behemoth just spoke of.

I don't know if there is a stream, or if Behemoth is tricking Con into being quiet. Whatever the case, it worked. Con is quiet for the moment. More than ever, I am cheering for the mighty Behemoth. I believe he is capable of such a feat. Upon the first sight of Behemoth, it is not hard to imagine that he is capable of accomplishing anything. He is pure might held in a human-like body.

Behemoth uses a different technique from the other two, and it is even different from when he sent me and my family to freedom. He is now going for maximum distance. If he is to make the water he spoke of—if there is water at all—he will have to send Con a good mile and a quarter. *I believe it can be done. Behemoth can do anything he wants to.*

He backs up several feet from the launch site. He takes long strides toward the circle, sort of skipping and hopping. As he approaches the mark, he draws back, and the pole bends in his massive and powerful hands. The pole is almost directly behind his back. It is like putting tremendous tension on a *spring coil* that I saw once. A man about to strike a tree at a point waist-high with an ax would be in a similar position.

He starts his swing forward with a deafening war shout. The pole bends into a lazy U shape in his hands. Then, the net swishes forward so fast that it was hard for me to realize what happened. *Surely I didn't see what I thought I just saw.* The blur of the net zipped by, but Con did not. Instead, he simply dropped to the ground. *The strain on the net was too great, and it gave way, bursting at the bottom.* Or so I thought.

It wasn't until I noticed that Con was not moving as he was lay on the ground that I realized what had happened. And when thirty or so pieces of him separated and fell in different directions, my horror was confirmed. Even if I had the words to describe what I just witnessed, how would I tell my wife what happened to her brother? Some things are better left unsaid.

CHAPTER 16

The mighty Behemoth, my master, lost the last event and walked away dismayed. The other Nephilim looked around at each other and shook their massive and yet surprised heads. This is the closest I had ever come to witnessing a group of Nephilim truly impressed with something.

Then something happened that surprised and distressed me. The Nephilim competitors from all the groups pulled out their swords, took the blades in their hands, and began to pat the ground with the handles in unison. At first, I didn't have any idea what this meant. When Behemoth turned and glared at his admirers, I soon realized that the sword patting after this feat of sheer gruesomeness was an acknowledgement of the greatness of his feat.

I also realized that these creatures are truly mad. With all the powers and abilities, they possess, it was the discovery of a never-before-seen way to destroy a human being that excited their admiration. I have also realized something else: Behemoth has just come to the same conclusion.

He stood and turned about slowly, gazing the field. He seemed sickened at the sound of the pounding swords. He had a snarl on his lips, and then he looked solemnly at the diced body of what used to be a man. If only I could have known what he was thinking at this time.

I wasn't the only one wondering the same thing. The others in his group of Nephilim were regarding meeting each other's gazes. They seemed to be wondering the same thing. A slight smirk of a smile cut across their faces. They knew. I feared for Behemoth. I now understood that his toughest fight will come after the Games. They now know his weakness.

The next event doesn't involve a volunteer. It is the spear throw —a simple contest of strength and aim. These creatures are at their most deadly with a spear in their hands. They can kill you from any distance. Any distance. They seem to know exactly how far to lead a moving target.

Once, I watched Nape spill a barrel of berries on top of Ashtoreth's lap. He didn't do it on purpose, but he wasn't going to stick around to see if master Ashtoreth was going to forgive him either. He panicked and ran for it. He would have been much saver if he had hit his knees and begged for mercy. He would have at least had a chance. After Ashtoreth wiped the berries off his cloak, he casually retrieved his spear that was leaning against a tree. He seemed to deliberately let Nape get a quarter of a mile or so away.

Instead of peering back over his shoulder, Nape should have made haste. The last time I saw Nape peek over his shoulder, he had a relieved grin, as if he were about to get away. We never saw Ashtoreth's hand move. Never saw the spear in flight. Just a blur in the air. Nape's head no more than made it halfway around when he abruptly stopped in mid-stride. Still standing, the spear pinned him to the ground. He never knew what hit him. Thankfully. I knew he was a dead man running the moment he decided to flee.

Every member of the group of seven has to compete in at least one event. Ashtoreth is the contestant representing our group in this event. He is very, very good. But then, they all are. There are living Nephilim, and there have been weak Nephilim, but there are no living weak Nephilim. Weak Nephilim never make it to maturity. I see why.

Another simple contest: hit the target with the spear. I am so relieved that people are not the targets. I am also sure that the people feel the same way.

The target is a tree. It is about three feet thick. Solid oak. Very hard. I was wrong. I can now see that the target is a small green lizard, about the size of a regular man's hand. It is dart-like quick. Jittery. Impossible for even a quick-handed man to catch. But these are not men. They are Nephilim. Nothing is impossible to them.

They are standing about 300 feet away from the target. They are holding *small* spears, about 12 feet long and weighing approximately 75 pounds. The next event, I understand, will involve the *larger* spears. But not this one. This is a contest of quickness and accuracy.

I was wrong again. Now I fully understand. I had hoped that my people would not be involved in this one event. But alas, this is not the case. A volunteer must hold the lizard by the tail with his hand while his master attempts to hit the squirming, fidgety lizard with the head of his spear from a distance of 300 feet. Here is the catch, as usual: the closer the volunteer holds the lizard at the base of its tail, the less it can squirm. A test of nerve for the volunteer.

The first Nephilim takes his position, and so does his volunteer. The small spear looks so tiny in the giant's hand, more like stick than a weapon. The quivering hand of the volunteer grasps the lizard's dashing tail and places it inside the circle on the side of the oak. The lizard's sharp claws latch onto the bark and immediately squirm this way and that, desperately attempting to make its escape. A difficult target indeed.

Sensing that this is too much movement, the volunteer moves his grip close to the base of the tail which stops the movement considerably. This pleases the volunteer, who displays a wide grin and turns his head to signal he is ready just as the spear plows through his hand, the lizard, and buries halfway through the tree.

I don't believe he ever felt it, because he didn't start to scream until he looked back at the tree and saw his hand missing. He clasped his wrist with his remaining hand, held the stump close to his face, and watched as where his hand used to be turned into a spouting fountain of blood. It counted as a hit, though. "Next," said the judge.

The next volunteer's hand was trembling nervously as he held the lizard by the tip of his darting tail. It wasn't until now that I fully understood the point of this contest and the point of the Games, and why the volunteers of a conquered village were used in such a manner.

I thought I heard the judge say something at the beginning of the Games, when the three leaders were at the circle, about *demonstrating that it is our destiny to rule the humans forever,* or something like that.

The whole point of the Games is to quench the fever these creatures have for competing and to show the humans how insignificant they truly are in the lives of the Nephilim. That the human God is no match for their God, Lucifer. This is why a few families are allowed to live: to spread the terrifying news of the Nephilim.

The spear was releases and caught the lizard's foot as it plunged deep into the oak. The volunteer, who had closed his eyes, opened them and was ecstatic that his hand was still intact. He remained that way for about three seconds, until the other spear followed the first and took his head off at the shoulders, leaving another human fountain of jetting blood. Message received: grasp the lizard by the base of the tail and lose your hand, or grasp it by the tip and lose your head. Understood!

The judge took his thumb, grasped the end of the spear protruding through the tree, bent it back and forth, and snapped off the head. Then he used two fingers to pull the other end from the tree. They were ready for Ashtoreth and his volunteer.

Now I was worried. I could see the outline of the skinny, young volunteer and recognized him as my cousin, Rex. I feared for him also. In a minute he would be handless, or headless. I hoped he would choose to go through life handless —and go through life. I would lend him my hand and help with his crop, and gather his food, and fight his enemies. I couldn't very well lend him my head.

He gritted his teeth, clamped his eyes tight, and began to yell. At first, I thought this was usual behavior. But would I have been any different? Ashtoreth wore a smile on his face as he let the spear fly so quickly it was hard to tell he moved at all. Amazingly, the bottom edge of the spear pierced the lizard's tongue when it flickered for a taste of the air and pulled it out of his mouth by the root.

The judge called a conference with another Nephilim. This must have been a first of its kind. Based on the fact that the volunteer wasn't handless, and the lizard was still alive, the second Nephilim was declared the winner.

Rex was overjoyed that he was alive. He hopped and clapped his hands. A smile spread across his entire face. He did have a beautiful smile with pearly white teeth. I was so happy for him. I saw him broaden his mouth and noticed the brightness of his even, perfect ivory teeth just as the spear passed through his mouth and exited the back of his head. He hit the ground with a perfect hole where his perfect teeth used to be. Nephilim are terrible losers.

CHAPTER 17

Ashtoreth had lost the first part of the spear completion on a technicality. He lost by a tongue. Rex lost his life because he was too happy to be alive. Life and death are a thin line indeed to tread around the Nephilim. Ashtoreth still has a chance to redeem himself, though.

The judge calls the next part, *"The Drive."* This is a contest of strength and spear velocity. The object here is to see who can drive the spear the furthest into the tree. The *big* spear is used for this test—20 feet long, 300 pounds and razor sharp at the head. Another oak tree is selected, since the one used for accuracy is only three feet thick. I have seen an angry Nephilim drive a spear through the entire breadth of a tree trunk ten feet thick before.

I don't see how the humans are going to be a component of this contest. A large oak, about eight feet thick or so, has been chosen, and the three Nephilim have measured the required distance. So far, no volunteers are being gathered. So far, no death is required. It would actually be a real pleasure to watch these creatures compete against one another, save for the pending gruesome deaths which naturally accompany anything involving the Nephilim. They are made to kill.

The first contestant begins to run at the target with his spear held in his right hand, poised on his shoulder. When he nears the line drawn in the dirt, he launches the heavy spear with all his might. Again, just a blur. The spear takes less than a second to travel the 300 feet distance.

There is a noise that I can hear coming from the spear, but the sound does not keep pace with its movement. It is too slow and trails by a good second. Another sound follows —a *crack* sound —when the spear strikes the bark of the oak. It too is too slow for the speed of the spear. The bark flies, the spear buries itself, and then I hear the sounds. It is like some sort of sorcery. Surely nothing can travel faster than the sound it makes.

The first Nephilim's spear is about half in, half out of the tree. I don't see them measure in any way. How will they tell who won if they don't measure the distance? I don't understand.

The next Nephilim does the same thing with the same results, and the spear goes about the same depth. Again, no measurements. Can the judge measure something so precisely with just his eyes?

Then Ashtoreth completes his attempt. And just as before, it appears very close to the other marks. Who won? I don't understand. Something is wrong. Why are the Nephilim guards stirring about? I am starting to worry again.

I was too hopeful that men weren't going to die in this event. There are Nephilim. These are the Games. Men will die, and not pleasantly.

The Nephilim have gathered the volunteers that were the easiest to catch. They are forming a human stack of four men, one behind the other, and strap them to the tree. I see now why they tested the depth of the spears that had protruded through the oak, and the horror of this game is revealed.

Men are screaming for mercy in shrieking cries. I can hardly stand to listen. I put my hands over my ears, but I can still hear them. The first Nephilim makes his run at the tree, and then a blurry hand flashes. The cries stop. All four men are pierced. All four are dead. The judge holds up five fingers, which means to bring five volunteers for the next attempt. This time the screams are louder, because an extra man is added to the death.

And so, the contest proceeds. One attempt, four dead men. Second attempt, five dead men. Third attempt, five dead men and one badly wounded, but still alive. Get it. The winner will be determined by the total number of men killed and the most severely wounded among the survivors. *How do they determine the most severely wounded?* By which one dies first. This is timed.

With the next attempt, each contestant penetrates five men goes deep into the sixth. Unfortunately, the spears do not go deep enough to kill instantly. The sixth man is dropped on the ground, and the Nephilim judge counts in his head until the man stops breathing.

The second Nephilim's volunteer dies in just a few seconds, and he is declared the winner. The first Nephilim's man dies a couple of minutes later; he took second. Ashtoreth's man is still alive and moaning in pain, trying to hold his own intestines inside his stomach.

I don't know who he is, and don't want to. I am sorry to see he is still alive, and apparently so is Ashtoreth. Because Ashtoreth walks up to the man, looks angrily at him, and then buries his spear through his chest and a couple of feet deep into the ground.

He lifts the dead man up with his right hand while still skewered on the end of his spear. He peers at the man's lifeless face closely and then flings him from his spear with a flip of his wrist. I have done something similar before with a foul piece of meat at the end of my fork.

CHAPTER 18

Sword Play—That's what I thought I heard the judge say. A Nephilim always carries his sword nestled inside a sheath and attached to his muscle- bound hip. I have never seen one without it. Just like sandals, it is part of their wardrobe. They never leave home without it. Why would creatures as powerful as they need to have a sword at all times? Simple: to keep from being killed by an armed Nephilim. There is no love lost between Nephilim, nor is there any relaxation. A careless Nephilim is a dead Nephilim.

To watch a Nephilim handle a sword is breathtaking. If you can indeed see it, it's more of a twinkling steel blur. They have a variety of swords for different occasions. They vary in length and weight depending on what they're killing. The lightest is about 150 ponds, which seems like a stick of wheat shaft in their hands. The heaviest is about 300 pounds and is used more serious matters —like killing another Nephilim. I have never seen a Nephilim fight another Nephilim. I am told it is something to behold. "You people would not believe it" was the exact words.

All of a Nephilim's swords have one thing in common: they are razor-sharp. The pastime of a Nephilim is spent sharpening his blade. They do it mindlessly, without thinking. Their hands move on their own, sharpening the blade, sharpening the blade. If they have an idle hand, it will be sharpening the blade. It is as natural an act as breathing.

They are using a smaller sword for the first event. I can only imagine what is about to happen to the men of my village.

I have been wondering about the pen of oxen off the left of the field. I assumed they are there for food. But perhaps not. The preferred food of a Nephilim is goat and sheep. The do eat beef, but they prefer goat. This is another curiosity of the Nephilim: they eat only meat. They can, if they have to, eat fruit and some vegetables. But if it is available, they eat meat. I have guessed they each eat 150 to 200 pounds of meat a day.

Someone once asked why they prefer goat or sheep to ox. I was told it has something to do with the beast they live on when they are in the land across the ice. They eat so much of this beast, similar to an ox, that they become saturated with the taste if it. I don't know what they mean by, "across the ice." They are not the kind to lend much to details. If you are not satisfied with my answer, then you can ask a Nephilim the next time you see one. If you have the nerve.

The judge goes to the pen, kneels down, places the palm of his hand under the brisket of an ox, then stand and raises his arm over his head. The ox's legs are dangling and sometimes mocked galloping. Then he does the same thing with his other hand, and walks out of the pen with two 2,000 pound oxen over his head and makes his way to the center of the field.

The best swordsman in our group is Asmodeus. He is joined by two other swordsmen. It is obvious that an ox is going to be used in the event. Every time I think that people are not going to die in an event, they do, so I won't even let the thought enter my mind this time.

This appears to be similar to the opening of the Games to determine the order. Except this time it will be the unlucky oxen that will be sliced to pieces with the twinkling sharp swords.

The first swordsman lays his sword against the ground to indicate that he is ready. The judge tosses the ox in the air about 15 feet above the swordsman. It is over in less than a second. I could hardly tell he moved at all. Seven cuts, all at different angles, all in the blink of an eye.

The ox seemed to be unaffected completely. It never moved or seemed to flinch. The thought entered my mind that he missed him. Then the animal slowly stared to disassemble. A separation of body parts. When the ox hit the ground, it resembled the way our village butcher has them laid out, ready for purchase: beheaded, all four legs quartered, the trunk cut in halves down the spine, and the entrails in one pile to themselves. Perfect. I am amazed at this.

The next animal is done the same way by the next swordsman. A different style — he went to one knee in order to finish the last cut —but the results were the same: a perfectly butchered ox, all done in about a second.

Next, it would be great swordsman Asmodeus. I am curious how he can do better than the others. How are they judged? Every time I think this, something bad happens. Why is another ox not brought for Asmodeus to butcher?

Then I notice the guard Nephilim bringing arms full of volunteers. I knew it! These creatures can't go for very long without the death of my fellow men. They squirm, they struggle, they twist and contort their bodies in ever manner to try to escape the grip of the Nephilim. It is impossible. If I could, I would swoop down and kill all this vile creatures and save them all. But I am but an ant.

The volunteers are thrown to the ground. About 20 men or so are wondering in what gruesome manner they are about to die. Then the judge reappears with another ox held quietly above his head in his right hand .In his other hand are large sticks of wood. They appear like something that would be used to stake a man out for execution.

It looks like Asmodeus will get his chance with the ox after all. Some of the guards bring some kind of large black barrels and more wooden stakes. In a few minutes, the fate of the volunteers will be revealed. The judge throws the ox in the air, Asmodeus' blade flashes in the sun. The ox is cleanly dissected just as the others. Perfectly.

The judge motions for the swordsmen. He is about the announce something important. The volunteers are circled around by the guards so they can't make a desperate attempt to run. My heart is ponding, fearing in agony for my friends.

Everyone becomes deathly quiet. A sickening hush. And then the judge speaks:

"Time to eat." The volunteers happily start a fire with the wood and begin preparing the meal for the Nephilim. I'm somewhat hungry myself. I wish I could find an apple.

CHAPTER 19

I am still waiting for the *Sword Play*. The carving of the oxen was merely an exhibition to scare the villagers even more. They derive pleasure this way. They believe it is more exhilarating to terrify humans than to actually kill them. Killing is too easy. What challenge is that? So, I have figured they are scratching two itches with one finger: deciding the winner of the Games, and satisfying their urge to kill their hated rivals and enemies, the wee little humans.

It doesn't make sense to me, not now, not ever. Why are the humans, my people, their rivals and enemies? We are no match for them. They are ten times bigger, stronger, faster, and smarter. They are over-equipped for the jobs they have. They have every human characteristic multiplied by ten — physically and mentally.

They are all lacking, however, in the ingredients that makes God's children like Himself: love, compassion, sympathy, empathy, and kindness for one another. These qualities are entirely absent. They have no compunction to acquire them, so they frustratingly compete and fight each other.

I believe this is why Behemoth is sometimes lost in lonely reveries. That is why he is different. He knows it. He senses it. This is why he makes attempts to be human —feeble attempts sometimes, but efforts nonetheless. The other Nephilim sense this in Behemoth also, and they hate him for it. All those human feelings have eluded them completely. This is why they will try to kill him. And it is for this, that I must try to help my master if I can. He has saved me. I would not be a Child of God if I did not try to save him.

A shattering scream of some colossal monster shakes me from my contemplation. A giant animal of some sort is making its way to the grounds. I can't see it yet, but I can feel the earth tremble from each of its long strides. The sound of its scream is even louder than an angry Nephilim war cry.

Over a hill in the horizon, I can see it stomping the ground with giant hooves, shaking its massive head at the tiny men harassing the beast, forcing it to come in the direction of the field. It appears to be angry and coming against its will. The men are some of the Nephilim guards. And yes, they are forcing the animal in this direction on purpose. I can only surmise it is part of the next competition. *It* is the volunteer.

I have never seen this giant beast before. I have seen drawings similar to it inside a cave once. But, just like the Nephilim, I attributed it to folklore. And just as I did with the Nephilim, I am learning differently.

It has a long body, and longer tail, and an even longer neck. Its head is flattened on the top and shaped like an adder's. Its legs are powerfully built, for they have to be in order to support its massive girth. It must be 200 feet from head to tail, and its weight is many thousands of pounds — 100,000, probably. As large as the Nephilim are, they are tiny standing next to this creature.

I would say that it looks like a grazing animal and not a meat eater. I am curious as to what they intend to do with it. It does not pose a danger other than trampling someone. I am guessing the challenge is to see who can kill it the quickest or with the least amount of blows, perhaps. But it appears to be the only one. Just like the other events, I am ignorant as to the point of it all.

And just like the other times I have tried to guess; I am wrong again. Because the scream I heard that shattered the air did not come from this giant animal, but from the three giant beasts that are following it. The first giant was merely the lure to get the three other beasts to follow. The real creatures the Nephilim must battle are far more formidable. They are the most terrifying creatures I have ever seen. I bang my fist against the side of my head to see if my brain is failing me.

These beasts are not as big as its prey —the Nephilim's lure — but are terrifying killers and eaters of flesh. Each walks upright on two large, muscular back legs, like a man. Its front legs are useless —more like shriveled hooks than arms. Its head is large, its jaws are larger still. Its teeth are long and look razor sharp. Its skin resembles snake scales, so dense that it appears impenetrable by sword or spear.

No man or group of men would dare go up against such a beast. But the Nephilim are not men — they are beast themselves. A killer beast versus a killer beast. As mighty as the Nephilim are, I figure they have met a mightier beast than themselves. The thought enters my mind *that I wish this beast would kill all the Nephilim*, but another thought erases it: *What would we do with the beast that killed the Nephilim? They would be a worse pestilence, more deadly than the first. Better the Nephilim win and die in combat than be consumed and digested in the gut of these creatures from hell.*

The three swordsmen dash in a dead sprint toward the beasts, yelling blood-curdling screams. Each one has singled out the one beast he will attack. Despite the evilness that flows through these Nephilim's souls, they are completely unafraid of anything to do with battle.

They fear nothing. They know only to fight. The bigger the challenge, the better they like it. If they weren't so vile, they would be the most enviable creatures to ever walk the world. Indeed, as I watch them sprinting at near 100 miles per hour directly at the jaws of these deadly beast, swords twirling and flashing in their mighty hands, I find myself picturing what it would be like to be a Nephilim. I am a child again, a hero of old… My God, my God, they are magnificent to watch.

The first, or second, or perhaps even Asmodeus himself—at this distance and with the speed at which this is happening, it is hard to tell who is who— whichever the case, a swordsman has reached his beast of prey and attacks. The monster is at least 40 feet tall at least, but is not quick enough to stop the swordsman from mounting its back, as we might mount a donkey or camel.

The other two swordsmen have done the same as the first. They have avoided the snaps of the deadly jaws and have each mounted a beast. This enrages the giants, who are twisting and contorting their necks, snapping and hissing, spiting, and flashing their saber teeth in a desperate attempt to catch old of a leg or an arm —anything they can clamp down on and shred the unwelcome riders to pieces.

One by one, the riders gain their footing, and with great balance and agility, they stand upright as the beasts spin around and around, snapping at the riders like a dog chasing their tails. It is not easy to stand, but now they are attempting to walk along the creature's boney spines toward the middle of their backs.

This angers the animal all the more. They begin to jump, leap, and scratch with their massive feet at the annoying riders. At first, it looks as though one of the swordsmen is about to be tossed off, but then he regains his balance. Another slips and hangs on by one of the brute's scales, fighting off the flailing teeth with his sword.

It doesn't work. The beast catches him in its jaws. I can now see that it is Amadeus who is caught in the death grip of the saber teeth, which are at least six feet long and as sharp as the blade in Amadeus' sheath. But he cannot use his sword because both hands are being used, with all his strength, to prevent the jaws from closing and snuffing out his life.

I understand what they are attempting to do. They are trying to sink their swords into the heart of the monsters. The only way is from the top. But as one swordsman draws back to launch his blade, he is jolted by the hysterical animal and cannot put all his might into plunging into the beast's back.

The winner will be the one whose mount fall dead first. One swordman has gotten a plunge into his creature's chest but has missed the heart because the creature is still spinning. Another is struggling stay upright but is now in a good position to drive his blade deep.

Asmodeus sees what is about to happen. He pushes with all his strength the jaws of his monsters, forcing them apart, and pulls his body out of the way of a mighty clamp-shut. The teeth chime as they crush against each other. Hanging by one tooth, I see his sword drop to the ground. He then flips himself onto the top of the beast's snout. Reaching down, he takes hold of the nearest saber tooth, pulls with all his might, and uproots the tooth clean from the monster's bloody mouth.

Meanwhile, the other swordsman drives his blade into his creature's back. It seems to paralyze the beast in a stilled flinch. However, it does not go down. Asmodeus, standing on atop of his monster's snout, right between its two beady eyes, slowly raises the tooth above his head. He and the monster are stare at each other, eye to eye.

Asmodeus is about to drive the monster's own tooth into its skull. I wonder why they didn't attack the beasts' heads with their swords earlier. I learn that the beasts' skulls are a foot thick with granite-hard bone, and the poor creatures' brain are only about the size of a human hand. It is much easier to attack their hearts, which weigh over 1,000 pounds.

But Asmodeus has no choice. The other swordsman's creature is about to topple.

With a monumental plunge, Asmodeus buries the creature's tooth deep into its skull. A tooth, being much larger than a sword, finds the tiny brain with its blunt edge. This creature, too flinches, paralyzed, but toppling over like a fallen tree. It dies one second before the other beast, whose heart had been pierced by the other swordsman's blade. In this case, killing the head precede killing the heart by a single second.

Just before the creature hits the ground, Asmodeus steps off, landing lightly. He raises his hands in triumph. For the first time, all the other Nephilim gathered at the Games cheer. It is hard to impress a Nephilim, but this does. Even the mighty Behemoth smiles at Asmodeus when he returns to his group. It is an acknowledgement of great honor, one that does not happen often.

CHAPTER 20

There are two of the giant creatures left roaming the field. The third swordsman dismounted the monster he was riding when it became obvious, he was not going to win the contest. The much larger *lure* is also alive. I suspect it will be used in the next event.

A flash of silver glitters across the sky. The lone meat-eating monster flinches and drops to its knees, dead. In the foreground, I can see a spear lose altitude and arc to the ground. It had passed through the beast's body and pierced its heart in less time than it takes for its heart to beat once. I didn't see who threw the spear. I guess they couldn't let the dangerous beast wander about.

A group of about 30 or so Nephilim juveniles descend upon the dead monster. I have been told that when they are at a certain age, they get an uncontrollable urge to join the Nephilim Nation and travel about with the clan and learn the ways of their kind. They are raised by the human parents until the age of the irresistible hunger named the *Calling*, and then they must go.

These youngsters look to be teenagers. Only about ten feet tall, and have not developed the thickness of muscles of the Nephilim masters. They weigh no more than 700 pounds. They began to hack the carcass of the beast with axes and carry it off in chunks laid across their shoulders. It will now become a meal for the clan. Another group does the same for the monsters killed by Asmodeus and the other competitor. Nothing is wasted.

I've learned that they grow herds of this ancient, never-seen-before giant beasts for food and for the games, of course. It takes large amounts of food for the Nephilim. I don't know where the actual Nation they speak of is located. I am told it is thousands of miles away, lying somewhere *across the great ice bridge.* I am glad it is far away. I have also been told that the Nephilim all originate here in the land of Canaan. I do not understand why.

There is the one giant creature left alone in the middle of the field. It lowers its head occasionally to nervously graze on the lush grass, then suddenly lifts its head and bellows like an ox, anxiously waiting for a return call that never comes. It is alone in this strange country and is frightened like a lost child. I am afraid for it as well. It will be the next volunteer, I fear. I feel such sorrow for this wayward giant that I have the urge to save it from the unspeakable fate which awaits it. *Shrink this beast, O'Lord, that I may tuck it away in my tunic safe, like the toys of my youth.*

Three Nephilim take to the field. I recognize Mammon even from this distance. I do not know what the next exercise is, but I'm sure it will not be good for the forsaken beast. None of the three participants have weapons. *How are they going to kill a beast of this size without a weapon?* I wonder. Nothing is happening. Three Nephilim have the beast surrounded but are just staring at the terrified being, which is so large the giant warriors seem like mites.

They begin to close in tighter around the colossus, that is confused as to what it is supposed to do, so it bellows a cry. My ears ache, and the report that bounces off the mountains and returns in an echo is almost as loud as the original. Yet, Mammon, as well as the other two competitors, tightens the circle closer still. When will they attack, and with what? I am confused, just like the hopeless animal.

They are doing nothing but staring at the forlorn brute, who looks like it is about to make a run for the strange-acting men who appear as though they are seeing who can get the closest to it.

They have now stopped advancing, sensing that the animal is about to try an escape through a gap. Then one of the Nephilim steps forward in slow, methodical steps, advancing closer and closer still. He gets to within a few feet of the creature and does nothing but stands gazing the animal's eyes.

The beast looks this way and that, and finally seeing how close the Nephilim is to him, it stares back angrily, hoping that he might frighten the pesky little flea away. But when it meets the Nephilim eye to eye, something strange happens. The giant beast cannot seem to break the lock the contestant has on its now aching eyes.

I now understand what this strange contest is about. Remember that I told you earlier that a Nephilim could stare angrily into one's eyes for a period of time and it caused their head to ache? Same thing here. Each one will see if it can bring this mighty giant to the ground merely by looking hard into its eyes. The catch is that the animal has to look into the warrior's eyes as well. No look, no lock, no win.

Each Nephilim has only so long, then the judge raises his hand and he must back away and let the next have a try, and so forth until there is a winner. But the first competitor has a lock onto the animal's brain, and it is weakening. I know firsthand how it feels, for I have found myself caught in the lock of the mighty Behemoth himself and brought to my knees in agony in only a matter of seconds.

Once in the lock, it is hard to break free from the relentless power of the Nephilim brain. The beast starts to wobble from side to side and then drops down on its front knees. All of this happens after the lock has been broken. The duration of its effects last's about thirty seconds or so. Then you recover. The after effects are a terrible headache. That's as far as the first partaker gets the animal: its front knees.

After the beats regains itself, the next challenger steps forward. It isn't long before it is in another Nephilim brain lock. The second challenger has his hands behind his back with one foot forward. His brow is furrowed in concentration. The animal is in a trance. It starts to act like it is playing, if the beasts can play. I imagine that all beasts play when they are pups. It is a strange sight indeed to watch a creature that weighs 100,000 pounds revert to the playfulness of its youth.

It runs and bucks the way I've seen young calves do. The ground shakes with each touchdown of its gigantic back hooves. It rears up and paws with its front hooves. Upright, it must have towered 90 feet into the sky. It was amusing to see. I begin to wonder, *is the challenger causing this to happen on purpose? Is this part of the competition?* I now know that the object is control of the animal. One might attempt to bring the beast down or put it in a trance and have it at your command.

Each challenger will be judged accordingly. This is strictly a mental contest of keen concentration.

The playful creature shakes it relatively small head from side to side, like a fly is buzzing inside its ear. Then it starts to circle round and round, its head following its tail the way a dog does just before it lays down for a nap. It finds the perfect spot and circles itself down on the ground with a thud, its tiny head at the end of its long neck snuggled upon its hunch. It sleeps. Again, the crowd of Nephilim pound their spears onto the ground in praise. This was impressive.

The noise of the pounding spears brings the sleepy animal back to life and it regains its feet. It is now Mammon's turn to impress. He casually walks toward the unsuspecting simpleton. He has his arms folded in front of him as if he is about to go for a stroll at his leisure. The unusual carelessness of Mammon works, as the animal has unwittingly caught the glare of Mammon's penetrating eyes.

The lock takes hold of the beast. Mammon's brow furrows in a row of undulating muscle. A large vein rises across his forehead like a winding river, and soon tributary veins branch in different directions. The creature is at Mammon's mercy.

He strolls right up to it, which causes the mighty animal to bend its head down to the ground. Then it begins to lick and lap its three-foot-wide tongue at Mammon, the way my appreciative dog is happy to see me. Mammon pets the monster on top of its head. The whooshing sound of its 100-foot-long tail cuts the air, which I can hear plainly.

And then, to everyone's amazement, the gigantic beast flops over on its back. The rumble of the collapsing body could have been heard in the next village. Mammon begins to rub its bulbous belly, which activates one of its back legs in a mock scratch. In a few seconds, the beast is in a deep sleep. Mammon does not wait for the tapping of the spears. He bends at the waist, raises and holds up one hand, and makes his way off to his group.

A Nephilim boy makes his way to the creature and abruptly kicks it on the head with his foot. It raises his head from the ground and is groggy. The boy places a large collar over its smallish head and ties a rope around the collar. He orders the beast to rise and leads him off toward the horizon with its massive tale swishing the air in delight.

CHAPTER 21

Ronwe is the only one of the group yet to compete. I know that they all have to participate in at least one event —something they excel at. Ronwe is the best at talking. I am wondering how they will manage a talking contest. He is also very clever. It is this cleverness where the next event lies. All the Nephilim are clever, but how will they determine who is the *most* clever? I don't know.

Ronwe and two other Nephilim are listening intently to the judge speak. I'll have to get closer to hear what is taking place. I also have to stay out of range of their super senses. It's almost impossible to spy on a Nephilim up close. I must try to get a little closer, though.

As I understand it, in this event, an object—the identity of which is unknown to the others—must be hidden by one of the clever Nephilim. The task of the other two is to find it. It's a war of wits, as the seekers can ask three and only three, questions of the hider. The hider must answer honestly and with only one word. The contest can be won either by finding the object or by keeping the object from being found. They call this event *Hide and Seek.*

The three hiders and seekers sit in a circle. They have already hidden their objects during the commotion of the earlier events. No one saw them. I didn't see them either. The two seekers will ask the first hider their three questions and must return in ten minutes with the object —or they lose.

The first Nephilim seeker speaks, "Is the object alive?" he asks.
"No."

"Is it larger than my hand or smaller?" he asks his second questions.
"Larger"

"Is this object in sight now?" Was his third question.

"Yes." was the final answer. The first seeker is off in search.

Ronwe, studying the hider judiciously, and then says coyly:

"I have only one question to ask of you:
Judging by the blood on your hands,
Our object was once alive and now it's through,
Because you have killed it, where it stands."

After a long pause, the hider responds: "Yes."

Ronwe gets up, walks unconcernedly to where the camels are tied, gently pushes one finger against one, then another, and on the third push, the animal topples over. Ronwe snatches it up and tosses it at the hider. The hider looks dejectedly at the dead animal and nods. The hider had killed it, stiffening its legs with iron poles pushed down through its limbs and along its spine. It looked alive, standing among the other camels. I never noticed. Ronwe won the seek.

The circle is reassembled with the same three players. Now it's Ronwe's turn to answer questions about the object he has hidden. *Can he say just one word?* I wonder.

"Is this object alive or dead?" ask the first seeker.

"Yes, I guess," answers Ronwe, smiling.

"What do you mean? Is it alive or not? Asks the second, annoyed by the previous answer.

"What I mean to say,
Is that it is in neither way —
Neither alive nor dead,
But both at once instead.

The two Nephilim ponder the strange clue. Nephilim enjoy riddles and often bemuse one another this way. Ronwe is the best at it, and even Behemoth occasionally smiles at his riddles. I never understand any of them —just like now. What is dead and live? I don't know.

"Is this an animal?" asks the second.

"Yes indeed; is your lead."

"Is this an animal that is among us now?" asks the first.

"Yes of course; you have your source."

"I know what the answer is, Ronwe," says the second, rising to his feet. "I'll be back." The second Nephilim seeker heads straight for one of the giant tents. The tents of Nephilim are made strange. They are round at the bottom and taper in at the top, like an upside-down cone. I suppose it's so they can stand inside them.

One of the tents contains ice, brought from the land they came from, *over the ice bridge*. The seeker searches the ice tent, returns carrying a small block of watery ice, and throws it on the ground in front of Ronwe.

Ronwe watches the melting ice dissolve at his feet. He then nods at the second seeker, confirming that he had indeed solved the riddle of the animal that is both alive and dead. Soon, a snake begins to wiggle and slither away.

The final hider takes his place in the circle, awaiting the three questions about the object he has hidden. Ronwe bows his head toward the second seeker, signaling for him to go first. Since the second seeker has the prerogative, and since Ronwe asked last during the first round, he returns the nod to Ronwe, indicating that Ronwe may ask the first three questions this time.

Ronwe studies the hider's eyes before speaking. Nephilim cannot inflict pain on one another the way they do on humans or animals, so the hider looks back without emotion. Then Ronwe asks:

"The origin of the object you have hidden —is it carried or ridden?"

"Ridden, "the hider answers reluctantly. Ronwe focuses intently as the hider forms his words.

"The object of which you have concealed —is it contained within this field?" Ronwe gestures around the circle.

"Yes," the hider answers, growing more dismayed.

"The object of which you are so aloof —Is it a piece of the monster's tooth?" The hider smiles at Ronwe hatefully.

"You gave it away when you spoke," Ronwe says smugly, "for your tooth in the front is usually broke." The hider wiggles his tongue across his front teeth, then spits the piece of the monster's tooth — found during an earlier game—at Ronwe. A disgruntled snarl soon covers the chipped tooth of the hider. Our group had another victory.

CHAPTER 22

I can't understand what they are saying, but I am under the impression that the competition is going to come down to the final event: *The Toss and Catch.* The groups are tied, I think. I lost count, but it looks like whoever wins this event wins the prize.

This is the demonstration that the mighty Nephilim from the other camp displayed while I was a spy. This one requires volunteers but at least there is a chance that they will be caught at the end of their flight.

Behemoth will be the hurler in our group and Urobach will be the catcher. The rules are simple: grab a volunteer and throw him as far as you can. If the catcher gathers him in and he is alive, it is measured. A pair gets three attempts.

The first hurler takes hold of the volunteer around the waist. It is natural for the volunteer to start kicking and screaming —they all do this. It seems so foolish from a distance for a man to act this way, but I suppose I would do the same as he. Even the bravest of men act this way. We are all brave until we are in the hands of a Nephilim; then all bravery retreats. This is true of everyone.

The object is to get the volunteer to spiral into the wind for maximum distance. The squirming of the frantic volunteer makes this difficult. From the group of volunteers, I hear someone yell out, *"Be still! It is for your own good. Don't you understand that?"* It is funny how the same person who is doing the yelling will be doing the squirming and crying in just a few minutes. We are all like that, though. Bravery comes from proximity. The farther away, the braver.

The hurler is tempted to thump the volunteer to relax him and hush his screaming mouth, but the power in these creatures' fingers is tremendous. Thumping is a common cause of death around the Nephilim. Many have gone that way. It is funny, but I don't think the Nephilim were ever trying to kill them. They were *accidental* thumping deaths, I believe.

The first hurler is called Bathem. He grasps his volunteer around the waist and the kicking and screaming begin. He holds his volunteer up to his face and frowns at him, then drops his hand to his waist and sighs. He wanted the volunteer to look him in the eye, but the man knew better. If you have ever been in the painful lock-gaze of a Nephilim, you will never look one in the eye again.

Bathem didn't want to hurt the man, but merely cause him to pass out. Bathem figured it was easier to throw a spiral with an unconscious volunteer than a wriggling one. He considered thumping him, but the skulls of puny humans are fragile.

Bathem is a formidable hurler. He is one of the names I can remember spoken by the other Nephilim in our group. They had dealt with him before. I would have liked to have known more about the Games. It sounds sacrilege, but these creatures and their history would be interesting to know.

The Toss and Catch is the final and most important event. As best as I can tell, it has something to do with the days when the Nephilim were the protectors of the earth from the invasion of the *Beasts of the Sky*.

The Toss and Catch was used as a way of communicating commands during the warring periods against the *Beasts of the Sky*. Commands were hurled form one site to the other. The helpful little people would memorize the orders and repeat them. It was important that the little recorder arrived safely.

Since those days, this is the most sacred of the events. Because of the Toss and Catch, the Nephilim were able to defeat the beasts that were physically superior, save for the communication of the Nephilim and the little people. All of the Games are adapted from the *wars*.

Bathem and his catcher stand 100 yards apart, tossing and catching their screaming volunteer in a warm-up round. On the sidelines, Behemoth grabs another volunteer while Urobach nonchalantly kicks a lifeless body out of the way.

When Bathem is ready, his catcher drops back nearly a half mile. The catcher has to be fast and nimble. He may have to run up several hundred yards, or back several hundred yards, or to the right, or to the left. It is hard to say where the man may drift against the force of the air. If he spirals, he will go straight and far. Spirals are hard to come by with a fidgeting human.

Bathem runs up to the launch line and hurls a perfect overhand toss. The volunteer begins tumbling end-over-end and gains good height. But he soon begins to flatten out his arms and legs and drift far to the left. He loses altitude quickly. The catcher starts sprinting toward him, but Bathem shouts, *"Let him go,"* and the catcher stops. A thud and a poof of dust. *"Next volunteer,"* says Bathem.

A volunteer is pitched to Bathem. He snatches him from the air and begins to instruct the hysterical man.

"Keep yourself in a tucked position, like a ball," he says hopelessly, as he has given up on a spiral. This is the same thing he told the other, who is now a pile of guts about 600 yards away. The volunteers don't listen to anything they are told, only the resounding sound of their own screams. They are too busy trying to squirm away from the death that awaits them.

The volunteer suddenly stops squiring as Bathem says," *If you want to live, curl yourself into a ball."* The volunteer seems to understand and curls himself into a ball with his knees pulled into his chin tightly.

Bathem is not as large as Behemoth and some of the others. He is about 17 feet tall and weighs about 4,200 pounds. All Nephilim have large hands for their bodies, but Bathem's are relatively small. He is having trouble griping the man he is about to toss when he is in the ball position with one hand. He also has to be careful not to grip too tightly around the ribs. Ribs are even easier to break than skulls.

Bathem's approaches the line and grunts as he launches the man from his hand. The man-ball is rotating rapidly and gaining height. The catcher only has to take a few steps back, claps his hands, and smothers the human ball into his chest. A clean toss and catch of about 800 yards. Bathem seems pleased.

The next hurler is the one I saw giving the demonstration the day I was spying. His name is Abbodon—the prince of wars. He is massive.

Bigger than even Behemoth. His body is well scarred. A deep gash runs across his right eye and brow, making him look even more menacing. He is about 26 feet tall and must weigh in excess of 8,000 pounds. His chest is about four feet thick. His hands are large, even for his body.

He knows how to make the tiny men spiral. I have seen him do this before. He will be all but impossible to beat.

"Stiffen yourself, hands over head," he growls at his volunteer, who is standing in the palm of his open hand. The volunteer obeys willingly and becomes like a plank. Abbodon clutches him around the waist and waves at his catcher to back up. "I will end this now," he shouts at the catcher, waving for him to back even further.

He starts his run-up toward the line with the volunteer held over his head, much like a spear toss. As he approaches the launch line, his strides lengthen and he plants his left foot at the line. Abbodon is going to use all his strength on this toss. His right arm flashes forward. A red spray of blood and entrails rains down on the ground from the man who disintegrated the second he left Abbodon's hand.

I once became good at throwing eggs a long way and had an egg to shatter in my hand in this manner.

"I was afraid of this." I heard Abbodon say in disgust. "Why are you human men so soft?" he mumbled to himself. "I'll have to take some power off my toss," he said as he looked humorously at the next volunteer, whose eyes were opened so wide in terror that they appeared to be solid white.

This seemed to anger Abbodon, and he backhanded the terrified volunteer into a hundred pieces. I have seen the backhands of Nephilim before, and I know what they can do. After they destroy a human body, they always seem even angrier because they have to remove the human body parts from their hand. They are easily annoyed by the frailty of humans.

Abbodon motions for the catcher to come a bit closer as he knows a full-force toss will disintegrate the volunteer as he leaves his hand.

"Stiffen yourself, hands over head," he rumbles once more at his volunteer, who, like the first, is terrified—and considering what has just happened—for good reason.

Abbodon is apprehensive. He is the favorite in this event. If he wins, his group wins, and he wins the prize since he is the leader.

He has become so powerful that he has to restrict his toss. He seems to be concerned about Behemoth, who has stopped warming up and is staring mechanically at Abbodon. It is clear they don't like each other. One of them will win the prize, one will not.

Abbodon launches his man, perfectly. The man is spinning rapidly and traveling far. The catcher starts to back up, and then backs up some more. He catches the man over his shoulder expertly. The judge places a mark at the spot of reception. It is 900 hundred yards, well over a half mile.

"A record!" I hear shouted from someone. Behemoth glares at Abbodon. Abbodon cuts a quick glance back and begins to laugh. Behemoth places his hands on his hips and says confidently. "Well done, Abbodon. You came so close to winning" Abbodon does not look amused at Behemoth's words.

CHAPTER 23

Behemoth resembles a statue as he poses with his hands on his hips. His daunting dimensions inspire awe and wonder as he defiantly stares down his nemesis, Abbodon. Behemoth is 24 feet tall, weighing 6,500 pounds of bulging muscle. He looks like granite. Even among the Nephilim, he is startling. Magnificent is the only word befitting him.

Behemoth has his volunteer in hand and is ready. "You understand what to do," he says quietly to the bewildered man, who is trembling nervously yet seems to understand what he must do to survive the Toss and Catch.

The man-mountain of granite, iron, muscle and blood begins to stride toward the line. With longer and longer strides, he plants a foot; dirt piles up from the force. He lets fly —not with all his might, for fear of breakage as the man leaves his hand — but hopefully with just enough of his prodigious strength.

The man-spear begins to twist in violent rotations, cutting through the sticky air. This is going to be far. But the man's hands drop to his sides; it is very difficult for one to hold their hands above their head at 200 miles per hour against the resistance of the brazen wind. They all do this —no one can hold the point the entire distance

Urobach stands on the line to beat. He drifts to his right about twenty yards or so and is about to put his hands out to make the catch. He looks down, and then quickly draws in his hands. A fellow villager splatters the ground five feet from the line to make. One attempt. Only the catch is counted. Urobach did right.

The men from my village scatter, trying to avoid the sweeping hand of Asmodeus as he scoops up the next volunteer who will become the spear. One is caught and flung to Behemoth, who snatches him out of the air and begins to prepare him for his flight.

"Stiffen as hard as you can, hold your hands at a point tightly above your head," he commands. The volunteer understands and assumes the position. The same approach is taken, the same heave, the same result. This time, however, the volunteer splatters the ground within 10 feet or so of the mark to make. Not quite as far as the first. One attempt left.

Behemoth is frustrated and storms toward the pen of volunteers. His massive arms are swing from side to side. The ground thumps with each stride. He is in a fit of desperation.

He looks over the pen, and, remembering the weights of each, he snatches the heaviest remaining man from my village. I see him and know that it is Buer, a friend. He squirms, the same as I suppose we all would. Behemoth holds him around the waist in his right hand while appearing to search the camp for something.

He spies what he is looking for and makes his way to a tree. He picks up a large rib bone from the beast that was vanquished and eaten earlier. Anguish is in his eyes, along with the desperation.

"I truly hate to do this to you, Buer. But I must win," he says loudly and remorsefully. He breaks a piece of the flat bone into a section about three feet long, then breaks two more pieces about the same length.

Buer's eyes look like white glass as he watches what Behemoth is doing, shaping the bone with his teeth into the exact configuration he desires. The image of what happens next will stay in my mind forever.

Behemoth lays Buer on his stomach and takes his razor-sharp thumb nail, laying open a line alongside Buer's spine. The blood-curdling sound of Buer's scream echoed off the mountain, and tiny bumps rise on my arms. Behemoth rolls Buer over and does the same on each of his sides. How Buer stays conscious is beyond reason. It would have been better had he fainted…

Behemoth places the edge of bone, about three inches wide, inside the split skin. A portion about two feet high creates a fin on Buer's back and sides.

"You must rotate." Behemoth growls through clenched teeth, his jaw muscles tightening in desperation. He threads a rawhide string around and around the split skin to hold the three bone-fins in place. The last piece of rib bone, about three and a half feet long, is braced at the front edge of the fin and Buer's spine, running to his hands, which Behemoth holds above his head. The raw hide is tied around the wrist and the bone. Now Buer's hands have to stay above his head.

Behemoth grasps the barely conscious Buer and holds him up to the judge, "How do you feel, Buer." Buer screams in agony. The judge nods to acknowledge that the man-spear is alive. Behemoth rolls Buer over and softly says, "Forgive me, Buer, but I have to win.

Behemoth waves Urobach to back up. It is easier to make a catch running forward then running back. Better to be too far back than not far enough. A fumble loses the Prize. Behemoth looks at his new creation and he wonders if it will hold up. He moves the bone fin on Buer's spine with his thumb. Buer howls in pain.

Behemoth takes the necessary long strides, coils his arm back to the cocked position, plants and fires. Buer spins so quickly that I can hear the air sputter as he glides through the blue sky. He keeps going and going, higher and higher. Not even Behemoth expected this distance. Urobach surely didn't, for he must sprint at a dead run after the man-spear that has just soared over his head. *He'll never catch him*, I think to myself.

Urobach has waited too long to make his break. I've heard them say it's hard to judge the distance when the spear is straight overhead. Urobach is looking back and sprinting at about 75 miles per hour. Then he launches himself in a full layout. He leaps about 100 feet in the air, holding his right hand outstretched, and grasps Buer between his thumb and third finger. He slides to a stop without Buer touching the ground.

The judge speeds to the spot. Buer is dizzy from the rapid revolutions but manages to moan while trying to steady his head, which is moving in circles. The judge holds up his hand and booms, "Behemoth wins the Prize." If the villagers from 50 miles away had been listening intently, they could have heard the announcement.

The other Nephilim are yelling, *'Foul! Foul!* "There is nothing in the rules that says you can't modify your spearmen." the judge declares. Then he turns to Behemoth and shouts, "Come with me, Behemoth, and meet your Prize."

Abbodon stands in front of Behemoth, glares into his eyes. Behemoth steps forward, almost touching Abbodon, and glares back. "There's about to be a fight," I think to myself. I have often wondered what happens when Nephilim fight each other. The only thing that can kill a Nephilim is another Nephilim. I hope Behemoth wins.

Two titans stand eye to eye, chest to chest. I wait for the first blow. Then, Abbodon bows his head slightly to Behemoth, cracks a tiny, brief smile, and walks away dejectedly. Behemoth jogs to Urobach and glides within a foot of the catcher who just won him the Prize with his sliding, two-finger catch.

They gaze at each other for a few seconds without the slightest expression. Then Urobach holds up Buer to his waist. Behemoth takes him in his hand, and Urobach walks away. Behemoth quickly unties the cords and carefully removes the bone fins he had gruesomely attached to his volunteer just minutes earlier. Buer faints, and Behemoth gently lays him on the ground, nodding his head in gratitude.

He strides to the convoy and the Prize that has dominated his thoughts for years. He gaits is like that of a king, full of pride for his queen and kingdom. But kingdoms are grueling to acquire, and more grueling still to hold.

CHAPTER 24

The Queen's smile is as lovely a thing as has ever been bestowed upon my eyes. She slides her tanned leg from the sedan chair, and the slit skirt reveals the feminine shapeliness of her thighs. Every square inch of her 18-foot frame is stunning. She is the most beautiful woman to walk on the earth, by a tenfold.

Yes, I would say a tenfold would be correct. The Nephilim men are everything the human men are, times ten. The same would have to apply to the lovely Queen. It is all I can do to restrain myself. I have the uncontrollable urge to dash down from the protection of my little hill and grovel at her gorgeous feet. I would die instantly. I am contemplating whether it would be worth it.

What has happened to me? I am under a spell of enchantment. I cannot look at her without becoming intoxicated with her beauty. I am walking toward her. I must get closer. I must not be seen. Oh God, why have you forsaken me? I can't look at her, or I will die. I cannot not look at her, or, I will also die. I am caught in a spell that is leading me to my doom, and my master will be the one who will end me.

I will be saved, for a volunteer from another village has darted from his group and is in a dead sprint toward the Queen. He is loping rather than running, and sometimes skipping like an elf, as in the days of our childhood. He slides to a halt on the ground and begins to kiss the feet and ankles of the amused Queen. She laughs, Behemoth laughs, and every Nephilim in the entire field laughs. The loudness jars me to my senses.

Behemoth pinches the lovesick little man between his two fingers and flings him back to his group with a flick of the wrist. Then another man, and then another, can no longer contain the love spell and makes a break for the smiling, laughing, and absolutely charming young Queen.

As this one and that one slide around her feet, she holds her two lovely hands up to her voluptuous bosom and turns slightly to the side, sighing at the love-starved fools. Her amused smile seems only to excite them all the more. I have seen male dogs take to a master's leg in the same manner. The Nephilim men are not angry but laugh amusedly as they toss this one and that one back to their respective groups.

The Nephilim boys seem to enjoy peeling away the little hunching puppies and carrying them back to their groups. They seem to have been anticipating this. The villagers are helpless against the Queens' captivating splendor. The Nephilim seem to understand. It is merely part of the ceremony.

After the men have been stilled by the boy Nephilim as much as possible, the Queen takes Behemoth's hand and stands before the judge. They are truly a handsome couple. As they are being married, the ugly thought enters my mind: how puny and ugly we humans are in comparison.

What I have just witnessed from these *men-times ten* has cast me in a melancholy mood. We are truly insignificant compared to the mighty Nephilim. We are merely specks in their eyes. And we should be. These are men. I am not sure what we are.

I have never felt smaller than I do now. I almost made a fool of myself by running to the Queen and mounting her leg like a forlorn pup. I will have to gain the courage to return to my wife and my sons, unashamed. How can I protect them? With what? I am but an insect waiting to be squashed underneath a mightier heel.

As I make my way to get closer to the ceremony, it occurs to me that my sadness is misplaced. I possess something the mighty Nephilim do not: I am made in the image of God. These ill-tempered creatures are not. I believe they all sense they are lacking this ingredient.

Despite all their powers, they are envious of that which they can never obtain, and which they see in the tiny humans as a daily reminder. The humans will be happy for eternity when this world comes to an end; they will not. Being separated from God will turn any man ill-tempered. It is my belief that underneath the invincible wall of muscle, they are lost in the world, and they know it.

I zip from tree to tree, hoping to be undetected. I sense that something is going to happen after the ceremony. Mammon, Urobach, Ronwe, and the others are watching intently. They have just helped Behemoth win the Prize that they all covet. What will they do next? I don't trust them. I know Behemoth doesn't. He is statuesque as the Judge is awarding him his prize, but his eyes dart from Judge to Queen to his fellow teammates.

"You may go now," says the Judge, "You have won a glorious prize, Behemoth, and may the Sons of God be with you." These princes are the Sons of God, the fathers of the Nephilim. I have always been told that the Sons of God are the fallen angels that chose to follow Lucifer. This explains these creatures' size and power. I had always assumed these were folk tales.

The legend goes that the fallen angels had to acquire the blood of three animals to be able to take human form and mate with the daughters of man. This explain how the offspring were born with human characteristics, combined with those animals they mixed with. It all makes sense. It's true. It's all true. It all seems like a dream, a nightmare, except there is no waking up, because it is real.

Behemoth seems pleased that he has won such a prize. Pleased, not joyful. Not delighted. Not thrilled. Not jubilant. But pleased. He is worried. But now the others in his team are gone. They seemed resolved that they had agreed to help Behemoth and have left in peace.

Behemoth was the leader. I do not know how he became the leader. They have done their duty, I suppose. Next time, it will be their turn to compete for the prize. They seem to accept that. They left one by one. They seem to have followed the caravan back to where they came from. The games are over now. Maybe Behemoth looks worried over nothing. If I had won what he just won, I would be singing to the top of my lungs. Behemoth is more composed than I.

I would like to get a little closer so I can hear what Behemoth is saying to his bride. I am trying to move as quietly as possible. Behemoth and the queen are standing in the shade of a massive oak. They can't take their eyes off of one another. They are no longer speaking but lustfully gazing into each other's eye.

I am about 200 feet away, nestled behind another large tree. Just like Behemoth, I too can't look away from the mesmerizing queen. Then Behemoth says in a loud tone:

"Stop gawking from a distance, Compel, and come meet my Queen," he says, still taking in the loveliness of the Queen's beautiful blue eyes and without once looking my way. I was honored. I obliged. In a flash, I was standing beside Behemoth and his Queen.

As I was literally gawking at this creature of beauty, my mouth hung open like a fish with a thumb in it, a slimy string of drool sliding down my chin. It enters my mind that I might be offending my master. I am also hoping that he understands that I am a mere man. I am still alive, so he must understand.

My garment is extended in the front. I believe a dead man would be the same. It is impossible to restrain the involuntary. I momentarily gain my senses and look at Behemoth who is bemused by me.

"This is the prize, Compel. I take it you approve," he says humorously.

She cuts her eyes toward me. I go light headed. Her beauty and sensuousness are overwhelming when you are merely observing from afar, but when she looks at you this close, it is beyond what a mortal man can withstand. She looks me in the eye; my knees weaken. She parts her lips in the slightest smile, and I am so in love with her I cannot stand. I fall to the ground like a boiled noodle. I hear them both laugh.

I roll over on my stomach and try to gain my feet. Behemoth extends his finger to assist me.

"Why did you come back, Compel?" he asked.

"I thought I could help you, Master," I answered.

"Help me with what? My Queen? Believe me, Compel. I don't need any help with her

"I am so sorry to hear that master," I say as I am again drooling at her exquisiteness.

They both laugh uproariously, the sound booms in the air. Then a high-pitched whistling sound. Behemoth raises his hand in a flash and catches a spear that is inches from his chest.

CHAPTER 25

Behemoth held the spear in one hand and swung the startled queen behind him with the other. His eyes darted this way and that, desperately pausing, and then twitching, searching to detect the slightest movement from the direction of the spear that was meant for his heart.

I am jolted from my spell and begin to roll on the ground, searching for the nearest tree, stump or even clump of dirt for protection. I roll up next to the large oak, ease to my feet, and hide my body on the opposite side from the attackers. I am scared of dying. If Behemoth dies, I die.

Behemoth has the spear in lunging position. He is crouched down and pivots from side to side, hunting for the smallest movement, hoping to return the spear to its owner, point first. I can hear the muscles and tendons in his bulging thighs strain as he pivots. When it is deadly quiet, you can hear the tensed muscles of a Nephilim contract against one another. It is a creaking sound, much like a door neglected of grease. This is all I can hear right now.

Behemoth motions for the Queen to join me behind the oak. She quickly obeys without a word. I look up at her, and she puts her hand on my head and presses it against her thigh. She looks terrified.

The alluring aroma of her perfume eddies into my nostrils. I turn my head toward her and peer straight up. Her bosom swells out about two feet and is incredibly sensuous. Even from down under, the opulent features of her lovely face are striking and magnificent. She looks down at me as I am mesmerizingly examine her loveliness. She parts her lips in a slight, nervous smile, and my knees begin to buckle. She holds me up with her hand. I have to focus or die.

I regain my wits again when I immediately look down beside her knee. Her tanned skin is beckoning me. The calf of her leg is perfectly shaped. Her angles are flawless. Her feet are immaculately feminine and dainty for a woman 18 feet tall, and yes, sensual. Why am I thinking these thoughts as my master is under attack? Because I am human? What is wrong with me? I must get a hold of myself.

Behemoth is still crouched but is not moving. Perfectly still. Listening. There is no movement. No sound. He stands erect but is still attentive to any sound or movement.

I say, "Could it be a prank, master?"

"Not even Ronwe would think this funny, Compel," he whispers. "The spear was meant to kill me. Welcome to the world of the Nephilim, Compel. Tell me how you like it." He still is not taking his eyes from the distant yonder.

"Be careful, Behemoth," murmured the Queen.

"I most certainly hadn't planned on daydreaming right now, Sheba," he murmurs back.

Sheba. Now I know what her name is. Just in case she has any of the male's temperament, I will call her Queen. Good, I am myself again. I can think clearly, so long as I don't look at the Queen. But my master is in big trouble. He doesn't know where his attackers are, or how many, or where the next spear may be coming from, or even if there is an attacker at all.

"You disappointment me," Behemoth shouted loudly, "An ambush! Come now! This is no way for a warrior to act."

"Who said we were at war? Really, Behemoth you are such a bore," echoed the familiar voice of Ronwe from the woods. Then he appeared from the shade, casually strolling toward us with his usual brash smile.

"Don't trust him, Master," I said cautiously.

"Though she only lived fifteen minutes after she gave birth to me, my mother would be proud of the fact that her son didn't grow up stupid Compel," Behemoth said just as cautiously.

"Come closer, Ronwe. I want to hear if you can manage to spout your silly rhymes with your head missing. It would not surprise me to hear that your chattering mouth can still bore me without your body to support it."

"Really Behemoth, is that the best you can do? You know if I wanted to kill you, you would be through." Ronwe had made it to within ten feet of Behemoth. It looked like a fight to me.

"That's close enough, Ronwe? I would not press my luck."

"You are concerned about a little thing like luck."

"And what should I be concerned with, Ronwe?"

"I would think it is to know…when to duck."

Just as Ronwe said it, he ducked his head forward. Behemoth never saw the spear that zoomed just above Ronwe's back and buried itself deep into his stomach. I saw the head of the spear plunge about two feet through the other side of mighty Behemoth's back. He stood for a moment, tried to pull the spear out of his stomach, and then fell backward, flat on his back. The spear jutted forward out of his stomach the same two-foot distance that had been protruding from the back.

When Behemoth hit the ground dead, my fate was sealed. I knew I would die a horrible death. I looked up at Sheba. She looked uncertain as to what to do and puckered her lips in the manner of a child who is about to cry. Even that expression is beautiful.

"What will happen to you?" I asked her bravely, knowing that no matter whether I acted bravely or cowardly, I would die. I might as well act bravely.

"I don't know, Compel. I think I am about to become the queen to them all." As she said that, Urobach, Astaroth, Andras, Asmodeus, and Mammon appeared from different directions into the open and surrounded us.

"I will protect you with the remainder of my life, Queen Sheba. I ask but one favor of you."

"What is that, my tiny warrior? You have but to ask," she said kindly.

"Would you remember me in your thoughts? And tell those that will listen that I died bravely. The story might eventually reach my wife and children someday. Dying goes easier when it is remembered."

"I will, little one," she said with the smile that I will soon die for.

I let out a scream to the limits of my lungs and scurried from behind the oak tree to the side of Behemoth's body. I grabbed the handle of his sword but could only manage to pull it out of the sheath with great difficulty. I couldn't pick the heavy sword entirely off the ground. I hear a discord of laughter.

I let forth another yell, pulled the sword with all my might, and began to swing it toward the enemy, when suddenly, Behemoth took hold of my shoulder with his bloody hand.

"I'll take it from here, Compel. This is more my kind of fight."

He quickly rose to his feet, grasped the end of the spear protruding from his stomach, and in one blinding flash pulled the spear out and back handed it completely through Mammon. Mammon's eyes grew as large as plates before he fell to his knees, dead.

Behemoth made a pirouette with his sword and flashed it at Ronwe's throat.

"You had better not miss," Ronwe shouted as the blade flashed. His head spun several revolutions and landed by the base of the oak tree. His eyes widened, and he gasped his last words:

"These didn't work out worth a piss." His eyes and his mouth shut finally, forever.

Andras charged so quickly that I could hardly see him move. He locked Behemoth around the shoulders and began to push him backwards. They must be moving 50 miles per hour in reverse. One tree and then another was uprooted by Behemoth's back.

Then Behemoth flipped Andras around and began to push him backwards at the same speed. A trench was dug deeper and deeper from Andras' two resisting feet. Behemoth pushed him until the trench was about ten feet deep. They stopped against a giant tree with even larger roots. Behemoth grabbed a root and plunged into Andras' mouth. It exited the back of his head in a spray of blood and brains.

Behemoth hopped out of the trench, looked up, raised his hand, caught the spear that Astaroth had launched, twirled, and flung it back to its owner. Astaroth ducked, and the spear passed through Asmodeus' chest and buried into the tree behind him so quickly that Asmodeus turned to watch his own heart make one beat still attached to the spear. He fell limply, dead.

"Do you really want to challenge me, Astaroth?" Behemoth thundered.

"The usual Behemoth, no." Astaroth bellowed back. "But the Behemoth with a hole in him, maybe."

"Ask Ronwe, Urobach, Mammon, Asmodeus, and ole Andras their opinion on Behemoth with a hole in him, Astaroth," Behemoth labored the words. He looked like he was weakening. Astaroth could see that as well, yet he did not attack. He merely stared at Behemoth, contemplating his chances.

Nephilim stare at each other as if they are trying to read the other's thoughts. I was never able to find out if they actually might. I believe that at some level they could. Perhaps not the exact thoughts, but rather their intentions. A subtle sign in the eye, a quiver maybe. I don't know if this is the case, but the stares are so intense that my head began to hurt in just a few seconds, even from a side view.

"I think I can take you down, Behemoth," Astaroth said calmly.

"If you are able to wield your sword the way you can your jaws, you might," returned Behemoth even calmer.

Half of Astaroth's upper lib smiled, and then he nodded. He took a step forward and said,

"The Prince of Darkness is with you today, Behemoth. I think I'll join the others and go home."

"A wise decision, Astaroth," Behemoth retorted. "But the God of these little people is not with me, or you, or any of us." Behemoth took one step closer to Astaroth. His face became forlorn and he said:

"Ever since I was born bloody, I have felt that I didn't belong here. You have felt the same?" Astaroth dipped his head. "Why? We have everything we want." Behemoth glanced at me. "Except what these little ones have. Wives, families, love of their fellow man. We have none of these."

"How can you say that, Behemoth? We are the kings of the world. We rule them. We are invincible. Look at you and your Sheba." The words inevitably came out of Astaroth's mouth, mechanically, as if he were asking a question.

"We are not invincible. We kill each other easily enough, and we are not long for this world," said Behemoth

"Surely we won't kill each other until we are all gone, Behemoth."

"No. That feeling I can't rid myself of, tells me that their God is about to end us first."

"How can he do that? We can't be killed except by each other's hand."

"Can you swim?" Behemoth asked.

Astaroth stared perplexedly at Behemoth and shook his head. "You know Nephilim can't swim, Behemoth," he whispered to himself. Our heavy muscles don't float." Then he mumbled to himself and walked away staring at the ground emptily.

For the first time, the silly rumor I heard about the crazy men building a giant ark in the middle of nowhere made sense. I had better get to a scribe and tell this story soon. I will give it to the crazy men and their big boat. It does look rather cloudy.

PART 3

CHAPTER 1

Ike closed the book and gazed irresolutely at Harrison and Shannon. He didn't carry a demeanor of a man surprised by what he had just read. He placed the heavy book down and shuffled his way to the counter.

"Who wants coffee?" he asked cheerfully. He poured himself a cup of cold, black coffee, pausing for a moment, listening politely for an affirmative. Hearing nothing, he made his way to the door and turned on the lights.

"That was a hell of a story, wasn't it," he said, chuckling at the last couple of words. "I don't know about the copyright laws, but I'm gonna try to get this thing published." Again, he was chuckling as he said it, completely amused, but he was alone in his amusement.

"This is the only copy of this book, you know." Ike was pointing at the book, waiting for of any kind of words to be spoken, but his audience was not in a talkative mood. "Hollywood goes for this sort of thing. You know they like monsters." After the poor choice of the word "monster" drew only the uneasy silence, Ike decided to keep his mouth shut.

Harrison and Melissa were looking gravely at Clayton and Shannon, who looked like a couple who had just received a terminal diagnosis from their family doctor.

"You two going to be alright?" Coach Harrison asked as gently as he could muster. "Is there something we can do to help?" He thought to himself if this was the proper response, but he didn't want the awkward silence from them to continue. Ike's clumsy attempt at humor wasn't working.

Clayton lowered his head and put forth his hand toward his wife, who took it forlornly. The other three people in the room wanted to console them at this moment, as they could see the pain etched on the parents' expressions. Clumsy silence seemed the only answer for now.

If they had truly received a terminal diagnosis from their doctor, they would have known exactly how to respond. But what do you say to someone who just received the diagnosis that their son was a Nephilim? What is the proper response to that? One hour ago, they had never heard of a Nephilim, but now they had to comfort a couple who just got the news that their son was one of these Biblical monsters with a penchant for killing.

What's the correct way to say, "I'm sorry your son is the offspring of Satan?" Harrison was dumbfounded at his own thoughts. *A Nephilim is in our midst! What do I do now? What do I say? Who do I tell? Pinch me, Melissa, and wake me from this stupid-ass nightmare.* Unfortunately, his wife was having the same thoughts.

Ever since he first saw Gabe, he felt an unreal dreamy sensation in the presence of the child. In a strict clinical sense, he thought it was the way the brain protected itself from the absurd. But then again, he had never had to deal with the absurd for more than a second or two before. This was a permanent sensation: a dream from which you can't awaken.

It suddenly occurred to him that it was similar to getting *dinged* in football. That light-headed feeling caused by a slight concussion when two helmets collide. But those go away after a while. This sensation was hard to get out of your head. It lingered.

"What do we do now, Ike?" Clayton feebly asked, his head still down, afraid to make eye contact with anyone yet.

"I don't know, Clayton. I wish I did. I'd tell you." Ike was fumbling for words.

"What do we do, Clayton?" Shannon raised her head and waited for her husband to raise his also. "We can't sit here and feel sorry for ourselves for the rest of our lives."

"Why can't we!" Clayton shouted bitterly, with his head still down. "Why the hell can't we just stay right here and feel sorry for ourselves, huh?" Clayton's shouting tapered to a hysteric whisper. "I've got no idea what to do." His voice cracked as he tried to resist crying in front of the others. Men's mores.

"Do you believe all that shit, Ike? That book didn't read like a book that was written in those days." Clayton said, searching for a footing.

"No, it was translated and modernized, Clayton. This story was written in some strange language centuries ago. Somebody rewrote it and made it modern. Hell, it's just a translation. It could be completely a myth, like the stories I was told as a child." Ike replied. He caught himself doubting his own words because he now thought that this story was probably true.

"No, Ike, it's true," Shannon said, her voice trembling. She was shaking her head as her tone grew louder. "Our son is one of them. He has all the same characteristics of the… what were they, Nephilim?"

"Wouldn't the giant David fought—ah Goliath—wouldn't he have been supposed to be one of them? He didn't seem like one of those creatures, did he?" Clayton asked curiously.

"No, Goliath was just a tall dude. He was nothing like one of the Nephilim I just read to you," Ike replied. "Nobody knows what the Nephilim were really like."

"Nobody till now," Shannon said gravely.

"Oh, now, we don't know that any of that crap was true. It's probably some wild-ass story passed down and exaggerated more with each century." Clayton said, still searching for something positive to say.

"What about Gabe, Clayton!" Shannon exploded. "Weren't you listening? That is our son's people! He's just like them, for Christ's sake!" She began to sob. "He's going to continue to get bigger and stronger and smarter."

"And meaner," Clayton interrupted. "You forgot meaner!" Clayton lost control and was now somehow furious at Shannon for being negative. "What do you want me to do, Shannon?! Huh! What the hell do you want me to do?!" How the hell did he get here?!" Clayton turned toward Shannon as he spoke. "Would somebody please tell me how the hell he got here?!"

"Why are you looking at me like that, Clayton?" Shannon said defensively. "Why are you looking at me like that?" She got to her feet. "Do you actually believe that I had an affair with one of those fallen angel things that speaks in rhyme and shit? Do you think I might have noticed that? Don't you think I might have noticed?"

"Not necessarily," Melissa chimed in. "They were very clever and would have disguised themselves to blend in with the times. It looks like to me that you would have never known the difference."

Shannon turned toward Melissa with a hateful look on her face. Melissa shrank and then said sheepishly, "I didn't mean to imply that's what happened. I'm just saying, if they existed, you wouldn't know it." Melissa was embarrassed and wanted to find a hole to crawl into.

"Look, Shannon, we're not accusing you of being unfaithful," Harrison said, coming to the defense of his wife, "We just don't know what to think of all this. We don't think you had an affair."

"Well, I do," uttered Clayton. "There is no other explanation for it. We were having trouble getting pregnant. You can say what you want to about women, but you all think that a man that can't get a woman pregnant is not much of a man. So, you figured you would just go out and find yourself a real man."

After a pause and some very unnerving stares, Shannon said calmly, "Do you really suppose that, Clayton? Do you really think I have been unfaithful to you?"

"No, I don't really believe that," Clayton had an *ah shucks* air to his demeanor. "No, of course not."

Shannon went to Clayton and hugged him passionately. "I would never, ever do that to you, Clayton. Never. I love you with all my heart. I don't know how he got there." Shannon was desperate and showed it.

"Wait a minute," Ike interjected Ike, looking puzzled before resolving. "Never mind."

"What were you going to say?" Harrison asked curiously.

Ike chuckled for a second and grunted, "I was going to say, *how do we know that Clayton isn't one of them?* But it occurred to me that those guys were smart and clever." He looked like he could have slapped his own forehead.

"And you forgot good-looking, Ike." Clayton added sarcastically.

"Oh, you know what I mean, Clayton. I didn't mean any offense by it. My brain is damn near fried by all this, man. I don't know what

I'm saying right now. All I know is I'm on your side." Ike stuck his hand out, Clayton took it.

"I know you're confused, Ike, but how the hell you think I feel?"

"I think we're all confused right now," the Coach said.

"All I know is, we've got to come up with some kind of plan," Melissa added.

"We?" said Clayton timidly. "You guys don't have to get involved in this."

"We are already involved in this," the Coach declared.

"Amen," Ike resounded.

"I'll help any way I can," Melissa spoke softly.

CHAPTER 2

"So what do you suggest we do about Gabe," Clayton said while searching for sympathetic eyes.

"We do nothing right now," Ike spoke smoothly. "We don't need to alert him that we know about him."

"That would imply that he knows what he is," interjected Harrison.

"I think he knows what he is," Clayton said nervously. "My son is so brilliantly smart. He stays on the computer. He probably knows." Clayton paused confusedly. "My God, did you hear what I just said... my son. Is this thing we're talking about my son? Did one of those monsters come out of you, Shannon?" Clayton was tormented by his own thoughts.

"Before we can come up with a plan, there is one thing we need to know," chimed Melissa.

"What's that?" asked her husband.

"Well, how did that big-ass Nephilim get in her womb?" Melissa acted offended, as if he shouldn't have to ask. "If she didn't have sex with one of those angel-demon things, then what gives?"

"Why am I getting the feeling that you don't believe me?" Shannon felt Melissa was accusing her again.

"Look, I'm not accusing you of anything. I'm just saying that your husband is not any taller than I am, that's all." Melissa's tone betrayed her skepticism.

"Mind what you are saying, woman!" Harrison was clearly embarrassed.

"Mind what I'm saying," she shot back defiantly. "Since when do I have to mind what you say?"

"Now come on," Ike intervened. "We've got to work together, remember? What we don't need right now is bickering."

Melissa put her hand to her head like she had a headache. "I'm sorry, sugar. I'm sorry, Shannon." Melissa was trying to hold back tears. "I don't know what is wrong with me. I need to sit down before I faint." Harrison pulled a chair up to her, and she plopped down.

"She really has been feeling poorly lately," Harrison sounded apologetic, though he hoped nobody noticed.

"The weirdness of this has got my head spinning." Melissa was pressing her temples.

"I've done nothing but think about how this could happen for 12 years," Clayton said frustratedly. "This Nephilim explanation is the only one that makes sense. But how we could have a Nephilim for a son doesn't make any sense." Clayton sat in the chair next to Melissa and continued, "Over at the clinic, they told me that he was an alien of some sort; that his DNA was not completely human; that it was a genetic thing. I don't know what to believe."

"That could very well be it," Ike said as he stepped into the center of the group. "It could be possible that both you and Shannon are carriers of the Nephilim gene." Ike looked around, waiting to see if the others were following his logic. They looked receptive, so he continued. "Over the centuries, through some cosmic accident, humans got some of the recessive Nephilim gene in them."

"That actually makes sense to me," Coach Harrison said convincingly. "It has to be genetic. Like when two parents have brown eyes, and they manage to have a blue-eyed baby." He looked around for approval.

"That could be it, Clayton," Shannon said as she put her arm around her dejected husband. Clayton nodded, checking the others' expressionsS. They seemed to agree.

"I've already considered that," he said, "though not a Nephilim gene, of course. I've heard of the giants of the Bible, but I never knew what they were called. It does really make sense. Well, it makes about as much sense as anything else does." Everyone seemed to agree. Melissa shrugged her hands and nodded to make it unanimous.

"I don't understand something, though, Ike," Clayton said, still perplexed. "Why doesn't the Bible say more about these creatures than it does? It mentions a couple of passages, and that's it. Why?"

"The Bible doesn't say much about a lot of things that would blow our minds." Ike replied, entering teaching mode. "You have to remember that this was at a time when angels and demons patrolled the earth. The Bible makes a very big statement about these creatures.

"It says that God was so discouraged at man— and these Nephilim were considered men, that He decided to destroy the world and all that was in it. Do you think that if regular ole people were doing just regular ole sinning, God would have brought a worldwide flood on the earth?

"Think about it," Ike continued to teach, "If that were the case, He would need to destroy the world every century or so, right? What I'm saying is there is as much sinning now as there ever was. Regular people sin. They just do. They always have. But at the time of the Nephilim was different.

"These men, if you can call them men, brought sinning to a different level. They took over the world. God had to destroy them. That's the only way they could be defeated." Ike turned solemnly toward Clayton and Shannon and quieted his tone as he spoke:

"The Nephilim had one goal: to destroy mankind. And mankind had only one answer, to destroy the Nephilim. But they couldn't do it. And since they couldn't do it, they needed help. So God decided that since His creation couldn't take care of the Nephilim, He would end it all—man, Nephilim, everything.

'The Nephilim have one goal,' Ike turned his head away from the others and gazed out the window of his store. "To rule over and destroy man. It is in their nature. That's what they do. That's all they do. The Nephilim and man cannot coexist on this planet. The Nephilim must be destroyed."

'Are you suggesting what I think you're suggesting,' screeched Clayton.

'That's exactly what he's saying, Clayton,' Shannon spoke softly. 'I've known for a long time that my child didn't belong here. And you have too.' She looked up at Clayton, who was shaking his head in disbelief. "You knew this wasn't going to end well," she told him.

"No!" Clayton shouted.

"You knew how this was going to end!" Shannon shouted back. "Don't tell me you didn't know or feel it in your heart that we would someday have this conversation. Don't do this to me now Clayton."

Clayton cut his eyes around the room at the others. They seem to be looking at him curiously. He perceived that they wanted confirmation from him, waiting for him to make it unanimous, waiting for him to agree that the only answer for a bigger, smarter, stronger twelve-year-old is to kill him now, while it was possible.

"What the hell is wrong with you people!" Clayton bellowed as loudly as he could muster. "He is still our son, Shannon." Clayton was pleading. "How can you listen to what you are saying? There is no proof that he is going to be at war with the world. He has never killed anybody, or else we would know. Somebody would come up missing if he had killed them."

"Listen to what *you* are saying, Clayton," His wife was still speaking calmly. "*We would know because somebody would have come up missing. The only reason you believe he hasn't killed anybody yet is because nobody has come up missing —yet. You didn't say you don't think he is capable, or that he wouldn't.*"

"This is ridiculous. We can have him put in custody. In a facility somewhere." Clayton was sounding more desperate.

"A jail?" Said Harrison.

"Yeah, a jail or something. It beats the hell out of killing him! I can't believe I'm having this conversation with my own wife! Shannon, he's your own son, for God's sake." Clayton wiped the tears that were running down his cheek with the cuff of his shirt.

"That's right, Clayton. For God's sake, he is my son. And it is for the sake of God that he has to be destroyed." Shannon's voice became so low that the others had to strain their ears to hear. "He is no longer my son. He stopped being that years ago when I saw that he was not of this world, when I saw how cruel he could be. We have to do this, or someone else will."

"Then someone else will because I'm not going to have anything to do with this because—" Clayton stopped suddenly as something caught his attention: a dark shadow at the window. He looked up, saw nothing and dropped back down in his chair and starred at the floor.

Outside, Gabe had leaned against the building silently. Curiosity had caused him to follow his parents. Superhuman hearing had allowed him to perceive everything that was said. Tears trickled down his cheeks, and he muttered in a whimpering voice, "My God, am I one of them?" Disbelief flushed his face. "Oh No! No! I don't want to be one," he mumbled, looking dreadfully into space, lip quivering. The human in him forced him to formulate desperate plans. The Nephilim in him forced him to make terrifying ones.

CHAPTER 3

"What we're saying here, Clayton is it's not reasonable to think that we can keep him a secret much longer," Ike said in the most reasonable way he could. "I can't believe that somebody hadn't done something already. You have to admit, other than just a few gawkers and an occasional passerby, Gabe has been kept a pretty good secret.

"How much longer do you think that's going to keep happening. Huh? It's just a matter of time before word gets out and then what? The only reason that people haven't been crawling all over this place is because he's just another crazy-ass Indian tale, right? Nobody believes it right now, but that's going to change. You know it will."

"That's right," Harrison jumped in. "I told some buddies of mine back home about Gabe and they thought I was full of shit…I mean, they thought I was joking. I couldn't help but tell 'em. I had to tell people about it or go insane. It didn't matter; they thought I was insane anyway." Coach was chuckling a little at the end.

"I've told Mama and one of my cousins," admitted Melissa.

"And I've told people myself," Ike confessed. "Now think that about everybody in town. Hundreds of them have told people. They can't believe the whole town's crazy. People in authority will be coming to check this out. It's just a matter of when."

"What will you do then, Clayton?" asked Shannon harshly. "What about the reporters? The tabloids? The government? The doctors? That clinic over there has left us alone for now, but that's because we were going to sue them. He's getting bigger, and stronger and meaner too,

Clayton. You know it's true. What's going to happen when he starts to kill people, if he hasn't already?"

Clayton looked at Shannon with agony in his eyes. *What was his wife saying about their son?* "What do you mean, if he hasn't yet?"

"You know, that kid that came by the house with one of his friends from school. What was his name? Razz's friend."

"Yeah, that wasn't Razz's friend. It was some kid that he just met that day. Nobody knew who that kid was. We thought that Gypsy's dropped him off and came back and got him." Clayton paused and pondered for a moment. "What are you saying happened to that kid, Shannon?"

"I don't know what happened to that kid. Gabe was playing with him one day and he was gone the next. Have you never wondered about it?"

"No, I've never wondered about it because I never had a reason to wonder about it. Sure, Gabe is cruel, but he has never hurt anybody. That I know of."

"That you know of." Shannon shrugged her shoulders.

"Even if he hasn't killed anybody yet, Clayton," Ike saw his chance, "you know that he is going to. That's what he does. That's all his kind does. They kill, period. If not today, then tomorrow, if not here, then somewhere else, but he is going to kill. He can't help himself."

Clayton began to shake his head no. Ike came over and put his hands on Clayton's shoulders and twisted his head around so Clayton had to face him.

"Look at me, Clayton, and understand this. He is not your son. He is some kind of malfunction of nature. He's not supposed to be here. Just like those dinosaurs in that movie *Jurassic Park* were never supposed to be here with us humans. A Nephilim is not supposed to be here with us now.

"I know you don't want to hear this, but you've been dealt a really shitty hand here, brother. I don't like this any better than you do, but it's up to you to do something about this." Ike let go of Clayton's shoulders. They both stood in silence for a moment. The only movement was Clayton occasionally wiping away streaming tears.

"I'll help you, brother." Ike continued, "I'll help you with this."

"With what, Ike?" Clayton sniffled. "With killing my son? Why are you so G-D gung-ho with killing him?"

"What do you want to do, Clayton?" Harrison couldn't restrain himself. "What do you want to do? Tell me and I'll help you with it. I don't feel good about this killing mess myself." He paused a minute and continued, "Maybe we can trap him somehow and have him put somewhere safe." Harrison was feeling pretty good about his idea and was looking for approval.

"Yes, that's the best idea." Clayton finally heard something he liked. "We will just ask Gabe to give himself up to some research facility or clinic somewhere and he'll be safe and can't hurt anybody."

"Will he just give himself up like that?" Ike sounded skeptical of this idea. "I don't want to have to kill either, believe me. He has a distinct advantage when it comes to combat, but will he just come willingly. You know how smart he is."

"Yeah, I think he will." Clayton sounded confident and was starting to see a way out of his predicament. "I think I can just explain to him it is for his own good, and he will go along with it. He's smart and reasonable and I…"

CRASH!

The glass shattered in the front window of the store. Glass was ricocheted off the counter and floor. The startled group looked up in horror at the hulking Gabe standing before them. He looked menacing with his bulging arms spread away from each side. He was breathing hard, and his teeth were clenched in tightly muscled jaws.

"Gabe, what are you doing here, son?" Clayton was trying to act calm. "We were just talking about you. We have some good news, son."

Gabe grabbed the cash register from the counter and flung it toward Clayton. The electrical wires sparked as they were uprooted, and pieces went in a hundred different directions as it shattered against the floor.

"I've heard what you have planned for me, he said smugly. "I've also heard what I am. I've already figured out that I was a Nephilim, but until I listened to your rather assuming reading, Ike, I had no idea what I know really as. Now I know."

"You've also heard what we have planned for you too, Gabe," said Coach Harrison hopefully. "Why don't you just calm down and come with us? We will take good care of you and nobody gets hurt, right."

"He's right, son," Clayton continued his point, "Just come with us. We'll go home for now, and in the morning, we'll think of the best thing for you. I love you, son, and I don't want to see anything happen to you."

Gabe turned his eyes toward his mother. He stared blankly at her.

"What about you, dear old mom? I hadn't heard any word from you yet, at least while I'm standing here. But you said plenty just a few minutes ago." He started slowly walking toward Shannon. She didn't move at first, then she started toward her son in the same slow, mechanical way as Gabe was at her. She stopped about three feet in front of him, looking almost straight up at her son.

"Yes, I think that would be the best thing for you, Gabriel." She smiled when she said his name.

"You haven't called me Gabriel for a long time," he said, smiling back at his mom. Then he bent over and placed his hands on his knees. His face was within a foot or so of his mother. He still wore a smile when he whispered:

"By the way, I hate this G—D name. That damn Gabriel was nothing but a fag angel anyway. What kind of pussy goes around blowing a trumpet? Since I come from a long line of angels, I should know." The smile evaporated from both their faces. A maniacal scowl came across Gabe's face. Fear came across his mother's.

"I heard what you said," he continued, spitting out his words bitterly. "That I'm no longer your son. Hell, you were as anxious to kill me as that dried-up piece of Indian shit over there." Gabe cut his sinister eyes toward Ike and then back to his mom.

"What am I supposed to do?" Shannon said with the same bitterness. "I'm not even supposed to be alive, right. Don't you things kill your mothers while they're giving birth to you?" Shannon was within a couple of inches of Gabe's face.

Gabe smiled at her words as if they amused him.

"You're right," he said and then he gently kissed her on the check. He brought his face closer to hers. He looked solemnly into his mother's eyes, and she into his, and then he whispered softly once again into her ear,

"A problem that can be easily rectified." Then he snatched up Shannon and flung her ragged body at Ike. They both slammed into the wall with a thunderous crash. Lanterns, dishes, stuffed animals, toys and other items crashed to the floor. A wind-up monkey clanged a pair of cymbals repeatedly and made monkey sounds, which for the moment, was the only sound in the store.

CHAPTER 4

Gabe dashed through the broken window and stopped, frozen in his tracks, and deliberately turned to look back at the humans. Clayton and Harrison hurried to Shannon and Ike, who were sprawled unconscious on the floor. They frantically threw store merchandise this way and that as they uncover the bodies. Clayton cradled his wife's head in his arms and screamed," Shannon!". No response.

Clayton cut his watery eyes toward his son, who was still standing like a 10-foot statue, his eyes focused on his lifeless mother. Then he made eye contact with his pitifully weeping father. Clayton couldn't tell what was on Gabe's mind at that moment, because his son showed no emotion. He neither smiled nor frowned, but peered through the gloom of the night. Gabe looked down at the ground for a moment, took one step back toward the store, put his hand forward, reaching toward them, but suddenly changed his mind and darted off into the night with a swish.

"Is she alive?" shrieked Harrison.

"Yes, she's breathing," Clayton stammered. "I don't see any blood or anything broken. See about Ike."

Harrison jumped over a pile of rubble to the moaning Ike, who was trying to sit up. Meanwhile, Melissa was dialing 911 on her cell phone.

"Not yet, Melissa." Clayton pleaded. "Don't call the police yet. Give me a chance to think of something."

"I'm calling 911 for an ambulance, Clayton," Melissa shouted in response.

Clayton nodded his head feebly.

"We have to get the police involved, Clayton," Harrison said, making no attempt to be polite. "He's out there, and he knows who he is, and what he is, and people are going to get hurt." Harrison shook the despondent Clayton by the shoulder. "There's a chance they can still get him to surrender and take him away safely," Harrison reassured him.

Clayton began to shake his head and said violently, "He tried to kill his mother. They are going to have to kill him." Then he cradled his unconscious wife in his trembling hands and sobbed uncontrollably.

"If they can. If they can," said Harrison while he was trying to help Ike stand.

A Helpmein Police Department car screeched to a halt. One officer stood at the broken glass front, and another proceeded to the four shaken people and the one badly hurt. Seconds later, the ambulance arrived. The medical attendants scurried about with a wheeled stretcher and started administering to the still-unconscious Shannon.

Ike was now walking around, rubbing the back of his neck. "Is he all right?" one of the attendants shouted, nodding toward Ike.

"I'm alright." mumbled Ike. "Just a mild case of whiplash, I think."

In a few seconds, they had Shannon's head strapped with tape to the gurney and wheeled her to the ambulance.

"I don't know what to do," Clayton said, confused. "Do I stay here and try to save my son's life, or do I go with my wife to the hospital?" Clayton was reduced to a sobbing, blithering shell of a man.

"Go with your with wife, damnit!" an angry and irritated Ike screamed at Clayton. "We'll take care of Gabe," he added, much calmer.

"We will?" Harrison eyed Ike.

Ike waited for Clayton to be out of earshot and then whispered to the Coach, "Hell no. The police can handle this. I'm going home to soak my bruised old ass in a tub of hot water. I'm beat."

Police officer Jason Myers walked up to Harrison and asked what had happened.

"You know that giant kid that goes to school here, don't you?"

"Yeah, I've seen him a time or two. He's got some kind of growth hormone problem. Did he do this?" The policeman took out his pad and started writing.

"Name."

"Gabriel Rinehart."

"Age."

"Twelve, I think." Ike agreed with Harrison with a nod.

"Description."

"Nine or ten feet, 500 to 600 lbs. Looks like a Nephilim."

"What was he wearing?"

"Harrison stammered a minute, "I think the first person you see that's 10 feet 600 would be him."

"Ok, we'll go pick him up," the officer said with a flip of his pad.

"Yeah, good luck with that," Harrison said mockingly.

The police officer slightly tugged the brim of his hat, nodded and headed back outside.

"What do you think the police will do about Gabe?" asked the stressed Coach, addressing Ike.

"How do you think this is going to end?" Ike peered up at Harrison coyly.

"I think they're going to have their hands full with that dude."

"Damn right. And how to you think they'll finally get him?"

"With bullets."

"Damn right. Now get your wife and go home," said Ike. Then he stopped, thought for a second, and said, "You got a gun?"

"Yeah, why?"

"I'd keep my door locked and set up with that gun, just in case the police can't take him."

Harrison laughed out loud. "Do you really think that a locked door is going to stop him?"

"I just hope that bullets stop him." Ike looked serious about what he had just said, or at least Harrison took it that way.

CHAPTER 5

Gabriel Rinehart, a newly unleashed Nephilim warrior, was on the loose. He was roaming somewhere in the Helpmein, South Dakota night. He had just become self-aware of his heritage, and now his destiny. Though he was only twelve years old, he was nothing that mere mortal men had ever seen or encountered —not for a least four thousand years, that is. The encounters that occurred four thousand years ago didn't go well for the mere men.

But mere men have evolved since that time. They have developed technology that has given them great advantages over their enemies. Indeed, a man is at the very top of the food chain and has been so since the beginning —except for a few hundred years during the time when the Nephilim roamed the earth. It took God himself, with a harsh solution, to solve that problem…But that was then…

Helpmein police officer Myers cleared his throat. "All-points bulletin. All-points bulletin. Be advised and on the lookout for a white male, twelve years of age, approximately 10 feet tall, and approximately 600 pounds. No distinguishing marks. Looks like a Nephilim. Over."

"What the hell is a Nephilim?" his partner, Officer J.B. Gentry, asked as he was listened to Myers, who spat the ridiculous words into the radio mic.

"I don't know, but that's what he said."

"I know that's what he said, but I don't know what that is. You might want to change that part."

"I thought it might have something to do with his condition. Maybe that's the medical term for giant or something."

"Good point."

In a South Dakota state trooper car, the driving officer, David Fox, looked at his partner, Kenneth Foster, who looked back at him. They both broke out in laughter.

It can be a lonely job being a South Dakota state trooper. Miles and miles of road with little traffic to patrol —especially at night —makes the nights seem even longer and lonelier. It was not an altogether unnatural event for two patrol cars to pull off the curb of a lonesome stretch of unfrequented highway and shoot the breeze for hours. A hilarious prank call like this gave them a perfect excuse to make a visit and waste some time. Any action, even a prank would help pass the time.

"We're only a few miles away. We can stop by the station and see who's behind this call?"

"Yeah, let's do it. We haven't been by there in a while. Obviously, they want some company."

In the County Sheriff's patrol car, four miles from Helpmein, Sheriff Billy Upton was not amused by what he just heard on his official police radio. Sheriff Upton was sixty years old, a thirty-two-year veteran of law enforcement. He was a sniper in Vietnam and became a bounty hunter upon his return from the war. Upton, a big, burly, tough old bustard with a grizzled voice, was not a man to be trifled with.

He enjoyed a good practical joke as much as the next guy, but not on an APB over an official police frequency communique. He had no tolerance for such nonsense. If discipline was so vexing in the Helpmein office, he would just have to stop in and dole out a small sampling. *Heads are going to roll,* he thought.

"Where do we begin to hunt for this kid?" inquired officer Gentry.

"Somewhere around here," answered Myers. "He couldn't have gotten far from here. Where would he go? He's some kind of giant, but he's still just a kid. He won't get far. Somebody will see him wandering about, or he will probably just go home."

"Why did you put out that APB?"

"I had to. He likely to have killed two people. That woman may be dead for all we know right now. I had to. This is a serious charge, but I don't think he is really a danger. He probably didn't mean to hurt anybody. It was just an accident. He'll go home if we don't find him first.

"I hope you're right," added Gentry. "I saw him before. Man, I'd hate to try to do something with him," he admitted.

"Yeah, he's a big boy, all right, but he won't be much trouble for us, I don't think. After all, he's just a kid, for Christ's sake." Myers didn't sound too worried about this Nephilim, whatever that was.

"Have you seen this guy before, I mean up close?" Gentry asked with a scowl.

"Yes, I mean, I've seen him. Everybody's seen him."

"No, I mean have you ever taken a good look at this guy."

Myers shrugged.

Gentry took the cue. "He's more than just a twelve-year-old big kid. He's got muscles in places I don't even have places. And the way he moves around—he moves quick, too quick for his size. I ain't never seen anything like this guy."

"What are you babbling about?" Myers was already growing weary of Gentry because he had heard about this kid so many times and was, frankly, tired of it. "I've heard all those bullshit stories too. How high he can jump, and how strong he is and all that crap. J.B., listen to me, he…is…just…a…big…kid…period." BANG!

The "d" sound hadn't made it all the way out of Myer's mouth when the steel rebar flashed between them. It passed through the front seat, the back seat, and into the trunk. The trunk flung open and bounced once or twice against the latch. All of it happened in less than a second.

"What the hell was that!" screamed Myers, staring wildly at the perfectly round one-inch hole in his windshield.

"Somebody just shot at us! Pull over!" Gentry was already hunkered down in the floorboard.

"No, I saw something sparkle between us. Didn't you see it?" Myers was pulling the patrol car to the curb.

"I thought I saw something flicker. I thought it might have been the hot bullet maybe."

"You don't see a bullet. This was something else." Myers was so shaken he still had both hands in a death grip on the steering wheel.

"Somebody shot something at us, that's for sure." Gentry's attention was momentarily fixed upon the shaking hands of his partner and the steering wheel he had a death grip on.

"Who?" quivered Myers. "Who would try to kill us with some sort of cannon? Or what the hell was shot at us?"

"Why don't we pedal our asses back to the office and regroup." Gentry was shuddering a little himself.

"Way ahead of you, buddy." Myers was slinging the gravel from the shoulder of the highway.

"Hello." Sheriff Upton's voice reverberated through the Helpmein Police Department office. Beth Simpson made her way to the front desk. She was the dispatch operator, the clerk, and the secretary. One wears many hats in a small-town police department.

"May I help you, Sheriff Upton," she said as she approached.

"Where is everybody," he growled.

"There are only two officers on duty tonight, and they went on a call. An assault call," she answered him with equal verve.

"Who the hell called in that stupid APB?" He said with even more of a growl.

"That wasn't a stupid call," she said, feeling a little defensive. "The perp was our resident giant kid. You've probably heard of him."

"Yeah, I've heard of him and I don't believe a word of it. In fact, this place has always been a little weird to me. You've always been a strange place with that fancy-ass clinic and that billion-dollar school built for a bunch of dumbass Indians. And this stupid-ass name, Help-me-in—what kind of name is that?

"And now you've got a giant kid. I'll tell you one thing," now he had got himself worked up into a frenzy, "If I find the dumbass that made that APB, I'll kick his ass." The sheriff whirled and headed for the door but stopped to make one last declaration: "I'll even find that supposed giant and spank his ass too while I'm at it. Probably the only spanking he's ever had in his whole life anyway…" The last word was growled after the door shut behind him.

Troopers Fox and Foster were about one mile from the Helpmein Police station. Fox had left his car at the patrol station and was riding with his friend just to pass the time. Not an uncommon practice for that area.

They were having an enjoyable conversation about this giant kid who was rumored to inhabit the community. Almost everybody in the state of South Dakota and North Dakota for that matter—had heard the rumors. But rumors of spirits, goblins, UFO's and strange goings-on were pervasive in that state.

One more tale about giants was to be expected. Bigfoot was seen once or twice a week somewhere around there killing chickens, emptying garbage cans, carrying off wayward husbands all night and getting them drunk, and just generally causing all kinds of mischief. In fact, Bigfoot was blamed for everything that was generally unexplainable.

Suffice it to say, rumors of giants rolled off the minds of most people the way a drop of water rolls off a duck's back. But still, it was fun to talk about, and when the APB came in, it made the trip up to Helpmein even more fun to talk about.

"It's the next left, isn't it?" Fox wasn't sure how to get to the station.

"I've never been to the station up here," admitted Foster when something flashed across the road, making a large shadow in the glow of the headlights.

CHAPTER 6

"What was that, a moose?" an unsure Foster shouted.

"No, too big for a moose, and besides that, it moved way too quickly. It had to be a car or truck." Fox replied, though he didn't sound very convincing.

"We would have heard it, and it would have crashed," countered Foster

"I don't know. Let's go back." Fox said as he stopped to turn his patrol car around.

They drove slowly to the spot where they both thought the thing had darted across the road.

"Shine the spotlight around and see if you see anything, Ken," Fox anxiously suggested.

Officer Foster flipped on the powerful spotlight, a standard piece of equipment in every South Dakota patrol car, and pointed its bright beam in sporadic maneuvers alone the embankment.

Nothing.

"Shine it on the other side if you want to," said Fox, convinced that whatever it was, it was probably gone by now.

The light beam slowly made its way across the top of the car with each twist of trooper Foster's wrist until it lit upon the middle of Gabe's stomach, where he was now standing beside the patrol car.

The startled Foster methodically lifted the beam up the Nephilim's body—to the chest, to the neck, and finally to the menacing face of Gabriel Rinehart. The bright beam caused Gabe to raise a hand to shade his eyes. Foster shut the light off, and he and Fox gawked in awe at the giant, who resembled a monster from a movie poster.

"Hello," Fox squeaked.

"My God, David," Foster yelled, "It's true. He's real."

"Son, I'm afraid I'm going to have to put you under arrest," said Fox in a voice that resembled Mickey Mouse's. "Would you please stay still while I get out of the car?" Fox didn't get out of the car, but remained seated, unable to move or take his eyes off Gabe. The two patrolmen scrunched closer together, resembling frightened schoolgirls watching a late—night scary movie. Gabe half-expected them to hold hands.

"No," Gabe answered.

"No what?" Fox mumbled.

"No, I won't stand still."

"Why won't you?"

"Because I can't do *this* if I don't move."

Gabe bent down, put his hands under the car and easily raised it up on two wheels. He peered the driver's window at the two patrolmen, who were piled one on top of each other against the passenger door. He took one of his fists, bumped the window and shattered the glass, and said:

"I believe you can now appreciate the gravity of this situation."

"Don't do it son. It may kill us if we roll down the embankment." Fox pleaded.

"Unlikely, both of you are against one side. If you brace yourself properly, only minor bruising will occur. Of course," he said as he raised the car up and over, "I could be wrong."

The patrol car flipped three revolutions and came to rest on all four wheels. Gabe was right. Both men were battered, bruised, and dazed but alive, and thankful for it. Neither felt like exiting the car, instead, they fumbled about trying to find the radio handle. The horn, of course, was stuck on "honk", blaring through the neighborhood like a tornado siren. Residents spilled out of their homes, and clamored sleepily investigating the commotion.

In a few moments, Sheriff Upton pulled alongside the embankment. Fox and Foster had crawled out the broken window and were making their way up the bank when Upton barked, "What happened to you?"

"A giant flipped us down the embankment," Foster panted as he clawed his way to the top of the highway shoulder.

Sheriff Upton was not amused. He planted his fists on his hips, and a scowl darkened his face. Foster reached down to give his partner a hand with the last few steps. Both were out of breath and still visibly shaken. Fox's knees quivered— a sensation he hadn't experienced since he was a boy.

"You guys want to tell me what happened here?" Upton growled.

"I told you —a giant flipped us over," Foster repeated.

"Is everybody around this shithole crazy?" Upton's voice now dripped with sarcasm.

"He told you, damn it, what happened!" Fox, who hated Upton's guts, exploded.

"I ought to shoot both you drunk bastards. You drove your damn car off the road, and now you make up this crock. A giant did it? Really? I ought to run both of you in." Upton's disgust now mixed with sarcasm.

"We told you, you crazy old bastard, what happened!" Fox shouted, stepping into the crusty sheriff's face. The crowd of residents stopped murmuring and turned to watch what looked like an impending fight between a county and a state officer.

"Yeah," laughed the sheriff. "I'll just ride around and find this car-flipping giant myself. I'll bet he's something—woo-wee! Why, I'll bet he's jolly and green. Oh, wait, I forgot!" Upton mimicked a little girl's voice. "He probably climbed back up his beanstalk. You guys are pathetic." Sheriff Upton walked back to his patrol car in disgust.

"When you find him, be sure to tell him to get his ass back up that beanstalk, you pompous asshole." Fox shouted as Upton sped away. "I hope he finds him," Fox said to Foster in a much calmer tone. "I hope he finds him and gets his ass kicked."

"If he finds him," added Foster, "he's going to get his ass kicked—if not killed."

"I don't really give a shit," was Fox's summation.

"I hope backup gets here soon. It's going to be a long night," Foster's sighed.

Sherriff Upton was still seething with anger. He was driving with anger too. Perhaps that's why, when he saw the bull elk running a half mile or so ahead of him on the stretch of Co Rd 41, he failed to slow down. Rogue bull elk are common sights running alongside the shoulder of highways in this part of the state. Indeed, more elk are killed by vehicles than are shot by hunters.

They are also the third leading cause of vehicular deaths for humans in the state. Some years, they even overtake drunk drivers. Distracted driving is still number one, and that's exactly what Sheriff Billy (Wild Bill to some) Upton was guilty of when he realized he was getting dangerously close to the galloping elk. He was within a hundred yards or so when he lifted his foot from the accelerator.

That's a funny-looking elk, he thought. *It looks kinda like a man.* He turned his defroster on high and speed up to get a closer look. *It is a man. Can't be, I'm doing 40. Well, I'll be damned! Am I seeing this right? He is a giant of some sort. I don't give a damn. He's coming with me.*

The sheriff pulled alongside Gabe, who was at pretty good canter. Upon noticing that the police car was staying the same pace, Gabe darted to the middle line of the highway. The stupefie, but still angry sheriff pulled beside Gabe and rolled down his window.

"Pull over, boy. Pull over now," Upton screamed in his raspy voice.

Gabe raised his 14-inch-long middle finger and flipped the bird.

Upton attempted to get even closer, but Gabe sped up. Then Upton followed suit. Then Gabe accelerated some more, and so did the angry sheriff. Finally, Gabe floored it in a dead sprint.

Sheriff Upton looked down at the speedometer when he finally got beside Gabe: *70 mph!* He pulled his revolver from its holster, and pointed it out the window, and took aim.

Gabe looked over his shoulder and swerved alongside the window, one foot from the revolver. The wind made a whistling sound as it whizzed around the sights on the barrel. Gabe saw the tendon on the sheriff's forefinger tighten as he flashed his right arm into the window and snatched the bulky sheriff through it.

Gabe saw the sparks in the side mirror of the driverless car as the revolver bounced along the highway behind him. The car veered to the shoulder as he raised the screaming, bulbous sheriff to his shoulder. He maintained 70 miles per hour just long enough to stay ahead of the debris from the crashing car.

Then he slowed down to about 50, because he had to balance Upton in a sitting position on his shoulder with one hand. Not an easy proposition when the rider weighs 250 pounds and is squirming and crying like a baby.

"You've given me the perfect opportunity to actually demonstrate an axiom the native kids say whenever they gather around the pool at school," Gabe said to Upton, "when the irresistible urge for tomfoolery overcomes them, and they push each other in with the following precursor." Gabe cut his eyes up to the squalling sheriff to see if he was following.

"What the hell are you saying?" Gabe thought that's what he said. It was hard to tell between sobs and the whistling wind.

"Can shit float?"

And with that, Gabe made a hop, and pushed with his right arm, and launched the screaming, crying, cursing sheriff into the night and in the direction of a pond that he could make out in the field. The screaming and cursing stopped when he heard the tremendous splash.

I'm assuming shit can float, Gabe thought as he slowed down to a comfortable 40 mph.

CHAPTER 7

Officers Gentry and Myers eased into their headquarters' parking lot. They felt ashamed to be taking solace inside their own fortress instead of on the streets trying to apprehend the person or persons who just tried to murder them. Bravery is for the heroes on TV; they were just common folk with families. No, they agreed, it was better to go inside and call for help. The department employed five other officers. It was time to call in everybody. Everybody!

The front door opened with the same familiar swish it always did, except that a piece of the metal door jamb fell to the floor. Looking up, a huge dent was impressed into the metal jamb that crossed the top, like someone had thrown a bowling ball at it.

"Hello," hollered Myers, patiently waiting for Beth Simpson to say, *"Yeah,"* like she always did.

No answer.

"Beth, you back there?"

Nothing. Dead silent.

Both officers pulled their pistols from their black leather holsters, and their trembling hands held them tightly. Nothing appeared out of the ordinary. The florescent lights were just as bright. The computers were making their slight computer hum. The desks were in place, the chairs in place, papers where they were supposed to be. But no Beth. *Where was she?*

"Something's wrong here," whispered Gentry.

"Shh," Myers put his finger to his lips.

"If somebody's in here, they know we're here," said Gentry, sarcastically and little miffed at the hateful way his partner angrily shushed him.

"Somebody's in here and has done something with Beth."

"How do you know?" This time, Myers was really pissed at his dense partner.

"Where the hell is she? What happened to the door?" Gentry said loudly, not caring anymore if the perp heard him or not.

"Let's search the place," Myers continued to whisper.

"I got a better idea," whispered Gentry back.

"What's that?" said Myers, turning around in a circle, carefully and patiently waiting for a good idea.

"Let's run like hell," suggested Gentry.

A slight giggle sound came from the backroom — or they thought it was a giggle. They weren't sure, but they both heard something.

The two scared policeman looked longingly at one another. One encouraging word from either and they would have bolted for the door. But then, there was Beth? She could be in real trouble, hurt bad, or worse. They couldn't abandon her. Still, bravery looks good on TV; in real life, not so much. Nevertheless, they were hired to serve and protect, and though cowardly they may be, they had a job to do.

Myers pointed with his pistol toward the back and motioned Gentry to follow him. Funny, they never noticed how deathly quiet the office was until right now. The bottoms of their black, corrugated-soled shoes made a squeaking sound with each step. The squeaks seemed to get louder and louder with each nervous step, which agitated them both.

Both men's hands were shaking terribly as they were halfway down the hall that led to the backroom. The untimely thought of *Barney Fife* popped into Gentry's head as their hands seemed to be shaking in unison. In a morbid sense, he found this briefly humorous, and a slight smile appeared on his lips and then just as quickly disappeared.

Two more steps and it would be on. The missile- launching maniac would soon have his chance again. Maybe this time they wouldn't be so lucky. Their hearts were racing, palms sweaty, hands shaking, knees knocking…BANG!

The bathroom door flew open. It was only due to great alacrity, fueled by their heart-pumping, adrenaline-rich blood, that the two officers were able to avoid being plastered in the face. Out stepped Beth Simpson.

"Whew! Whatever you do, don't go in there. Man, those jalapeño peppers in that guacamole dip have torn my stomach up." Beth was playfully waving her hands to dissipate the imaginary stink.

Then she focused on Myers and Gentry with the barrels of their guns fearfully pointing at her. She threw her hands up and backed against the wall. The shaky pistols were still pointing at her, and the eyes of her co-workers were wild with fear.

"O.K., if you want to smell my shit that bad, knock yourself out." A nervous smile twitched across her lips.

Gentry and Myers exhaled a relieved sigh and dropped their revolvers to their sides. All three people began to laugh…Then a sudden shadow appeared behind them, and they whirled into the stomach of Gabe the Nephilim. A collective gasp of horror gulped down their throats.

Standing before them was the majestic figure of a man-monster… They stared straight up into the placid face and glaring eyes of Gabriel Rinehart. The two petrified officers raised their pistols quickly. Gabe seized hold simultaneously of the guns, one in each hand, and in a flicker used his thumbs to bend the barrels backward. Then, in slow motion, he removed his hands from the officers' trembling pistols.

Gentry and Myers scanned down and saw the barrels of their own guns pointing straight back at them. Beth Simpson shrieked and clasped her hand over her mouth.

"Officer Gentry, your pulse is 190," Gabe said with fake concern. "I can hear your heart pounding against your chest. You need to relax, take deep breaths. We wouldn't want you to die before I get the chance to kill you."

Both officers dropped their useless guns to the floor and ran for it. Gabe reached out and grabbed each officer on the shoulder and held tight.

"Do you find the irony as sweet as I?" Gabe mused whimsically as Gentry and Myers were running in place and going nowhere. They both stopped moving their feet and looked back gloomily at Gabe.

Gentry quivered, "What's the irony?"

"I always heard that it was the law that had the long arm." Gabe laughed loudly and abruptly stopped, and then an intimidating frown came over his face.

"Look, son, we have nothing against you," Gentry was trying to pathetically bargain for his life. "Why don't you give yourself up and we'll forget the whole thing? Why, busting a glass window ain't nothing. You won't get nothing but a slap on the wrist for that. Why foot, I've done a lot worse things than that when I was boy."

Myers nodded his head in agreement with his partner and began to laugh like a lunatic. Then they both laughed like a lunatics.

Gabe began to join them with a mock lunatic laugh. The men felt better. They might have defused the situation, they began to think. *We might get by with this and live.* Gabe continued to laugh sarcastically and said dryly:

"The only difference is you are not a Nephilim." and he laughed louder, and they laughed quieter until the laughter stopped.

"What's a Nephilim?" Myers asked humbly. "We were wondering what that was? Wouldn't we, JB?" Gentry nodded, and they both smiled meekly.

"Do you really want to know?" Gabe asked the two officers with earnestness, like they had struck a nerve of sincerity with him. "I'll show you."

He took hold of both men by the front of their shirts with his massive hands, lifted them to his shoulders, and pressed them up to the 12-foot ceiling. Their backs were tight against the sheetrock. Gabe's arms were not fully extended. His elbows had a good 25 degrees of angle left in them.

He braced himself and began to press Gentry and Myers against the ceiling tighter and tighter. The men began to moan and shriek in pain. The timbers on the rafters began to creak.

Beth Simpson, who had been too frightened to move, sensed what was about to happen to her two partners and bravely latched around Gabe's arm. Her feet were dangling a foot off the floor, and she began to scream, "Don't do it! Don't do it!"

Gabe looked at the frantic woman dangling from his right arm and frowned at her. Then a faint smile briefly showed.

"You have guts, lady," he grunted to her. "You certainly have more than these two gently used to have." He took in a deep breath and was about to make his final thrust upward and end officers Gentry and Myers but held his position.

He looked up at the two screeching men he had pressed tight against the ceiling, and then at the screaming woman dangling from his arm. Then he looked over at a window and caught his own reflection in its mirrored effect. He stared at himself, the men, the woman.

Suddenly, his throat began to contort, like he had a baseball travelling upward, trying to escape this mouth. It was like the unusual way a rooster clears his throat before he crows for the first time in the wee hours of morning light. He seemed to have no control over his mouth. He hacked a cough and bellowed his first Nephilim War yell—a yell so loud that all the windows in the room shattered outward like a bomb had exploded inside the police station.

CHAPTER 8

"Gabe! Stop! Don't do it, son," said Coach Harrison, standing at the police station's front door. Ike stood beside him with his .306 rifle pointed at Gabe's head. "You don't want to do that," the Coach continued in a calm voice.

"But I do, I really do," retorted Gabe, while snarling at Ike.

"We can't let you do this, Gabe. You know that," barked Ike.

"You mean you'd put a bullet in my brain and end me, Ike?"

"To save lives? Yes, of course." Ike tensed his finger, applying more pressure on the trigger.

"To save lives," quipped Gabe, "I think you'd want to kill me even if you only heard I illegally removed one of those mattress tags, Ike."

"Not true. I don't want to kill you, period."

"Didn't sound like it a few minutes ago." Gabe's arms became to quiver from the strain of holding up two men and a woman. "Would you please let go of me?" Gabe said, annoyed at Beth, who still dangled around his arm. "Do you really think that with a man with a high-powered rifle pointed at my head, you're the one preventing me from crushing these two men?" Beth dropped to the floor and backed away.

"If you put those two men down and give yourself up, I'll put the rifle down. I could have already drilled you, Gabe, if I wanted to."

"It's the only way, Gabe," added the Coach sternly.

Gabe slowly lowered the two depleted officers from his shoulders and gently set them on the floor. They both bent over, clutching their stomachs where Gabe's palms had pressed, but they weren't seriously hurt. Gabe raised his hands in surrender.

"Lock him up, JB," Ike said.

"Follow me," groaned Gentry, holding his bruised abdomen. Both officers and Beth were having trouble hearing, as their eardrums still ached from Gabe's glass-shattering war yell.

Gabe followed him. Ike and Harrison trailed behind, Ike's rifle still timidly pointed at Gabe's head. Gentry opened the creaking cell door. Gabe ducked down, stepped inside, and heard the cell latch slam shut. The distinctive *locking* sound reverberated inside the cell. Gabe didn't turn around but kept his back to the four men. Staring solemnly out the barred window near the ceiling, he said softly:

"My blood is calling me to fight… My first thought that I can recall ever having was that I had enemies about me. My first feeling I can remember was loneliness. Where were my people? I felt this from the beginning."

After a pause, he continued, "Are you familiar with the common cuckoo? The female lays her eggs in other birds' nests— like the reed warbler's or willow warbler's nests, for example. The mother warbler raises the cuckoo with her own chicks. Apparently, she's too stupid to know the difference, even though the cuckoo chick is three times the size a warbler's." He chuckled and tapped his chest.

"You know what's really cool, though," he said, turning around to stare stolidly at his quieted audience. "When the Cuckoo is about a week old, it begins to push the tiny warbler chicks out of the nest one by one to their deaths, until it's the only one remaining. The heedless parents continue to feed the giant, apparently clueless that this is not their own…I know how that cuckoo feels." He turned back toward the window.

"You'll never know how irksome it is to be fostered around beings inferior to yourself. You're surrounded by weakness and ignorance, which only pushes me to become smarter and wiser—like how an irritant goes into an oyster and comes out a pearl.

"I long to be with my kind, to be challenged, to become my best. What have I accomplished playing your sports?" He cocked his head over his shoulder and glanced at his dumfounded audience. "It would be like you defeating a ferocious colony of ants." He turned his head to the window again.

"That's it," he said, his voice louder as if he'd an *eureka* moment. "That's the analogy I've been searching for. Tell me, what would you do if you suddenly found yourself a member of an ant farm? Would you gloat over the fact that you're their superior? Or would you go mad, knowing that you can never escape their world and must forever acquiesce to a lower denominator?" Gabe sighed.

"There's only one thing wrong with your analogy, Gabe," said Ike shrewdly. "I don't believe a colony of ants could capture me and hold me in a cell." Ike was irritated at Gabe's boorishness. "We're more than ants, Gabe. We're men."

"You're right," Gabe quipped, "You're mants—half man, half ants."

"Then tell me, Gabe," Ike asked coyly, "What are you?"

Gabe turned and looked at Ike. "Out of here!" he said coyly.

Gabe took one step, leaped toward the window with his right arm extended and bashed the barred window from its casing, tumbling to the ground outside in a somersault move. The window was still in his hand, the quarter-inch steel rebar ends exposed through the concrete. Off he dashed.

Gentry, Myers, Coach, Beth, and Ike took turns looking at each other, startled and annoyed at the same time. Then Gabe suddenly stuck his head back in the window and addressed himself drolly to everyone except Ike:

"I was thinking, did you find the ant analogy puerile and fatuous… Now that I've thought about it, so have I." Then Gabe regarded Ike, saying, "But I found your analogy simply asinine, since I'm standing here and you're standing there." Then he was gone.

Gabe dashed around the building, turned the corner, and slid to a stop one foot from his startled father. Clayton looked up at his son, and they regarded each other in silence. Gabe lowered his head.

"How's Mom?" he asked sadly.

"She is conscious now and is going to be alright," a gloomy Clayton sighed.

Gabe nodded his head and said hopefully, "Good, good."

Clayton thought that he detected, for the first time in a long time, a twinge of sincerity in his forlorn son's voice. Gabe made a move, but Clayton took hold of his wrist.

"Don't do what I know you are going to do, son," Clayton's already reddened eyes began to leak tears again. Sirens of many approaching police cars rang through the night. "They will hunt you, and they will kill you, Gabe."

Gabriel took his long index finger and gently touched one of the tears streaming from his father's cheek and rubbed it between his finger and thumb, as if he had never seen a tear before.

"And it will be glorious, Father," he whispered softly with a watery gleam in his eye. "I will make you proud of me, Father. I will die like a warrior. For a warrior I am, and a warrior I will be for the remaining time I have left." He cast his moist eyes out into the night. Clayton felt him shudder. Then he said yearningly:

"I have often wondered how I would end. Though I tried to picture it as hard as I could, I could never see my plans for the future. The others have plans: A fireman, a doctor, a football player. They are going to get married and have children of their own someday. But for the Nephilim son, there are no plans.

"What would I become?" He paused for a moment and looked down at his weeping father. "A laboratory subject to be studied is all that awaits me. I'll have none of it," he said bitterly. "You should have had the doctors abort me before I was born, Father. Now I must abort myself."

The siren's blare was getting closer.

"I should thank you now, you and Mom. I had a good childhood. If only I knew what love is, I should think that I would feel it just about now. You did well under the circumstances, but it's time to end it now." Gabe looked at the approaching police cars and shouted, "If I'm going to leave this world! I'm going out fighting!"

Then he shook loose his father's hand from his wrist and wheeled to face the policemen.

"Wait, Gabe," Clayton pleaded feebly, "There is another way. You can choose to do good with your life. Think of all the good things you could do. You could be a hero of old; a man of renown."

Gabe stopped and looked at his father. Then the beam of the police car lights lit upon him. He was still looking when the sound of the megaphone cut through the air: "PUT YOUR HANDS ON YOUR HEAD AND LAY FACE DOWN ON THE GROUND."

Gabe turned back around and put his cupped hand up to his forehead to shade his eyes. The rifle shot rang out…

CHAPTER 9

Gabe flinched slightly. Then he looked distressedly back at his father. Gabe looked down at his shirt and slowly pulled up the tail. Blood was trickling down his rippling stomach.

Clayton gasped.

Gabe released his shirt and squinted into the lights again. Twelve officers were now advancing on foot with pistols drawn. Gabe screamed out the Nephilim war cry—the blood-curdling yell summoned from ancient DNA of an extinct race. The ferociousness of it stopped the approaching officers in their tracks as their minds were now concerned about their aching eardrums.

From behind the group of policemen came another report of a rifle. This time Gabe grimaced in pain and slapped his abdomen with an open hand. He staggered backwards and looked down at his stomach. He turned toward Clayton with a stunned and panicked look on his now childlike face. Paleness overtook him. Then he toppled backward, landing flat on his back.

The policemen surrounded him in a gawking manner, the way hunters approach a just-fallen rhinoceros. Clayton pushed his way through them to his prostrate son. Gabe 's eyes were closed. Clayton cradled his son's head and rested it on his lap.

Through the crowd pushed another man, a man carrying a high-powered rifle: County Sheriff Billy Upton by name. His shoes were still making a slight squishing sound with each step. His clothes were still dripping wet. His ire was temporarily dampened, however, when he saw the giant lying motionless on the ground but was rekindled the moment, he saw that someone was weeping over this monster.

He took the rifle barrel and nudged Gabe on his bloody stomach. Clayton slapped the barrel away from his dying son. This act of disrespect infuriated Upton, and he quickly took the butt of his rifle and rammed Clayton in the forehead. Clayton toppled to the ground, holding the bulbous lump that was only gaining size by the second.

"Why did you do that, you damn idiot!" Clayton screamed.

The Sheriff became outraged. He came forward a couple of steps so that he was standing over Clayton and drew back the butt of his rifle again so he could dole out "a sampling of respect for the law." The other policemen grimaced at what the old bastard Sheriff was about to do.

The butt of the rifle was about to make contact with Clayton's face when a large hand blurred upward and cupped the butt still. Gabe's eyes flung open; the Sheriff's mouth flung open. Gabe launched the rifle like a missile. The Sheriff spilled backward. Gabe flipped to his feet in one move.

The pissed-off Sheriff rose angrily and pulled out his pistol. Gabe took hold of his damp shirt and hurled him around in a circle. His flailing feet struck other policemen on their jaws, and one by one, they lost control of their weapons and toppled to the ground. On the last revolution, Gabe let go, and Upton whirled through the air like a Frisbee. Twenty feet later, he bounced a time or two before he stopped rolling. He groaned in agony.

Gabe looked down at his father, who was lying on his back, starring at his forsaken son. Gabe looked panicked and, for the first time, scared. He bent over in pain, placed his hand over his wound, and jogged toward the woods.

The policemen were scurrying to recover their weapons and regain their senses. Clayton leaped from the ground and shouted between his sobbing breaths, "Please let me get him. He's hurt bad. He won't get far. Please, he's my son. He won't hurt anybody else." Clayton's voice quieted, "He's bleeding to death. He's only twelve, for God's sake. Let me be with him, please."

One of the officers nodded his head and waved his pistol toward the woods. "He's your responsibility," the officer said, and then put his hand to the back of his aching head. The others didn't seem anxious to protest the officer's decision.

Clayton looked miserably at the blood drops on the ground, grass, and brush as he tracked Gabe on his winding path through the woods. His only hope at the moment was to find his mortally wounded son alive. The one thought that pierced his mind like an ever-dulling razor was this: *It was only twelve short years ago that he crawled on the floor and pulled himself into the safety of his father's lap, laboring with goo's and baby smiles to tell his father that he felt safe now. Nothing was going to happen, not now.*

The nostalgia made Clayton weep even more. *It's not that boy's fault,* he continued to think. *He didn't ask for this. He didn't ask to be born into this world. There's good left in him, I know it. If I could only find him in time, I could tell him that.* Another thought made Clayton shudder to himself, *I don't ever remember telling him that I loved him. Not since he was a baby, anyway, not since he could understand what it meant. Please be alive son, I have to tell you something.*

Next to a large oak tree knelt Gabe, on one knee and slumped over. He supported himself with his shoulder leaned heavily against the tree. His head was down, and blood and saliva streamed from his mouth.

Clayton approached hesitantly, afraid that he was too late and wanting to postpone knowing it. The giant boy was motionless. Clayton put his tiny hand on the thick shoulder…Gabe turned his head quickly and looked immediately into his father's eyes.

Clayton had never seen this look in the boy's face before. He was primed to cry. He had been crying. He watched a large tear stream down an already made path. Gabe made a sobbing sound and shuddered under his breath.

"I don't want to die, Daddy," he cried, just like a scared-to-death little boy.

Clayton was perplexed at the thought that went through his own head at that second. *This was the only time his son had called him Daddy.*

Clayton put his son's arm around his neck. Gabe pulled his father in tight, then relaxed a little, mindful not to squeeze too tight as not to hurt the fragile little man. Gabe whispered in sobs, "I don't want to die, I don't want to die, I'll be good from now on, I don't want to die, Daddy. Please don't let me die, Daddy."

Clayton felt the enormous weight lean against him. He tried to support it as much as he could, but there was no use. All Clayton could do was support his son's head off the ground. Clayton looked up to the heavens and said quietly,

"Oh Lord, hear me just this once. Please don't take this boy now, not now Lord. It's not his fault. It's my fault. If it's your will, Lord, let it be done, but you couldn't have put him here for this. Not to end like this. You must have a reason." Clayton began to cry. He heard a sound and looked around and saw Ike, Harrison, Melissa, and yes, Shannon standing beside him.

"I heard your prayer Clayton," Shannon said as he knelt down and combed over her son's blond hair with her hand. Her mind raced back to another time when she used to do the same thing to a much smaller head.

"How did you get out of the hospital?"

"I made Melissa bring me, or I was going to walk," she said, even softer as she stroked Gabe's curls.

"It's time to go, Clayton," Ike said. "You've done all you could do. It's over."

Just then, Melissa stumbled and almost fell. "Woo, I have to go, Harrison. I fell faint."

"What's the matter with you?" Said her husband, concerned.

"I'm pregnant."

"What!"

"I couldn't find a good time to tell you—not with all this going on."

"Sit on that log. I'll give them our sympathies, and we'll get back to the car."

Harrison approached Clayton and Shannon, hugged them gently from behind, and said, "I've got to get Melissa to the car, but I'll be back." He left.

Ike knelt down beside Shannon and Clayton, looking at Gabe's pale face. "I'll leave y'all alone for a minute." They nodded, and Ike walked away.

"The thing is, he was so beautiful." Shannon said, beginning to cry while still playing with Gabe's thick hair. She ran her fingers through it the same way she used to when she could still hold him.

"He never had a chance, you know." Clayton had stopped crying but continued holding his son's head in his lap. "Not a chance…Why? Why was he here?" Clayton shook his head in frustration.

"Maybe we'll never know why he was here," said Shannon. "Maybe we're not supposed to know." They turned toward each other and embraced lovingly.

The boom of police radios and the clamor of paramedics making their way to the scene faded into silence for them. They continued hugging each other, wondering, as did everyone else, why Gabriel Rinehart was ever put on this earth.

CHAPTER 10
EPILOGUE

The Ford pickup truck's brakes squealed to a halt in the last remaining parking spot at the Mal M. Moore Athletic Facility. The reinforced shocks hissed with strained air, and the truck's bed lifted 18 inches when the size 27 EEE foot stepped onto the pavement.

Clayton had never seen this building before. He could describe in detail Bryant- Denny Stadium: the four majestic statues of Coach Wallace Wade, Coach Paul "Bear" Bryant, Coach Gene Stallings, and, of course, Coach Nick Saban. He could even describe how Coach Saban is leaning over and clapping his hands with encouragement.

Encouragement —that's what he needed right now. Clayton felt apprehensive about this meeting. He could tell over the phone, when Coach Jeremy Pruitt had called Coach Saban, that the celebrated coach wasn't taking any of it seriously.

He didn't think Coach Pruitt was taking it seriously either. He hadn't acted serious —not the way he had agreed to come to the tryout on a dare, nor the way he kept looking at his stop watch and laughing: 2.7 forty. It wasn't very encouraging when Coach Pruitt joked that he had to go home and go to bed so he could wake up from this crazy-ass dream in his own bed —or something like that.

The door to the facility opened. "Look, Gabe, tall ceilings." Gabe laughed because the ceiling was at least 30 feet high. Clayton soon spotted payers he had only seen on TV. The Adam's apple on AJ McCarron slowly rose and fell as he swallowed nervously. AJ hurried out the door, and the word *SHIT* was easily heard from the outside. *A nice-looking boy*, thought Clayton. Too bad he's so quick to use bad language like that. All activity stopped. Deathly quiet. Gasps echoed.

A girl named Kelsey, Nick Saban's assistant, came down the steps and stopped, wide-eyed, the blood gone from her pretty face, "Follow me," she quivered.

Sheesh, Clayton thought. *You'd think they were used to see big kids around here.* "Hey, there's Cyrus Kouandjio and DJ Flucker," Clayton whispered to Gabe. "There the biggest guys on the team. They're both six-six, three forty." Gabe looked over at the two flabbergasted offensive tackles and first-round prospects and chuckled.

He hesitated for a moment, placed his left hand on the handrail, and squeezed hard. The steel rail collapsed together. Gabe winked at the two tackles, whose mouths were agape, and then proceeded up the steps.

"Hey, I didn't know black guys could turn pale," laughed Vinnie Sunseri, the safety, who had come to raze the two giants, and then noticed that they were staring blankly at something. He looked up and froze, blank himself.

T.J. Yeldon and Dee Hart were coming down the stairs. They took one look, turned, and bolted back up the stairs with blinding foot speed. They scrammed past Kelsey, who seized the opportunity to join them close behind. Clayton looked back at Gabe, "Nice quickness," he said, and then observed the crumpled handrail and whispered sternly, "Gabe, we agreed: no more showing off."

"Sorry, Dad, it won't happen again," Gabe said regretfully.

The door to Nick Saban's office was still open. He had not yet pressed the red button that closes the door from his desk. Clayton and Gabe assumed the door was open for them, so they entered.

They were standing in front of the renowned coach's desk when he rose from picking a Little Debbie he had just dropped to the floor. He had a satisfied smile on his face, rather proud of his rescue. He shook the cookie rapper vigorously and was just about to tear it open when the shadow of something massive caused him to look up.

The coach, known across the country for his stern discipline, firmness and toughness, was stupefied and motionless. Clayton had never been these close to his hero before. Thoughts sprinted through his mind: *He looks so young for his age. I've never seen his eyes this big or his mouth open like that. He's lighter- complexioned than I thought, particularly his face. I wonder what he thinks of Gabe.*

The horrified look on coach's face slowly morphed into a slender smile. "You mean to tell me that this was not another one of Pruitt's pranks… He's real!" Coach Saban walked around the desk, put out his hand to Clayton, but never took his eyes off Gabe. Clayton shook his hand. Coach kept his eyes transfixed on the hulking Nephilim.

Gabe didn't know exactly what to do about the awkwardness of the moment, so he picked up a large, heavy steel old-world globe that was decoratively placed by the coach's desk and held it like a basketball between his two thumbs and middle fingers.

"Are you as strong as you look?" Coach asked gingerly.

Gabe crumbled the 100-pound globe between his fingers with the greatest of ease.

"Son, you don't by any chance know anything about the five-technique in a three-four defense, do you." The smile on University of Alabama head football coach Nick Saban widened — and so did Clayton Rinehart's.

THE END